THE FORTUNY GOWN

THE
FORTUNY
GOWN

ROSALIND LAKER

Doubleday

LONDON · NEW YORK · TORONTO · SYDNEY · AUCKLAND

TRANSWORLD PUBLISHERS LTD
61–63 Uxbridge Road, London W5 5SA

TRANSWORLD PUBLISHERS (AUSTRALIA) PTY LTD
15–25 Helles Avenue, Moorebank, NSW 2170

TRANSWORLD PUBLISHERS (NZ) LTD
3 William Pickering Drive, Albany, Auckland

Published 1995 by Doubleday
a division of Transworld Publishers Ltd

All of the characters in this book
are fictitious, and any resemblance
to actual persons, living or dead,
is purely coincidental.

A catalogue record for this book is available from the British Library.

ISBN 0385 405294 BII 024 1746

Typeset in 11/13pt Caslon by Kestrel Data, Exeter

Printed in Great Britain by
Mackays of Chatham Plc, Chatham, Kent

To Muriel and John in friendship always.

THE FORTUNY GOWN

CHAPTER ONE

If Nikolai Karasvin had not been stuck in a traffic jam in the rue Pierre Carron he would not have seen her there. Something about her gripped his gaze. With a quick, light step she was walking along the pavement in the soft April sunshine of the Parisian afternoon, carrying a piece of labelled hand-luggage that suggested she had just arrived in the city. She was looking in exhilaration at everything around her, but she failed to notice him, long-legged and relaxed, seated in the back of the chauffeur-driven 1909 Rolls-Royce.

He smiled to himself. It was a welcome diversion to watch her. Paris always had something new to offer. He was on his way to the Russian Embassy before keeping an engagement of his own, which had nothing to do with his diplomatic duties. If he had been driving himself he would not have come along this street, for with its exclusive establishments, such as the *haute couture* houses of Poiret and Landelle, there were frequent comings and goings of carriages drawn by high-bred horses that often shied at the motor traffic, causing hold-ups, which was what had happened today.

Appreciatively he noticed that she was tall with a good figure set off by her well-fitting cream jacket and long skirt, but she also had that gift inherent in Frenchwomen of imbuing whatever they wore with style. Not conventionally pretty, her face was interestingly piquant with a thin, longish nose, a firmly pointed chin, hazel eyes that were lively and sparkling, and a wide, inviting mouth. As for her hair, it was pale copper and piled up under her hat, a few escaping tendrils shot through by sunlight to a burnished hue.

Her gilded initials were clearly discernible on her leather hand-luggage: *J.C.* He wanted to know her name.

Juliette Cladel was glad she had decided to walk from the Gare de Lyon where she had deposited the rest of her luggage. It was a relief to find that her birthplace had not changed in the eight years of her absence as a pupil at the convent school where the final twelve months had been spent as a teacher of embroidery. The city still had its own particular pot-pourri, blending the aroma of roasting coffee beans with the pungency of garlic, the fragrance of blossom, the bouquet of fine wines, delicate perfumes and the whiff of expensive cigars. Paris exuded an atmosphere of opulence, pleasure and enormous wealth. Surely there was no better place in all the world to be when one was eighteen and life was about to begin at last!

She halted to put down her hand-luggage and buy a bunch of violets from a flower-seller, unaware that she was in the direct line of a stranger's vision from a few feet away. She raised the violets to her nose and closed her eyes sensually as she inhaled their scent. Turning to face her reflection in the window of a perfumery, she tucked the stems under her hat ribbon letting the blooms lie on the brim. It was then that she sensed she was being watched. Self-consciously she put a gloved hand to the back of her hair as she glanced to the left and right before picking up her hand-luggage again.

At that moment the traffic began to flow once more. Although Nikolai looked back she was already disappearing among the other pedestrians as she continued on her way.

Juliette glanced upwards at the numbers above the doorways as she went past, never having been to her sister's *haute couture* fashion house before. Denise, sixteen years her senior and her only living relative, widow of the late Baron Claude de Landelle, had been careful to choose the right address for her business where she could be sure of collecting the best clientele. Juliette knew that Denise would be far from pleased by her unexpected arrival in Paris, especially when she heard the reason!

10

Yet in spite of the trouble ahead it was wonderful to be home. Juliette was determined never to leave Paris again or at least not for as long as the exile that had just ended. In the weeks and months ahead she would get to know her birthplace again even though poignant memories of her late parents would always be associated with some parts of the city.

She had reached the Maison Landelle. Taking a step back, she looked up at the imposing frontage, which seemed to warn of the high prices to be expected within. As Juliette moved towards the entrance a liveried doorman swung open the door with its gilded cypher. She entered to face a wide marble staircase. At the time of opening the business Denise had opted for the style of décor that had become generally known as *art nouveau* and the effect was quite splendid. The walls were panelled in copper with embossed decorations of stately irises and on stands there were elegantly simple vases shaped like elongated trumpets, holding the fresh flowers that perfumed the air.

At the head of the flight with its swirling wrought-iron banisters, Juliette reached the reception area, which was enhanced by screens of Lalique glass, the designs both clear and opaque with light glowing through them from the silk-fringed lampshades held high by female figures of gleaming silver. She could hear the buzz of conversation in the salons. By one of the screens two women in large hats stood chatting, boned lace giving a swan-like look to their necks, the fashionable *S* silhouette of their figures achieved by fullness to the front of their bodices and to the back of their skirts. Juliette could only guess at their restrictive corsets underneath that aided this effect. Thankfully she had never yet resorted to such uncomfortable under-pinnings!

'*Bonjour*, mademoiselle.' A smiling woman elegant in black silk had come forward to greet her.

Juliette knew this must be Madame Millot, Denise's *directrice* and right hand at all times, for in any great couture house the woman holding this trusted position was the pivot around which the clientele and the staff revolved. She had to be dignified, calm and gracious at all times, whatever the crisis.

'I'm not expected,' Juliette said after explaining that she had come to see her sister after a long train journey.

'The Baronne de Landelle isn't here at the present time, but I

11

feel sure she would wish me to tell you where to find her. She is calling on an old friend, who is back in Paris today on a visit from Louisiana in the United States and is staying at the Hôtel Bristol in the place Vendôme.'

Juliette's face had lit up. 'Would that be Madame Garnier?'

'Yes. That's the name.'

Juliette hastened back down the stairs. Lucille Garnier was an old friend of her parents, looked upon almost as an aunt by Denise and herself even after she had gone to live abroad. The move from Paris had come about when Lucille's husband had accepted a high business appointment in New Orleans, promoting and protecting French interests. Lucille had made only one trip back since then and that had been for tragic reasons, but this time Juliette knew it would be for renewing old friendships and seeing her homeland again. Denise had been a poor correspondent, which had made Lucille's letters even more welcome at the convent, and all the more enjoyable since they were written from a faraway place where the customs of old France still lingered and yet so much was new and thriving.

Juliette took an omnibus to the Place Vendôme and her thoughts turned to her sister's success. She well remembered when Denise had first revealed her intentions of going into the fashion business. It was after Claude de Landelle's funeral when Juliette herself had been a year at the convent. Denise was furious that he had bequeathed the bulk of his fortune to the children of a previous marriage while she had been left a moderate income and the grand house in the faubourg St Germain for her lifetime unless she remarried.

'How can I live on a pittance?' she had stormed to her young sister, not having dared breathe her fury to friends and acquaintances out of fear of malicious gossip. 'It's Claude's revenge! Oh, he was generous enough at first, but then he began niggling about my so-called extravagance.' She paced the floor, biting her lip and fuming. As the visitors' room at the convent was chilly she had kept on her sable coat and it swirled about her ankles with a hiss of silk lining. 'Thank God I had the sense to stack away as much as I could into sound investments when I had a free rein with his money and made sure he gave me Cartier jewellery on every possible occasion.'

'Shall you marry again?' Juliette asked from where she sat. On the table beside her were the samples of embroidery and sewing that the nuns had thought her sister would like to see, for it was a craft at which she was beginning to excel, but Denise had not glanced at any of them.

'Marry again?' Denise had come to a halt at the question. 'Never! Old men get jealous and possessive. Younger men are never faithful. I know!' Her tone was bitter. 'I can tell you there is not a marriage in all Paris to compare with Papa's and Maman's.' She glanced at the clock. 'I'll have to go. Don't worry that I won't be able to afford to keep you here, because Claude made provision for your school fees and there's a small nest egg for you when you've finished your education.'

Juliette had liked Claude. He had had kind eyes, but perhaps they had saddened in the time since she had last seen him. 'That was very good of him.'

'He should have been good to his widow!' Denise tossed her head. 'But I don't intend to rot in poverty for the rest of my days.'

'So what shall you do?'

'My assets are my business instincts and my flair for fashion. I intend to capitalize on both.'

'But how?'

'That's all I can tell you at the present time, but I'll let you know later how my plans work out.'

Juliette had known that she would not hear for a long time. Denise's letters were infrequent. When one finally came it was headed Maison Landelle. Denise, totally without sentiment, had sold some valuable paintings that had been birthday gifts from Claude, one of which had been bought at auction by the Louvre and others going at exorbitant prices to an American millionaire. She had invested everything in a fashion house. With her social connections the right people came to view if not to buy, but had succumbed to day-wear that rivalled Maison Worth in cut and style while her sumptuous evening wear outshone many of Maison Paquin's wonderful ensembles. Within a week her order books were full and she had taken on twice as many hands as when she started.

'Are you selling cheaper than anyone else?' Juliette had asked naïvely when Denise came on one of her flying visits.

'No!' Denise gave a satisfied laugh, her mood light-hearted and entirely changed from her last visit. 'I'm far more expensive. That's

what makes my creations so exclusive and sought after. I've begun
to make lingerie too. Really lovely items that any woman would give
her eye-teeth to wear. That reminds me.' She dived into a pocket
and produced a parcel. 'I've a present for you.'

It was only a small package and when opened revealed a filmy
chemise trimmed with pink ribbon and delicate lace. Juliette gasped
with delight and held it up.

'It's gorgeous, but the nuns would never allow me to wear it. Oh!'
She was suddenly embarrassed.

'What's the matter?'

'It's so fine,' Juliette whispered, wide-eyed. 'Are you producing
lingerie that can be *seen* through?'

Denise smiled indulgently and took the chemise from her and
folded it up again. 'I'll keep this and start a bottom drawer for you.
You'll feel differently about such wear one day.'

'When shall I come back to Paris?'

'You have to finish your education first.'

The omnibus had arrived at the Place Vendôme. Juliette sprang
out and crossed to the Hôtel Bristol. It was a grand, aristocratic
establishment much patronized by royalty. In the vast lobby with its
marble pillars, potted palms and circular seating she heard plenty of
English voices among the well-dressed people milling about. If
Edward VII had been on one of his trips to France she might well
have seen him there. She made her way across to the reception desk.
There she asked for her name to be given to Madame Garnier. The
clerk rang through and then turned back to her with a bow.

'Madame Garnier's suite is Number Fourteen on the second floor.
She wishes you to go up.'

Juliette was about to take the lift and then changed her mind.
With everything becoming dearly familiar to her again after her
long absence nothing should be hurried. Every minute should be
savoured to the full. She would take the staircase instead. She
wondered if Lucille had felt the same when she had arrived earlier
today. Joy at the prospect of seeing this good friend again was
tempered by the thought of the hostile reception she could expect
from her sister, but with her plans made there was nothing Denise
could say or do that would sway her from her chosen course.

As Juliette crossed to the crimson-carpeted flight she was glad that
the few extra minutes it would take to reach Lucille's suite should

14

be time enough to compose herself before facing Denise's acid displeasure. She recalled how the nuns had wished her well in her new life, having accepted some time ago that their best needlework pupil had no vocation to join the Order and would not want to stay on indefinitely as a teacher of her skills. Unfortunately Denise never saw any viewpoint but her own.

Pausing with her hand on the gilded banister-rail, Juliette looked down into the lobby. What a splendid sight it presented! Almost like a flower garden with the women's large hats perched on their hugely padded pompadour coiffures and trimmed with every kind of bloom, massed ribbons and gauzes. Some had nodding plumes or, more sadly, whole exotic birds with wings spread out as if speared, tails upmost across the brims, the glass eyes glinting. She glimpsed the iridescent blue of a kingfisher and the gem-like gleam of a cockatoo. As for the men, there were the gleaming top hats of those formally attired, but there were also the bowlers of business men, the derbies of the newly arrived travellers and the panamas of those who had been strolling along the boulevards and the Bois.

As Juliette scanned the scene her gaze came to rest by chance on a tall young man standing on his own by one of the potted palms. The wide brim of his slouch hat hid his eyes from her as he read a newspaper folded to a single column, but the lower half of his face was striking, the cheekbones wide with pleasing hollows under them, his nose handsome, a worldly sensual mouth and a strong broad chin. Coming to the end of what he was reading, Nikolai Karasvin tucked the newspaper into the pocket of his coat as he raised his head and glanced across with an impatient frown at the lobby clock above the reception desk. Now she could see that his brows and lashes were as dark as his curly hair.

There was no doubt in her mind that he was waiting for a woman. His wife? His betrothed? Maybe an actress from the Folies-Dramatiques, or a singer from the Opéra. She hoped whoever it was would arrive within the next few seconds before she continued upstairs, for her curiosity was aroused. Then, unexpectedly, he looked up swiftly and his eyes met hers.

She caught her breath. His heavy lids had suggested that any glance from him would be moody and bored, but she had been mistaken. His eyes, fastening on hers in a way that sent a tremor through her, were sharply alert, a clear steel-grey and piercing. Not

15

a man to be crossed in any way! Even as their gaze locked, his deepened with warm recognition and yet she had never seen him before. Inexplicably she felt wildly drawn to him.

From his viewpoint she stood with a window-light falling full on her, making her stand out with her tawny hair and light clothes against the dark fleur-de-lys pattern of the wallpaper that flanked the stairs behind her. Although there was nothing coquettish about her, he could tell she was unable to break the look by which he held her across the distance between them. She was as magnetized as he was by the powerful, almost tempestuous attraction between them. If he had been able to touch her she would have trembled.

Then a couple talking loudly on the stairs distracted her. She glanced towards them and then back at him. He grinned at her, his eyes dancing. She was unable to resist returning a smile in their mutual enjoyment of the encounter. More swiftly than before she continued up the stairs.

Out of his sight she flung back her head exuberantly, for momentarily there was nobody else there to see her. What a dangerous exchange! She believed if he had not been waiting for someone he would not have let her go without speaking. It had always been instilled into her to look away from such predatory glances, but today she had ignored the rule wonderfully and was glad of it. Apart from anything else it showed her that at last she was in control of her own life!

CHAPTER TWO

Juliette found Lucille Garnier's suite at the end of a long corridor where it would have a prime view of the Place Vendôme. A tap on the door caused it to be opened by a neat-looking maid, who held it wide into a gilt-mirrored hallway.

'Madame Garnier is expecting you, mademoiselle,' she said in French, her accent revealing she was from Louisiana. She took Juliette's hand-luggage from her and showed her into a luxurious salon with crystal chandeliers and Louis Quinze furnishings.

Lucille rose immediately from one of the sofas and flung out her plump arms in a rustle of cinnamon silk, her rope of pearls swinging. 'Dearest child!' she exclaimed emotionally.

'*Tante* Lucille!' The pet-name of childhood had come spontaneously from Juliette's lips as she rushed forward into Lucille's embrace. They kissed each other's cheeks and hugged again. 'How is *Oncle* Rodolphe? Is he with you?'

Lucille shook her head. 'He hasn't retired yet and couldn't spare the time, but in any case he has never liked travelling and is content to stay at home.' She held Juliette by the shoulders at arm's length to study her fondly. 'How like your dear mother you've become when she was your age. I'd have known you anywhere!'

'As I would have known you! You're just the same!'

17

Lucille smiled a little ruefully at the compliment. 'If only my mirror could convince me of that!' Yet although she was almost sixty her complexion, aided by the right cosmetics, appeared remarkably smooth; the only wrinkles clearly discernible were the laughter lines at her twinkling blue eyes, for she had always had a lively sense of humour. As for her thickly puffed hair it had been skilfully tinted to its original golden hue, defying the passage of time, and in spite of being a large woman she was firmly corseted into the *S* shape that fashion demanded.

'Why didn't you mention in any of your letters that you were coming to France?' Juliette demanded happily as she removed her hat and pulled off her gloves.

'I wanted to surprise you by a visit to the convent and then bring you back to Paris to stay with me.' Lucille led her across to the yellow silk sofa where they sat down together. 'It's for that reason I booked this suite with an extra bedroom.'

Juliette was sitting bolt upright in her delight at this unexpected reunion that was adding to the excitement of the day. 'So you have surprised me just as you wished, although I forestalled your journey. I could scarcely believe my ears when I was told at Maison Landelle that Denise was calling on you here.' She glanced about quickly. 'Where is she?'

'Denise left just before I picked up the receiver to hear that you were in the lobby. I don't know how you missed her.'

'She must have taken the lift while I was coming up the stairs.'

'I'll ring the reception desk and see if she can be stopped before she leaves the hotel.' Lucille would have reached for the telephone had not Juliette stayed her with a touch on the arm.

'No, I'll have plenty of time to see Denise later. I'd like to talk to you on my own first.'

Lucille raised an eyebrow as she sat back again. 'If you want to spare me being a witness to the scene that's likely to erupt when she sees you, I'll tell you now that I've heard all about the telegram that Denise received from the convent earlier today. So why not enlighten me as to why you made this move so unexpectedly. Denise declared that you had only to ask and she would have made arrangements.'

Juliette arched her eyebrows quizzically. 'Did she? Yet Denise has never encouraged me to return. At first it suited me very well to stay on as a teacher and that was for two reasons. I was furthering my experience of dressmaking from one of the nuns in my free time and there was a special task I wanted to complete. Dear old Sister Berthe, who was always so kind to me, had asked me to help her finish the beautiful altar cloth for Chartres Cathedral that she had begun over a decade ago before her sight began to fade.'

'I recall your telling me about it in one of your letters.'

'When I put in the final stitches yesterday I had already packed my trunk.' Juliette looked triumphant. 'The Mother Superior had arranged for another nun to take over my classes and so there was nothing to keep me there any longer. What did cause a furore was my travelling without a chaperone! The nuns were quite frantic that I wouldn't wait to be accompanied, but suddenly I was so desperate to get home to Paris that I couldn't have waited another hour.'

'I can understand that.'

'If I may, I'd like to send a telegram from here to let everyone at the convent know I've arrived safely.'

'I advise you to take no more upon yourself at the moment. Leave that to Denise. As soon as I judge she's had time to get back to Maison Landelle I'll telephone to say you're here with me. You can speak to her too. Now tell me about that middle-aged suitor who had gained permission from Denise and the Mother Superior to call on you under a nun's chaperonage.'

Juliette sighed. 'Denise liked him because he is a prosperous man and has a fine house that she visited once. But he's more her age than mine and nothing would ever have made me marry him. Unfortunately the more I showed my lack of interest the keener he seemed to become. Finally he accepted that I was determined to remain single and became most annoyed about it.'

'Men in love can be very perverse. Denise spoke to me at length about the advantages such a match would have given you and how foolish you were to have thrown such a chance away. It's my belief her anger has its roots more in disappointment that you turned down marriage than in your leaving the convent as you did. To be frank, I've seen for myself that she wants to foist the responsibility for you on to someone else, just as she did by packing you off to the convent after your dear mother died.'

'I realize that and I can understand why. After all, she had no

19

children herself to make demands on her busy life and, although we're sisters, I'd played no part in her life either before or after her marriage. I don't hold it against her in any way. I was happy enough at the convent once I overcame my terrible homesickness. But I'll soon put Denise's fears to rest. I've made my own plans for the future in the career of my choice and will stick by them.'

'So you're going to work!' Lucille clapped her hands together approvingly. 'I'd do the same thing myself if I were young again. Before we talk any more, how long is it since you've eaten?'

'I had a snack at midday.'

Lucille promptly picked up the telephone and ordered coffee and pastries to be sent up at once. Then she settled back again against the cushions. 'I'm sure you'll excel at whatever work you intend to do,' she continued. 'I'm glad to see that your generation has more sense than mine. We thought only of being married and having babies. Every woman should have some individual freedom first.'

'Judging by my fellow pupils, I think I'm the exception.'

'Then think of yourself as the thin edge to a wedge. More and more opportunities are opening up for women in business and the professions. You haven't surprised me in the least, because through our correspondence I've seen your character develop and your will become strong. I have to admit I was delighted when you wrote of your first mischievous escapade as then I knew you were no longer the docile, malleable child that I remembered.'

Juliette's eyes danced. 'Thank goodness for that! I certainly had plenty of reprimands from the nuns in my early years, although my pranks were harmless enough. I knew you would never be censorious.'

'Indeed not! I don't wonder you became something of a rebel. I thought it was most unkind that your sister never let you come home to her for any of the holidays.'

'She did what she could for me in other ways. I never wanted for new clothes or books or pocket money and she came to visit me for a few hours three or four times a year.'

Lucille did not look impressed. 'So I should think!'

'As I grew older she seemed to become fonder of me and treated me as a confidante, pouring out her troubles. As for the holidays, remember how lucky I was to have a good friend in Gabrielle Rousset

20

at school. Her parents invited me to stay quite often and always when they were at their villa at Antibes where there was swimming and picnics and sailing and parties. I missed Gabrielle so much after she was taken away from the convent and sent to a finishing school in Switzerland.'

'Shall you be seeing her again?'

'Yes, as soon as it proves possible. We keep in touch.'

Then the coffee came in a silver pot with thin blue china bordered in gilt and the pastries proved to be as delicious as they looked. Juliette enjoyed every flaky crumb. Lucille chatted on.

'Luckily I've accepted no invitations for this evening, although I'm looking forward to seeing old friends again. I hope you'll stay for all or at least part of the six weeks I'll be at the Hôtel Bristol, but that must be as you wish. You must also feel free to come and go as you please with regard to your possible employment and if you've friends to see.'

Juliette put down her empty cup and saucer with a contented sigh. 'How you are spoiling me and I love it! It will be wonderful to stay here with you.'

'Good! That's settled then.' A gilded clock struck the hour with a tinkling chime, reminding Lucille of the call she had to make to Denise. The conversation was brief. Denise's voice came clear and terse over the line and was audible to Juliette.

'By all means have Juliette stay with you, Lucille, and I'll let the convent know she's arrived. No, I don't want to speak to her and neither am I in any hurry to see her. In any case I'm going out of Paris on business tomorrow for two days. I'll let you know when I'm back. Goodbye.'

Lucille replaced the receiver. 'So, Juliette, you have forty-eight hours' reprieve before you meet your sister.'

Juliette nodded. 'That's most opportune. It will give me the chance to find employment before she and I come face to face. It's what I would have liked to have done in the first place, but naturally I had to try to see her as soon as I arrived.'

'So tell me now what line your career is going to follow. Has it anything to do with your embroidery skills?'

Juliette gave a happy nod. 'I want to work in a couture house – not Maison Landelle, I assure you. I hope to get into Maison Worth.'

'You've chosen well.'

'I know from the way my needlework has been displayed in a recent exhibition that I'm too advanced to be an apprentice, but I could be a second-degree seamstress and rise from there. I've examples of my work with me to show what I can do.'

Lucille leaned towards Juliette in her interest. 'So what is your ultimate aim?'

'To have my own dressmaking establishment, but not in opposition to Denise. When it proves financially possible I'd set up in one of the bigger cities, but in range for getting to Paris easily.'

'Not a couture house then?'

'One would have to be in Paris for that.'

'Wherever you are I'll be your first client. It would break my custom of being dressed by Maison Paquin, but if I'm not too old and doddery I'll come myself to be fitted instead of everything being made for me on a *mannequin* to my measurements and sent to Louisiana.'

'You'll never be old!' Juliette protested vehemently.

Lucille laughed. 'What a tonic you are to me! You make me realize how much I miss young company with both sons in different parts of the world and grandchildren whom Rodolphe and I rarely see. I can't help wondering what Denise will say about your becoming a seamstress. Have you ever visited a couture house other than calling at Maison Landelle today?'

'No. I was too young to accompany Maman when she went for her fittings at Maison Worth, but Denise used to go with her when old enough to require more adult dresses.'

'Then come with me to Maison Paquin tomorrow. I'm going to choose a new wardrobe to take home. It will give you a real insight into the atmosphere and allure of high fashion.'

Juliette was enthusiastic about getting this chance. It was exactly what she needed, for to see everything from a client's viewpoint could give her extra authority when she applied for work. 'It will be so interesting! I heard much about it whenever Denise came to visit me, but it's so much better if I can see that side of the business for myself.'

'In the matter of clothes, what do you have with you?'

'Just overnight things in my hand-luggage with some spare shoes and so forth. I left my trunk at the Gare de Lyon, not wanting to take it with me until after tomorrow when I had found the right

22

permanent accommodation. Also, if I'd had it with me, Denise would have supposed I was landing myself on her.'

'Let me have the deposit ticket. I'll give it to my maid, Marie, who is a treasure I couldn't do without, and she can arrange the trunk's collection.' She rang the little bell that stood by the telephone. Marie appeared and the ticket was handed over. As she went again Lucille spoke of the evening ahead. 'I thought we'd dine at Foyet's. I'm sure we shall find the cuisine and the service as superb as I remember.'

'My parents often dined there. It was their favourite restaurant.'

'I know. That's why I thought it would appeal to you. Now I think you'd like to see your room and have a bath and a rest after your travelling today. I always lie down for a while before dressing for the evening.'

Juliette found her room to be as sumptuous as all else she had seen in the suite. There were fresh flowers in a vase, a large complimentary box of chocolates from the management as well as a basket of fruit. Everything was such a contrast to the stark walls and bare floors that she had lived with for so long. Although she was not in the least tired she flung herself backwards on to the satin coverlet of the bed, flinging her arms wide while she luxuriated in the downy comfort. It was not long before she heard Marie running a bath for her.

By the time Juliette returned to her room from a long, scented soak she found her trunk had been delivered and Marie was on her knees unpacking it. Seeing the package of needlework was still in the upper tray, Juliette asked her to put it in a drawer on its own as she did not want the items crushed. As this was done Juliette turned her attention to her dresses which had been hung up in the wardrobe. All her clothes had been made at the Maison Landelle and, although simple in style, they had been sewn by some of the best seamstresses in Paris. As a needlewoman herself she had always appreciated the exquisite workmanship.

When she was dressed and the maid had left the room, Juliette crossed to the window and looked out at the twinkling lights of Paris. She wondered where that interesting stranger, accompanied by the woman he had been meeting, was spending the evening hours. She hoped not to see them at Foyet's, for that would disturb her peace of mind. He had looked prosperous enough, judging by his well-groomed appearance and tailored clothes, to patronize, anywhere he chose. Maybe he had taken his partner to one of the other top restaurants or, if she was in the theatrical profession or otherwise not quite a true lady, they could be out to enjoy themselves at some more risqué place such as the Moulin Rouge. What fun that would be!

Her parents, Michel and Catherine Cladel, had spent an evening at the Moulin Rouge when they were newly wed. She learned of it when she was young and had asked her mother about a framed sketch on the wall. Although the lines drawn were sparse and the effect rather strange it was an unmistakable likeness of her parents merrily drinking champagne. Catherine, half-laughing as if the merriment of the occasion was still with her, explained how it came to be there.

'I had to persuade your Papa to take me,' she said, holding Juliette's hand as they stood looking at the framed sketch, 'because it wasn't a place where ladies ever went, but I'd heard so much about the scandalous can-can and out of curiosity I wanted to see it. I'm told it's still danced, but not so outrageously as it was in those days.'

'Who drew the picture, Maman?'

'An artist named Toulouse-Lautrec. We saw him there, but had no idea he might be including us in his sketching. About two years later your Papa came across the drawing in a shop and bought it. I chose the frame and we hung it here on our bedroom wall to remind us of a wonderful evening.'

They had had many memorable evenings throughout their marriage. Juliette could remember clearly how her parents had moved in a splendid social whirl, having their own box at the Opéra, always in the best enclosure at Longchamps, giving parties that filled the house with music and laughter, and all the time Catherine dressed only by Worth from head to toe. In all they had lived a charmed life, never dreaming it would end tragically.

It was not until Juliette began staying with Gabrielle during the convent summer holidays that she discovered that many marriages were very different from the loving and no doubt passionate union of her late parents. Monsieur and Madame Rousset moved in a similar social circle and on her first visit to Antibes Juliette was astonished to observe how they bickered and seemed to prefer the company of other people. Wide-eyed, she also witnessed discontent among some of the other couples who made up the house-party there. On the surface a bubbling joviality prevailed and all were there to enjoy themselves, but not necessarily with their own partners. Once she saw Gabrielle clap her hands over her ears and run from the villa when her parents' voices were raised angrily yet again behind a closed door. Juliette ran after her and found her sitting on one of the rocks by the vivid peacock-hued sea. It became apparent that the rock was Gabrielle's place of refuge.

'I don't know how I'd endure these holidays if you weren't here, Juliette,' she said on another occasion. 'At least we can get away on our own whenever we like. They don't want me under their feet.'

'That's why I'm invited,' Juliette replied sagely, pulling off her socks and shoes to dabble her toes in the water.

Gabrielle, brown-eyed and round-faced, pushed a fall of her soft brown hair back from her face. 'Thank goodness for it! Letting you come to stay is the best thing they've ever done for me.'

The annual happenings at Antibes gave Juliette plenty of food for thought as she grew more mature and spent quiet hours with her stitching. She began to wonder if Denise, who had always demanded to be the centre of attention, had resented the close relationship and devotion of her parents for each other. Then, when Denise was sixteen and emerging socially, her mother had caused her excruciating embarrassment by giving birth at the age of forty-three to an unplanned but totally welcome new daughter. Denise saw her sister lavished with the parental love that she imagined had never been directed with the same warmth towards herself and this became another cause of jealousy. Juliette was not very old when she began to realize there was a long-standing discord between Denise and her mother, for her sister's quick temper made life very difficult for everyone in the household at times.

Juliette still thought it strange that Denise, who set a high value on love, should have decided when she was twenty-four to marry solely for money a man more than twice her age. Juliette was present at the unhappy scene when Denise stood ready in her bridal finery and she herself was in a frilled bridesmaid's gown of blue organza and lace.

'It's not too late to change your mind about this marriage, my

25

dear,' their mother had urged, her gentle face distressed at the loveless step being taken.

'I've told you enough times, Maman,' Denise had snapped, 'Claude is very rich and, as you know, is highly respected in the government and other important circles. There is even blue blood in his veins and if he wasn't such a true son of the Republic he would use the title to which he has the right.' Her eyes glinted. 'In time I intend to see that he does. In any case, I'll be invited everywhere that matters and can have everything I want. That will make a change from here where Papa doesn't seem to like paying for anything these days.'

'How can you say that! You know he has business problems at the moment and yet he is giving you the grand wedding you wanted and no expense has been spared.'

'Only because he's glad to be getting rid of me!'

'You're so cruel! And on such a day!'

Juliette had watched the whole scene miserably, all the excitement generated by the wearing of such a pretty dress ebbing away. Somebody came to fetch her then, for the bridesmaids' carriage was waiting. She had looked back over her shoulder and seen the tears of hurt in her mother's eyes. Although she was unaware of it then, her mother had mentioned for the first time in her hearing that all was not well with the Cladel business empire. Eighteen months later her father suffered a fatal heart attack brought on by his financial ruin.

That was when Lucille returned to France in order to comfort the grief-stricken widow. She stayed as long as she could, but eventually she had to return home. Catherine found it impossible to readjust to life without Michel and sickened in her bereavement, falling an easy victim to influenza.

Immediately Denise took capable and compassionate charge. Juliette had long since concluded that her sister had felt needed for the first time. Denise had nursed her mother tirelessly, even though Claude, who due to his wife's pressure was using his title again, had engaged the best of medical care. It was all to no avail.

A tap on the bedroom door caused Juliette to turn from the window. It was the maid.

'Are you ready, mademoiselle? Madame would like to leave for Foyet's now.'

26

'Yes, of course.' Juliette picked up her wrap and beaded purse.

Lucille, waiting in the salon and resplendent in crimson brocade and rubies, nodded admiringly when Juliette came to join her. 'How pretty you look, my dear. Now we'll go.'

When they crossed the marble floor of the lobby Juliette glanced about under her lashes to see if the stranger was to be glimpsed anywhere, but he was not to be seen. Neither was he at Foyet's. She did not know if she was disappointed or glad.

CHAPTER THREE

'May I ask why you patronize Madame Paquin, whom Denise sees as her deadliest rival, and not Maison Landelle?' Juliette asked Lucille the following morning. They were setting out for the Maison Paquin in the carriage that had been hired with a top-hatted coachman for the duration of Lucille's stay.

'I shall buy some lingerie from Denise,' Lucille replied. 'She has told me she is unsurpassed in this line, not that she doesn't hold the same opinion about the rest of her creations. But I was one of Madame Paquin's first clients and she has looked after me for many years. I always know her garments will be comfortable as well as elegant, because she has every design made up to wear on trial herself before offering them to public view.'

'But Denise does that too.'

'Is that so? I didn't know.' Lucille's casual tone showed she had no intention of switching her patronage. Happy to have Juliette's company, she had asked her to take a free day before seeking work and Juliette had agreed, equally glad to make the most of their time together.

It was a warm, sparkling morning. The young foliage of the trees was fresh and green, not yet made dusty by summer. As they passed Napoleon's memorial column in the Place Vendôme the bronze plaques depicting his long-ago victories seemed to glow in the sun. Juliette looked about her as the horses clopped along. Motorcars were for speed and convenience, plenty of them tooting their horns on all sides, but an elegant carriage was still the best way to ride when wishing to see and be seen. And there was so much to see!

The tall old houses were still in need of paint, their weather-faded shutters flanking lace-curtained windows where flowering potted plants made bright splashes of pink and red. Rainbow-striped awnings spread wings over the café tables where people sat talking and drinking and watching the world go by. Along the Champs Elysées milliners' windows were full of hats as frothy and appetizing as the pastries in the pâtisseries; satin-ribboned boxes vied for places with pastel sugar almonds in every confectioner's; exclusive displays of jewellery glittered and sumptuous fabrics were swathed and draped in expensive shops.

'I'm glad we didn't drive direct to Maison Paquin,' Juliette said when the carriage eventually bowled into the gracious width of the rue de la Paix, Lucille having instructed the coachman to take a circuitous route.

'I wanted to see everything again as much as you, my dear,' Lucille answered.

Just before they passed through the portals of Number 3 into the courtyard beyond, Juliette glanced towards Maison Worth at Number 7. It was there tomorrow morning she would present herself and her needlework.

Within minutes of their entering Maison Paquin they had been welcomed by the *directrice* and then Lucille's own *vendeuse* was leading the way through luxurious salons. Juliette saw immediately that Maison Paquin was a favourite rendezvous for smart Parisiennes. Many sat chatting together, ornate hats close as gossip was exchanged. Others were being shown lengths of rich fabrics by *vendeuses* or were studying designs that had been specially drawn for them. Several had brought lap dogs with them and these tiny creatures, trimmed with bows, trotted about. Inevitably there was the occasional yelp when somebody inadvertently trod on one. This meant exclamations of distress from the nearest ladies and much petting and cooing to sooth the little victim. There were also a few bored-looking men, who sat or stood haplessly dangling hats and canes in their hands. Several fine-looking girls known as mannequins, the name taken from the dressmaking dummies used in the trade, paraded gracefully about in Paquin creations.

Lucille and Juliette were eventually seated in one of the smaller salons where they could view on their own the clothes that the *vendeuse* had selected for her client to see.

'You wrote of wanting a lace gown, madame,' she said to Lucille. 'There are several in exquisite Venetian lace for your consideration.'

At some unobserved signal the first of the mannequins to show clothes to Lucille came through a draped archway wearing an almond green morning gown. There followed more dresses for the same hours of the day as well as all the other changes of garments necessary for any fashionable woman from morning to night. Costumes for walking and calling preceded outfits for the races and motor drives, afternoon and tea gowns, dinner gowns and finally evening creations. Madame Paquin was renowned for her evening wear and each garment displayed seemed more sumptuous than the last. In Juliette's opinion those of Venetian lace were the loveliest of them all, although she would have preferred less ornamentation in the pearls and gold and silver trimming, the lace being beautiful enough in itself to her eyes. But in any case none of the clothes were for her and although her taste ran along simpler lines every one of the garments displayed would suit Lucille's Junoesque figure to perfection.

When all the ensembles had been seen more time was taken up as those that had most appealed to Lucille were shown again. Since she needed so many to take home with her not all could be decided upon in one session. In any case no final decisions could be made before a personal consultation with Madame Paquin, when modifications of style and colour best suited to Lucille would be discussed.

'The joy of couture clothes,' Lucille said later when she and Juliette were lunching lightly and deliciously at Voisin's, 'is that everything one orders is made specifically to one's exact measurements, even to the circumference of one's wrist. It's well worth the tedium of three fittings and sometimes more, because the result is always perfect. No dressmaker in all the world can compare with a Parisian seamstress. I only wish I could have asked for some clothes to be shown for you, Juliette. I'd love to buy you some pretty things, but I'm afraid Denise would hit the roof if she saw you wearing something by another designer.'

Juliette laughed, 'I know she would! But in any case I'll be a working girl very shortly and I'll have no need of anything as grand as those clothes we've seen this morning.'

The afternoon was spent driving leisurely through the Bois. Many other people of leisure were also in their carriages and in the tree-dappled sunshine the flanks of the high-stepping horses gleamed as if polished, harnesses shone and all the parasols, looking like pastel-hued mushrooms, were held in white-gloved hands. Lucille was extremely pleased when she and old acquaintances in oncoming carriages sighted one another and drew up alongside to exchange greetings. Invitations were forthcoming at once for her and Juliette, whom she proudly introduced. Although she had already accepted several written invitations from close friends, which had been awaiting her arrival, she found after consulting the small engagement book in her purse that she could accept each new occasion on behalf of Juliette and herself.

'There!' Juliette exclaimed triumphantly as they drove on again after the third halt, 'I told you that you hadn't changed! Everybody knows you at once.'

They discussed the invitations received, Juliette delighted to have been included. One was to dine that same evening, another to join a party at the Théâtre-Français at the end of the week and a third to the Opéra two days later. Juliette felt as if Paris were already taking her back to its heart. Then, suddenly, she saw approaching on foot the young man from the lobby whom she had not expected to see again.

He was strolling in deep and serious conversation with an older, equally well-dressed man who had a short, neatly-trimmed grey beard. Although there was little likelihood of the young man sighting her, Juliette felt her pulse quicken as the distance between them shortened.

Then came an unexpected development. The bearded man, happening to glance absently towards the carriage as it was drawing level, gave a start of recognition when he saw Lucille and quickly raised his panama hat. The young man turned his head sharply in the same direction, automatically following suit, and as Lucille bowed in gracious acknowledgement he saw who was sitting at her side. His intense, passionate eyes held Juliette's in the same flare of rapport as before. It was all over in seconds and although she did

31

not look back all her senses told her he was staring after her.

'That was Prince Vadim of St Petersburg and his nephew, Count Nikolai Karasvin,' Lucille said, not having noticed the exchange of glances. 'They're related to the Romanovs. I knew the Prince's late wife, Augustine. She was a fellow Parisienne and we were friends from our school days, writing regularly to each other after I left France. Sadly she died four years ago. Recently he married again.'

'Would the Prince be in Paris on vacation?'

'No, he has a residence here, usually winters in Monte Carlo and returns to Russia whenever he feels obliged to show himself at Court.'

'Does Count Karasvin lead the same kind of life?' Juliette almost held her breath in her eagerness to learn as much as possible about him.

'He has some minor diplomatic duties at the Embassy these days. When I was last in Paris he was still an assistant-student at Rodin's studio.'

'So he is a sculptor too!'

'It was a whim that his father indulged, according to Augustine. When I last saw him he didn't look as if he owned a franc, instead of which it's always been very much the reverse, but he kept odd company then.'

'Do you mean he led a Bohemian life?'

'He lived wildly with other artists in Montmartre. I know Augustine used to worry about him. But he's older now. At least twenty-five or so.' Lucille twisted in her seat to look penetratingly at Juliette. 'Why all this interest?'

Juliette assumed a nonchalant air. 'I liked the look of him.'

Lucille tapped the back of Juliette's hand with a warning finger. 'Never let yourself be bewitched by a man's fine looks, my child. Such men can be self-centred and faithless. It's far better to find a good, plain man for yourself. Reliability is what counts in the end. There's enough heartbreak in the world without inviting it.' She sighed as she looked ahead again.

The rest of the afternoon passed uneventfully. They had tea and ices before returning to the hotel. At the reception desk a letter with a crest was handed to Lucille. She opened it as soon as they entered the suite.

'It's from Prince Vadim,' she said after reading it through. 'He has

32

apologized for not knowing I was in Paris and invites us both to dine this evening.'

'How would he know you were staying here?'

'It's easy enough to make inquiries and there are only two or three top hotels where a woman of my standing would stay. More surprising is how he discovered your name, but no doubt the hotel gave it to him. I'll reply at once and decline through our having a previous engagement and send it by special messenger.' Lucille sat down at the secretaire and drew a sheet of paper towards her. 'I suppose he wants me to meet his new wife, which I must do eventually, but it will be painful for me, because I shall miss Augustine at his side. The men of that family have always been charming womanizers and poor Augustine had a very difficult time.'

Going into her room, Juliette could not help wondering if Nikolai Karasvin had instigated the invitation. Then she dismissed the idea. He would have no such influence on his uncle and most likely would not have been at the dinner party either. Yet she felt curiously in limbo as if waiting for him to make the next move.

When dressed early for the evening in one of her best silks, Juliette passed the time while waiting for Lucille by checking again the items of needlework she had put ready to take to Maison Worth in the morning. She had just added one more piece of embroidery when Marie knocked on the door and entered with a white beribboned box.

'This just came for you, mademoiselle.' She handed the box over and left again.

Mystified, Juliette sat down on the bed and removed the lid. Then she flushed with pleasure. Inside was a corsage of pearly-white orchids with green flecks rising from the deeper green surrounding the golden calyx. She took up the accompanying card and read it.

Mademoiselle Cladel. Since we are not to meet elsewhere this evening after all, I hope you will still spare me a few minutes of your time in the lobby now. Nikolai Karasvin.

She sprang to her feet in jubilation. If she took notice of Lucille's warning words about the Karasvins she would tear up the note and toss the corsage away. What he had suggested was in itself outrageous, for he was flouting convention completely. She checked the time. It would be at least another twenty minutes before Lucille appeared from her room. That gave ten minutes to keep Nikolai

Karasvin waiting in suspense, five in his company and then she could still be back in the suite before any awkward questions could be asked about where she had been. She was only too certain that Lucille would never condone such a meeting, but it was one she did not intend to miss.

After pinning the orchids to her green velvet waistband, Juliette went to the mirror and gave a few unnecessary touches to her hair. She could see the excitement sparkling in her eyes.

She watched the clock until the exact moment came to leave. Not even Marie saw her go from the suite. She thought Nikolai would expect her to take the stairs and so went to the lift instead, planning an element of surprise in her arrival and wanting to see him before he saw her. As she descended her heart began to beat a little faster.

When the lift operator sent the gates rattling back, Juliette stepped into the lobby and saw Nikolai standing by the pillar where she had first seen him. As she had anticipated, he was looking towards the stairs and was in profile to her. She began to stroll in his direction, taking in every detail of his features, studying him as she had been unable to do before. There was a powerful curve to the nostrils of his straight nose and a tan to his skin as if he rode a lot in the open air or had followed the increasingly popular sport of skiing. His whole frame bore out this possibility, lithe and athletic as if full of controlled energy. Another few steps and she would address him by name.

'Juliette!'

She halted abruptly. It was Denise who had called out to her, advancing with ostrich feathers dancing on her hat, a pale silk scarf floating about her neck, arms outstretched.

'I hadn't expected you to return yet!' Juliette exclaimed in dismay, able to see out of the corner of her eye that Nikolai had heard her sister call and had turned to look quickly in her direction.

Denise embraced her warmly, so full of high spirits that for the time being she seemed to have forgotten her previous fury. 'Yes, isn't it splendid! I had such a very successful business trip that I was able to conclude everything in time to return to Paris twenty-four hours earlier than I had anticipated.' Standing back, she tilted her head assessingly as she looked Juliette up and down. 'Yes, your hair put up in that new style suits you and you're as slim as ever.'

34

She began glancing about searchingly. 'Where's *Tante* Lucille?'

'Upstairs.'

'Then we'll go up to her straight away. She'll be glad to see me back.'

Just before the lift gates clanged shut Juliette saw Nikolai smile at her and shrug his shoulders in regret.

Denise talked all the way up and along the corridor about her new Mercedes that had been delivered during her short absence and in which her chauffeur had driven her to the Hôtel Bristol. Juliette scarcely heard her, angry with herself for having delayed going downstairs at once after receiving the corsage and even angrier with her sister for having returned to Paris so soon. She was further exasperated that she should place any importance on what would have been no more than a brief flirtatious encounter that should never have been contemplated in the first place.

In the suite Lucille was just emerging from her bedroom in her evening finery. Denise's affectionate greeting and her exuberance over her successful trip gave Lucille no chance to consider why Juliette should have been in the lobby to meet her. Then Denise, sitting back with a satisfied sigh, looked indulgently at her sister and unwittingly launched the topic that was destined to disrupt the present harmonious atmosphere.

'I've forgiven you for your hasty and foolish departure from the convent yesterday, Juliette. I knew I had this business trip coming up and intended to send for you afterwards. As for Monsieur Pellitier, I had no wish to force you into any marriage that was not to your liking. It was just that he was a dear man and I hoped you'd come to see that he would have made you a good husband. But never mind. There are plenty more fish in the sea and I shall make sure you meet the best of the eligible bachelors. We had better see about getting you all the clothes you're going to need, so come along to Maison Landelle tomorrow morning.'

'I'm sorry, but I can't do that.' Juliette spoke composedly from the chair where she sat. 'It's very generous of you and I don't want to hurt your feelings, but I've made up my mind to work for my living and to have a small place of my own, even if it's only one room at first.'

'Work?' Denise narrowed her eyes incredulously and sat forward. 'What could you do?'

'I can use a needle and in Paris a skilful seamstress and embroiderer will always find employment. I believe I have an eye for fashion too and I want to gain training for myself until eventually, away from Paris, I'll have a dressmaking business of my own. Tomorrow morning I'm taking samples of my work to Maison Worth.'

Denise screamed. There was no other way to describe the furious shriek she emitted, springing up from the sofa as if about to throw herself into hysterics. Lucille leapt to her feet in concern. Yet she was not in time to stop Denise darting across to deal Juliette a vicious slap across the cheek, sending her tossing back across the cushions.

'You little traitor!' Denise burst out on the same high-pitched note. 'After all I've done for you! What ingratitude! What heartlessness!' She would have struck Juliette again if Lucille had not been in time to grab her by the wrist.

'No, Denise! No! Calm yourself! This is no way to settle anything. Juliette has every right to choose a career for herself.'

'But not like this! She's stabbing me in the back!'

Juliette had also risen to face her sister. She had been relieved when Denise had proved amicable over her convent departure, but this display of temper was beyond comprehension. 'I don't understand you,' she protested in angry bewilderment. 'I only want to follow my own path in life.'

'But at my expense!' Denise, seeing she had dismayed her sister with her accusation, became calmer, although no less intractable.

'How can that be?' Juliette demanded. 'You made it clear enough that you wish to be rid of me through marriage and instead I've chosen my own way to relieve you of all responsibility for my future. I know from what you've said in the past that you consider Madame Paquin to be your rival and so I'd never sew for her, but surely Maison Worth would be neutral territory?'

'No! There's none as far as I'm concerned.' Denise's eyes glittered with sudden savage triumph as she delivered the ultimate blow to her sister's dream. 'I'll tell you something else! No matter how good your work, no *haute couture* house would ever employ you.'

'Would you have me blackballed?' Juliette's own rage burst forth.

'I wouldn't have to. Every door would be slammed in your face!'

'Why?' Juliette's demand was fierce.

'Use your intelligence! We are both Papa's daughters! He is still spoken of with respect in spite of his financial misfortune and everyone knows I was a Cladel before my marriage. In no time at all it would become public knowledge that we are siblings.'

'Where's the harm in that?'

'All harm! You'd never be trusted. New designs for a season are a closely guarded secret until the day they're shown as finished garments, and as soon as you revealed your identity you'd be suspected of being a spy. No couturier would risk the young sister of another head of a great fashion house being in his or her ateliers. The first question you'd be asked is why you were not giving me your support. The brothers Worth themselves would be held up to you as an example of close family bonds.'

'You know it's not a question of loyalty!' Juliette exclaimed in distress. She had not thought of herself being viewed in such a degrading light, but she could see how it might happen.

Denise drew in a deep breath. She was shaking, but she had regained full control of herself and was intent on gaining the upper hand. 'As it happens I believe now that you intended no treachery towards me, but unfortunately nobody else will. If you wish to test the waters for yourself, by all means go ahead and take your needlework samples wherever you wish, but you will cause me the worst humiliation I have ever suffered. I'll be ostracized by all the other couturiers as the one who tried to plant an informer.' Her voice choked deliberately on a note of appeal. 'I can't believe that you of all people would do that to me.'

Juliette, her eyes stark with disappointment at the destruction of all she had planned, raised her head a little as she answered almost inaudibly, 'You are right. Nothing on this earth would make me betray you in this matter. I'll go far away and find work where nobody will connect us as sisters. You need never fear that I'll compete in Paris with you.'

Denise concealed her satisfaction, but triumph was not hers yet. Gossip flew swiftly and even if her sister was working far from Paris it could still filter back that there was a rift between them, and that would be even worse if Juliette should begin to make her own mark in the fashion world. So far there had never been any threat to the good name of Maison Landelle and Denise was determined that not even the slightest shadow of a family scandal should fall across it.

She had always spoken of her convent-based sister in the fondest terms, continually on guard against any criticism being pointed in her direction for not having the girl to stay with her during the vacations.

'If you wish to overcome this setback I've put in your path, Juliette, you can work for me.'

'No! That's out of the question! I'm not being ungrateful, but it would never do! I have to progress and rise through my own efforts. It's vital to me!'

'Listen. I'll take you on as if you were any other applicant for work at the Maison Landelle. Your sewing ability is commendation enough. If you're as capable of advancement through your skills and intelligence as you believe, it will come to you through those in charge of each section of the business. Gradually you'll be fully trained in all spheres. Isn't that what you want?'

'Yes, but—'

'There'll be no privileges and you would have to adhere to the strict discipline that has to be maintained. But you'd have to live with me, which society would expect, and scrimp along on your wages as a beginner, because I'd pay you no more and no less than others engaged in the same tasks. It will give you a chance to rise by your own merits as if you were a stranger to me. Only out of working hours would we ever be as sisters.'

Juliette wanted to trust Denise, but to live with her and to work under her jurisdiction would be impossible. Then Lucille, as if reading her thoughts, spoke directly to her.

'Think carefully, Juliette. Take your time and weigh all that has been said. I'm sure that Denise would be the first to admit that it won't be easy for you in any way, but then you never expected to follow anything but a difficult path.'

It was true what Lucille said. Abruptly Juliette turned her anguished face away, struggling with her emotions. Denise watched her, more anxious for her sister's acceptance than she was prepared to reveal, because such an important reason for an affirmative answer had shot into her mind that she did not know how she would brook a refusal. She tried persuasion on another line.

'I know your opinion about an early marriage now, so don't fear that I'll put pressure on you ever again. I'll allow no man to pester you and the subject of matrimony need never be raised unless you yourself should wish it. We'd be starting afresh. The two Cladel sisters united in harmony.'

There was a long pause and then Juliette, her eyes stark, faced her sister again. 'You never wanted me in your home before. Why should you change now?'

'I never had any patience with children and you were better off where you were. Now it would embarrass me to have you living elsewhere. People would talk.'

'At least you're being honest with me.'

'Think back for a few moments. Have I not confided my personal problems to you several times since you grew older? Surely that is a basis to give you confidence that we have the joint ability to sustain our relationship. Had you not returned to Paris I doubt we would have seen each other again very often, but since you are here we have sibling duties that bind us, however much you might wish it otherwise.'

'I've never wanted the blood tie between us to be broken!' Juliette declared in a tortured voice. 'It's my personal liberty that I must defend.'

'Then out of working hours you shall have it,' Denise conceded. 'All I ask in return is that you conduct yourself respectably. Don't reject my goodwill. Be tolerant and let the arrangement be made.'

Juliette drew in a deep breath to keep a tremor from her considered reply.

'So you would keep your vow always to treat me as an ordinary employee at the Maison Landelle.'

'You have my promise. *Tante* Lucille is your witness.'

Juliette straightened her shoulders resolutely. 'Then I will do my best for you as I would have done for any other employer.'

Neither sister noticed Lucille heave a silent sigh of relief. Her great fear during these minutes of conflict was that Juliette in her torment would refuse the employment offered and end up sewing in a sweat-shop far from Paris. It would not have given the right experience for a prestigious future and even her health could have suffered. So many seamstresses died young of tuberculosis from poor working conditions.

'I ask only one favour, Juliette,' Denise continued. 'I want you to agree to the wardrobe of new clothes that I mentioned earlier. I'll need you to promote my ensembles whenever you appear anywhere

39

that matters socially.' She gestured appraisingly. 'Look at you now with those orchids pinned to your waistband, allowing the blooms to hang in just the right way. I noticed that detail as soon as I clapped eyes on you in the lobby. But some time ago, as soon as your figure began to develop fully, I could tell that you were like me in having inherited Maman's gift of wearing clothes with ease and elegance. Papa was quite a dandy too and so I suppose we get it from both of them.'

Lucille nodded in endorsement. 'Your sister is right, Juliette. She's not flattering you.' A twinkle close to mischief appeared in her eyes. 'And I agree that those orchids are perfectly placed.'

Juliette could tell that Lucille had most surely guessed the corsage was from an admirer and how the meeting with Denise in the lobby had come about. The fact that there was no sign of condemnation in her friend's eyes lightened Juliette's heart considerably. She was sure Lucille had also been romantically adventurous on occasions. The thought encouraged her as she answered her sister.

'If I can look half as well in Landelle clothes as Maman always did in her Worth ensembles I'll feel very proud to wear them.'

'You will.' Denise was prepared to be magnanimous in victory. 'Now enjoy whatever you and Lucille are planning for this evening. Tomorrow morning have your things sent to my house and present yourself at the employees' entrance to Maison Landelle. We'll start as we mean to go on.'

'Yes. I'll come in the morning, but until *Tante* Lucille leaves I'll stay on at the Hôtel Bristol.'

Lucille intervened quickly, not wanting to be the cause of any further dissension between them. 'No, Juliette, my dear. Circumstances have changed since that was decided. As you will have much to learn I think you should be with Denise to talk over the events of each day. But I shall count on seeing you for the engagements to which we have been invited and also whenever you can spare time to be with me.'

'That will be often!'

Denise was ready to leave. 'That's all settled then.' She made her farewells, kissing both her sister and Lucille, and then she was gone.

But Lucille was thoughtful. There had been a smugness in Denise's expression as she departed that stirred a certain mistrust. It was impossible not to wonder what was in her mind. Then Juliette was indicating the orchids at her waist. 'Do you want to know his name?' she inquired evenly.

Lucille read the determination in her face that was enabling her to cope with the switch from her original plan. 'I believe I can guess. It explains the urgency of the Russian invitation that arrived earlier. But be wary. Remember what I said about handsome men and the Karasvin males in particular.'

'Don't worry! I'm in Paris to work, not to lose my heart.'

As Denise descended in the lift she smiled to herself in satisfaction. It had suddenly come to her during the dispute that it could be to her immense advantage to have her sister at Maison Landelle. Her only regret in not having a child of her own was that she could not boast of having established a family business and that had caused her to harbour a secret envy of Maison Worth. But with Juliette trained and then making the right marriage, there would be offspring to draw into the business. There was no doubt the cloud of her sister's unexpected return had turned out to have the proverbial silver lining.

CHAPTER FOUR

When Juliette arrived at the employees' entrance of the Maison Landelle she was shown where to hang her hat and jacket and was given a crisp white apron to wear with a bib at the front and straps over the shoulders to tie at the back. Then she was taken to Madame Tabard, who was in charge of the sewing atelier.

'The Baronne let me know you were coming, Mademoiselle Cladel. In future you will arrive at seven o'clock – not at eight as you did today – and you will work until a break at noon for refreshment. Then you will leave your sewing apron on your chair, because cleanliness is of utmost importance when handling costly fabrics. Let me see your hands now.' She gave a nod when Juliette had displayed them. 'Good. I see you take care of your nails, which is what I expected in your case. Some girls have to be taught the first day. After that if a beginner, whether apprentice or seamstress, snags a fabric or soils it with a grease-spot it can mean instant dismissal. So clean, neat hands all the time. Is that understood?'

'Yes, madame.'

'Your day will end at six o'clock unless there is a rush of work for the completion of the new season's clothes or a special order or some other need to get work done before a certain time. The fact that you are the couturière's sister will make no difference to how you are treated here, except that you will be addressed as Mademoiselle Cladel as befits your position as a future head of Maison Landelle.'

'Is that necessary? I don't want to be marked out from my fellow workers.'

'But you have to be. How do you suppose you'd hold respect and keep a disciplined fashion house later on if the start wasn't made now? Not even a *directrice* gets appointed from her own training ground for that reason. You may face some hostility.'

'I hope to prove there's no need for it.'

'That will depend on you. I've been told that in addition to excelling in embroidery you were taught to dressmake by a nun who had been an experienced seamstress before taking the veil, but you can consider that just an apprenticeship. Here you will be shown all the finer details of couture. Now show me the samples of your work that I see you've brought with you.'

Madame Tabard realized as she examined the work that this new girl had been taught all she needed to know of stitching. Afterwards, as was the custom, she took Juliette on a tour of the whole establishment, for it was considered necessary that each new employee should view the various stages involved in the making of a garment from its drawn design until ready for the client. Juliette was shown some designs, each with samples of the allotted fabrics pinned to it. She knew that the next stage for any *haute couture* garment was to be made up as a *toile*, the name taken from the light fabric used.

Madame Tabard led her on to the cutting room where the male cutters and their assistants were hard at work. Juliette looked through a glass panel set in the wall of the corridor at the embroiderers engaged in their intricate tasks and was able to see into several of the sewing ateliers before she followed Madame Tabard into the one where she was to work. The seamstresses, each in a white apron like her own, sat at long tables. All of them, even the apprentices who were picking up pins or fetching reels of thread, hushed their quiet chatter as Juliette entered at Madame Tabard's side. On the way there the woman had told her that everyone had been informed, either directly or by the atelier grapevine, that the Baronne de Landelle's sister was joining the workforce.

'This is Mademoiselle Cladel,' Madame Tabard announced.

Juliette smiled at everyone there. '*Bonjour.*'

They all replied, some mumbling the words. Two or three gave her a cautious smile in return and several eyed her levelly with curiosity, but she could see that the majority were uncomfortable in her presence. Madame Tabard spoke to the senior first-degree seamstress at the table. 'I'd like Mademoiselle Cladel to sit beside you for a few weeks, Aude.'

'Yes. I can move Françoise to the end of the table,' the woman replied. Then she gave Juliette an amiable nod. 'I'll have some work ready for you when you return.'

From there Juliette was shown the pressing room, the storerooms and also the packing-room where sheets of tissue paper billowed and rustled as the costly clothes were placed in the green and white striped boxes of Maison Landelle ready for delivery.

'As you have seen for yourself,' Madame Tabard continued as she led the way from the ateliers up an uncarpeted flight to the showrooms and salons, 'everything connected with the making of a garment takes place downstairs in an area that the client never sees. Neither do they see the design studio on the floor above the salons. You will only see it when the Baronne takes you there. It is her domain and that of her designer, Monsieur Pierre.'

Juliette knew that Denise relied heavily on Pierre Clemont as did other couturiers on their designers when, like Denise, they had no atelier experience themselves. Yet Denise decided the season's line, made preliminary sketches and introduced the touches that gave Landelle clothes their individual mark of distinction.

The luxury of the salon floor struck Juliette anew after the starkness of the area she had just left. In the mannequins' *cabine* the girls were getting ready for the day, some sitting in front of their mirrors and putting discreet touches of rouge on their lips and cheeks. Fluffy powder puffs made clouds as arms and shoulders were dusted. None were yet in the clothes they would display later, but in négligés supplied by Maison Landelle over beribboned corsets, their stockings black or white. Juliette noticed there were two mannequins with red hair like herself. Both smiled at her, as did most of the others, and wished her well. All were intrigued; but they had no need to be wary of her, even though she was the couturière's sister, since her work would not overlap theirs. Then it was back downstairs again and she took her place beside Aude, who gave her a pink velvet skirt and told her what had to be done.

'If you have any problems over work you're given,' Aude added,

44

'always ask me or Jeanne, who's sitting at your right hand. She's a first-degree seamstress too.'

Nobody else spoke, all conversation having faded away at Juliette's return. When she had threaded her needle from the reel an apprentice had placed in front of her, Juliette let her gaze travel around the faces bent over their work. Her guess that each seamstress glanced under her lashes at her as soon as her attention was diverted made her decide to speak out.

'I hope you'll soon get used to me, everybody, because I'm here to stay. That is if I don't snag my material or – worse – soil my first task with a grease-spot.'

The unexpectedness of her declaring herself to be vulnerable to the threat that had hung over each one of them as beginners made some of the younger ones giggle in surprise.

'Would you really be thrown out?' one asked. 'After all, you're—'

Juliette interrupted firmly. 'I'm a new seamstress with much to learn and I'll stand or fall by the standard of my work.'

Another spoke to her. 'Have you served an apprenticeship?'

Juliette, who had begun to sew, told of the nun's instruction. Gradually those around the table became more relaxed and began chatting together again, although they did not draw her into their conversation.

The room where the women ate their packed lunches had an electric plate on which coffee could be heated. As Juliette opened her lunch packet she was exasperated to see that the Hôtel Bristol chef had given her pâté de fois gras, hard-boiled plovers' eggs, dainty rolls and a chicken breast garnished with aspic and cradled in a lettuce leaf with asparagus tips. Everybody else had bread and cheese. Tomorrow she would prepare the same for herself.

It was mid-afternoon when a bold-looking seamstress, clearly egged on by her neighbours, asked Juliette an edged question. 'Are you wearing a Landelle dress now? I seem to recognize the cut of the collar.'

Juliette looked straight at her. 'Yes, it's one of my convent dresses.'

'But what happens next? Shall we be sewing some of the grand gowns just for you?'

'I expect so,' Juliette replied evenly. 'I won't be sufficiently qualified.' As she renewed her sewing she could feel the chill of the seamstresses' hostility seeping out towards her, but she would not make any excuses for herself by saying nothing had turned out for her as she had originally planned. Then, next to her, Aude rested her needle and spoke up.

'I think we're very fortunate to have somebody in our midst who will be wearing the result of our efforts. It will make a refreshing change from sewing for the unknown clients upstairs. Perhaps Mademoiselle Cladel will let us see her in some of the finished garments.'

There was silence as all watched for Juliette's reaction. She looked at Aude in surprise and relief at the tactful intervention. 'I'd be glad to.'

There was a murmur of interest and approval around the table and Aude gave a nod of satisfaction. 'Well said, Mademoiselle Cladel.'

There was a diversion then as a fitter came from upstairs with two gowns that needed additional trimming to suit the client's wishes and the rest of the day was uneventful as far as Juliette was concerned. Before going home she thanked Aude for her intervention, thereby helping her through some difficult moments.

'I've no wish to flaunt my benefits,' she said. 'All I wanted was to be an ordinary trainee here, but that doesn't seem to be possible.'

Aude looked at her sympathetically. 'Don't worry about it, even though you're not out of the woods yet. I know it's not unusual for the son of a head of a business to start from the factory floor, but a girl who is the sister of the couturière of a fashion house can't expect the same tolerance from other women, especially when some of them have hard and difficult domestic circumstances. Drunken husbands, dependent elderly parents, widowhood, a sick child and so forth. I've heard it all.'

'They come to you with their troubles?'

'Yes, they do. Sometimes if it's a broken heart no more than a few words of comfort are needed, but I've had desperate cases sometimes when a poor girl is pregnant. So whenever you encounter jealousy or what seems to be unreasonable spitefulness, just spare a thought as to what those seamstresses might be going home to every evening and try to be tolerant. After a while everything will settle down. If you're not proud – and I don't think you are or else I wouldn't have intervened on your behalf as I did – all will be well and you'll gain their respect. You'll also have their loyalty in the years ahead.'

'I hope so and I appreciate your kind advice.'

That evening Juliette went straight from work to Denise's large house in the faubourg St Germain. Her sister was already at home and came to meet her in the spacious hall with its graceful crystal chandeliers and Persian rugs in russet hues.

'So you found your way here all right. How did your first day go?'

'It was very interesting and all my work was approved.'

'Good. I'll take you upstairs and show you your room. It's where you slept for a few nights after Maman's funeral before I took you to the convent, but it's been redecorated since then.'

Juliette looked around her as she accompanied her sister up the curved flight. Nothing was as she remembered it. 'You've changed everything since I was here.'

'Yes, Claude hated the upheaval of decorators and I sent him off to the family villa in Tuscany until it was all done. Incidentally the villa is mine now. I managed to get him to sign it over to me when we were on our honeymoon there, but I never seem to have time to take a vacation these days.' She opened a bedroom door and entered ahead of Juliette. 'You have your own bathroom. I had one installed for every bedroom.'

This was the height of luxury and Denise was proud of it. Even the best hotels had a meagre number of bathrooms and few, if any, grand homes in France could offer guests the individual facilities to be found in her house.

'I shall appreciate that,' Juliette said. She could tell that her trunk had been unpacked since its delivery from the hotel, for her hair-brush and hand mirror were on the dressing-table. The room was light and restful in soft green and white, very different from the dark décor of eight years ago when she had sobbed herself to sleep in the grief of bereavement every night.

'Remember the chemise I brought to the convent?' Denise said, pulling open one of the drawers in a tall chest. 'You'll find it here with all else you will need in nightwear and lingerie. I'd thought these would be part of your trousseau, but now that you're in Paris you'll need them. The housekeeper took away all the underwear decreed by the convent and after dinner we'll talk about the new Landelle clothes that you're to have. I brought some designs home with me.'

For a few moments Juliette felt as if she could not breathe. She clenched her teeth at the manner in which Denise was high-handedly sweeping her along as if she had no will of her own. Then she reminded herself that this was part of the agreement made and once the initial stages were over she would be at liberty again. At least Denise was doing everything out of goodwill and she must be glad of that.

Her fluctuating colour must have given her away, for Denise suddenly regarded her with rare understanding. 'If I seem over-bearing at times it's just my way. You should know better than anyone it's how I've always been and ever will be. But I want you in the business and I'm pleased you're here, even though I didn't expect to be when I first heard you'd left the convent.' She moved to the door. 'Come down as soon as you're ready.'

After taking a bath Juliette put on a set of the new lingerie, which was of softest lawn trimmed with hand-made lace and satin ribbons. After the thick cotton of the past there was a sensuous pleasure in feeling these dainty garments against her skin. She continued to be aware of them even when she had put on a dress and re-done her hair. Downstairs she found her sister in a salon panelled with flowered Lyonnais brocade. Denise was glancing through the designs she had mentioned and on one of the tables swatches of various fabrics in all colours were piled high.

'Pierre sketched some of these today for you,' Denise said, looking up as Juliette came towards her, 'and the rest are ideas we had in the pipeline, so nobody else will have anything just like them. I've already made some changes and,' she added indulgently, 'you may have a few suggestions of your own. But we can discuss all this later.'

Over dinner the talk was inevitably of Maison Landelle. As Lucille had said, Denise had never had anyone before with whom to talk over the day's happenings and now she was able to chat away, knowing she had her sister's intelligent attention. It had been the same when she had poured out her pent-up troubles on the convent visits. And, above all else, she knew Juliette would keep to herself whatever she was told in confidence.

When the time came to look at the designs Juliette selected several and then made a final choice. It was difficult to persuade Denise to dispense with the extra frills and loops on some of them, but eventually they reached a compromise on each design. Only on the evening gowns did Denise refuse to budge. She was determined to uphold her reputation for magnificent evening wear and anything too simple would not be to her standard.

'People will always be eager to see what my sister is wearing and in the evenings I want you to dazzle. But night or day you'll be the best advertisement I could have, because, even though I wear my own creations you have youth on your side.'

It seemed churlish not to fall in with Denise's wishes and since the evening gowns were beautiful, Juliette acquiesced and agreed to all the designs.

'That's good.' Denise was satisfied. 'Another advantage you'll have in wearing these clothes is that you hold yourself with a statuesque pride.'

'Do I?' Juliette raised her eyebrows with a smile. 'It must come from all the times I was punished by having to stand with a book on my head!'

Denise knew it was more than that. 'Now choose the fabrics and the colours that you like best.'

There was no dithering when Juliette made her choice. Denise was able to see that her sister knew instinctively what would be right both for herself and each particular design. Juliette looked amused when Denise commented on this with approval.

'I learned about choice long ago from you.'

'From me?' Denise was surprised.

'I was too young to notice Maman's clothes, except that she always looked pretty and had a sweet fragrance about her. But at the convent where everything worn was the black of the nuns' habits and the sombre shades to which the pupils were restricted you would burst on the scene looking like an exotic peacock. From your first visit I noticed every detail of your attire. The rich patterns of your dresses, the intense and sometimes deep colours of the shaded fabrics, even to the silk lining of your furs and the summer gauzes on your hats. A love of fashion was awakened in me and has been with me ever since.'

'You never told me!' Denise said wonderingly, quite overwhelmed to discover she had been such an inspiration.

'My passion for sewing was for the day when I could enter the world of *haute couture*.'

Denise felt triumph burst anew within her. A family business was truly destined for Maison Landelle! She wished that Juliette were already fully trained and the time had come to find the right husband for her, a rich man malleable enough to allow his wife to continue working between babies and who could be made a director, thus ensuring his support and interest from one generation to the next. And she, Denise Landelle, would become a legend in her own time just like the couturier Worth himself!

Quite overcome, she threw up her hands joyfully and then clasped them as if her dream were already realized. 'How fortunate it is that you have Titian hair!'

She was thinking of the sensation her new evening gowns would cause when Juliette was seen in them.

Juliette's measurements were taken the next morning before the clients arrived. She observed the meticulous care of the fitter and remembered Lucille's words as her wrists were measured.

When it became apparent that in spite of the haste none of the gowns would be ready for the evening at the theatre, Juliette chose to wear a topaz chiffon from the current Landelle collection and it was adjusted to her measurements. She was dressed and ready to go downstairs to await Lucille when Denise came into the bedroom with a jewellery case. She opened it to reveal a necklace and earrings of pearls.

'These were Maman's. I intended to give them to you on your wedding day, but now I think you should have them to wear whenever the occasion arises.'

Juliette, deeply moved, embraced her sister. 'I had no idea. I thought everything was sold to meet Papa's debts. Have you anything of Maman's for yourself?'

'Yes, a ruby brooch. That was all she kept.'

'I'll treasure these pearls always.'

Lucille noticed the pearls as soon as she collected Juliette in her carriage and they set off for the Théâtre-Français together. 'You're wearing Catherine's pearls.'

'You remember them?'

'Naturally. They were your father's gift to her when you were born. So it's right and proper that they should be yours.'

Juliette touched the pearl necklace lovingly. Denise had not told her that. Perhaps she had forgotten.

At the theatre their host, Monsieur de Bourde, was waiting

for them in the foyer and took them to his box where his wife greeted them warmly and they were introduced to the other couples who made up the party. Juliette was given a chair where she would have a superb view when the curtain went up. Ivory opera glasses had been handed to her and she scanned the boxes opposite as well as the rest of the auditorium in case she should see Nikolai, but it was in vain. Soon she was enjoying the music and spectacle of the operetta and was too absorbed to notice the arrival of a party of latecomers, who took their seats in the third row of the *fauteuils d'orchestre*. The highlight for her came in the last scene before the interval when a group of dancers created a delicate rippling and swirling of gossamer silk veils patterned asymmetrically in wonderful colours until the whole stage dazzled.

Juliette joined in the thunderous applause. Then, as the curtain descended, she turned enthusiastically to Madame de Bourde. 'Those lovely veils! What a spectacle!'

'They're called Knossos scarves by their designer, Fortuny. I first saw them in a ballet performed in the Comtesse de Béarn's private theatre in her house here in Paris. I've heard that those veils are being adopted as a fashion accessory by some women.'

'I'm not surprised. They'd be very flattering.' Juliette was turning the pages of her programme. When she found the designer's name she read it out. 'Mariano Fortuny y Madrazo. I see he designed all those splendid lighting effects too. His name sounds Spanish.'

'That's what he is. He was born in Granada, the son of a very distinguished artist, not far from where my husband and I have stayed on vacation. That's how I know. Apparently there's a custom in Spain of linking the father's name with the mother's for a child's name, but normally he's known just as Fortuny.'

'Is Fortuny married?' Juliette felt she wanted to know as much as possible about this talented man.

Madame de Bourde raised her fan and whispered behind it. 'He associates with a divorced woman! They live together!'

So Mariano Fortuny was not afraid to flout society! The rose-tinted lights of the auditorium were beginning to lower again. Juliette made up her mind to ask Denise more about the designer at breakfast next morning. To her disappointment the Knossos scarves did not appear again.

The foyer was teeming with the departing audience waiting

for carriages and cabs when Juliette was addressed by someone close by.

'*Bonsoir*, Mademoiselle Cladel. Did you enjoy the performance?' It was a Russian-accented voice, deep and beautiful, that she had never heard before, but which she knew instantly.

Her lips parted in a quick, indrawn breath. As she turned her head she saw Nikolai was beside her, even more powerfully masculine and attractive at close quarters. He was smiling at her with a recognition that seemed to go back far beyond the few times they had glimpsed each other.

'Yes, I did,' she replied quickly. 'Especially the wonderful scene with the Knossos scarves.'

'Ah! Fortuny.' He nodded approvingly. 'A master in many fields of invention. I've been an admirer of his theatrical lighting effects for some time.'

'I knew nothing about him until this evening.'

'I'd like the opportunity to tell you more. I'm sure you're keen to know how and why his theatrical lamps and illuminating devices are being adopted all over the world.' His eyes were dancing at the obviousness of the ploy he was using and she was equally amused.

'Not particularly. I'm not technically minded. It was his use of colour that appealed most to me. Is his work the reason you came here this evening?'

'No, although he only works with the best, such as Diaghilev's *Ballets Russes*, La Scala operas and so forth. Unfortunately I was late going in this evening as the friends I was to meet here were not in time.'

She recalled his impatience when he was waiting in the hotel lobby. 'I think you are always on time yourself!'

He grinned. 'How did you guess that? Yes, I am, except in certain circumstances when time loses all meaning.'

She wondered if that was when he was sculpting. 'Did you miss much of the performance?'

'Only about ten minutes.' Then he gripped her arm and steadied her as someone jostled past and the contact brought her close to him. She realized that she had been separated from those she was with, for the crowd was constantly moving forward and edging through, but she did not care. Neither she nor Nikolai made any attempt to draw apart again and he lowered his voice on a smile,

52

even though none could overhear anything either of them said in the babble of noise. 'I saw you in the interval. If I had known any of the party you were with I'd have called at your box.'

'So that we could be formally introduced?' she questioned quizzically.

He laughed quietly. 'I fear I've rather taken that for granted since my uncle and I are acquainted with Madame Garnier.'

'She was with me in the box.'

'I didn't see her!' He threw up a hand in exasperation. 'If I had I'd have been there. Instead I watched for your leaving.'

'You've given me the chance to thank you for the beautiful orchids you sent me at the Hôtel Bristol.'

'That attempt at a meeting was a fiasco. Who was the lady that whisked you away?'

'My sister whom I live with. If she had known I was going to speak to a stranger without a chaperone—' She left the sentence unfinished, rolling up her eyes expressively, and he laughed with her.

'Socially it was unforgivable of me, but I couldn't take the risk that you'd vanish for ever if I didn't make some attempt to contact you. I asked your name at the reception desk.'

'You instigated the dinner invitation too, didn't you?' She was amused.

'Yes. One would have been forthcoming, but I wanted no delay.'

'You're being very frank.'

'And you're being very tolerant. Since both of my previous attempts failed to result in a meeting would you agree to my making a third try? This time I'll ask your sister's permission first.'

'It would make matters easier.'

'Then let's—'

But Madame de Bourde, all unwittingly had come blundering between them. 'We thought you were lost in this crowd, Mademoiselle Cladel! Come along quickly! You're keeping everyone waiting. The carriage taking us on to supper has been blocking all the rest for minutes! Oh! How I hate this crush!'

Juliette looked back over her shoulder as she was hustled away. Nikolai called to her. 'What's your address?'

She answered, but was not sure he caught what she said. He grinned and shook his head in mock despair; although that might have been at yet another untimely interruption. Then he was lost from her sight in a sea of silk top hats. She was undismayed. He would soon find her again.

At breakfast next morning Juliette spoke of Fortuny to her sister. Denise was eating a croissant with strawberry preserve and was unenthusiastic about him.

'I admit those Knossos scarves are quite pleasing, but not as a fashion accessory. They're so large. Why would any woman want to swathe herself until she looks like a Greek statue? As for Fortuny's ability in the theatre—' she paused to shrug his achievements away '—that's only because he knows a lot about lamps, being a photographer as well. So you can tell what he is in all, can't you? A jack of all trades. In the end that kind of person comes to nothing.'

Juliette could not help wondering if Denise was jealous because she had not designed those scarves. 'I can't agree. On the strength of what I've seen on a single occasion I'd say he was greatly talented.'

Denise smiled indulgently. 'Naturally you were impressed. Everything is new to you yet, Juliette. There is really nothing unusual about whisking scarves about on the stage. Isadora Duncan does it all the time. She's to dance again in Paris next week. We'll go to see her and take *Tante* Lucille too.'

When the evening came Juliette thought the barefoot dancer in her loose, flowing robes was marvellously fluid and vibrant in her movements and her grace with a long trailing scarf was a delight. But it was not a Knossos veil and the dream-like effect was missing. Juliette's curiosity about Fortuny remained unsatisfied.

CHAPTER FIVE

Two letters bearing the Karasvin crest were delivered to Lucille within half an hour of each other. The first was from Prince Vadim with another dinner invitation two weeks hence for herself and Juliette, which she was able to accept this time, but the second was from Nikolai and caused her deep concern. She read it through several times and then paced the salon of her suite holding the letter he had enclosed and which he asked to be forwarded to Juliette as he did not know her present address.

She sat down in a chair and rested her forehead in her hand. What was she to do? Nikolai's letter to her had been brief, but to her eyes very revealing, showing that his selfishness was limitless. She had to consider Juliette before all else. When she had first warned the girl about the Karasvin men she had never supposed for an instant that Nikolai might loom as a shadow across the girl's life.

Lucille reviewed all that had happened. The giving of orchids had not seemed important, for it was typical of Karasvin men with their wealth and eye for beautiful women to make such a gesture. It had given Juliette pleasure upon her arrival in Paris and that had been all that mattered. Before that there had been the sighting in the Bois had followed, making excitement throb in the girl's voice afterwards, even though she had been unaware of it, and then had come that tell-tale radiance in Juliette's face when she had told of meeting Nikolai in the theatre foyer. In all it added up to very little, but Lucille could not dismiss from her mind a line once written by Victor Hugo that a single glance could plant a flower in another's heart.

If only it had been any man other than Nikolai that had sent a glance at Juliette! Lucille remembered how in one of Augustine's last letters she had written of how ruthless he was with women, causing her to despair of him. Too handsome, too rich and too spoilt had been her summing up of her nephew by marriage.

Slowly Lucille rose to her feet, unsure how long she had agonized before finally reaching her decision. In her bedroom she unlocked her jewel-case and put the letter at the bottom under the trays, then turned the key again. Her conscience would plague her, but Juliette's well-being came first. Had not she herself, after many innocent, romantic encounters, finally fallen in love with a similar handsome womanizer, who had left her so broken-hearted that she had married kind, sensible and dull Rodolphe. She did not deny that time healed, but it never filled the emptiness left in the heart.

Juliette was delighted that the first of her new dinner gowns was delivered in time for the evening at Prince Vadim's. It was of heavy cream satin with a pattern of roses in a deeper shade with folds at the back ending in a slight train and a *décolletage* that skilfully avoided showing the cleavage.

'This modest whim of fashion gives all of us women a kind of mono-bosom,' Juliette joked at one of the fittings. 'I can only hope that mine won't look like a pumped-up cushion!'

'Yours', said the fitter on her knees as she adjusted the hem, 'could never look like that, although I've thought differently about the pictures I've seen of the Gibson Girl. But then she has never been dressed by Maison Landelle. You will always look as nature intended.'

Juliette could see for herself that her figure was not disguised when she stood before her bedroom cheval-glass as Denise's maid fastened the last of the tiny hooks and eyes at the back of the gown. She understood now what it was truly like to wear couture clothes. Her simple convent garments and those she had worn on vacation had been beautifully made to her exact measurements, but as she was never in Paris there had been no fittings. This gown was in a different category altogether. Her narrow waist, held in the gown's under-bodice, was smooth as a stem, not the minutest pucker anywhere. She might have been sculpted in this gown by Michelangelo – or by Nikolai. The thought made her eyes sparkle. In less than an hour she should be seeing him again!

Yet when she and Lucille arrived at the Prince's house and entered the gilt and green salon she knew instinctively, even without looking around, that Nikolai was not there. She had pictured him coming forward at once to greet her and her disappointment was acute. He was late! How could he not have arrived on time! It must be the traffic. She smiled as she was presented to the other guests and made light conversation while all the time she waited for Nikolai to appear in the doorway. Then the Prince happened to mention casually that his nephew had returned to St Petersburg on important family affairs. All the lustre faded from Juliette's evening.

'When will he be back?' she heard herself ask bleakly.

'Who can ever say what the young will do?' the Prince replied jovially, greatly taken by her. He considered himself to be a connoisseur of the arts and of women and this fine-looking girl with her seductive figure and innocent yet passionate mouth delighted his eye.

Juliette wanted to cry out that Nikolai had most surely left a message for her, but at the same time she realized what a foolish notion that was. Clearly she had read far more into the way Nikolai had looked at her than had ever been meant. She swallowed hard.

'What of his interest in sculpture? Would not that bring him back to Paris?'

'It can only be a hobby for him, no matter that he is exceptionally talented. He has responsibilities and commitments in Russia that he can never relinquish. His duties stand before all else.'

'Is any of his work on public view?'

'Not at the present time, although he has exhibited on half a dozen occasions at the invitation of the *Société Nationale des Beaux-Arts* in the Salon at the Grand Palais, which is a considerable honour.'

'Yes, indeed!'

'As you're interested in sculpture, I have a bust of myself that my nephew did about two years ago if you care to see it.' Taking her answer for granted he took her white-gloved hand into his, smiling

57

into her eyes through his black-ribboned pince-nez. 'It would be a pleasure to show it to you later.'

But he had no chance. His second wife, eagle-eyed and twenty years younger, had no intention of being another betrayed Augustine and it was she who showed the ladies the bust of her husband after dinner. Juliette went forward to study it closely, although with the exception of Lucille the rest showed only polite interest. Cast in bronze, it was strongly and vigorously sculpted into a penetrating likeness that had brought searingly to the surface the weaknesses as well as the qualities of the aristocratic man whose likeness it was.

'This bust should be in a better light!' Juliette exclaimed involuntarily. It was set back in an alcove where even by day it would be in gloom.

Her hostess made a deprecating little gesture. 'The Prince doesn't really like it, but accepts it is an exceptional work of art.'

Juliette could see how it would offend the Prince's conceit, for although it showed the laughter corners of the eyes, courage in the line of jaw and resolution in the chin it did not flatter in any way, the mouth fleshly sensual and there was a sagging to the handsome jowls. She saw Nikolai had signed his name on the base and had to restrain herself from running her fingertips along it. On the drive home she and Lucille discussed the sculpture.

'Nikolai Karasvin has his own individual style,' Lucille said after consideration, 'but the influence of Rodin is there. With the exception of certain great masters, there's probably never been a sculptor more committed than Rodin to depicting the truth of what he sees in men and women. The Prince's nephew is following the same decisive lines.'

When Juliette had alighted at her home Lucille, alone again in her carriage, breathed a sigh of thankfulness that the evening was over. She had seen for herself how the news of Nikolai's departure to Russia had taken all the light from the girl's face. It was as if a bright candle had been snuffed. But Juliette would learn a lesson from this disappointment. By the time Nikolai returned, if ever he did, she would be far more sophisticated and used to the irresponsible ways of men. She would not be easily snared again.

At home Juliette, having been helped out of her gown by Denise's maid, sat in front of her dressing-table mirror to brush her hair. As soon as the maid had gone from the room, her offer of further help declined, Juliette stopped the strokes and let her head drop disconsolately. It was over with Nikolai before it had begun. She would never allow herself to be so vulnerable to any man again.

It was very hard for Lucille to leave Paris when her vacation came to an end. Her conscience continued to trouble her over the letter she still had in her jewel-case, but there it must stay. She and Juliette both wept on the platform of the Gare du Nord as they kissed each other's cheeks and embraced in farewell. Denise, who had already said *adieu*, glanced surreptitiously at her watch as she waited by the open door of the carriage. Within it Marie, excited to be going home while dreading the sea voyage, waited for her mistress to enter, the jewel box on the seat beside her.

'Don't stay away so long again, *Tante* Lucille,' Juliette implored as she and her friend drew apart.

'Not if it lies in my power,' Lucille promised in a choked voice. 'Be sure to keep writing.'

'I will.'

Lucille paused on the step of the carriage and, regardless of Denise being within earshot, spoke earnestly to Juliette. 'Remember if ever things don't go well and you want to leave Paris, you can always come and live with Rodolphe and me.'

Juliette felt some surprise. Had Lucille guessed how deep her disappointment had been that Nikolai had gone without leaving her a message? She shook her head gently. 'You told me I hadn't looked for an easy path and nothing has changed.'

Denise snapped into the conversation. 'I should think not. Nothing worth having comes easily as I know to my cost!'

From the open carriage window Lucille exchanged a smile of understanding with Juliette. Denise had not the least idea of what either of them meant.

When all that could be seen of Lucille was her fluttering handkerchief as the train chuffed away into the distance, Juliette continued to wave until it was out of sight.

As soon as Juliette's new wardrobe was finished Denise launched her into society with a series of dinner parties and musical evenings. From the first occasion Juliette was included in all the return invitations and many others as well, for young people of her own age, mostly the sons and daughters of Denise's acquaintances, drew her into their circle. All knew she was being specially trained at Maison Landelle. Some of the girls, who hankered for a chance to do something more concrete with their lives other than preparation for eventual marriage, declared themselves envious of her chance, but Juliette knew that none of them had any conception of how hard a seamstress worked.

She was popular with the young men, her dance programme always full within minutes of her arrival at any private party or ball. Although she liked two or three more than the rest, even permitting a kiss now and then, she remained uninvolved, and since she and the other girls were never without a chaperone nearby no complications ever arose.

With Lucille gone from Paris no more invitations were forthcoming from Prince Vadim. Occasionally Juliette saw him with his wife at the Opéra, or in a restaurant. If they passed her she was graciously acknowledged with a slight bow, but they never stopped to speak and she knew nobody else who could give her news of Nikolai. As time went by she was sure he had not returned or else she would have seen him somewhere at the functions she attended. It was a wonder to her why she could not erase the image of him from her mind. It was even painful to accept that he might have forgotten her by now. Once she even pricked her finger on this thought while sewing, but a little drop of spittle erased the tiny spot of blood from the fabric.

When writing to Lucille, Juliette often covered several pages entertainingly about her work as well as her social activities. Once she wrote that nothing had surprised her more at Maison Landelle than to discover it was anything but a peaceful place and she had been told it was typical of all the other couture houses. Whenever a new client came there was competition between the *vendeuses* as to who among them would become her personal *vendeuse*. If it was believed that an unfair advantage had been taken a storm erupted as soon as was possible out of earshot. The *directrice* had to cope with temperamental clients, who screamed and cried with disappointment when they decided a finished gown did not suit them after all, or something else had seemingly gone wrong. There were arguments at the sewing tables, squabbles in the pressing room, fitters displayed their fury when some alteration was not done to their specification and sometimes hair was pulled in scraps that flared up in the mannequins' *cabine*. Occasionally Denise herself stormed through the workrooms.

Juliette viewed it all like a spectator at a circus, intrigued by everything. At first her work was simple and mundane, however rich the fabric, but she was never bored and took a pride in the seams and hems and tucks that flowed out from under her needle with barely visible stitches. Then she advanced to setting in panels of silk, velvet and net, as well as those of silver-gilt threaded with diamanté imported from Turkey; others were necessary insertions to maintain the mono-bosom effect. Fastening intricate trimmings from lace to bobbin-fringes was another of her tasks.

It pleased her that she was no longer given the easier work and the more difficult it became the more she felt she was passing another milestone. Sometimes she found she was sewing a garment for herself. Denise was increasingly promoting Landelle designs through new outfits for her.

'You turn heads wherever we go,' Denise enthused on one occasion when several orders came in for the design her sister had been wearing the evening before. She often regretted that Juliette could only be seen at weekends or in the evenings after work, but that could not be changed, for the whole future of herself and Maison Landelle depended on her sister's full training. 'I think you should have a soft green silk for your new gown for the Longchamps races.'

'Won't I match the track too much?' Juliette joked. 'I could be lost against it.'

'You're right,' Denise answered, failing to see she was being teased, for she had almost no sense of humour. 'Let's make it apricot. All the citrus colours are so dramatic with your hair.'

Later Juliette paraded in her apricot ensemble for her fellow seamstresses as she did with all her Landelle clothes. If there was a half-train to a garment her fitter's assistant would always gather it up to avoid it coming in contact with the stairs and floors of the ateliers, even though these areas were kept spotless to protect the precious fabrics from being soiled in any way.

It was when Juliette was wearing a newly-finished blue chiffon *robe de dîner* and was waiting for the fitter's assistant to accompany

61

her down to the atelier that one of the two red-haired mannequins, named Yvonne Rouband, came along. They had always exchanged smiles, but rarely spoken. This time the young woman paused to compliment Juliette.

'That blue suits you very well, Mademoiselle Cladel!' Yvonne was looking very fine herself in a striped gown she had been displaying. They began chatting about the colours they liked to wear.

'Are you ever allowed to wear pink or red?' Juliette asked.

'Not here,' Yvonne replied with a laugh, 'but I'd love to appear in scarlet and I have a crimson blouse at home.'

'I feel the same yearning for scarlet,' Juliette agreed, 'and I should think you look splendid in crimson.'

'Thank you!'

In her own mind Juliette thought Yvonne looked marvellous in everything she wore, even the simple clothes in which she came to work, for apart from her good looks she had a beautiful figure with full breasts and tapering hips.

'As you can see,' Juliette continued, 'I'm on my way downstairs to display my new gown. Could you give me any tips as to how to do it professionally? I think it would amuse everyone.'

'I'd be glad to,' Yvonne said willingly, 'even though you really need no instruction, because so much of being a good mannequin is in the walk. But if you insist, then go slowly along this corridor for a few paces and then turn to look back over your shoulder. After another three or four paces do a half-turn and look the other way. I'm talking about display in the limited space between the tables of the ateliers. When coming through the salons there is much more space for a mannequin to move around.'

'Is this right?' Juliette asked as she looked back the second time while following instructions.

'Excellent! Do the same again and this time try making the ruffles on the half-train dance a little by kicking out slightly as you turn.'

Later Juliette gained more tips from Yvonne, who showed her how to swirl a cape, toss a scarf carelessly over the shoulder, the most graceful way to dip one's head in order to display a hat specially created for the ensemble and even how to hold a parasol to show sleeves to advantage. They chatted whenever they met.

It was when Juliette was sewing in the atelier that she happened to hear Yvonne being discussed by two of the most sharp-tongued seamstresses at another part of the sewing table.

'It's true,' one was saying, 'she's been an artists' model for some time. I always thought she was as vain as a peacock about her figure. It's not enough for her to flaunt herself with clothes on, but she reveals herself with them off!' They both sniggered.

'How did you find out?' asked another seamstress on the opposite side of the table.

'My sister's new beau knows Yvonne. He works in the Montmartre gallery where the artists hang their work, hoping for a sale. Several nudes of her have been displayed and sold.'

'How could she pose with no clothes on! I'd die of embarrassment!'

'So would I!' There was another explosion of malicious giggles.

Juliette, busy with her sewing, thought to herself that their assumed shock probably had its roots in jealousy that Yvonne had such a superb figure. Aude, snipping threads with her scissors, spoke for Juliette's ears alone.

'If these particular seamstresses didn't live at home they might be thankful to earn a few extra francs in honest work. Yvonne has to find rent for her room and I know she's been saving to bring her sister to Paris.'

'But she's Maison Landelle's best mannequin. Isn't she paid accordingly?'

'She may get a little extra, but all mannequins receive a low wage.'

Juliette spoke to Denise about the mannequins' wages that same evening. 'Why aren't they paid more?'

Denise raised her eyebrows incredulously. 'What a notion! Why should they be? All they have to do is walk about in the most beautiful clothes in Paris. *Mon Dieu!* I wish my daily routine was as easy as theirs!'

'But it can be very hard work too. Just think what they have to put up with when a difficult client explodes with temper.'

'I admit that some clients can be cantankerous, but most of the girls would be mannequins for no pay at all if the truth were known.'

'Whatever do you mean?'

Denise regarded her cynically. 'I'd have thought that by now you'd have heard enough tittle-tattle in the ateliers to know that in being a mannequin a working girl has a better chance of meeting rich men

63

than anywhere else. No other kind comes to the salons of a couture house. Three of my mannequins have the most favourable addresses through being mistresses.'

Juliette gasped. 'I hope you don't take that chance into account when you fix the girls' wages.'

'Of course I don't! What a foolish question to ask! I pay the same rates as most of the large couture houses, the others pay far less. So if you're angling for a rise in your own wages it's too soon yet.' Denise held up a placating hand quickly. 'All right. I see by your expression that you weren't. Now let's end this discussion before we fall out. Things haven't been going too badly up until now.'

Juliette flushed. Peace had only been maintained because many times she had bitten back retaliatory answers, reminding herself that she and Denise had struck a bargain. No good could come of constant disputes.

CHAPTER SIX

The first time Juliette was followed she was not aware of it at first. She had been given time off from the atelier while a cut finger healed and had decided to go to Rodin's studio on the rue de l'Université in the hope that she might see some of Nikolai's sculptures there. It was as she was waiting to cross the street that out of the corner of her eye she saw a woman sketching her from the pavement nearby. Since Paris was full of artists she would have thought no more about it if the woman had not darted across the street ahead of her to continue drawing as she approached.

It was then that Juliette realized the woman was one of the notorious dress spies who, knowing her identity, had seen she was wearing one of Denise's new autumn designs, perhaps even knew she was the first to wear it. These spies rushed their information to manufacturers, who in turn competed with each other to bring cheap copies into the shops in record time.

Hoping for Denise's sake that the spy had not managed to get all the finer details of the buttons and braiding on the jacket and skirt, Juliette broke into a run and glimpsed the surprised fury in the woman's face as she darted past. Passers-by also turned their heads at her speed. She ran the rest of the way and when she reached the studio she darted through the open double doors that were standing wide.

Astonishment as well as breathlessness brought her to a standstill. It was a vast place and the scene was of bustling and noisy activity. She had always supposed that sculpting took place in silent concentration, as it would do in a private studio, but here several sculptor-assistants were at work clad in linen overalls and the only sculptress among them wore the traditional triangular cap that kept her hair free of the tiny chippings that flew from the marble she was chiselling. All were engaged in individual tasks. As far as Juliette could see only two were working from life, one model being an old man and the other a mother cradling a baby in her arms. It was a wonder the child did not wake, for all around was the hammering of scaffolding being erected and sculptures being crated for transport, the rumbling of trolly-wheels pushed by work-boys over flagstones, shouting, whistling and a whole cacophony of sounds echoing and re-echoing among the high rafters. Dominating everything were the great high 'Gates of Hell', sculpted by Rodin himself, about which she had read so much, for the work had been commissioned by the State and was still unfinished after many years.

Juliette took a few steps forward, feeling singularly out of place in her bright corn-yellow costume amid the muted greys, terracottas, whites and browns of that cavernous studio. One of the sculptors, spotting her, thought she looked like a living flame in her vivid attire and tawny hair topped by a plumed hat. He was in the process of re-arranging screens on wheels that were shielding from general view his nude model presently waiting on the stand with a kimono thrown about her shoulders. Leaving his task, he strolled across to the new arrival.

'Mademoiselle?' he said inquiringly, certain she was not a model and wondering if she was one of Rodin's latest conquests. In spite of the *Maître*'s age and grey beard women still found him immensely attractive. 'I'm Anton Casile. May I be of any assistance? If you want to see the *Maître* he's at one of his other studios.'

'Oh, no. I've no wish to trouble him. I came hoping to look at some sculptures.'

'You've come to the right place,' he remarked drily.

She caught his amused glance and smiled. 'It's not Monsieur

Rodin's masterpieces that I wish to see, but work by another sculptor. It's that of a Russian whom I met a little while ago.'

'To my knowledge there's only ever been one Russian here. Is it Nikolai Karasvin?'

'Yes. So you know him.' It gave her pleasure just to hear his name spoken.

'He and I, with some fellow artists, often enjoyed a few bottles of wine together, discussing and arguing about art at a café table all the night through.' So, he thought to himself, she is another of Karasvin's conquests and not the *Maître*'s as he had first supposed. 'But he has gone away. Did you know that?'

She nodded, feeling again the painful tug of disappointment at Nikolai's departure. 'It's his work I'm interested in,' she said deliberately.

'Of course.'

She heard the mocking tone in Anton Casile's voice and knew she had failed to convince him. 'So have I made this visit in vain?' she persisted.

'I'm not sure.' Anton turned to speak to one of the work-boys going past with a bucket of wet clay. 'Marcel, are any of Karasvin's pieces still here?'

'There's the *Athlete* and a couple of others.'

'Put that bucket down and show them to our visitor.' Anton smiled at her again. 'Mind you don't slip on any wet clay, mademoiselle. It gets dropped around when we're working and isn't always cleared away as quickly as it should be.'

'Thank you. I'll take care.'

Marcel led the way. Juliette followed, looking about at all there was to be seen, for this was an entirely new world to her. When she expressed interest in racks of various chunks of marble Marcel explained that they came from different places and the quality varied, some much easier to work than others. A huge block of Carrara marble stood alone, looking like a giant iceberg left high and dry on the flagstones. There were also shelves of seemingly forgotten works of art, for bronze and plaster figures as well as horses, feet, hands, limbs and torsoes all jostled each other and gave the effect of curious frescoes against the walls. Finally Nikolai's sculptures were reached.

'There you are!' Marcel said with a sweep of his hand towards

67

them. 'That's *The Athlete* and next to it is *Sea-Bather*. Cloths are covering the third one because it's unfinished.'

'But the cloths are damp. When is he expected back?' Hope had made her voice tremulous.

'Don't ask me, mademoiselle. It's my job to keep unfinished works damp or else the clay will crumble away. I'll go on doing it until the *Maître* or somebody else tells me to stop. I'll leave you here. You'll find the way out, won't you?'

Left on her own Juliette lost all sense of time, even the din of the studio seeming to fade away. Both the finished works were cast in bronze, the athlete caught in the last strenuous effort to pass the winning line, his face tortured and every straining muscle of his nude body taut with the final burst of energy and power. Stark and dramatic, it was as if at any moment the figure might speed from its base into the distance.

The sea-bather was a woman, lusty and seductive and beautifully shaped, sitting nude with one leg tucked under her, her back arched and her elbows high as she combed back her wet hair with her fingers. This figure was as tranquil and at ease as the other was alive with furious movement, but in no way was it over-shadowed. Each sculpture commanded attention in its own right. Juliette viewed them both for a long time, first from where she stood and then from every angle, knowing that unlike a painting a sculpture had to be looked at as a whole from all sides.

Finally with a soft sigh of appreciation she moved away, glancing again at the covered sculpture as she wondered what was concealed and if it would ever be finished. Then she went back through the various sections of the great studio. She stopped only to study the anguish and torment and beauty of the figures that gave Rodin's gates such splendour.

She did not see Anton Casile again and guessed he was at work behind the screens. When she emerged into the sunshine there was no sign of the spy. She walked home leisurely, her mind full of the magnificent sculptures she had seen.

A few days later Juliette needed some binding at work. Seeing the apprentices were all busy she went herself to fetch some. Nothing at all usable of surplus fabric was ever thrown away and pieces left over by the cutters went into large lidded chests. She knew that the fabric she was working on had been popular recently and she expected to find what she wanted very easily.

It was as she was sorting through the multi-coloured collection of pieces that she happened to find a narrowly pleated length of silk in what at first looked coppery in colour, but when she pulled it out it swirled about her hands like a soft snake, its sheen creating a shimmer of gold and coral as well. Fabrics were often pleated in various widths, but this was entirely unusual, the pleats so narrow as to give the illusion of a deep rippling of the silk. She knew she had never seen the original garment, for she would not have forgotten it. Almost without thinking she held the gentle fabric to her cheek and it seemed to cling in a caress.

Fascinated, she began to search in the chest to see if there were any more pieces. Three more lengths came to light and she realized she was holding the sections of a kind of gown that might have been worn by a woman of Ancient Greece. She could only suppose it was one of Monsieur Pierre's designs that had been made up and discarded, for it was not his usual style at all.

Taking the pieces with her, Juliette went to the cutting room. 'Do any of you know anything about these cast-out remnants?' she asked the cutters and their apprentices.

All shook their heads. She was more successful with one of the seamstresses who specialized in pleating.

'Yes, I remember it,' the woman said. 'It's about a year ago that Madame la Baronne called me to her office where she and Monsieur Pierre were trying to discover how the pleating was done after it had been unpicked. In all my years I've never seen narrow pleats quite like them. Whoever made it must have some trick of the trade unbeknown to the rest of us.'

'There are some eyelet holes. What was it laced with?'

'Thin cords rolled of the same silk.'

Juliette returned to the chest where she had found the pieces but although she rummaged through all its contents, and did the same with the other chests to see if she could find the original ribbons for the lacing, nothing came to light. She could only suppose they had been thrown away.

'What are you doing, Juliette?' It was Madame Tabard.

Juliette straightened up. 'I came originally to find a scrap of binding, but I became interested in this pleated silk.'

69

'You haven't time to waste. Put it back and take whatever it is you're looking for. Next time send an apprentice.'

Juliette was highly reluctant to relinquish the silk in case by unlucky chance somebody should decide to cut it up before she could retrieve it again. Swiftly she rolled the pieces together and thrust them deep down at the side of the chest.

She could hardly wait for the day's work to be finished and to get home to ask Denise about the pleated garment that had been so ruthlessly taken apart. When she had changed for dinner she went to the garden room where her sister sat in a cushioned basket chair reading a newspaper. The doors were open to the green lawn, the flower beds and the evening air. She paused to greet her sister.

Denise answered without taking her eyes from the newspaper. 'What a lot of depressing news there is to read these days. A runaway horse killed an old woman on the rue Royale, there's been an earthquake in Japan, the Kaiser is enlarging his army and some peasants have created more trouble in Russia.'

Juliette sat down in a neighbouring basket chair. She always read any snippets of news about Russia in case the Karasvin family should be mentioned, but that had not happened yet. Instead she had learned much about a vast country that had barely raised her interest in past geography lessons. *Le Figaro* had reported the brutality of arrests there and the merciless prison sentences imposed on the pathetic-sounding trouble-makers. It made grim reading. The Tsar should learn a lesson from what happened to Louis XVI of France, although such a tempest of revolution was unlikely to flare up anywhere ever again.

'Today I found some most unusual pleated silk in one of the chests,' Juliette began.

'Did you?' Denise answered absently, turning a page to the social column. She liked to keep abreast of any news concerning her clients.

'I was told the manner in which it was pleated remains a mystery.'

Denise lowered the newspaper to look at her. 'You must mean Fortuny's Delphos robe. I managed to get one from his Venice workshop. Not under my own name, of course. I didn't want the word spreading that I was at all interested in what he was making, but I had heard a remark here and there about his garments and wanted to examine one for myself.'

'I didn't know he designed clothes for women other than for the stage.'

'He doesn't. They're just shapeless nonsense, supposed to be inspired by some ancient Delphic statue, but anyone in *haute couture* can see that they are in no way related to fashion. In any case, what can he hope to achieve stuck far away in Venice? Nobody would go all that way for an inferior garment when Paris offers only the best. In my opinion the Venetian air has addled Fortuny's brain.'

'I'd like to buy that silk for myself,' Juliette said. It was the custom at Maison Landelle to let the seamstresses purchase surplus remnants at a reasonable price when the fabric was at least two years out of season or rejected for some other reason. 'I realize that it's only been in the chest for probably less than a year.'

'That doesn't count in this case. It was not my fabric originally and should have been burnt. I don't know why it wasn't. So let Madame Tabard set the price and remember I never want to see it again. That means not using it to make one of your pretty little evening purses out of it as you have with other scraps that you've bought. Make shoe-bags for your footwear or cover some coat-hangers. Anything that is normally out of my sight.'

Juliette smiled. 'I promise!'

She knew Denise hated to be beaten by anybody or anything and the sight of the pleated silk would be an anathema to her, reminding her of a mystery she had failed to solve.

For weeks the silk lay untouched in its tissue paper in one of Juliette's drawers. She had not forgotten it, for it was linked hauntingly in her mind with the ethereal beauty of the Knossos veils and, far more important, the last time she had seen Nikolai Karasvin.

Afterwards Juliette could never be entirely sure when she had reached the decision to join the pieces of silk together again. She happened to be alone at home on an evening when Denise was elsewhere and she went back upstairs after her solitary dinner to take the silk from the drawer. Carefully she spread the pieces out on her bed and was able to see exactly how the sewing should be done.

It could not have been simpler. She re-sewed the original seams together and the result was a cylindrical robe that would hang straight from the shoulders when laced through the tiny, exquisitely-bound

71

eyelets, leaving the neckline *bateau*-shaped and giving the effect of bat-like sleeves. On another evening she laced the shoulders with rolled silk ribbons, the hem already edged by Venetian hands. Then she took off her own dress but hesitated before she put on the new garment. Surely her petticoat would spoil the line of the gown, for it must hang sleekly when worn. She took it off and on impulse removed everything else too.

She slipped on the gown. Even as she crossed the room to the full-length cheval-glass a gasp escaped her at her own reflection, something that had never happened when viewing herself for the first time in any of the Landelle clothes, lovely though they were. She saw that the tiny pleats of the Delphos robe clung shimmeringly to the contours of her figure without any violation of modesty, revealing and yet skilfully concealing while emphasizing her feminity and the freedom of her body beneath.

What Fortuny had begun with the veils he had brought to fruition in creating this glorious, deceptively simple and yet sensual gown that was fine enough to pull through the proverbial wedding ring, and yet was first and foremost a celebration of the female figure. Even the rich copper-gold of the silk glowed and deepened with the slightest movement, the hem gently rippling. Whenever she stood completely still the pleats of the skirt curved slightly inwards from calf to ankle, almost like a mermaid's tail, the hem spreading out on the floor and concealing her feet. She marvelled again at the genius of the designer. This exquisite gown made all the other evening gowns she possessed seem archaic with their boned bodices and extravagant decoration.

Yet she would never be able to wear it. Not only would Denise be offended, but she herself had promised to keep the silk forever out of her sister's sight. After twirling once more before the mirror she took off the Delphos robe to lay it back in the drawer. To her surprise, now that the pieces had become a garment again, the pleats coiled like a skein and she could see it was the perfect way to keep it uncrushed.

In the morning Juliette went early to work and searched again in the chest. She thought that perhaps the designer's label might have been thrown in with the pieces. Unfortunately she did not find it.

72

CHAPTER SEVEN

Throughout the time she had spent in Paris Juliette had corresponded with Gabrielle Rousset. The exchange of letters with her former school friend was infrequent, each being busy in her own sphere, Gabrielle's entirely social. Then Gabrielle wrote of Derek Townsend, a thirty-year-old English merchant banker, whom she had met in Monte Carlo where they had fallen deeply in love.

Juliette was pleased for her, but unfortunately the courtship was not running smoothly, hampered by Derek's business commitments that kept him in England for weeks at a time and the determined opposition to the match by Gabrielle's mother, although her father, always at loggerheads with his wife, approved. It was an impasse that would prove difficult to overcome.

When Juliette had been exactly a year at Maison Landelle she was upgraded to first-degree seamstress. She had been doing advanced work for some time and the main difference now was that she received instructions as to what adjustments were needed after fittings from the fitters themselves. She and the other seniors then delegated work within the capability of lower-grade seamstresses, keeping the most complicated work for themselves.

'Madame Tabard has always had every confidence in your ability,' Denise said one evening at dinner in a rare moment of praise. 'She would have upgraded you earlier if she could have been sure that it would not cause dissention among two or three other seamstresses awaiting a step up.'

'It was the right decision.' Juliette was thankful she had not been given priority sooner. Her relationship with most of her fellow workers remained good, but it was a delicate balance.

A triumphant letter from Gabrielle the following day gave the good news that finally she and Derek were to marry, thanks to her father who had threatened her mother that he would give them permission to elope if she persisted in opposing the match. Madame Rousset's objections had crumbled in the face of the scandal that would have resulted.

So we are to meet again at last, dear friend, Gabrielle continued in her neat hand. *Mother and I are coming to Paris for my bridal gown and trousseau. She is making the best of the situation and now intends to outshine all her friends with her daughter's wedding! My only regret is that we are to get everything from Maison Worth and I had hoped that you would sew my bridal gown, but she is insistent and my father says we must try to avoid any more terrible scenes.*

Although Juliette explained the situation, Denise took offence immediately, seeing the Roussets' decision to go elsewhere as a slight to herself.

'I would have thought,' she said sarcastically, 'that since you and Gabrielle were supposed to be such friends that the order should have come to Maison Landelle. When I think how I allowed you to visit the Roussets when you were at the convent I'm even more surprised!'

Nothing Juliette could say would pacify her.

The reunion between Juliette and Gabrielle took place on a warm June day at four o'clock on a Saturday afternoon at the English Tea Rooms near the Opéra. Juliette was already seated at a table when her friend arrived in a primrose muslin gown and a pretty hat. Juliette sprang to her feet and Gabrielle's brown eyes lit up joyfully in recognition. She hastened to Juliette and they embraced exuberantly, laughing and talking at the same time.

'It's been so long, Juliette!'

'How wonderful to see you again!'

'It seems like yesterday and yet so much has happened!'

74

When they sat down Juliette would have ordered tea with lemon and pastries, but Gabrielle shook her head. 'I wanted to meet you here for us to have an English tea together.' To the waitress she said, 'A pot of tea for two with milk not lemon, scones and jam and also fruit cake.' Almost shyly she faced Juliette again. 'I'm trying to become as English as possible in readiness for living in London, although Derek says he wouldn't want me to change in any way, because he loves my French accent when I speak English – Oh, how I wish I'd studied harder during English lessons at the convent! – and my mannerisms and everything else about me.'

'I'm sure he does. My English is a little rusty too.'

'No, you always had a gift for languages – not only English but Italian and Spanish too.'

'You exaggerate! We only had Spanish for half a term when those two Spanish nuns came to study Sister Berthe's special embroidery, but the other two languages I did enjoy learning. Have you met any of your future in-laws?'

'Not yet, but Derek's mother and his brothers and their wives are all coming to the wedding. I wanted you to be my bridesmaid, but' – here Gabrielle shook her head with some of her old sadness from the past – 'I'm to have six of my cousins and nobody else. You see, I've had to compromise on several issues.'

'I understand,' Juliette reassured her sympathetically. 'But the worst is over. You can look to the future now.'

Gabrielle smiled again. 'What of you, Juliette? Never have you written of any man being important in your life.'

'There isn't anyone. I thought there might be once, but nothing came of it.' Juliette shrugged regretfully.

'Did you fall in love?'

Juliette shook her head quickly. 'I didn't mention anything about love. It was just someone I found attractive.'

Gabrielle listened attentively to her friend's account of the brief episode with the Russian. 'At least you've found out that one man can overshadow everything, even though you thought yourself dedicated to a career.'

'I am still! That didn't change!'

With a wave of her hand, Gabrielle dismissed the protest. 'After Derek and I are married I want you to come and stay with us in London. He knows so many people and I'll watch out for a charming

75

bachelor and make sure you meet him straight away.'

Juliette laughed. 'Are you turning into a matchmaker already? I thought one had to be a plump mature matron to fill that role. But,' she added humorously, eyeing the tea being set before them by the waitress, 'I think you've every chance of becoming the right size very quickly if you indulge in a spread like this every day in England!'

They saw each other again several times before Gabrielle and her mother left Paris after the final fittings. Denise, still harbouring her pique, had her petty moment of revenge when the wedding invitations arrived. She declined hers and forestalled Juliette's expressing a wish to attend.

'It will be at the height of the rush when clients want everything ready for the autumn season. No other first-degree seamstress would be granted time off just then, and when we first arranged your training you yourself insisted that you were never to be granted any exceptional privileges.'

Juliette accepted the situation, but it was a bitter disappointment for her and the bride.

September was as busy as Denise had foretold. Juliette was putting the final stitches to an evening gown when she happened to glance towards the interior windows of the atelier, which looked out into a hallway and the cutting rooms beyond. Yvonne's sister, who had come to Paris some time ago, was going past. Although Juliette knew her by sight she had never met her. She wondered if the girl had come to apply for work and then thought no more about it as her sewing absorbed her again. Later over dinner, when Denise's careful tone showed she had something on her mind, Juliette still did not make any immediate connection with Yvonne or her sister.

'There's something I'd like you to do for me,' Denise said, toying with her wine glass as if uncertain how her request would be received.

Juliette was interested. 'What is it?' she asked.

'I've an important Russian client coming to Maison Landelle tomorrow. She has light auburn hair very similar to yours and she'll only view clothes displayed by mannequins with the same colouring.'

'You've Yvonne and Isabelle.'

'That's just it. Unfortunately Yvonne is away sick and, as you once

76

told me she has taught you how to display clothes, I'd like you to fill the gap temporarily.'

'So that's why Yvonne's sister was in the building today! Did she say what was the matter?'

'At first that it was a bad cold, but the *directrice* had her suspicions already and a few astute questions brought out the truth. Yvonne has had an abortion.'

'Poor Yvonne!' Juliette exclaimed compassionately.

Denise frowned impatiently. 'Don't be sentimental! There's no excuse. Whatever trouble Yvonne is in she has brought it on herself. Any woman can say no.'

'You're not going to sack her?'

'I think so. I don't want her coming back tearful and too weak to stand for hours and all the rest of it. It's happened with other mannequins over the years and usually I find it best to get rid of them. It would never do either for clients to suspect what has happened.'

'There's no reason they should if Yvonne takes enough time to recover. I'll stand in for her as long as you like on condition you don't sack her.'

Denise glowered. 'One can't be soft-hearted in business. I could get red wigs for some of the other mannequins.'

'I don't think that would please your client.'

'Very well.' Denise gave in ungraciously. 'Yvonne did teach you the tricks of a mannequin's trade and that in itself is helping in this crisis. There'll be no need for you to display clothes to anyone other than my Russian client. Her uncle is Prince Vadim. Although you went to his house once you won't have met Countess Anna Dolohova, because it's over two years since she was last in Paris.'

Juliette drew her in breath. No doubt the Prince had any number of nieces, but could this woman be Nikolai's sister? Although it was foolish to still be interested in him he continued to haunt her. Sometimes, lost in realms of fantasy, she thought it might be because he still thought of her, but in the cold light of day this possibility had to be dismissed.

'Tell me about the Countess,' she requested.

'She was widowed soon after her last visit and is enormously rich. The Russian aristocracy never heed the cost of anything and she has always spent a fortune with me, which is why I want nothing to go wrong. This time I'm expecting an even larger order, because she'll be replenishing her entire wardrobe after two years in black. It means she must only be shown clothes in subdued colours, because Russians still observe a third year of mourning, but there need be no restrictions on the actual designs and all evening gowns will be *décolleté*.'

'I'll do my best for you,' Juliette promised.

'I know you will.'

In the morning Juliette had to try on some of the clothes that would have been shown by Yvonne and was viewed in them by the *directrice* as well as the Countess's *vendeuse* and her fitter, all wanting to be sure that everything would fit well. Fortunately Juliette's measurements were virtually identical to Yvonne's and all was satisfactory.

'What's the Countess like to deal with, Hélène?' Juliette asked the *vendeuse* who was helping her out of the last gown she had been viewed in, the other two women having gone. Hélène was always pleasant, unlike some of the other *vendeuses* and also the fitters, who took upon themselves a status according to the rank of the clients to whom they were personally assigned. Although Hélène was *vendeuse* to two British princesses and three royal duchesses, who were considered equal to Russian royalty, she gave herself no airs. Members of minor European royal families came next in importance, but Frenchwomen whose titles went far back into French history, gave special esteem to those in couture houses who attended them.

Hélène put the discarded gown on a padded hanger. 'The Countess is very charming and dignified, but if she's displeased she's a terror. So watch out!'

'Thanks for the warning!'

By now clients had begun to arrive. When Juliette went into the mannequins' *cabine* the girls were all in various stages of dress and undress. Dressers' nimble fingers fastened hooks and eyes, smoothed down the folds of skirts and dealt with the tiny loops of sleeve buttons. Their assistants darted about, fetching clothes from racks, shoes of the right colour and whatever accessories were needed. Yet it was organized chaos, except when a mannequin's squeal told of a glove momentarily misplaced or a hat-pin driven in too hard. The senior dresser sighted Juliette.

78

'Over here! The hairdresser is waiting for you.'

Juliette's hair was brushed until she thought it must surely pop from its roots and then to her dismay was dressed over padding to give the exaggerated pompadour that fashionable women favoured. When the rest of her long tresses had been pinned into a coil like a rose on the top of her head she was claimed by a dresser named Sophie.

'It's day gowns and calling costumes first for you and Isabelle.'

When the two of them were dressed there came the waiting for Countess Dolohova to arrive. Isabelle, in grey velvet, buffed her nails while Juliette, in cinnamon silk, observed the little dramas going on when shoes pinched, a corset lace broke and a mannequin gave vent to wrath after parading for over an hour in the same gown for a client who still could not make up her dithering mind. Then there came the signal from Hélène that she had brought the Countess into the best of the individual viewing salons. Juliette, who was to go in first, went forward.

'Good luck!' Isabelle said.

Juliette gave her a grateful smile and went through into an anteroom to turn in the direction of the salon where the Countess would be waiting, Hélène in attendance. But as Juliette entered through the draped archway a spasm of joy hurtled through her. Nikolai, his back half-turned towards her, his hat and his cane in his hand, stood talking to the Countess, who sat gracefully against the tasselled cushions of a sofa, her sable coat thrown back from her shoulders. Clad in black, Anna Dolohova's rich tawny hair set off her triangular, finely-boned face with the thin arrogant nose, curved brows and darkened lashes giving drama to the violet-blue eyes.

'We'll meet later then, Anna,' Nikolai was saying. 'It will be good to see Boris back in Paris again.' He grinned at her impudently. 'I'll leave you now to your orgy of new clothes.'

'Don't tease!' she replied good-humouredly, making a little pretence of kicking out her foot at him. 'You never change.'

'You may count on that,' he gave back in the same vein. '*Adieu* until this evening.'

He drew away, intending to go out of the door that still stood open to the reception area, but he took no more than a single step. He had caught sight of Juliette just as her hands jerked up involuntarily as she would have made her presence known to him.

79

But his reaction at seeing her was not at all what she had expected. For no more than a second or two there was dazzled disbelief in his eyes that was immediately swept away as a glacial fury engulfed him. 'You didn't write!'

His pent-up outburst was equally astonishing to the Countess. 'Nikolai!' she murmured in protest. 'What are you saying?'

He did not seem to hear her, but took a step nearer Juliette. 'At least you could have given me the address of this place if you wished to keep me at a distance when I returned! I didn't have to know where you lived!'

She was too bewildered for a retaliatory anger to rise in her. 'I don't know what you're talking about! How could I write? I had no address and in any case when you left Paris I'd no idea if you'd ever be back. Not even your uncle knew.'

'But I sent you a letter telling you why I'd been called away and asked Madame Garnier to—' He broke off as realization dawned on both of them. 'So she didn't forward it to you as I requested?'

'No,' Juliette replied quietly. She felt shattered at such a betrayal of trust by Lucille, even though she knew that her friend would have had her best interests at heart.

He was as devastated as she. 'I must ask you something, Juliette,' he said, forgetting he had never addressed her by her Christian name before. 'Would you have written to me if you had received my letter?'

'Yes!' she replied without hesitation, realizing that throughout the eighteen months that had passed neither of them had forgotten the other.

On the sofa the Countess gave a discreet little cough to remind them of her presence. Nikolai became animated at once and took Juliette by the arm to draw her forward. 'I'm delighted to introduce you to my sister Anna, Countess Dolohova.'

As the introductions took place Juliette could see Anna's astonishment beneath the surface politeness. It was easy to realize that the Russian woman was thinking that never in her life before had she been introduced to a mannequin. For her it was akin to being expected to exchange social pleasantries with a servant. Nikolai, oblivious to his sister's reaction, went on to tell her that he and Juliette had last spoken in a theatre foyer.

'We discussed Fortuny. Isn't that so, Juliette?' He wanted her to know that he remembered everything.

Juliette nodded. 'I've seen nothing of his on the stage since then.'

'Neither have I. But that can be put right very quickly. He has created several lighting innovations at the Opéra in the new production opening next week. He also had some influence on the costumes, which should please you. Anna shall be chaperone. Won't you, Anna?' He had tossed the question over his shoulder, taking an affirmative answer for granted as he continued talking to Juliette. 'So tell me your sister's name and where I can call on her to ask permission to escort you as we arranged at our last meeting. Would she be at home if I went there as soon as I leave here?'

Juliette, her eyes sparkling, could guess the further consternation of the Countess at being expected to chaperone a mannequin. 'No, my sister isn't to be found at home at this time of day, but she's not far away. Denise happens to be the *couturière* of Maison Landelle and is in her office now.'

Anna spoke up in surprise. 'Do you mean the Baronne de Landelle? I'm well acquainted with her! But I didn't know she had a sister.' There was a different note in her voice and Juliette could tell that the Countess was relieved to find that she might just be socially acceptable after all.

'I was away at a convent school for a long time. In fact, I saw Nikolai for the first time on the day I came home to Paris.' Briefly Juliette explained that she was standing in for a mannequin who was indisposed and that normally she was sewing garments and not displaying them.

'But why are you a seamstress?' Anna inquired incredulously. 'I should have thought the Baronne would have found – well – a pastime more suited to you.'

'But it isn't a pastime. It's my career.'

'I suppose you come into the category of The New Woman!' Nikolai interrupted, knowing his sister's resentment over her own lack of freedom throughout her marriage and subsequent mourning might erupt into spitefulness. 'I admire you for it, Juliette! It's time women gained recognition of their rights.'

Anna had become impatient with this interlude. 'You must go now, Nikolai. You are holding up everything with your presence. Go and see the Baronne. Mademoiselle Cladel has been delayed long enough in showing me all I've come to see.'

He turned to Juliette. 'Say you're not otherwise engaged this evening and will join Anna and myself when we go out to dine. An old friend will be coming too if he gets back to Paris in time.'

'Yes, I'm able to come.' Nothing could have prevented her from accepting.

He wrote down her telephone number and address in his diary and she told him where to find Denise's office. Then he left the salon, pausing at the door to look back at her. His satisfaction at the outcome of their reunion was as transparent in his expression as it was in hers.

'Now,' Anna said as the door closed after him, 'there should be no more delays. So let me see what you're wearing, Mademoiselle Cladel.'

But as Juliette paraded to and fro Anna's mind was on more than the gown. She had been astonished by her brother's behaviour. He had been like a man in love. But why? He'd had other women far more alluring and never shown his heart so transparently. Maybe he found Juliette more of a challenge than the rest, sensing a difficult chase to get what he wanted from her. He had even spoken of her, although not by name, one snowy afternoon at home in Russia when he was particularly cast down by circumstances controlling his life. Anna recalled it was in his studio, there being three hundred rooms in their father's palace where Nikolai had his own spacious apartment. She herself had come home for a while in her widowhood while selling the house near St Petersburg where she had known only unhappiness with her late husband whom she had loathed, the marriage having been arranged without her wishes being consulted and her protests crushed. Nikolai was working in clay, sculpting a young woman's head. He saw she had brought him some mail, which she had taken from a servant who had been on the way upstairs with it.

'Is there anything from Paris?' he asked at once, his hands becoming still.

She glanced through the letters and shook her head. 'No. Were you expecting something important?'

He resumed his task and did not heed her question. 'I'm impatient to get back to France. There's work at the studio I left unfinished. So often the momentum goes if a project is left too long.'

'As soon as Father is confident there'll be no more disturbing uprisings in the district you'll be free to return.'

82

'Free!' he echoed bitterly. 'I'm as tied as any peasant on the land.'

She sympathized with his predicament, but in her opinion it was infinitely better than hers had been at any time until widowhood had suddenly and mercifully released her and left her a rich woman. At least away from home Nikolai had enjoyed the liberty that was a man's privilege, was even allowed to study sculpture as he wished. She knew that their father had believed it was a passing whim that Nikolai would tire of in time, a mere excuse to sow wild oats in the most exciting of all cities before settling down to marriage at home and a more ordered way of life.

Instead Nikolai had proved himself dedicated from the start and she had understood better than anyone how torn he was between the creative work he loved and the duties imposed on him by their Uncle Vadim, which involved an entirely different, intensely social existence. His being attached to the Embassy was a compromise settled by the Tsar himself when their father, fearing that Nikolai might break away for ever, had anxiously sought advice from his son's imperial godfather.

Anna wanted to cheer up her brother. 'Come now,' she urged consolingly, 'things aren't as bad as all that. Remember it was in your own interests as much as Father's that you should return to ensure that matters were kept under control since you'll inherit everything one day. I know that you and he have quarrelled often enough about your radical views, but be thankful that when a crisis arose he turned to you, knowing that anything you chose to say to a disgruntled mob of peasants would have far more effect in making them see reason than anything that he voiced.'

He shrugged impatiently, pausing to wipe his hands on a damp rag as if the blackness of his mood had come between him and his work. 'If Father had taken more notice of the events of the last few years and had used his influence to lessen the heavy burden of taxes, which cause the peasantry such unbearable suffering, these crises might not occur.'

Politics bored her. She thought he might begin to elaborate on his theme and was quick to divert him. 'Things change here, there and everywhere. Be patient. Life is full of unexpected happenings.' Somewhat smugly she had smoothed the black taffeta ruffles of her sleeve. 'Who would ever have anticipated that Leonid would die as conveniently as he did?'

83

Nikolai, who had been her confidant since childhood, being only a year older, regarded her with a flash of macabre humour. 'I've never asked you, but did you poison him?'

Surprise made her burst out laughing. 'No, of course not!' Then more soberly she added, 'but often I was sorely tempted. If I'd known how to keep suspicion from myself I'd have done it.'

'He would have deserved it. It sickens me to see you in mourning for that brute.'

She shrugged resignedly. 'It does me too, but I have to bow to convention for the sake of Father, the aunts and the rest of the family. But as soon as I'm out of mourning with all its restrictions on my social life I shall emerge like a butterfly from a chrysalis.' She had been circling the clay bust as she spoke, but came to a standstill as she studied it more closely and there was curiosity in her voice as she commented on it. 'This is going to be very fine. You've had an interesting model for this work.'

'But not a professional model. She's a girl I met only briefly in Paris and I'm relying on my memory.' He had begun working on the head again as if mention of the girl had drawn him back to continue moulding the delicate cheekbones, concentration returning to him.

Now as Anna studied Juliette's face she knew that this was the one and the same he had been sculpting from memory. Then she jerked her thoughts back to clothes when another mannequin entered as Juliette left. How dull these garments looked!

It soon became apparent to Juliette and Isabelle as they displayed alternately one ensemble after another that the Countess was becoming increasingly disappointed. Nothing was pleasing her. Once Hélène caught Juliette's eye expressively. This was followed by a telling grimace from Isabelle as she passed Juliette under the archway. They all knew how furious Denise would be if the Countess should leave without ordering anything.

Suddenly, while being hooked up at the back in the first of the evening gowns, Juliette realized what was wrong. Anna Dolohova was bored with mourning clothes and sombre shades. Maybe she felt she had shown respect for the late Count Dolohov long enough! It did not matter that any garment she viewed might be in the colour she had requested, in her present mood she saw only bleakness in the overall presentation and that had ebbed away any interest in the clothes being shown to her.

84

There was no time for Juliette to change out of what she had on, but she looked about quickly and saw a mannequin in a scarlet and gold spangled cape coming from another of the salons.

'Quick!' she said to her dresser. 'Find something vivid for Isabelle to wear next! And for me after that, or else there won't be a single sale!'

As she swept forward in a rustle of olive green satin to parade again she whipped the scarlet cape from the mannequin, ignored the shrieks of protest and whirled it about her shoulders with a dazzling sparkle of spangles. Hélène looked at her in horror as she appeared, but Anna's whole attitude changed.

'That's delicious! Why has everything else been so dreary? That scarlet looks wonderful with your hair as it will with mine.' It was the first time she had addressed Juliette throughout the showing and her face had become animated.

'Reds are fine for us if they have an orangey tint and are carefully coordinated.' Juliette swirled the cape away from her shoulders, letting it spread out like a vivid petal as she displayed the gown, and even that met with Anna's approval as it was viewed in a new light. 'One of the day gowns I showed you is also available in russet red. Would you like to see it? There's another in emerald and many of the ensembles are in bright topaz, apricot, coral and a lovely pumpkin shade.'

'I'll see them all.'

Juliette thought to herself that the Countess was like a woman desperate for the sight of a flower garden. Hélène was still bewildered by the turn of events, but satisfied that everything was going to be well after all.

Afterwards Denise was similarly pleased, although she did not like having to admit that her original judgement had been wrong. She sent for Juliette and to come to her office.

'You used your wits in the nick of time, Juliette. The Countess is returning tomorrow to discuss with me the clothes she liked best and it looks as though her order will be three times larger than last time. But there is something else. Count Karasvin came to see me as you know he intended.' Denise hesitated, getting up from her desk to come round and face Juliette. 'I'd prefer you not go out with these people this evening. He's not the right company for you. Surely you have enough beaux in our own circle to please you?'

'What is your objection?'

'The Karasvins are selfish, extravagant people used to having their own way in everything, powerful through past feudal laws in their own country and equally so through their vast fortunes everywhere else. I don't want your head turned.'

'I can't think of anything more unlikely,' Juliette said confidently.

'I could still exert my authority and forbid you to go.'

Juliette knew it was an idle threat. Denise's sisterly concern, although genuine, could not outweigh the importance to her of not offending the Countess on the brink of a huge order.

'You mustn't worry about me, Denise. To reassure you I'll tell you where we went and everything else when I come home. Well, almost everything,' she added teasingly.

Denise did not smile. 'I'll be home later than you, because I'm attending a civic banquet with Monsieur Noiret and there's dancing afterwards followed by a champagne breakfast. You can tell me all about it later tomorrow.'

Denise left the house at seven o'clock with Monsieur Noiret, a distinguished banker in his fifties, and then Juliette went upstairs to get ready. As arranged, Denise's lady's maid had laid out the gown chosen for the evening complete with shoes and accessories, but Juliette had everything put away again.

'I've decided not to wear that gown,' she said. 'No, you needn't wait. Whatever I choose will have fastenings I can manage myself.'

The lady's maid was puzzled by this change of mind, which had not happened before, but in the wardrobe there were at least four evening gowns with tiny buttons at the front.

'So don't wait up for me,' Juliette added. 'Just set an alarm clock for the Baronne's return.'

'Yes, mademoiselle.'

As soon as the door had closed after the woman Juliette crossed the room and turned the key. From the first moment of Nikolai's invitation she had known what she would wear and at the same time keep a promise she had made to Denise. Her sister being out of the house had made the whole operation easier than she had expected. Swiftly she pulled open a bottom drawer and lifted the Delphos robe from its tissue paper. Briefly she held it close to her, almost in an embrace of reunion, and then put it on. It seemed to her more beautiful than ever, the tiny pleats shimmering about her in changing hues of coral-red, copper and gold as the light played on them. The neckline when tied was not low, but left the base of her neck scooped free. Her only jewellery was a pair of gold earrings that Lucille had given her one birthday.

She had a variety of Landelle evening jackets and capes, but she did not want to wear anything that would be out of harmony with the gown. Instead she took a wrap of creamy diaphanous chiffon, which she had bought herself that day as being as much like a Knossos scarf as she could find. Full of anticipation, she went downstairs to await Nikolai's arrival. The doorbell rang even as she reached the hall.

CHAPTER EIGHT

Nikolai saw her as soon as he was admitted. She stood poised at the foot of the staircase, the lights of the chandelier flaming her hair, her silken gown agleam over the contours of her figure. He went towards her, his admiration apparent.

'You look wonderful!'

'This is my Delphos robe by Fortuny!' Happily and unself-consciously, she twirled around for him, the tiny pleats swirling out in their gleaming fire colours.

He stood regarding her with deep pleasure. 'Have you been all the way to Venice to buy it since I saw you this afternoon?'

'Only in spirit,' she declared merrily, her mood matching his.

'I want to hear all about it.' He handed her a boxed corsage and watched her take out a spray of the same ivory orchids that he had given her before. Her whole face revealed her delight as she pinned them on.

'These are my favourite orchids, Nikolai!' She wondered if he would guess that it was since the first corsage he had sent her.

'I have to tell you there's been a change of plan. My sister can't come with us after all.'

'Is that so?' She met his eyes, knowing that Denise had been most strict about her chaperonage that evening, but she saw he had no doubt that she would still go with him and she instantly made up her mind. 'At least there is no need for us to delay any longer.'

He swept her out of the house. A taxi-cab was waiting and within minutes they were being driven away, the light of the street lamps flickering across their faces.

'I've booked a table at Larue's in the rue Royale,' he said as they talked.

'I've never been there.'

'I'm not surprised. Until very recently it was just another restaurant, but it's been bought by Monsieur Nignon, who was formerly a renowned chef himself, and now it offers the best food in all Paris. Russian dishes are a speciality.'

'Are we to dine *à la Russe*?' she asked eagerly.

'If you would like that.'

'Yes, indeed!'

When they arrived at Larue's it was Monsieur Nignon himself, black hair smooth as paint and a red carnation in his silk lapel, who came forward to welcome them.

'*Bonsoir*, Count Karasvin! Mademoiselle!' There followed two deep bows, 'What honour! My best table awaits you.'

An orchestra was playing light music and the restaurant with its white and gold décor, an abundance of mirrors and seating upholstered in rose velvet, was well patronized. On all sides the women's jewellery sparkled. As they were led to their table Juliette did not notice at first what an effect her appearance was having on all those around her. She was used to glances in her Landelle clothes, but it began to dawn on her that something far greater was happening. People were staring, knives and forks stilled, glasses of wine remaining poised in mid-air and whispers gathering momentum. It was her Delphos robe! She had let the chiffon wrap waft away from her shoulders when entering the restaurant and could guess how the light was playing across the pleats to create their unique effect.

A group of young army officers, dining alone, sighted her as she approached and when she drew level they sprang to their feet with flirtatious grins, raising their glasses to her in tribute. Nikolai saw her acknowledge their homage with one of her generous smiles. He was not in the least surprised that she was dazzling everyone – and certainly shocking some – in her revolutionary gown that proclaimed she was naturally clad without whalebone corsets, padding or those layers of petticoats that no other woman in the room was without.

When they were seated on the banquette at their table, which was set in a recessed alcove amid a bower of flowers, Nikolai ordered aperitifs. Juliette had not expected to cause such attention in her choice of gown. There was every likelihood that someone present had recognized her and that sooner or later Denise might hear about it, but that was unimportant now. Nothing should cast a shadow over this evening. Her happiness radiated from her.

The aperitifs had been served. When she would have taken up her glass to drink with Nikolai he toasted her first.

'To you, Juliette, for coming into my life.'

It was a perfect start to the hours ahead.

Monsieur Nignon returned after a suitable interval to discuss the menu with them. There was to be caviar served with tiny glasses of ice-cold vodka and also bortsch, since Juliette had never tasted it, but made according to his own recipe into a soup supreme. Other dishes included quail *à la Souvaroff* and Monsieur Nignon could only blow a kiss in the air as he failed to find words to describe its perfection.

'Such a favourite with the Tsar's late father, Alexander III,' he told Juliette, Nikolai having heard the tale before. 'I served it every time he came to dine at the great house in St Petersburg where I was chef in my younger days. Once I was summoned to serve it at one of the Imperial banquets!' Even after a lapse of some years pride over the occasion still shone out of him. 'But I digress. Let us return to the menu for this evening. May I suggest veal in white wine garnished with gently sweetened crabapples?'

The dinner was to end with fresh sugared berries served with cream in a Russian silver *trompe l'œil* dish that had been a gift from Tsar Alexander after the banquet. It was left to Nikolai to choose the wines unerringly. Before Monsieur Nignon went again Juliette asked him why he left Russia when his skills were so highly appreciated.

'Ah, mademoiselle!' He put his head on one side and smiled. 'Paris called me all the time I was there. Finally I couldn't stay away any longer.'

'I thought that would be the reason. I felt the same way when I

90

was far from Paris.' Then when he had gone again she turned to Nikolai. 'I know it was the study of sculpture that brought you here originally, but your homeland must draw you in the same way.'

'At times,' he admitted with a frown, 'but I resented having to leave Paris as abruptly as I did so soon after meeting you. Unfortunately I had no choice.' He went on to explain all that had happened and how it had taken time before he was able to return.

'You did right to stay, but how do you reconcile your creative work with the demands made on your time by your Embassy duties?'

His jaw set grimly. 'It's a compromise to which I was pressured by the Tsar himself when I was considerably younger. Now I'm honour-bound to uphold it.'

She was sympathetic. 'I was also compelled into a compromise at my sister's insistence, but it's possible to live through these restrictions. They can't last for ever.'

For a moment he hesitated as if about to disagree with her, but then his brow cleared as he smiled again. 'That's enough gloomy talk for this evening. We're here to enjoy ourselves. And what was it you were going to tell me about your Fortuny gown?'

Juliette made Nikolai laugh as she described how she had discovered it in pieces and sewn it together again. 'So,' she concluded merrily, 'this is the first time I've worn it!'

'A perfect choice for our celebration!'

She raised her eyebrows quizzically. 'Is this a celebration?'

He leaned forward. 'You know it is. Today we found each other again!'

Although he spoke lightly in keeping with the easy flow of their conversation there was a depth of feeling behind his words. He would have said more, but two waiters arrived to serve the caviar and the vodka was poured into thimble-sized glasses.

Every course proved to be as delicious as had been promised. They ate leisurely, taking their time. If other diners left and more came they did not notice, absorbed in each other. She recounted how she had gone to the studio to see his work.

He was surprised. 'I didn't know you'd been there.'

'Do you mind?'

'No, quite the reverse. When was this?'

'A few months after you'd gone away. I spoke to Anton Casille and he said he knew you well. I suppose he forgot all about my visit.'

'He's moved to Florence. I missed meeting him again by a matter of days. You saw my two figures, did you?'

She knew Nikolai wasn't waiting for praise, for he had shrugged carelessly, as if his sculptures were no more than apprentice pieces. Her guess was that he was like Rodin in never being fully satisfied with his own work.

'I like them both,' she said firmly, 'for being so physically alive and sensual. The woman looked to me as if she had been caressed by Poseidon himself or maybe just by the sea.'

If he was surprised by her outspokenness he did not show it, although his lids drooped slightly over his lazily handsome eyes as if he were reassessing her. 'And *The Athlete*?'

'To me it seemed as if winning the race would be a kind of rebirth for him.'

He released a slow breath in satisfaction. Juliette had shown a deeper insight into his work than he would have deemed possible. Then he realized that it was his own cynicism that had caused him to doubt what she might say. Juliette was never going to disappoint him in any sphere. More than ever he wanted to make love to her.

'What about the clay figure still under cloths in the studio?' she asked. 'Shall you finish it now that you've returned to Paris?'

'The *Bacchante*? It is finished.'

She was taken aback. Somehow she had assumed that he had travelled with Anna, who had only arrived from St Petersburg a few days before.

'You were in Paris and we didn't meet!' she exclaimed involuntarily.

His brows drew together fiercely and he leaned forward. 'There's a good reason for that! I'd have turned the city upside down to find you if I hadn't believed that you'd chosen not to have any further contact with me! As it was, I threw myself into the work I'd left unfinished, scarcely surfacing for food, drink or rest to try to get you out of my mind.'

She guessed that her supposed rejection had hurt his pride and even his ego. It was probably the first time in his pampered life he had ever suffered a supposed slight. 'In future you must learn not to jump to conclusions,' she advised. 'Consider the possibilities first.'

He relaxed, grinning. 'You're right. Would you like to see the *Bacchante* at the studio before it goes on exhibition with the other two figures?'

'I would very much. Do you paint as well as sculpt?'

'Not since I first came to Paris, because by then I only wanted to be a sculptor. Naturally I still sketch first whatever I have in mind to do and then I make a number of small models until I find exactly what I'm aiming for in the finished work. But what of you? When did you discover your flair for sewing?'

Their conversation flowed easily along while she described her convent days and the circumstances that took her there as well as the holidays she had with Gabrielle, and how they had only met once since then when her friend had come to Paris for her trousseau. 'She's living in England now and has invited me to visit her whenever I can, but that will have to wait until my training is finished. Have you ever been to London?'

'Yes, a couple of times. I was there two weeks ago on a quick visit to buy myself a British sporting car, but settled on a Grand Prix Benz instead.'

'Does it go very fast?'

He laughed. 'Not fast enough for me. Would you like me to teach you to drive?'

Her eyes widened. She did not know personally any women who drove, although she had seen those of her own sex behind the wheel of a staid motorcar now and again. 'Yes!' she exclaimed eagerly. 'When shall I have the first lesson?'

'As soon as you like.'

It was arranged and they finished the final course of their meal to which the sugared berries made a perfect conclusion.

'So what would you like to do now?' he asked over the coffee. 'Shall we go dancing?'

Juliette had already mentioned that her sister would not be home until dawn and nobody would be waiting up for her. She clapped her hands together eagerly. 'Take me to the Moulin Rouge. I've always wanted to go there!'

Nikolai's eyebrows shot up in surprise and he threw back his head on a laugh. 'My dear Juliette! If that's what you wish of course we'll go.'

A blaze of light welcomed them to the Moulin Rouge. It was very crowded in the theatre hall. Although it appeared at first that there was not a spare place to be had, Nikolai was known to the *maître d'hôtel* and they were given a table for two in an advantageous position. As before Juliette attracted notice and several men, merry with wine, threw her kisses from their fingertips. Nikolai ordered champagne. She was exhilarated by the vibrant atmosphere. It was all so colourful, noisy with laughter and hazy with the curling smoke of good cigars. Here, as at Larue's, all were in evening dress, although at some tables the men had not removed their jauntily-angled silk top hats, which showed they were with women of a low class. Busy waiters in large white aprons darted between the tables, carrying loaded trays. Champagne corks popped spasmodically in various directions. An air of good humour prevailed everywhere and the music of the orchestra made Juliette's feet tap.

She was certain that little had changed since her mother had sipped champagne here as she was doing now. It was still not a place a gentleman would expect to bring a lady, but Nikolai had indulged her and, judging by the velvet looks he was giving her, she wondered impishly if he would be able to refuse her anything.

'Well?' Nikolai asked smilingly, entertained by her excitement and having heard from her on the way how she had long wanted to follow her parents' footsteps to this famous place. 'Has the Moulin Rouge come up to your expectations?'

'Oh, yes! I love it. No wonder my mother did too! I think we're at the very same table where she and my father sat.' She spoke less in jest than she made it appear.

'Perhaps we are.' Reaching across the table he covered her hand with his. 'I'm as glad as you that we came.'

'Thank you.'

'Would you like to dance now?'

The floor was full of couples rotating to a Strauss waltz, the men white-gloved with coat-tails flying. Nikolai put his arm around Juliette's waist as he led her into the throng, but the dance ended even as they reached the floor. Almost at once the orchestra struck up a tango. He swept her into its steps and her gown rippled out in waves with every graceful sweeping movement. Several of the couples drew back to watch them and more followed suit until they were tangoing on their own in the middle of a wide circle of spectators, the men appreciating the glimpses of Juliette's slim silk-stockinged ankles as her gown swirled out before whipping back again. She and Nikolai did not realize at first that they had become the sole focus of the establishment, people at the tables having begun to strain their necks to watch.

Juliette had danced the tango before when at parties, it being a new dance popular with the young, but this was the slow version she was dancing for the first time, which was banned by Denise and older people in her circle as too *outré* and erotic. But how glorious it was! How sensuous! And Nikolai was such an excellent dancer! They swayed and dipped together as if attuned exactly to each other's bodies, almost as if they were one. His smiling eyes met hers deeply as if he could read her thoughts, but in spite of that being impossible it seemed to Juliette that, known only to themselves, there was a passionate intensity to their perfectly matched movements.

Thunderous applause greeted the end of the tango, for those who patronized the Moulin Rouge were there to enjoy themselves hugely and were demonstratively appreciative of any entertainment, whatever the form. Several women jumped up from their chairs in a wish to be Nikolai's partner in the next dance as he hastened Juliette through the applauding crowd back to their table. One bright-haired blonde addressed him by name and kissed his cheek exuberantly, leaving a pink imprint which he wiped away with a napkin as soon as he was seated again.

'Do you always create such a stir when you leave a dance floor?' Juliette teased mischievously.

'*Mon Dieu* no!' he shook his head humorously. 'You're casting a spell over everywhere we go tonight!'

'It must be my Delphos robe! Perhaps it has magical powers,' she joked.

He shook his head again more seriously. 'You've magic enough of your own.'

She saw very well that he was not joking.

They did not dance again, but sat talking through the polka that followed and then it was time for the nightly cabaret, extra lights setting the stage aglow. It was a splendid show, one brilliant act following another, the comedians very funny, the jugglers talented and the acrobats' feats spectacular. The singers, male and female, had superb voices and the dancers, all pretty, were lavishly costumed and be-feathered. The can-can was the grand finale with the sweating orchestra pounding out the music. Black-stockinged legs kicked high with a gleam of thighs in a mass of lacy frills. When the girls streamed down the steps from the stage into the hall itself to continue their wild steps, the audience was on its feet, singing and shouting and clapping, for the can-can had lost none of its power to excite and inflame. As the dancers threw themselves down one by one into the splits at the end there was such a roar of appreciation in the charged atmosphere that it seemed as if the roof were threatened.

Nikolai and Juliette were among those who left afterwards. It was the early hours of the morning and yet Paris was still vibrantly alive with passing motorcars and carriages. Flower-sellers thrust nosegays at passers-by and restaurants with full tables within streamed out lights.

'Let's walk,' Juliette suggested.

Nikolai had been about to hail a taxi-cab, and he took her hand instead as they strolled along. He had lived in Montmartre when first coming to Paris and he described the tiny studio and the cramped living quarters that he'd had not far from the *Moulin Rouge*, but higher up on the slopes of La Butte. He and his friends had patronised the *Lapin Agile* café, a favourite place for the Bohemian element. Picasso, Utrillo, Van Dongen and a dozen other struggling artists and sculptors, some of whom were beginning to make a name for themselves, had been among his drinking companions.

'Have you ever been back to your first studio?' she asked.

'Not for a long time.'

'I'd like to see it one day.'

'I'll take you.'

They began to make plans as to where else they would go together, apart from the driving lessons he was to give her. There were no passers-by just then and he drew her to a standstill under a tree. They stood facing each other, dappled by the lamplight through the branches.

'You're so lovely, Juliette,' he said huskily. 'God knows what lies ahead but if it means anything to you I want to see you again and again.'

She was very still, no movement except her gentle breathing and the dancing of her little gold earrings, for she was deeply moved by the tenderness with which he was gazing at her. 'I want that too,' she answered softly.

She moved into his arms as he caught her close. Then his mouth was warm on hers, his kiss slow and subtle at first as if in discovery, but soon his embrace tightened and she clung to him as his surge of passion ignited her into an abandoned response such as she had never experienced before. When he took his lips away from hers he drew back his head and she, her eyes still closed, felt his hand stroke her hair and then the side of her face. A delicious tremor went through her as if a current of love had passed between them. Only then did she raise her lids in a return to awareness of her surroundings, almost like a waking sleep-walker.

They smiled at each other and kissed again. Then they strolled on once more, having no further need of words, until dawn began to lighten the sky. His arm was about her, her head resting against his shoulder. At the house she gave him her key and when he had unlocked the door for her she paused on the threshold.

'It was a wonderful, unforgettable evening,' she said.

'You made it so for me.'

'*Bonsoir*, Nikolai.'

As Juliette went upstairs she recalled his words as to the uncertainty of the future. Perhaps he has been remembering how they had almost lost each other once already through a withheld letter, or how the demands of duty might at any time snatch him away from her again. As for herself, her plans for the future had not included getting out of her depth in love with anybody, which was now a stark possibility that she had to face. Perhaps through their joint wills she and Nikolai would find a way to take every moment as it came with no regrets afterwards.

CHAPTER NINE

Next morning Denise slept late as she did sometimes after an exceptionally late night. Juliette went to work as usual and did not see her sister until summoned to the office at mid-morning. Although Denise was looking out of the window Juliette could see by her whole stance that she was in a towering rage, fingers drumming on her folded arms.

'You wanted to see me, Denise?'

Denise turned immediately, thin-lipped with temper, her eyes flashing. 'What in heaven's name did you wear yesterday evening? A friend rang to tell me she'd heard you'd been immodestly dressed in the company of Count Karasvin.'

'It's not true!' Juliette was indignant.

Denise's tirade went on unabated. 'And if that were not enough, the *directrice* is trying to placate two clients in the salon who saw you at Larue's and they're clamouring for gowns in the same coloured pleated silk that I know did not come from here! How dare you go anywhere in other than a Landelle design! I assume you made the garment yourself?'

'It's a Delphos robe by Fortuny.'

Denise was aghast. 'Where did you get it?'

'I told you a while ago that I had found it. The pieces were in the remnant box and you said I could have them. It wasn't my original intention to sew them together again, but the idea became irresistible.'

'How could you!' Denise clutched the back of the chair in front of her at the desk as if to keep from attacking her sister physically. 'You've created a scandal and shamed me! Don't you know that in a Delphos robe you're *en déshabillé*? Respectable women would never wear one in public! Even at home it would only be when dining alone with their husbands.'

'Surely you are exaggerating? There's nothing new about loose-fitting gowns being worn in public.'

'And by whom?' Denise countered savagely. 'Only fast women leading a Bohemian life with no morals whatever!'

'That's a sweeping judgement of women wanting freedom of movement in their clothes!'

'Don't argue with me!' Denise hissed, her lips drawn back over her teeth. 'I'll remind you that I'm not only your sister and guardian, but your employer too. Did you go anywhere else other than Larue's?'

'Yes. To the Moulin Rouge. Anna Dolohova had another engagement otherwise I don't know if Nikolai could have taken me there as I requested.'

Denise was momentarily beyond speech and let her hands rise and fall expressively. 'I've heard enough. You'll not see Count Karasvin again and you'll destroy the Fortuny rag.'

Juliette spoke determinedly. 'I'll do neither.'

'You'll do as I say if you want to stay on here!'

'Then I must leave.'

'No!' Denise struggled to control herself, suddenly seeing how close matters had come to her losing all she was aiming for. 'I'll not let you go to another couturier! You haven't been trained to be of use to someone else! I'll move you from the sewing rooms. I know you've been looking forward to studying design with Monsieur Pierre. I'll let you start there today.'

Juliette raised her eyebrows incredulously. 'What are you saying, Denise? I don't have to be bribed to stay. If you want me to continue working for you I will and gladly, but I can't agree to your terms about either Nikolai or the gown.'

'I realize that.' Denise sank down in the chair at her desk. 'You always were stubborn, but at least promise me you'll not wear the Fortuny gown in public any more.'

'All I can vow is that I'll not cause you distress about it ever again.'

Before Denise could reply there came a tap on the door and the *directrice* entered looking anxious. 'Madame! The clients are insistent! Nothing I've said—'

Again Denise turned furiously on Juliette. 'There! See what you've done! I'm likely to lose two valuable accounts and more when they spread their dissatisfaction throughout society!'

'Why not just tell them the truth?' Juliette exclaimed in exasperation. 'Find something else to please them instead. There are some beautiful tawny silks in the storeroom that weren't used in the present collection. They're not the same as Fortuny silks, but would look elegant if pleated in the Landelle way.'

Denise sprang to her feet again, her face hard and maliciously triumphant. 'You can fetch that silk and try to placate those women. I'm giving you your first chance to handle clients diplomatically!'

The *directrice* was dismayed. 'Madame! Is that wise? It's you whom they wish to see.'

But Juliette was out of the door, and when the *directrice* would have rushed after her Denise called her back. 'No! Let my sister try. It will be a hard lesson for her whether she wins or fails.'

Juliette did not fail. The two women were pleased to see her since she had worn the gown. Soon they plied her with demands and questions. She explained that the gown had been designed by Fortuny and then displayed a selection of the silks in autumn shades that she had fetched, suggesting alternative designs from ideas of her own. They left quite satisfied.

'I've promised them the designs will be ready for them to see tomorrow,' Juliette reported back to Denise.

Her sister's cold expression did not change. 'Very well. Take your ideas to Monsieur Pierre and tell him what you have promised. As I said before, you'll work in his studio until further notice.'

The designer was not a temperamental man or else he could not have worked well with Denise. She had told him some time ago that her sister would take her place eventually when she retired, and so it came as no surprise when he received a message that Juliette was being transferred to his studio.

When Juliette entered, sample lengths of the silks chosen by the clients over her arm, she found Pierre adjusting the sleeve of a *toile* on a *mannequin*, which was like all those used in the ateliers in being on a mahogany stand with a polished knob above the neck of the body-shape for easy handling. Dapper in his appearance, Pierre was short with fair hair brindled with grey and a neatly pointed beard. He looked over the top of his gold-rimmed spectacles at Juliette and waved her forward.

'Toss the silk over the back of a chair and tell me what's been going on downstairs. I gather there was quite a crisis.' When he had heard everything he nodded towards a drawing-board. 'Put down your ideas in rough sketches for these two pleated gowns and we'll work together on them afterwards.'

The outcome was that he and Juliette worked late until the designs were ready for the clients when they came in the morning. Denise, before going home, came to see what was in progress. Only Pierre knew that for once she made no suggestions of her own when seeing the finished sketches.

When Juliette arrived home a maid informed her that Denise had gone to bed and that Count Karasvin had telephoned twice. She tried to get through to him at his apartment in one of the grand mansions in the rue de Lille, but a manservant told her he was not yet home.

She was undressing when there came a rattling of gravel against her window. Opening it cautiously, she looked down. Nikolai stood on the lawn, grinning up at her.

Amused, she whispered, 'Are you mad? What are you doing here at this hour?'

'I came to say good night,' he answered and then heard her fascinating, throaty little laugh that he liked so much.

'How many vodkas have you had?' she asked mock-censoriously.

He shrugged merrily. 'I lost count.'

'I thought so. Go home now.'

He was more sober than she realized, having become so possessed by the need to see her that he had left a party early to come here. The light in the room behind her made a red-gold aura of her hair, and, although she had thrown on a wrap, he could see her cleavage. 'Come down,' he requested seriously.

She hesitated as if torn by indecision, but then she shook her head. 'Go home,' she repeated and closed the window. The curtain flicked back into place.

Almost at once she turned out the light, wanting him to think she had gone to bed, and finished undressing in the dark. When she did lay her head on the pillows somehow she seemed to know it was only then that he went away. A few moments later she heard the faint clang of one of the double gates close after him.

The furore created by the Fortuny gown continued the following day as gossip spread about the daring garment worn by the Baronne de Landelle's sister and the salons were busier than usual. The *directrice* found herself inundated with demands to see this new gown that had not been shown in the collection. The more adventurous women wanted to try it on, although with no intention of wearing it in public. As before, Juliette was sent for and knew she faced a harder task this time, but her quick-wittedness enabled her to overcome the problem. She took five of the *vendeuses* to the storeroom and made the storekeeper bring out every silk that was in a vivid autumn tint, some having been on the shelves for a long time. She tumbled the shimmering lengths into the *vendeuses'* arms. When they walked behind her into the salons an effect was created by the heaped and flowing silks as glorious as if a Venetian painting of the Renaissance had poured forth its splendour.

'Any of these silks,' she said as the luscious fabrics were draped, twirled and spread out in display for each group of seated clients, 'will pleat and hang perfectly. Not, of course, as Fortuny does it, but then he has a secret method. Yet,' she added, lowering her voice to a confidential whisper, 'there's another secret of the Delphos robe that I discovered by chance.'

'What is it? Do tell,' they whispered in return, agog with interest.

'No corsets!'

There were gasps and giggles and gloved hands were clapped over mouths to smother laughter that sprang involuntarily from surprise and, in some cases, shock. But nobody walked out, for the women who had come here because of the gown were all intrigued that a respectable young woman, sister of the Baronne herself, had dared to wear it in the name of fashion, even if they would not themselves. They asumed it had been to attract notice to Maison Landelle, which had succeeded.

On Sunday as arranged, Juliette went for her first driving lesson with Nikolai in his Grand Prix Benz. She was ready and waiting when he drew up outside the house and ran down the steps to him.

'What a splendid machine!' she declared. It was a deep yellow two-seater elongated raceabout with a handsome brass radiator and headlamps. He had sprung out to greet her, but he still had to get back in first again as the gear and brakes baulked the driver's side of a sporting car. Denise watched dubiously from the window as they drove away.

Juliette had lots to tell him about the scandal she had caused in the Delphos robe. Word of it had reached Nikolai through Anna, and he and Juliette laughed about it together. There seemed so many other topics to talk about that amused them, for they were both in high spirits and out to enjoy themselves. He drove some way out of Paris into a quiet village before he drew up and instructed her in the rudiments of driving.

'Let's see you start,' he said, jumping into the seat beside her after cranking the engine, for she had failed to turn it over sufficiently for it to burst into life when she switched on the trembler coil.

'Here we go!' Juliette depressed the clutch, engaged the gear and they were away. She found it easy enough to control the thick mahogany wheel and she learned quickly after the initial false starts and erratic jolts were overcome. Those whom they passed on foot, on bicycles or in motorcars, stared at the sight of a young woman at the wheel of the strange sporting car, tendrils of her coppery hair flying from her eager face, a smiling young man beside her.

They had taken a picnic, for it was a mild September day, and sat on a plaid rug by a river, eating the food Juliette had brought and drinking the wine that Nikolai had provided. Her obvious happiness was matched by his own. Before they left again he kissed her as he had done in the lamplight of Paris.

The salons at Maison Landelle continued to be crowded as the days went by, many new orders resulting when the new pleated designs were shown, for clients could see that these were not only lovely garments but were also totally respectable. As a result, a trend was sparked off that made vivid autumnal colours and an abundance of pleats the height of fashion.

Apart from the extra work, which meant there was no slackening of pace in the ateliers of Maison Landelle, a number of complications did arise when clients wanted to change the colour of clothes already ordered, but eventually everything was sorted out. Denise could scarcely believe that so much good fortune could have come her way through her sister's indiscretion, for not only had she gained new clients, but all the other fashion houses had to follow the trend Maison Landelle had set for the most stylish colours for the winter.

She discussed Juliette's initiative with Pierre, who advised her to let her sister have a voice whenever the two of them discussed new ideas.

'Juliette has an instinctive flair for fashion and colour,' he said, 'as well as the nose necessary in this business that enables one to scent change in the air.'

Denise possessed it as he did – that indefinable sixth sense that so often led couturiers simultaneously onto the same trail. 'You're sure Juliette has it?'

He nodded. 'Only yesterday she showed me some sketches she'd done, all with the softer lines that you and I discussed only the other day. She pointed out that the *S*-shape has been in too long and should be modified drastically as it was no longer in keeping with the new freedom that women are gradually winning for themselves.'

'Very well, Pierre. We'll include her in future. If all goes well I'll start letting her have an insight into the business side of everything.'

By now Nikolai considered Juliette to be a capable driver and it was a great day for her when she drove through the Paris traffic for the first time. After that she took it in her stride, hooting back at taxi-cabs when they cut in on her, the sporting car's horn loud and magnificent.

Nikolai's Embassy duties and Juliette's late working hours on occasion prevented them seeing each other exactly when they wished, but it made their times together all the more valued. They went to an opera that had been costumed by Fortuny and were able to see Nijinsky dance with his ethereal grace before the season of the *Ballets Russes* came to an end. They attended the preview of an exhibition where Nikolai's *Bacchante* held pride of place. Already it had been bought by an American collector and was to be shipped to the United States.

There were many Sunday afternoons when they went to the Louvre and other galleries. They liked to wander through the gardens of the Palais Royale, depleted now by winter, but still unexpected touches of colour were showing here and there. At other times they were to be found amid the statues of the park at the Luxembourg Palace or strolling leisurely, always hand in hand, by the Seine.

If rain forced them to take shelter they took refreshment at marble-topped tables in tiny cafés. She had coninually swept aside her sister's protests that they should have a chaperone. Her time with Nikolai was too precious to have another person at her side. Both of them liked these quiet sessions when they could talk and draw closer together; later in the evening, unless they dined grandly at Larue's, they would have supper at one or another of the many little restaurants, her favourite being where balalaikas were played and male dancers in costume with Cossack hats danced wildly. Once Nikolai joined in, more than a match for the other dancers, his yells mingling with theirs, and Juliette sprang excitedly to her feet to clap to the reckless rhythm. When the dance ended the dancers and the orchestra applauded him as did everybody else in the restaurant, he doing the same according to the Russian custom.

When he returned to the table, laughing and exhilarated, Juliette flung her arms about his neck exuberantly. 'Nikolai! That was fantastic! I didn't know you could dance like that!'

He held her tight about the waist, his eyes bright. 'There's so much you don't know about me yet, Juliette!' Then he acknowledged a cheer with a raised hand before he and Juliette sat down again to resume their interrupted supper.

At these little places Juliette would sometimes see a seamstress or someone else from the work force of Maison Landelle with whom she would exchange a smile, but neither she nor Nikolai ever saw anybody from their own social circles. She thought sometimes that she was happier when with him than at any time in her life before.

Juliette had never borne any malice towards Lucille over the withheld letter. She did not refer to it when first writing after discovering what had been done, but told of meeting Nikolai again and how she had enjoyed his company. As she had expected, Lucille returned the sealed letter when next she wrote, but did not make any reference to it. Their correspondence continued as if nothing untoward had ever occurred. It was a misjudged action that was forgotten by mutual understanding. If Lucille continued to have misgivings about the relationship with Nikolai that was never expressed.

In contrast Denise still voiced her disapproval openly to Juliette. 'You're abandoning all your old friends,' she pointed out sharply. 'You couldn't see Count Karasvin more often if you were engaged to him.'

'He's not in Paris for ever,' Juliette replied with a casual shrug, 'and there's no question of an engagement. We like each other's company. As for deserting my friends, that is not true, because I see them whenever I can. They understand that I've little free time at the present moment.'

'He'd never marry you anyway, so it's as well you're being sensible.'

Juliette flushed. 'I know that Nikolai with his Romanov connections will be expected to take a wife of aristocratic birth and I haven't a drop of blue blood in my veins. Our ancestors probably cheered every time the blade fell at the guillotine.'

'Don't say that!' Denise grimaced, clapping her hands over her ears.

Juliette smiled ruefully and took her sister's wrists to pull them gently down again. 'I was only trying to emphasize the gulf that lies between Nikolai and me. The rules of class aren't easily broken, especially by someone so tied by the rigid society to which he belongs. You must remember that I've seen plenty of it among the clients of Maison Landelle.'

Juliette gave no indication of how difficult it was to keep herself anchored to reality and not give way to foolish hopes and dreams.

Denise was fully reassured by Juliette's practical attitude. She realized that not for the first time she had underestimated her sister. It meant she need not harbour any fears that her plans for the future of Maison Landelle might be ruined by Juliette's being swept away by love. It was highly likely that Juliette might have been alerted to the state of affairs from the very beginning when Anna Dolohova made some excuse not to accompany her and Nikolai on their first evening together. It had been Denise's own conclusion that the Countess had resolved to do nothing to help a romance between her brother and her couturière's sister. Although always charming when the occasion demanded it was noticeable that the Countess had never

106

invited Juliette to the parties held in the mansion taken for her sojourn in Paris. Denise would have had to admit that she had never heard that Nikolai was ever there either, but thought that was probably because he would not attend without Juliette.

Then Denise took added comfort from the thought that Anna Dolohova would be vigilant in making sure that her brother did not make a fool of himself by suddenly declaring honourable intentions against all odds. The Countess would have strings to pull and could bring Imperial pressure to bear. Yet Denise's concern was not centred entirely on a possible threat to what she wanted for herself from her sister. She had become fond of Juliette, as far as she was able to care for anyone, and proud of the united sibling strength that was blossoming at Maison Landelle.

In her relieved frame of mind she decided that with work finally under control in the ateliers she would make a trip to England before Christmas. She could even be sure the *directrice* had a right hand in Juliette for quelling any crisis. The purpose of the trip was to visit silk mills in Macclesfield, which was the heart of the British silk industry, and also another mill in London, the owner of which had had the initiative to send her some very attractive samples.

'You must send me a cable if anything goes wrong,' Denise insisted as she departed.

'Nothing will,' Juliette answered cheerily. 'Go and look at those silks and enjoy yourself in London too.'

'Send me a copy of the ball-gown you design. I have to approve it. Remember that!'

'I will.'

The motorcar bore Denise away. Juliette rubbed her arms as she went back up the steps, for it was still early morning and the air was frosty. She and Denise had both been specially invited at Nikolai's instigation to the New Year's Ball at the Russian Embassy and Denise, in a benevolent mood, had said she might design a new gown for herself under the Landelle label, only adding that it must not resemble a Fortuny robe.

Juliette knew as Denise did that the couturier, Poiret, was stocking a few Fortuny gowns in his boutique, but whether they were being purchased it was impossible to tell, for as yet none were to be seen publicly.

After the talk with Denise about the Romanovs and other

107

problems, Juliette had realized just how much her life had become centred on Nikolai and the time they spent together. She knew it was unwise. Her work had not suffered, but the fact remained she was totally in love with him. More than once recently she had found herself glancing at the clock when she was at the designing table, finding she was thinking more than was sensible about the hour when they would be meeting.

That had to stop. Her will was strong and somehow she would manage it. In the meantime she was going to a moving-picture theatre with him this evening and then to supper afterwards. On Sunday afternoon they were going to see where his old studio was in Montmartre.

It was a long time since Juliette had been in Montmartre by daylight. She had gone with her father to a gallery there where unknown artists displayed their work, hoping a buyer would pay enough for an absinthe and a solid meal. She remembered she had become hot and tired and her father had bought her a lemonade. A painting had been purchased of ballet dancers tying their shoes and she had loved it, but it must have gone in the sale of his effects at the time of the bankruptcy, because it was not in Denise's house.

When Sunday came Juliette and Nikolai left the sporting car parked and walked hand in hand up the steep, narrow streets of the Butte, which was crowned at the top by a windmill. When the nightspots and brothels had been left behind Montmartre had the same rustic charm of the past. With its old houses and cobbles and even with the trees bare of leaves it was easy to see why so many artists had chosen to paint what was on their doorstep instead of more exotic views.

Nikolai drew her to a halt as he pointed to the sprawling, untidy buildings clustered on the hillside that were the studios of any number of artists and known as the Bateau-Lavoir.

'That lopsided window on the second floor of the third studio along was my place and where I worked, lived and slept when I came to Paris after a year at the St Petersburg Art School. It's where I sculpted the two heads and a figure that resulted in my becoming one of Rodin's pupils.' He was also remembering that it was there he'd kept his first mistress, discovered how to drink companions under the table and enjoyed many new experiences, learning a great deal about art, women and how to exist on a few francs like everybody else, never tapping the funds in the bank that had been arranged for him.

Juliette glanced sideways at him. There was a faraway look in his eyes as he gazed at the ill-formed buildings, his thoughts obviously in the past. It was a chilly day and as he stood there in his warm tweed coat, scarf and wide-brimmed slouch hat she found it easy to picture him coming up this hill as a youth, eager to immerse himself in the Bohemian life of Paris. After a few moments she plucked at his sleeve.

'You're looking nostalgic and you're too young for that.'

He laughed, turning to her, and tucked her arm into his. 'You're right! It wasn't really all that long ago and I was here barely six months, but so much has happened since then, especially meeting you. We'll go now to the *Lapin Agile* and have a glass of wine.'

On the way there they met a street photographer, his tripod over his shoulder, his camera-box in his hand, who was returning from taking winter scenes of Montmartre for postcards. He promptly offered to take a photograph of them together. When he had taken it Nikolai wanted one of Juliette on her own. She protested, laughing, but the photographer captured her holding her hat, her scarf and skirt billowing out in a sudden gust of wind, and congratulated himself on a perfect picture. He gave Nikolai his card and said the photographs would be ready at his shop within a few days.

The warmth of the green-shuttered *Lapin Agile* was welcome after the chill outside. They sat at one of the tables and Juliette looked about with interest. It was quite busy, people smoking and talking at the tables over wine, and the walls were decorated with a conglomeration of art, including plaster figures, a striking oil painting of a harlequin left behind by Picasso among various other paintings, some so darkened by time and tobacco smoke that it was evident that their particular donors had long since departed from Montmartre.

When ordering the wine Nikolai was hailed exuberantly by two artists he had not seen for a long time and he invited them and the young women in their company to sit down and have some wine. They accepted gladly and another two bottles were brought. There were introductions followed by an exchange of news and the women talked to Juliette while politics were discussed by the men, although she would have liked to join in. When she heard the young women were models she asked if they knew Yvonne. They did and one of them added gravely, 'She had a hard time with that wretch who put her in the family way and then deserted her. Yet when he died of booze in a pauper's bed she sat nursing him to the end.'

'I didn't know,' Juliette said sadly. 'Poor Yvonne. She always looks so lovely and yet she's had such trouble.'

'He used to get all her money out of her, but she's all right now that she's only herself to keep, because her sister has married a butcher. She has a nice little place of her own now.'

Juliette knew Yvonne had changed her address since she had returned to Maison Landelle. She also knew it was in all probability due in no small part to her own successful insistence that top mannequins be paid more. Denise had not been easy to persuade, but as a result of the higher wages two exceptionally good mannequins had joined Maison Landelle from another house.

Inevitably the conversation of the men had switched to art and the three young women entered the discussion on Cubism, which was sweeping so many canvases. As it grew dusk outside more people came in and were drawn to the same table through mutual acquaintanceship and the lively talk necessitated the ordering of more bottles. The air grew thick with tobacco smoke and the talk came hard and fast. Eventually the group grew so large that they all moved with glasses and wine bottles to a central rectangular table where there was more room. Nikolai ordered bread and cheese for everyone. Afterwards he and Juliette joined those who streamed off to the Moulin de la Galette dance hall where admittance was cheap and all was informal, nobody in evening dress and all the men, as well as the women, kept on their hats. Plumes and ribbons bobbed around the dance floor with high bowlers, derbies and caps.

'Are you enjoying yourself?' Nikolai asked Juliette as he whirled her in a riotous gallop.

She threw back her head joyously. 'I'm having a wonderful time!'

It was late when they left, arms about each other. She asked him why he had not returned more often. He frowned as he answered, his jaw set.

'It's not easy to be a part-time artist among those whose lives are dedicated solely to art. I'll not come back again.'

She brought him to a halt, gripping his lapels and giving him an impatient little shake. 'But you are in your heart! That's all that matters.'

He folded his arms gently around her and looked at her tenderly. 'Darling Juliette. No wonder I love you.'

She caught her breath. 'I think you said you loved me.'

'I have from the start.'

'Why haven't you told me before?'

'I've been hoping that all the complications of my life would be smoothed out by some kind turn of fate, but unfortunately that hasn't happened yet.'

She touched his face tenderly with her fingertips. 'I love you no matter what comes.'

His embrace tightened. 'I never want to lose you!' Then he kissed her as passionately and hungrily as if even then they were on the brink of being torn apart.

When Nikolai collected the photographs taken in Montmartre he gave Juliette the one of them taken together, which she put in a silver frame on her dressing-table. He kept the one of her in his wallet.

CHAPTER TEN

The New Year's Eve Ball at the Russian Embassy was one of the great occasions in the social calendar. Denise used it as a chance to wear one of her own magnificent evening gowns, thick with pearls, with a view to advertising Maison Landelle in a new sphere, for it was the first time she had attended the ball and many foreign women there would normally only patronize Maison Worth.

Her visit to England had gone well. While there she had begun to have misgivings about having given Juliette licence to design her own gown, but she need not have worried. The girl looked remarkably lovely in softly shaded cream and peach silk *chiné* as she danced with Nikolai in the last waltz of the old year.

The orchestra suddenly stopped, bringing all the dancers to a standstill, and struck up a triumphant chord to herald in 1911. Bells began to ring throughout the city. There was the hoot of motorcar horns and fireworks began soaring into the sky above the Eiffel Tower. At the ball streamers made rainbows over those greeting each other. Denise, looking for Juliette to give her good wishes, saw that she had both her hands in Nikolai's as they stood smiling at each other, creating an oasis of intimacy in the midst of the celebrations. Then he lowered his head and they kissed.

Denise felt a sickening sense of dread. She knew the look of love when she saw it. All her anxieties about her sister returned a thousandfold. Something must be done to break up this close association before it was too late. At the moment she was too confused to think of anything, but she would watch out for the first opportunity to do whatever was possible.

Nothing presented itself for three weeks and then Pierre unwittingly gave Denise the chance she had been wanting. He spoke of Juliette's affinity with silk in all its forms and said how he thought some acquired knowledge about weaving and the origins of silk would greatly benefit her in time to come.

'You're right,' Denise declared. 'I want her to have the best grounding possible in all realms of the fashion business.'

When Pierre had left her office Denise rang for her secretary and dictated a letter to a business acquaintance and his wife in Lyon to make preparatory arrangements.

Nikolai, managing to get some leave from his Embassy duties, rented a studio of his own and moved in with his tools, materials and several small blocks of Pitacci and Soissons marble that he had bought at various times for future projects. He was like Rodin in preferring to work in clay and have the result cast in bronze, but the medium of marble was still his choice at times.

When he was settled in his studio the *Maître* himself came to view his premises and see what work he had in hand. Rodin, always well dressed since success had finally put an end to his years of poverty, made an impressive figure in his silk top hat, immaculate clothes and cream chamois gloves. He was broadly built with a craggy brow and a thick grey beard still tinted in places by its original red, his black-ribboned pince-nez glinting on his acquiline nose.

'Don't stop work,' he said when Nikolai had shaken his hand in welcome. Then Rodin waved aside the chair that Nikolai's assistant would have placed for him and went forward instead to view the sculpture of a young man in Carrara marble on which a hammer and chisel were being used, sending tiny chippings flying into the air. The model knelt on the stand, looking up over his shoulder in a pose that brought out the muscles of the neck, shoulders and thighs. Rodin nodded approvingly at the vibrant, pulsating life already captured in the marble.

'When are you going to rid yourself of those petty-fogging duties at the Embassy, Karasvin?' Rodin was violently opposed to this talented sculptor being thus tethered. 'You know as well as I do that you're throwing away valuable time there. Any fool could dance attendance on visiting dignatories and write a few letters, but as I first told you long ago, to be able to sculpt is a God-given gift and you've no moral right to relegate it to second place.'

Nikolai's face grew taut. 'Do you think I don't still wish to be free? Nothing has changed regarding those conditions laid down when I was seventeen and I was so desperate to become your pupil that I would have promised anything.'

Rodin inclined his head understandingly. What concerned him was that too many lengthy lapses in sculpting would eventually kill initiative and drain the gift from this Russian's talented fingers. So far that had not happened, but nobody knew better than he himself what anguish it could be when domestic and other problems came between an artist and his work. Now it was easy to see that his one-time student was sculpting like a man long starved of food. Rodin felt a word of warning would not go amiss.

'Do me one favour, Karasvin. Promise me that when those wretched duties continue to drag you away from this studio you'll never seek consolation in the bottle as you did once. You went through a bad patch then and made yourself the most notorious young man in Paris. Worst of all, your work suffered.'

Nikolai stopped his work and shrugged ruefully. 'Never again, *Maître*. I was younger then. It did me no good in more ways than one. You almost threw me out. I've always been grateful that you didn't.'

'It would have been a waste. Did you do anything worthwhile in your studio at home when you were there? We talked when you returned, but I don't think I asked you.'

'A few pieces that I had cast into bronze.'

'Good. At least you're still keeping your hand in whenever possible and you'll have a studio waiting when eventually you go home to live. Russia has given us all great literature, music and glorious ballet, even a number of artists, including the monks who created the icons, but the world has yet to applaud a particular sculptor from that vast land. Remember that.'

Nikolai grinned. 'I will.'

When Rodin had gone again Nikolai continued working even after

114

his tired model had dressed again and left. He was missing Juliette, whose sister had sent her on a visit to Lyon.

'I'm to learn all about the weaving and dyeing of silks.' Juliette had been excited by the prospect. 'Such knowledge will be invaluable to me.'

'How long shall you be away?'

'A month. Two months at the most.'

'So long!' he had exclaimed in dismay.

She had flung her arms about his neck. 'I wish you could be with me, but I'll write. You'll be sculpting in your new studio and you won't miss me at all!'

He knew she was hiding her own pain at leaving him and to suit her he replied in the same vein. 'Then you won't expect me to come and see you.'

She melted and clung to him. 'I'll die if you don't!'

So he had spent three cold March days in Lyon. Juliette had been as overjoyed to see him as he was to see her, but the couple with whom she was staying, Monsieur and Madame Degrange, were conscientious about her chaperonage and at no time were they ever alone. The Degranges were hospitable and Nikolai gladly accepted their invitation to dine at their home every evening, there being no other way he could see Juliette at the end of the day.

She was not the only guest staying in the house. The Degranges' Italian son-in-law, Marco Romanelli, was there too. A dealer in fine fabrics, he had been a widower for four years, his late wife having been the Degranges' eldest daughter, Françoise, whom he had first met when on business at the silk mills of Lyon, which still brought him back to the city from Venice at irregular intervals. Juliette introduced him to Nikolai on the first evening.

'Here's somebody you'll be interested to meet, Nikolai,' she declared as Marco Romanelli entered the salon where they were talking together. 'Signor Romanelli knows Fortuny very well and is buying undyed silk velvets for him among other fabrics for his own business.'

Nikolai had shaken hands with the Italian, who was as tall as himself with a larger and broader chest, his build more that of a La Scala baritone. A goodlooking fellow in his thirties, his face almost square and olive skinned, his chin deeply cleft, Marco was at ease with himself and everybody else. In the few words exchanged he spoke French fluently, which was a relief to Nikolai, who knew no Italian.

'Why undyed silk velvets?' Nikolai asked with interest. 'And why not silks as well?'

'Fortuny likes to use his own dyes and print his own patterns,' the Italian explained. 'I import a great deal of Lyonnais silk in my business, but not for Fortuny. I get undyed silk from Japan for him. He'll use no other. Mademoiselle Cladel told me that you and she have been interested in Fortuny's work for some time.'

'I've long admired his innovative effects in the theatre and, more recently, his designing skill in another sphere.' Nikolai grinned as he glanced deliberately at Juliette in her Delphos robe. She was wearing it with a full length silk-chiffon dévoré evening coat to avoid shocking her host and hostess. But she had worn the gown for Nikolai and he knew it.

Her face had flushed with pleasure at his compliment. 'I've told Signor Romanelli how I came across my Fortuny creation by chance in pieces and sewed it together again.'

Nikolai guessed she would have avoided revealing her sister's somewhat dubious attempt to discover its secrets. 'It was a lucky find.'

'I agree.' Marco Romanelli's quick, almost boyish, grin was accompanied by a crinkling at the corners of his brown eyes. 'I haven't asked yet if I'm permitted to tell Fortuny the story.'

'Of course you may,' Juliette replied light-heartedly. 'If you're sure it will please him.'

'I know it will. He'll want to hear what I thought of the result.' He stepped back and threw his hands wide. 'I shall tell him it's *bellissimo*!'

Nikolai nodded in agreement. Merrily Juliette twirled around once as if she were a mannequin again and then they all laughed together. All three of them were aware of the conviviality that their being a trio created.

They were interrupted by its being time to go into dinner. There were other guests present and to Nikolai's disappointment Juliette was seated some distance from him and Marco Romanelli had the place at her side. The conversation was generally depressing. A retired French general held forth on the threat he foresaw in the way the German Kaiser was rearming his forces on an extensive scale.

116

Nikolai held the same view on the danger involved, but it was difficult to be attentive when he could not stop looking in Juliette's direction. To his joy she frequently caught his eye and he was rewarded by a twinkling smile. The lovely sight of her kept flooding his heart. Her pearly skin seemed to glow against the coppery silk of the gown, its tiny pleats shimmering across the alluring rise of her breasts.

To Nikolai's increasing annoyance he found he was being watched in his turn by the Degranges' twin daughters, who at sixteen seemed even sillier than most girls of their age, batting their lashes at him and trying to draw his attention with fatuous remarks.

After what was to Nikolai a long and tedious meal, in spite of the excellence of the food and wine, he and Juliette and the Italian came together again in the salon where coffee was served. They had some animated discussions, Nikolai and Juliette arguing quite fiercely on one point to their mutual enjoyment, and before the evening was out they were on Christian names terms with Marco and he with them.

The next day Marco took Nikolai to the Degrange silk mill. Juliette was already there and had been since early morning. She was learning to weave under instruction and seemed not to hear the deafening clackety-clack of her own loom and the rows of others all around her. She flashed Nikolai a radiant smile.

'If the result is any good you shall have a new neck-tie out of it.'

The rest of the day would have been long for Nikolai if, after a tour of the mill, he and Marco had not lunched together and then hired a carriage to drive through the historic quarters of the old city and also to the heights to take in the view from Fourvière. He learned, as Juliette had already, that Marco was born in Milan, the youngest son of a close-knit family consisting of five boys and a girl, their father being a prosperous financier. In adulthood, after the death of their widowed mother, they had gone their separate ways. Three of Marco's brothers had emigrated to the United States where they had started successful businesses while the fourth had become a captain in the army, only to be killed in a tragic accident.

'As for my sister,' Marco concluded, refilling their glasses, for they were drinking wine together in an hotel bar after the drive, 'she is a nun nursing at a mission hospital in Africa.'

'How did you get into the silk business?'

117

'It was not by my choice. I'd had hopes of becoming a doctor, but that was to no avail. The reason was that my uncle had no sons, although he has rectified that since through a second marriage. In Italy blood-ties are strong and my father felt obliged to let his brother take me as his heir to learn his silk business from the floor up. Fortunately I became interested in the work and by twenty-five I was well-established in full management of the mill. It was then that my widowed uncle married a woman many years younger than himself.' Marco shrugged expressively. 'I found her too attractive for her good or mine.'

'So what happened?'

'I left when matters began to get out of hand between us. Before all this happened, I had met Fortuny several times and supplied him with silks for his theatrical costumes until he began to favour Japanese silk instead. After my departure from the mill I had a spell in the retail silk trade and happened to visit Venice on business. I went to see Fortuny again and during the course of conversation he told me about a local wholesale business for sale. It dealt with the import and export of luxury fabrics. On his advice I investigated and found it would be a venture I could build up and expand far beyond its bounds at that time. This was six years ago and I'm pleased to say all has been as I hoped.' He sat back in his chair. 'So there you have it. My career so far.'

'You've no regrets?' Nikolai took a mouthful of wine.

'None now. I met my late wife through the silk trade and I'll always be thankful for that, even though our marriage was tragically short.'

'I'm sorry,' Nikolai said genuinely, for he liked this man and sympathized with his loss.

'There's not a day when I don't still miss her.' Marco shook his head and then briskly looked at his watch. 'Drink up! We promised Juliette we'd be at the mill gates to meet her and it's almost time.'

On the second day, after Marco had finalized his orders, he and Nikolai went with Juliette to a silk farm where later hundreds of silkworms would hatch and munch their way voraciously through mulberry leaves, while elsewhere the cocoons of others would be unwoven in the first stage of making the world's most beautiful fabric. Nikolai found it all interesting, but it was a less pleasant visit when on his last day the three of them went to a dyeing plant in a local village where Juliette was to have some raw silk dyed to certain colours and Marco was advising her. The stench of the place was nauseating and they were all glad to leave.

'How quickly your time here has flown, Nikolai,' Juliette said sadly during the final dinner party. They had already arranged with Marco that he should contact them when he was next in Paris, for he had also come to the end of his stay in Lyon.

'How long do you think it will be before you return home?' Nikolai asked her.

She was uncertain. 'I can't say exactly when that will be. I'm to start learning all about screen and block-printing next and also some of my designs are to be woven. I have to see that through.'

When the time came for them to part Nikolai kissed her as long as he could with the chilling frown of Madame Degrange's shocked expression fixed on him and her giggling daughters peeping round the door.

'I'll miss you every day, Juliette.' He resented being overheard.

Her eyes were loving. 'I think of you all the time. And I'll keep writing to you as often as possible every week.'

She kept her word, but another month went by.

Eventually he received the good news that she would be returning the following week. There was also a message from the Embassy curtailing his six months' release as important diplomatic developments required his presence. Since the role he always played was a very minor one he swore in exasperation at this interruption of his work once again.

When Juliette arrived back in Paris Nikolai was waiting on the platform as she stepped off the train. They rushed into each other's arms, he sweeping her off her feet as they kissed, heedless of stares.

They talked all the way on the drive to her home. She wanted to know if he had finished *The Crouching Man*, which was what he had called his present work, and was sympathetic when she heard of his having been called back to the Embassy.

'Is there much left to do to it?' she asked.

'A little. Whenever I have a spare hour I go to the studio.'

'I want to see this new figure and your studio as soon as possible. Now I'll give you your present from Lyon.'

He opened it and saw it was the silk tie he had been promised.

'This is splendid! But I thought you were weaving emerald silk.'

'So I was! And I saw you quail at the colour! I'd already planned to make you a tie in the kind of grey you like.'

'This is perfect!' He pulled off the one he was wearing and replaced it with hers. Proudly she adjusted it for him and he caught her hands and kissed them.

Denise came home early and found her sister talking on the telephone, catching up with friends she had not seen for so long. Juliette left the telephone as soon as she could and they kissed each other's cheeks. Denise was more glad to see her than would ever have seemed possible in the past.

'I want to hear everything,' Denise declared eagerly. 'Your letters were so informative but there's still much I want to ask.'

She was soon impressed by all Juliette had learned of the silk trade and even more so by the lengths of silk imprinted with her own designs that she had brought home. There were feather and fern prints in silver on a luscious blue, ivory on black, and cinnamon on cream; stylized blossoms in pale pinks and blues created a lilac tint and other delicate patterns were in amber, ripe corn and pumpkin yellow.

'Monsieur Degrange will be writing to you,' Juliette said, relieved to see how pleased Denise was with the designs. 'He would like to use my patterns and colour combinations, but I thought we ought to have exclusive rights to them for eighteen months, or even for two years, before the release of the fabrics on the open market.'

Denise's eyes sharpened speculatively. 'Just as manufacturers serving the crowned heads of Europe withhold materials from their swatches that royal ladies have selected for themselves.'

'That's right. More important, it would give added prestige to Landelle clothes if the fabric designs didn't appear under any other labels.'

'I'll think about it,' Denise promised, seeing the possibilities of the idea, 'but I'm not sure I wouldn't let the designs be made up at the little silk-mill I visited near London. The price would be cheaper and the quality is comparable to what we stock already.'

The matter was left in hand for further discussion and preliminary enquiries. Denise congratulated herself once again on her own foresight in taking her sister into the business. She had forgotten the circumstances that had compelled her into it in the first place. Her jubilant mood faded somewhat when she heard that Nikolai had met Juliette off the train and they were continuing to see each other as if they had never been apart. If separation could not cool off the romance she must find some other means. But what? Whatever her anxieties, she must not turn Juliette against her. She was left in a quandary, hoping to find some solution.

When Juliette visited Nikolai's studio for the first time he was alone. It was late afternoon and he was working by the last of the daylight, his assistant having just left and the model no longer needed. He opened the door to her with a dark blue bandana knotted at the back of his head, white dust clinging to his lashes and linen smock. She had a basket on her arm covered with a red and white check cloth, a bottle of wine sticking out of it.

'I've brought supper for us,' she said after they had greeted each other. 'I thought it would be fun to eat here, because then you can work as long as you like and I'll be happy to sit and watch you.'

He praised her thoughtfulness as he took the basket from her and put it on a table. She glanced about her as she removed her gloves and slid the pearl-headed pin from her hat, which he hung with her jacket on a peg. She went at once to gaze in admiration at *The Crouching Man*.

'What can I say?' Her voice was almost breathless. 'You've looked into the soul of the model and seen all that was tormenting him.'

He took her by the shoulders and turned her towards him. 'Maybe he acted as a mirror to my own.'

Compassion for his predicament showed in her eyes. No artist should be torn apart as he was by demands on his life that ought never to have been allowed to interfere with his true vocation. She touched his face with her fingertips. 'I'm not here to interrupt your work. I want to be a quiet, undisturbing presence.'

Privately it amused him that she should suppose he could ever be other than totally aware of her presence. 'Talk as much as you like,' he said as he picked up a pumice stone to resume polishing the sculpture as he had been doing when she arrived. A bucket of clean water stood ready for washing it.

'Is that a long task?' she asked.

'Yes, it has been and always is when using pumice. Henri, my assistant, worked on it earlier today and looked tired enough for his

121

arms to drop off, which is why I sent him home. In any case I want to finish it off myself, because there comes a delicate point when marble can pass from being perfected to refined to a fault.'

'I never knew that. May I look around the studio?'

'Go ahead. Ask me anything else you want to know.'

She was intrigued by the great number of different tools in the rack. There were mallets, differently shaped chisels, hammers, scrapers, gouges, rasps and far too many others for her to ask the purpose of each one, as well as rolls of wire, which she knew would be used with wood when making supporting armatures on which to build up work in clay or terracotta. Pigeon-holed shelves were filled with the same kind of art clutter that she had seen in Rodin's vast studio. Behind a curtain was a tiny kitchen with an old cooking stove and a yellow stone sink with one tap. There was a kettle, a much-used coffee-pot and a cupboard that held cheap crockery from a street market. A door led to an outdoor privy in a tiny courtyard.

She wandered on around the room and came to a deep recess in which there was a table that had seen better days and benches fixed to the wall. 'I'll lay our supper there later,' she said. 'Was the furniture here when you took over the place?'

'Yes, it's just as it was, except that Anna insisted that I brighten the place up with that Russian shawl and cushions covering the leather couch.'

These items did make a brilliant splash of crimson, purple and scarlet, but nothing else gave any touch of comfort. Juliette smiled to herself. Nikolai had avoided bringing any of the luxurious trappings of his other life into the retreat. Even the facilities were as primitive as those he must have known in Montmartre.

Having explored the whole studio, she seated herself on the shawl-spread couch. Daylight was fading and he had switched on the electric light that shone directly down on him. She was half shadowed by the saucer-shaped lampshade, but her hair still caught red-gold highlights, her white blouse and dark skirt set off by the brightly woven covering and cushions behind her. He glanced at her with a smile and continued his polishing.

He liked having her near him as he worked. It was a new experience for them both. As they talked she asked him to tell her more about his childhood as she really knew little except that he had no brothers and Anna was his only sister. It had been a series of miscarriages that had undermined his mother's health and she had died just before he had first come to Paris.

'My parents' marriage was arranged as such matches always are for reasons of inheritance, property and land. My father was fifteen when the betrothal took place and my mother fourteen. They married eight years later when I suppose he was ready to settle down.'

'Surely such an archaic custom has died out now?'

'Not altogether. Young people are still subject to extreme pressure if they refuse to marry according to their parents' wishes.'

'Were your parents content in their marriage?'

'Against all odds, I believe they were. I know our home always seemed a happy place and was the centre of constant family gatherings with aunts and uncles and cousins coming for house parties in celebration of anything my mother could think of from birthdays to national feast days. Those were wonderful times in my childhood.'

'Please tell me about them.'

As he talked she could picture the wide green lawns and flower gardens where he and his cousins had played shuttlecock and hide-and-seek, pirates and Cossacks and explorers, the boys in sailor suits, the little girls in frilly dresses and if it was sunny, much to their annoyance, hats covered with dancing layers of white embroidery anglais. Later in life there was archery, tennis, dances, balls and parties as well as hunting and shooting for the older boys. Nikolai himself had been wild for riding and more than once had taken fast horses from the stables that had been forbidden him for their uncertain tempers. He had suffered a fall or two, but nothing had deterred him.

'So in the midst of all this,' Juliette questioned with keen interest, 'how did you discover your wish to sculpt?'

'The classic answer would be to say that it was from the time of making mud pies, but it wasn't like that. I had an uncle who liked to paint and sculpt in his leisure hours. When I was about ten he gave me a lump of clay to model whatever I wished. I remember I chose to do one of the hounds and when I'd finished in about an hour he stared at it so long and hard that I thought I'd made a terrible mess and he didn't know what to say for fear of hurting my feelings.

Instead he grabbed me by the arm and pushed me to another stand, stuck some handfuls of clay on it and told me to make something else. Even if he hadn't liked that first effort it would have been too late. The seed had been sown. Everything grew from there. It was that same uncle who persuaded my widowed father to let me have a year at St Petersburg Art School to assess my potential and then brought me to Paris when I was seventeen.'

'Does he still paint and sculpt himself?'

'Unfortunately not. He has developed arthritis in his hands, but his interest in art is as lively as ever. I visit him as much as possible whenever I'm at home.'

'Has he any of your work?'

'Yes. He has a bust of himself in bronze and another of his late wife. When he last wrote he offered to buy *The Wolf*, which was one of my early works that he saw when once in Paris, I'm going to ship it to him next week.'

'I've never seen it.'

'It's in that cupboard.' He nodded in its direction. 'I'll show you later.'

When he had done all the polishing he wished to do that evening, Juliette pulled the curtains across the windows and put a kettle on to boil for fresh coffee. He hung up his linen smock and hooked the bandana over it before he washed his face, arms and hands at the yellow stone sink. She spread the red and white check cloth on the table and put out the food from her basket on plates she had found in the kitchen. There was pâté, cold meats and cheese, salad for which she had brought dressing and a long loaf. Finally she arranged the fruit she had brought. Having found a candle in the kitchen she stuck it in a saucer and set it in the centre of the table. The harsh centre light would not reach them there.

Nikolai came from the kitchen, pulling his shirt-sleeves down into place. 'What a feast!' he declared appraisingly.

He poured the red wine and they sat for a long time over their meal, sometimes holding hands across the table. Afterwards she washed the dishes while he dried everything. Then he took out the bronze wolf from the cupboard and set it on a stand within the light. As with all his work it was dramatic, the animal fearsome and alert, sensing danger with its hackles risen. They discussed it together. It was when he was replacing the wolf on a shelf that a stack of drawings caught her eye. The top one was of herself.

Wordlessly, she took it up and then saw there was another of her underneath and yet more below that. The whole of the little stack consisted of sketches of her. He watched her in silence as she took them across to the table and spread them out in the candle-light that still flickered there. They showed her seated and standing, even glancing down as she knew she did at times of intense emotion when she wished to keep her feelings in check.

'When did you do all these?' Surprise had lifted her voice a note.

He came and stood behind her. 'While you were away. Remember that I mentioned once that I always make preliminary sketches for my next project.'

'So I'm to be your next model!'

'Not for the first time. I did a bust of you from memory when I was at home.'

She looked over her shoulder at him. 'Do you still have it there?'

'Yes, cast in bronze. It has a place of honour in my apartment.'

She returned her gaze to the sketches and smiled. 'So I'm to pose for you. It will be difficult to fit in sittings with our differing working hours, but we'll just have to take whatever time we can get. I'll enjoy being here with you away from other people.' A little laugh escaped her. 'La! This will be different from your other sculptures in that, as I can see from these drawings, I'll be fully clothed!'

He nuzzled the nape of her neck. 'Not by my choice,' he said softly.

She drew in a silent breath sharply at the suddenly changed atmosphere that his words had created. Slowly she leaned back against his chest, closing her eyes sensuously as his hands moved from her waist to cup her breasts caressingly and his lips travelled to her ear and into her hair while he murmured endearments. His tender fondling made her nipples rise through the satin of her chemise and the soft chiffon of her blouse. Her body began to throb with long suppressed yearnings. He had caressed her many times before during kisses and embraces, but then they had never been sure of remaining alone as they were now.

Slowly and yet willingly she turned to him, tilting her head back to meet his lips with her own. Immediately his arms were tight about her while she flung hers round his neck as they kissed wildly, his

125

mouth fierce, her own response exultant and abandoned. They were possessed by passion, all restraint flown. Nothing else existed any longer for her except him and her own desire sweeping her away towards the unknown. She did not know when he switched off the light, leaving them in the candle-glow, but it might have been in the last second before he gathered her effortlessly up in his arms and carried her across to the couch.

He uncovered her breasts swiftly, her chiffon blouse flying apart with a gleam of tiny pearly buttons, and with his stroking fingers and his tongue he explored the lovely shape of her, creating such delicious sensations that her spine arched and involuntarily she dug her fingers into his shoulders. With his every touch against her skin making her tremble ecstatically, he removed all her clothes, kissing every part of her body as it was revealed to him. When he moved away from her briefly she raised her arms and held them out to him as she waited during the few moments that he took to strip off and become as naked as she. He loomed over her, looking much like one of his own powerful sculptures in the aura of the candle. Then he was gathering her close, a warm and living and loving man, locking his passionate mouth on hers in a prelude for all that was to come.

His adoring exploration of her, banishing her last vestige of modesty in the most glorious ways, awakened her to new realms of pleasure that at times she found almost too exquisite to bear. She became so lovingly eager for him, the fount of her sensuality released by her intense ardour, that he waited no longer and entered her with a deep groan of joy. He swept her with him through all the rhythms of passion to a mutual and colossal explosion of total ecstasy.

In the quiet contentment that followed they lay close, silken limbs entwined, murmuring the talk of lovers. He pressed his lips to her palm when she rested her hand against his cheek and she smiled when he stroked back a long tendril of her hair, which had long since tumbled from its pins. Then after a while he began to touch her again with such intimate tenderness that she melted once more into his ardent love-making.

The candle was close to drowning in its own wax when Juliette awoke and sat up with a start. She had been lying within Nikolai's arm, but he was still sound asleep and her movements had not disturbed him. He lay magnificently sprawled, one leg against hers the other flung outwards, his foot over the side of the couch.

There was no clock in the studio. She left the couch and found her gold fob-watch amid the tumble of her clothes. It was three o'clock. Hastily she dressed. She hesitated as to whether she would wake him and then decided against it, but as she moved to the door in the near-darkness she knocked into a chair and the resulting clatter awakened him instantly.

'You're leaving!' He pushed back his hair with one hand, immediately swinging himself from the couch.

'I have to go.'

He took hold of her by the shoulders and drew her to him as he kissed her. 'I want to keep you with me for ever.' In their love talk he had sworn that he would love her always and nothing should ever part them.

'Let me leave now!' She was fighting her own wish to stay.

Seeing she would not be persuaded he released her reluctantly. 'I'll get dressed. Please wait. You'll not stop me from seeing you safely home.'

When they went outside he hailed a passing cab. Before long he was escorting her up the steps to her door, the cab waiting. He kissed her adoringly once more and this time she clung to him, the intimate hours they had spent together making them united as never before.

'Until tomorrow, my darling,' he said softly.

'Tomorrow,' she echoed in a whisper. But suddenly the true tomorrow seemed far out of reach.

CHAPTER ELEVEN

Posing for Nikolai was not the easy task that Juliette had expected it to be. She had thought he would make allowances for her not being a professional model and she would sit comfortably in a chair, but it was not to be like that at all. Previously on the telephone he had asked her what she intended to wear and, remembering her renewed promise to Denise, she had said it would not be the Delphos robe, which would have been her natural choice, in case the finished sculpture should go on exhibition.

'So what's it to be? Could you make something similar?'

'Slightly Grecian?'

'That would be ideal.'

So she made a simple tunic in cream silk without sleeves and with a round neckline. She took it with her to the studio in an anonymous cardboard box.

Upon her arrival Nikolai was waiting for her. She went behind the models' screen to change into the tunic. When she emerged he grinned his approval.

'Wonderful! Couldn't be better!'

He took her face between his hands and kissed her for the second time since he had opened the door to her and then led her to the modelling stand.

'Let me tidy my hair,' she insisted, for his fingers had disarranged some tendrils.

'I like it as it is. Don't touch it.'

On the stand he arranged her pose, taking her wrists to draw her hands down just a little behind her, and tilted her chin to the angle he wanted. She thought that if he asked her to be on tip-toe she might look as if she were about to take wing, but he did not mention that. Apparently satisfied, he crossed to the large window to pull a curtain half across it, explaining that shadow emphasized profiles to the sculptor's eye. He proceeded then to twist the stand on its castors, which rattled on the stone floor, only to stand back and study her before thrusting it round the other way. She raised her eyebrows half-mockingly, having staggered slightly.

'Are you trying to make me lose my balance?'

His concentrated gaze cleared as he saw her again as the woman he loved and not just as a model. 'Not at all,' he said with a smile. 'I just wanted to view you from every angle.'

He took up a sketch-pad and drew her from various view points. She was surprised how difficult it was to remain absolutely still. Twice her chin sank and he raised it again with his fingertips. But his pencil moved swiftly and the drawings were soon done.

'That's all for now.' He put the sketch-pad down. 'By the time you come again I'll have made a small clay model or two of your poses. Then we really can get to work, because the finished sculpture will be life-size.'

'May I see the sketches?' she asked as she stepped from the stand.

She had expected her poses to appear static, but it was quite the reverse. If he had drawn her with every breath she'd taken he could not have captured her more as a woman poised with energy and verve on the brink of some new venture. But what could that be? She almost asked him and was indirectly reminded of what needed to be said.

'Naturally I'll model for you as much as I can, but you have to remember that Denise wants me to go to England soon!'

Her sister had finally decided that the London silk-mill and another at Macclesfield were offering the best prices as well as delivery times for silk woven from Juliette's own textile designs. Denise wanted her to make the final choice.

Nikolai sighed resignedly as he embraced her. 'How could I

129

forget? But you shouldn't be away as long this time as you were in Lyon.'

She laced her fingers at the back of his neck. 'Of course not. Only long enough to see the first patterns come off the looms after I've decided which of my designs they shall have.'

'I think I'll go home for a short visit while you're away. There are a number of matters I have to deal with that are impossible to handle from here.'

'That's an excellent idea. Then we won't miss any time together.'

'That's what I thought too. Anna is going home at the end of the week to spend a few months to buy and settle in a new house and I'll travel with her. Have you heard from Gabrielle yet?'

'Yes. She and her husband are waiting to welcome me whenever I arrive.'

But he no longer wanted to discuss her going away and began to cover her face and neck with kisses. Soon they were making love for the first time since the night they had spent together. Never had he expected to want to cherish any woman for the rest of his life as he did her. What had happened to them was the rarest of all attractions in that at first sighting they had recognized, without quite realizing it, that in each other they had found the other half of themselves.

Denise was surprised when told that Countess Dolohova wished to speak privately with her in her office. There had been plenty of discussions about the large number of clothes the woman was taking back to Russia with her, all final fittings done, approval won and deliveries made.

Not having expected to see the Countess again until next spring, Denise's immediate thought was that this client wanted to bargain over the account. She had been wearied many times by rich women trying to beat her down when it came to paying or wheedling her to be 'nice' to them as good customers who deserved special 'consideration'. It was a hazard more common in *haute couture* than those outside the business ever realized, but she and the *directrice* always stuck to their guns in a smiling, tactful way.

Yet as Denise waited for the Countess to be shown in she dismissed on reflection the first possible reason for the visit. The idea of such a woman even deigning to talk money, especially as

130

she never even asked the price of any garment, was ludicrous. Anna Dolohova never lost an inherent haughtiness even when at her most charming. Puzzled, Denise rose from the desk to greet her as she entered. When seated Anna came straight to the point.

'As you know,' she commenced briskly, 'I'm leaving for St Petersburg at the end of the week, but I wanted to speak most seriously to you about your sister and my brother before I depart.'

Denise was alarmed. 'I don't understand.'

'Don't you, Madame la Baronne?' Anna spoke with an edge to her voice. 'Nikolai has told me he is in love with Juliette and intends to marry her. I see you are shocked and I share your state of mind. Believe me, I have nothing against Juliette, but the match is impossible. Nikolai has obligations at home that he cannot surrender under any circumstances.'

'I can't see Juliette ever wanting to leave Paris. Maybe they plan to live here and he'll make visits home as I understand he does from time to time.' Denise was clutching at straws.

'My father is in poor health these days. He's a proud man and would not admit it, but the call for Nikolai to return home to reside there permanently could come at any time. He will have to be there. There are too many problems that cannot be delegated. My brother is a talented sculptor, but he can sculpt as easily at home as he can here. Paris is a dream for any young artist, but there comes a time when reality has to take over.'

'Have you said all this to him?' In despair Denise was seeing every one of her wonderful plans for the future draining away like sand.

Anna sighed to herself. Out of her immense concern and sibling affection for Nikolai she had spoken bluntly to him, only to arouse his displeasure that she of all people should offer opposition instead of support. 'Everything I said to my brother fell on deaf ears. He is unshakable in his decision to return home with me for a short stay in order to arrange matters for a marriage to Juliette. So I felt compelled to discuss this crisis with you since it is of equal concern to both of us. If Juliette were a divorcée or an experienced woman of the world, as so many have been, I'd know it was no more than a passing *affaire*, but this time it is different.'

'In what way?'

131

'Because Juliette is young and beautiful and no doubt believes and encourages whatever he's promised her of a life together. He's convinced himself that it's possible, but I foresee only disaster for them both if everything isn't stopped before it's too late.'

Denise felt confused. 'How can you be so sure?'

'He is the Tsar's godson, madame! My father will turn to his old friend to intervene as he did once before when Nikolai's youthful ambition to be a sculptor in Paris for the rest of his life created an impasse that nobody else was able to overcome.'

'Young men in love can be very determined. Perhaps he will not listen to anyone.'

Anna shrugged and sat back in her chair. 'Then his life will be made wretched by ostracism at home and abroad as family links are severed and old friends turn their backs. Juliette will be unhappy on his behalf as well as her own, because when the first flush of desire wanes he will come to see her as a burden as well as a barrier to the social round he had enjoyed previously. The reason is that as his wife Juliette would never be received by the Russian nobility. Forgive me for speaking bluntly, but I have to emphasize that she is at present a humble seamstress. Doubtless you are training her for a more important position in your business, but she will still be a working girl. I have made inquiries about your parents and find that although reported to be most respectable persons they were nevertheless engaged in trade. My brother, while in Paris, has acquired ridiculously liberal and modern ideas, which are quite unacceptable in Russia. The situation is impossible.'

Denise had never hated a client before. Their money and their patronage had always enabled her to overlook their faults, but the Countess's words had made crimson rise up her neck to flood her cheeks as she forgot her own snobbery in this vicious snub that she saw directed at herself as well as Juliette. Cold fury erupted within her.

'What you are saying, Countess,' she exploded harshly, 'is that if Juliette had been Russian instead of French she might well have been in the crowd of poor starving people – working girls among them – who, a few years ago, were shot down by guards at the Tsar's own gates when they came unarmed to kneel in the snow to implore his aid!'

Anna sprang to her feet, her eyes blazing. 'How dare you! I shall

132

never enter this building again! I reject everything you've just made for me and do not ever dare to request payment!'

She pulled open the door and stalked out, leaving it wide behind her, ignoring the *directrice* and even an acquaintance who spoke to her. Pale and tight-lipped, she swept on down the stairs and outside into her waiting carriage.

'Maison Paquin!' she snapped at her coachman.

As the wheels rolled forward she sat glowering and drummed the ferrule of her folded parasol on the floor with every thought that pounded in her brain. There had been something else she'd been on the point of telling that upstart dressmaker, but now the moment was lost. Not even on the telephone would she speak to that creature again.

More than ever she was determined that Nikolai should finish with Juliette. If Nikolai had chosen a well-born girl, even as she herself had once loved a titled man whom she had not been allowed to marry, she would have fought tooth and nail to see that they wed, but she could not condone any betrayal of their class. All the troubles in Russia today were being caused by peasants demanding the right to vote, lower taxes, education and all else that belonged solely to their betters since they had neither the intelligence nor the manners to have a say in anything. One had only to see them fighting in the gutter over a crust to realize that.

Her thoughts slipped to the gorgeous clothes she would be sending back to Maison Landelle. Her only hope was that Madame Paquin would work her employees day and night to supply her with what she needed immediately to take back to St Petersburg, the rest to follow soon afterwards. So many evening and dinner gowns apart from all else. Surely, faced with such a stupendous order, Madame Paquin would be eager to oblige.

Anna stopped drumming her parasol's ferrule. Her frown cleared. She adored choosing new clothes.

When Denise had closed the door after the departing Countess she had sunk down in the vacated chair and rested her elbow on the arm as she put a hand to her head. She was shaking. What a terrible scene! Heaven alone knew how many Russian clients she would lose when they heard about her outburst.

Gradually her anger shifted against Juliette. Out of all the young men who had danced attendance on the girl during nearly two and a half years since her home-coming from the convent, she'd had to fall in love with a foreigner. In retrospect Denise supposed the Countess had come to her in the hope that together they could pit their wits to stop Nikolai and Juliette making the false step that could only lead to misery. But what was to be done? Denise recalled her own vehement opposition to her parents' advice that she should not rush into marriage with Claude de Landelle. The more they had wanted her to reconsider the more resolved she had become. Juliette would react the same way. The young always did.

Restlessly Denise moved back to her desk and sat abstractedly tapping a pencil at one end and then the other. The girl's trip to London should be brought forward. Separation had made no difference to the romance last time, but in Russia Anna Dolohova would ensure sterner measures were taken to make her brother see sense. It was a faint chance, but there was nothing else at the present time.

Denise's tumbled thoughts turned to another problem. How to explain the Countess's rejection of the clothes when previously she had been so pleased with them? Juliette would want to know why as would Pierre and the *directrice*. There seemed to be only one solution. She would instruct the doorman to bring the boxes straight to her when the garments were returned. After working hours, when she was on her own, she would go through them, remove labels and all valuable trimmings before packaging them herself to send to a woman in the provinces, who dealt in good cast-offs and paid well for any *haute couture* garments that on rare occasion had to be thrown out.

With this decision settled in her mind, Denise checked her anxiety-ridden face in a mirror and then composed herself as best she could as she rang for her secretary. The full account for all that Anna Dolohova owed was to be dispatched immediately. Denise was determined that the Countess should at least pay her dues. But the account was returned by evening with an accompanying lawyer's letter that stated none of the clothes had been to the Countess's satisfaction, and if there was any further communication the matter would be taken to court. Denise almost tore her hair. No couture house could risk the scandal of pressing for payment when valued clients were always allowed to take their time, especially when such

134

a fashionable woman as Anna Dolohova declared the garments to be below par.

Yet Denise's humiliation was not yet complete. The Countess did not send back the clothes in their original be-ribboned boxes, but bundled together in a canvas sack. It was the ultimate snub. Denise wept with helpless fury behind the locked door of her office.

Juliette was not surprised when the date of her going to London was brought forward. She knew how keen Denise was for the matter to be settled. A cable sent to Gabrielle brought an immediate reply that the change of dates for the visit were as convenient as those previously arranged. Juliette told Nikolai over the telephone. It meant she would only be able to model for him once more before she left and late the following Saturday afternoon was fixed.

At the studio Nikolai's assistant, Henri, opened the door to Juliette. He was a plain but agreeable youth with a shock of tow-like hair. Nikolai had already built up the clay on the supporting armature of wood and wire and it was taking its first shape. He paused to have a few words of smiling conversation with her before resuming his task. She studied the small clay models that were his replicas of how the finished sculpture would be. Even the slightly dishevelled state of the few tendrils of her hair which she had not been allowed to tidy back that first evening, were sensitively included. Behind the models' screen she carefully arranged the tendrils in the same way in front of the mirror hanging there.

'That's exactly right,' Nikolai said as she took up her pose on the stand. 'Perhaps the chin a fraction higher. Good.'

As the evening went by she was fascinated to see how the shaped clay was moulded into an unmistakable form of her under his strong, long-fingered hands. Meanwhile Henri was providing fresh clay when it was needed, scraping up dollops that inevitably fell to the floor and making sure that the wooden tools and cheese-wire were within the sculptor's range should they be needed, for these items were all that were used for work in this medium. When Juliette took a rest Henri made her and Nikolai fresh coffee, but Nikolai's became cold and remained barely tasted as he worked on all the time she was away from the stand. It was quite late when finally he called a halt to the session. Henri, eager to get away, gave the floor a final

135

clean and set everything to rights very quickly. As soon as he was gone Nikolai locked the door after him.

Turning back into the room, Nikolai saw that Juliette had already removed her silk tunic and stood ravishingly beautiful in her nakedness, her glorious hair hanging free of its pins. He went to kneel before her, enfolding her thighs in his arms as he pressed his kiss against her with all the devoted homage of a truly loving man.

On the eve of their leaving Paris Nikolai took Juliette to dine at Larue's where she had first worn the Delphos robe and where they had dined many times since. As a wrap she wore the Knossos scarf that he had given her on her birthday, its green silk soft and diaphanous as a sea-mist, its geometric motifs reputed to be inspired by Cycladic art in deeper shades with touches of gold.

At their favourite table with its concealing bower of flowers he took a Fabergé ring-box of white holly wood from his pocket. When she did not accept it from him he placed it in front of her.

'Please open it,' he urged.

Slowly she pressed the catch and the lid flew up to a dazzle of magnificent diamonds. Immediately her face became anguished, her lips tremulous. 'Oh, Nikolai! You know I wanted us to wait. We have so much to work out, so many difficulties to solve.'

'That needn't stop me from giving you a gift of love. If I choose to see it as being more significant towards our future then that is my privilege.' He took the ring from its velvet bed and explained that the three kinds of gold, which she saw gave such a lovely colour variation to the setting, was a Russian tradition with such rings.

'Rings of betrothal?' she challenged.

'Rings of love,' he countered with a smiling shrug that neither denied nor endorsed what she had asked. 'Let me put this on your finger.'

She could see how much it would mean to him, but instinctively she clenched her hands in her lap. They had discussed and argued the question of marrying ever since they had first made love. She had emphasized everything that common sense told her would be against their union, but he would not be persuaded. None was more aware than she of the intense snobbery and rigid lines drawn by high society, for she came in contact with it almost daily at Maison

136

Landelle. Not even the fact that she was a Baronne's sister would ever gain her an entré to gatherings of the old aristocracy of France and still less to that of Russia. She knew that her one and only visit to Prince Vadim's house had been tolerated solely through his old friendship with *Tante* Lucille. Love had not blinded her to reality.

Yet she did not want to spoil this last evening with Nikolai before they went their separate ways, however temporary the parting was to be. 'Let us wait with this ring until you've been home and talked everything over with your father. I don't want to be the cause of a family rift.'

He was determined. 'You won't be. My father has become more tolerant in his old age.'

She thought it a vain hope. Nikolai planned that after he inherited they should spend three or four months every year in Paris, which should make tolerable any social problems they had to face during the rest of the time. He had a cousin, who shared his own liberated ideals, whom he could trust to be his right hand and take over control of the great estate in his absence. Just the thought of living in Russia dismayed her. She had avoided hurting Nikolai's loyalty to his own country by reminding him that more enlightened nations thought of the Tsar as a tyrant. Yet he knew she abhorred, as he did, the terrible conditions of the Russian peasants that were being fully reported in the newspapers. It made no difference to her that Nikolai was resolved to make changes when the Karasvin estate was his, for his efforts would amount to no more than a drop in the ocean in the troubles of that vast land. She wanted to be no part of that oppressive system, even as the wife of the man she loved so much. It was an impasse that seemed insurmountable.

He had found her clenched hands in her lap and was gently but firmly releasing her fingers. 'I love you, Juliette. Surely that is enough for you to accept my ring as a constant reminder of what you will always mean to me.'

She let him draw up her hand and he slid the beautiful ring onto her finger. For a moment she could not be sure if it was the sparkle of the marvellous diamonds or the tears suddenly glittering on her lashes that made him appear to be already far away from her.

Later, when she had closed her bedroom door behind her, she

stood gazing at the ring before eventually she slid it from her finger and returned it to its box, which she placed in her jewellery casket. There it must remain, except when she wore it to please Nikolai. Perhaps one day there might be another reason as well, but in no way yet was it possible to see how that might come about.

CHAPTER TWELVE

The Channel crossing was not unpleasantly choppy. Juliette sat on deck with a plaid travelling rug over her knees until she put it aside and went to the rails, holding her hat in the stiff breeze, when the white cliffs of Dover appeared on the horizon. Nothing was to be missed on this trip that combined business with pleasure.

Her thoughts drifted to Nikolai, who had been travelling on a train with his sister for some hours already. His was a far longer journey and his purpose entirely different from hers. He had said it would be a tedious time *en route* to St Petersburg since he and Anna were not on particularly good terms at the moment. He did not give the reason, but she could guess and saw the strained relationship as the first sign of what he could expect to face at home. None could forbid his right to marry whomever he chose, no matter what displeasure it caused his father or anyone else in the family, but that was not the issue.

'Informing my father of my intention to marry you,' Nikolai had said before his departure, 'is a filial duty that I'm pleased to perform. He and I haven't always seen eye to eye and many differences still remain, but if he was overly strict when I was a child he was also just and I'm counting on that sense of justice now to spare any estrangement between myself and him in his old age.'

She knew he had been trying to reassure her about any possible family rift and it was as if he had not heard or heeded anything she had said to him. Yet now he was on his way, travelling in the luxurious family railway coach that Anna had sent for to be attached to the rest of the train, Juliette found it impossible to quell a tiny flicker of hope that in some unforeseeable way all problems might be solved. It was as though his decisive action had ignited an optimistic spark without her being aware of it at first. But now, physically detached from France on board ship in a kind of limbo, she was able to reflect on everything with a curious clarity.

Might it be said that she was even able to review the situation in the faint tint of a rosy light? If Nikolai's father should live to be very old – and by all accounts the Karasvin men were long-living if not struck down by the hazards of war and other disasters – it could be years before any thought need be given to residing in Russia. Perhaps by then the young Tsarevitch would have inherited the Throne and who knew what reforms he might introduce for the benefit of his poor down-trodden subjects. Everything in this new century was moving at a fast pace never known before, men even taking to the air and women breaking into realms that were formerly masculine strongholds. Surely there must come a time when the love of a couple from different classes would meet with tolerance instead of social ostracism?

During Juliette's reverie the white cliffs had come nearer. She moved away from the rails to prepare for going ashore. After disembarkation there was almost no delay in showing her passport or going through customs. The London train was waiting. Soon she was looking out at the lush green countryside of Kent, the pale golden sunshine lying softly over the thatched farmhouses, the many orchards and hopfields and the warm red, russet and brown brick-work of the conical oast-houses. After a glimpse of Chatham dockyard with Royal Navy ships lying alongside it was not long before she and Gabrielle were greeting each other affectionately at Victoria Station.

'You're here at last, Juliette! It seems aeons since we last met in Paris!'

'Why haven't you been back?'

'Impossible! Since Derek became a director of the Bank he's too busy to get away for any length of time and I won't go anywhere

140

without him. It's my pet excuse for keeping a safe distance from my mother.'

'Have your parents been to see you instead?'

'They've been twice.' Gabrielle rolled up her eyes expressively. By now she and Juliette were seated in a gleaming Daimler, a liveried chauffeur at the wheel. 'I'm always glad to see my father and he to see me, but my mother creates trouble as soon as she's across the threshold.' She chatted on as the London traffic closed in all about them. Suddenly she pointed through the window. 'Look! There's Buckingham Palace! Derek and I have been invited to a banquet there and other formal functions when the King and Queen were present. I must say that royalty does give a wonderful sense of occasion to any event.'

After gazing out at the Palace with its scarlet-coated guardsmen at the gates Juliette sat back in her seat again. The Daimler was sweeping down the tree-lined Mall. She regarded her friend humorously. 'What talk is this from a staunch French Republican? Are you becoming a royalist in your new land?'

Gabrielle burst out laughing and pressed fanned fingers across her mouth. 'Perhaps I am! Maybe it won't be long before you see me with a banner. Not as a Suffragette marching into Downing Street, but along the Champs Elysées and my banner will declare: "Bring back the Bourbons! All is forgiven!"'

Juliette shared the joke before she expressed her pleasure at seeing Gabrielle so carefree. 'You're so different. It's as if a burden has been lifted from you. I'm delighted to see you so happy.'

'Yes, I am,' Gabrielle declared eagerly. 'Being married to Derek still seems like a miracle to me. He came into my life like a knight on a white charger and took me away from all that made my life wretched.'

'Nobody could be more glad for you than I.'

'I know.' Gabrielle's voice softened. 'That's why it means so much for me to have you staying awhile. It's not easy for a foreigner to make English women friends here. The only new friends I've made have been among the French community, the rest are just acquaintances.' Suddenly her eyes twinkled mischievously. 'You won't find Englishmen unfriendly. A pretty face and a French accent act like a magnet to them. You're going to enjoy yourself in London! I'm giving a party for you and have accepted lots of invitations on your behalf as well as for Derek and myself. He's also booked seats for all the best shows and for the opening gala night of *Tristan and Isolde* at the Royal Opera House at Covent Garden!'

Juliette felt quite overwhelmed, having asked by letter only if she might stay awhile in England with them while on business. 'Have you forgotten that I'm here to work?'

'Of course not.' Gabrielle gestured dismissively. 'That can be fitted in somewhere.'

The Townsends' residence was in an elegant terrace of houses in Berkeley Square. When Derek came home he and Juliette met for the first time. She thought he looked older than his years, but then he held a highly important position and youthful looks would have been against him. Similarly his prematurely grey hair propelled him even deeper into an appearance of middle age, although his skin was clear, his jawline crisp and he was lean and trim in build.

'It gives me great pleasure to welcome you to our home, Juliette,' he said.

Gabrielle slipped her hand into the crook of his elbow, smiling up at him. 'Aren't we lucky to have her here! We'll lock Juliette up if she even thinks of going back to France before weeks and weeks have gone by.'

He caught Juliette's eye in a glance of understanding and then looked down into his wife's up-turned face. 'I'm sure Juliette will stay as long as she is able, but she is in business as I am and isn't free to do exactly as she might wish. You and I know what that means to our cost, don't we, my dear? We'll have to let her go when she feels compelled to depart.'

Gabrielle reached out a hand to Juliette in appeal. 'But you will stay as long as you possibly can?'

'You know I will,' Juliette promised. 'But it can only be for a few extra days. Another time I'll come just for a holiday.'

Later Derek spoke to Juliette on her own. 'My wife still suffers a great deal from homesickness. She has looked forward to your coming so much, not only because you've always been her best friend, but also because you represent all the better times of her childhood in France. Love of one's country becomes acute for the first few years away from all that was familiar.'

He did not know that his words had an echo for Juliette. Once

142

again she thought how impossible it would be for her to tear up her roots to live in Russia. 'You're very understanding.'

'As you were to Gabrielle in her convent days. She has told me many times that you were the only person she could trust in her unstable, unhappy youth.'

Juliette tilted her head. 'I think her memory has enhanced the role I played. I know now Gabrielle needed an anchor, even though I'm sure I didn't realize it at the time, and she will always need one. That's why I can see she has the right husband in you.'

'I'll never fail her.'

Juliette could tell that he was a man who would keep his word.

That night when Derek was in bed with Gabrielle he discovered there were tears on her cheek. Immediately he reached over to switch on the bedside light. 'Whatever is the matter, my darling?' he asked in concern, leaning over her again.

'I'm so afraid for Juliette!' She clung to him. 'I've a terrible feeling that when she leaves here it will be to go so far away that there's no telling what will happen to her.'

'Why ever should that be? She's only going back to Paris.' He spoke soothingly, supposing the premonition to be no more than his wife's own dread of something terrible happening that would cut her off for ever from her beloved France. He made up his mind to find some way to take her to Paris soon, but as yet he could not promise anything. 'Go to sleep. There's nothing to worry about. Imagination can play such tricks sometimes.'

'Are you sure?' She looked at him appealingly, anxious for her fears to be banished.

'Yes, I am. Now close your eyes.' He kissed her lids and she snuggled closer to him, seeking still further the security of his arms.

The lamp was switched off again. He was a sound sleeper and if it took longer than usual for Gabrielle to sleep he did not know. It was the first time she had not been wholly reassured by him over any qualm she'd experienced. She tried to take comfort from the knowledge that Juliette had always faced tribulation courageously, but that did not diminish her immense concern for her friend's future.

Juliette had arranged before leaving Paris that she would telephone the silk-mill owners in both London and Macclesfield after her arrival to make appointments with both. As it was, she had been in London a week before she was able to escape the entanglements of Gabrielle's social and sight-seeing round in order to get down to business.

The London silk-mill lay north of the Thames. Juliette had a very satisfactory discussion with the owner and approved the samples of finished work that she was shown, many fine fabrics being unrolled and displayed for her inspection. Some of the raw silk used was from English silkworm farms, but most was imported from China and India. She would have been prepared to allot the order to this silk-mill, but Denise wanted her to visit Macclesfield as well which meant withholding a decision for the time being. She decided to leave for Macclesfield in the morning.

'You can't possibly go tomorrow!' Gabrielle protested. 'In the evening we have a box for the Wagner gala performance!'

So the Macclesfield trip had to be postponed. Juliette wore the Delphos robe to the opera. Such a magnificent event demanded her best gown, although for the sake of her host and hostess, as in Lyon, she wore her silk chiffon dévoré coat with it to avoid creating a scandal.

The Royal Opera House with its gilt and crimson was a rich setting for a tremendous performance. The auditorium sparkled with jewels and the mother-of-pearl gleam of stiff shirt fronts. In the royal box a princess and her party added to the grandeur of the evening. During the interval Juliette left the box with Derek and Gabrielle to stroll the red carpet beneath the chandeliers, pausing when they were greeted by acquaintances, some of whom she had met already. Suddenly she was addressed unexpectedly by someone who had come unnoticed to her side.

'What a wonderful surprise to find you here, Juliette!'

She knew his voice instantly. Her companions, engaged in conversation, did not see her turn towards the man who had spoken. 'Marco Romanelli! Of all people!' she exclaimed delightedly. 'How are you? Why are you in London? We were to have met sometime in Paris.'

He laughed with her in their mutual astonishment at coming across each other so unexpectedly. 'I'm well and I've come to London on business.' He began craning his neck. 'Where's Nikolai?'

'He's far away in St Petersburg on a visit. How he would have

144

liked to be here to make our trio complete! I'm in England on business too, but combining it with a visit to a dear friend and her husband. I'll introduce you.' She would have attracted her host and hostess's attention, but he stayed her.

'One moment first. There's somebody who is waiting to meet you. As soon as I sighted you I pointed you out to him.'

Then she saw that a tall man of immense presence and striking good looks had come forward as Marco had done from the group of people they were with and stood there smiling at her. Every instinct told her who he was even as Marco made the introduction.

'Juliette, allow me to present Don Mariano Fortuny.'

She scarcely heard what else he said in her pleasure at meeting the designer whose work she had so admired. It flashed through her mind that Marco had told her in Lyon of Fortuny's passion for Wagner and how the composer's great works had inspired this brilliant man, not only in his theatrical work but in his paintings too, which would explain why he had come to this particular gala night. He was strongly built and handsome with a splendid nose, luminous blue eyes, thick, dark and well-groomed hair, a neat moustache and beard. Immaculate in his evening clothes, there was a dashing air about him as if he belonged to a more romantic era than the present day.

He bowed deeply to her. If he had added a flourish it would have seemed entirely natural to him.

'I'm honoured to meet you, Mademoiselle Cladel. Marco has told me the tale of how you found the Delphos robe discarded somewhere and sewed it together again. I should like to thank you for enhancing the gown with your elegance.'

From anyone else the compliment would have been effusive, but from him it was simply a sincere tribute and Juliette accepted it as it was intended.

'I'll never own a gown that will mean more to me.'

He nodded in satisfaction, pleased with her reply. 'You design clothes yourself, I believe.'

'I've some experience in that work, but my interests also include textile design, which is what brought me to England.'

'I'm leaving for Venice tomorrow and if ever you visit there I hope you'll call on me. I'd like to hear about your work and show you those textiles in my own designs that are displayed.'

145

'I'll remember your kind invitation.'

'Now I must rejoin my party. This has been a pleasure. Pray excuse me. *Adieu*, mademoiselle.'

Juliette turned back to Marco as Fortuny left them. 'What luck! Two splendid surprises in as many minutes! Firstly seeing you and then Fortuny himself! Now I want you to meet Derek and Gabrielle.'

For the rest of the interval Marco conversed with all three of them. When he heard that Juliette, accompanied by Gabrielle, would be leaving for Macclesfield in the morning he said that he would be visiting the silk-mills too.

'I'd intended to go at the end of the week, but it would be a pleasure to travel there with you both.'

It was agreed. Gabrielle was relieved. She did not like going far without a male escort. When the bell rang for the end of the interval Derek invited Marco to the party he and Gabrielle were giving for Juliette. He accepted at once.

It proved to be a very pleasant expedition to Macclesfield. Juliette and Marco conducted their own business during the day. Eventually she decided to give the Maison Landelle order to the London silk-mill after all as it offered the best delivery time. In the evenings Marco, who was staying at the same hotel, dined with her and Gabrielle, and afterwards took them to a moving-picture house. On the third day they travelled back to London together.

'I think,' Gabrielle remarked when she and Juliette had parted from Marco at Euston station, 'that Signor Romanelli is very attracted to you.'

Juliette shook her head laughingly. 'You've said that about practically every man I've spoken to since I arrived.'

Gabrielle smiled, but said no more.

A letter was waiting for Juliette when they arrived home, in a handwriting she did not recognize. As she opened it a silk label slipped out of the envelope on to the floor. She picked it up, realized what it was and read the letter eagerly. It was from Fortuny.

I was told that when you found the Delphos robe in pieces its lacings and label were missing. You have replaced the lacings. I enclose the final touch with my compliments.

Juliette rushed to show Gabrielle what she had received. 'He

146

would never have sent this label to me if he had been able to see any fault in my re-making of the gown!' she exclaimed. 'Now it will be complete.'

Gabrielle read aloud the wording of the label resting on the palm of her hand. '*Mariano Fortuny. Venice.* How thoughtful of him!'

'I wish I could have thanked him personally, but I know from Marco that he will be on his way back to Italy by now.'

When Juliette had sewn the label into the back of the gown's neckline she wrote to Nikolai of her good luck in receiving it. She did not see Marco again until the party on the eve of his departure. He knew about the label, Fortuny having told him, and his eyes twinkled at her enthusiasm for the gift.

'I've written my thanks to him at his Venetian home,' she said. 'The Palazzo Pesaro degli Orfei! Is it as glorious as it sounds?'

'Yes, indeed. It's one of the largest palaces in Venice and was built in the thirteenth century by the great Pesaro family. These days it's known as the Palazzo Orfei.'

'Is it on the Grand Canal?'

'No, a short distance away. Fortuny – or Don Mariano, as he likes to be addressed – has lived there since he moved out of his mother's palace, the Palazzo Martinengo, on the Grand Canal some years ago.'

Juliette was much in demand by others at the party and was not able to dance with Marco as often as she would have wished, but he was a very sociable man and at ease with people. Whenever she glanced across at him he was clearly enjoying himself and the women were finding his Italian good looks very attractive.

She had saved the supper dance for him. 'Shall you be seeing Nikolai in Paris on your way home?' she asked when the waltz ended and they joined those going towards the room with the buffet.

'Not this time. I've a busy season ahead of me.'

'Have you ever visited the silk-mills in Japan?'

'I was there three years ago. Were you thinking of my orders of silk for Fortuny?'

She nodded. 'I wish his Delphos robe could get the recognition it deserves.'

'You need never worry about Fortuny. He's such an individualist that public acclaim and success mean little to him and never will. He's a man in love with the past, its riches and its magnificent textiles, its works of art and its architecture. It's Venice's ancient links with the East that also make the city an ideal habitat for him. If he could robe himself like Marco Polo I believe he would be in his element.'

'Everything you say about him makes me still more fascinated by his achievements.'

When the party was over Juliette bade Marco farewell. 'Until we meet in Paris one day, Marco.'

'Until then,' he replied. 'Remember to give my regards to Nikolai.'

'I will.'

Juliette was now more than ready to return to Paris herself. Her business was settled. She had seen the first of her designs come from the looms and there was no reason for her to stay in London any longer, except that Gabrielle had so many more sights and events for her to see and attend. Nikolai had been unable to say exactly when he would return to France, but she was sure it would be any day now. She had received one letter from him. Except in his expressions of love it had been a restrained and concerned letter, saying how conditions had deteriorated since his last visit with more outbreaks of unrest. His father had installed armed guards at the gates, but he himself viewed it as a sorry state when he remembered the relative freedom and lack of fear that had prevailed in his childhood and formative years. Reading between the lines, she could also tell that the announcement of his intention to marry her had been no better received than she had anticipated. More than ever she wanted to be back in Paris when he returned.

'I really must leave on Friday,' Juliette said firmly at breakfast. 'I've looked up the times of the boat-train to Dover and I'll be in Paris by early evening.'

Both Gabrielle and Derek went with her to Victoria Station to see her off. Gabrielle wept uncontrollably, imploring her to take care and to return to them in England if ever she felt herself to be in any danger. Puzzled, Juliette looked at Derek for an explanation of such distress. He was reassuring.

'Gabrielle had some strange fancy that unless you were here with us to look after you all might not go well, but I think you are more than capable of managing your own life.'

'Indeed I am.' Juliette smiled into Gabrielle's anxious face. 'Don't worry about me. The world of fashion may be a jungle, but there's nothing that is life-threatening.'

Her encouraging cheerfulness had some effect. Gabrielle managed a watery smile at the final parting.

Paris was aglitter with early evening lights when Juliette arrived home. Denise was still at Maison Landelle. A hand-delivered note from Nikolai was waiting on the hall salver. Juliette tore it open and saw it had been written three days before. He had returned to Paris only to receive orders from his uncle to go to Brussels on diplomatic business, but he was delaying as long as he could in the hope of seeing her again before he left.

She rang his apartment immediately. His servant, knowing her name, informed her that he would be leaving Paris at noon the next day and was presently at his studio. Not stopping to change out of her travelling clothes, she darted from the house and hailed a taxi. Breathless with excitement, she saw the studio lights shining through the curtains when she arrived. She ran to open the door and rush in.

He was standing by the finished statue of her and spun round at her entry, his whole face tightening with joy and relief at seeing her. 'Thank God you're back!' he exclaimed hoarsely.

She threw herself into his arms and their kissing was violent and wild in a desperate seeking to assuage some of the lonely yearning for each other that had made being apart such torment for them both. Their clothes were scattered and within moments they were lying on the couch together, exulting in their reunion. Such passion possessed them that she cried out in an almost unbearable ecstasy when they both climaxed as soon as he drove into her.

In the delicious languor that followed they smiled at each other wonderingly, touched and stroked and kissed again, each loving the other's body, each feeling whole again in being together once more.

'You are my life,' he murmured, leaning over her. 'My only love and my darling.'

She raised her head and pressed her mouth to his once more, not wanting any talk yet of what he expected of their future or what it might hold. These present hours were their own, nothing of the outside world was able to assail them in this haven with its door locked against interruption and the curtains drawn. He made love to her again, but with no haste this time, his kisses and caresses pleasuring her in ways that stirred her passionate nature to renewed heights of desire. The night hours were passed in dozing and

149

love-making. Not until dawn did they sleep soundly, arms around each other, her hair lying like a coppery wave half over her face and across his shoulder.

In the morning Juliette did not know he had gone from the couch until he returned from the kitchen to sit on the edge of it, facing her with two cups of steaming coffee in his hands. He had thrown on the robe that the male models wore.

'Good morning, *chérie*.'

She sat up to see it was broad daylight and shook back her hair as she returned his smiling greeting. 'What time is it?' she asked, plumping up the cushions to lean back against them.

He handed her a cup. 'It's nine o'clock. Too early to wake you, but I have to go back to my apartment and to the Embassy before I leave from the Gare St Lazare at midday.' His face had grown serious. 'Maybe we should have talked last night, but we must now.'

She nodded reluctantly, knowing the time had come and dreading what she might hear of the trouble she had inadvertently caused between him and his family. 'Yes, I agree.'

His opening words chilled her through.

'I have to return home as soon as my mission in Belgium is done at the end of next week. My days in Paris are over.'

She was staring at him, her pupils dilated with shock. 'What happened?'

'I came to my senses,' he stated grimly. 'I've been living in a fools' paradise here in France, carrying on with my own life with no thought to how greatly I'm needed at home.'

'Is your father ill?'

He shook his head, frowning. 'No. He's in failing health, but then he is an old man. The doctor assured me that by taking care he will have many more years yet.'

'Then what caused you to make such a decision?' She was frightened. He looked so resolved, such a set to his jaw and a determined light in his eyes.

'It is the present state of Russia.' He passed his fingers across his brow, the scene of slaughter he had witnessed as vivid in his memory as if it were still happening. He saw again the starved and terrified faces of the crowd being dispersed by the Cossacks on horseback. The screams of the women, the crying of the children and the groans of the dying rang again in his ears as when he had stood there, a

150

helpless witness to the carnage. 'It was the second day I was home. I was on my way to see the Tsar when the road was suddenly blocked by panic-stricken people running from sabres in the hands of blood-lusting madmen. I leapt out of the automobile, but there was nothing I could do. A poor woman died at my feet.'

There was horror in her eyes. 'How is it all to end?'

'I don't know. Changes must be made and quickly. That's why I have to go back. I can't stay on here when there's so much to be done. I know many senior ministers in the government, some since my childhood. In many ways I have influence, but only if I'm at home and able to make my voice heard. Without being disloyal, I have to say that the Tsar is a weak man, too much influenced by his wife, who in her turn is dominated by that villainous monk, Rasputin, whom she thinks has more than once saved the life of the poor young haemophiliac Prince.' He took her free hand and pressed it within his own, his face wretched with appeal. 'Say you'll come with me. I can't go without you.'

Her hands were agitated, revealing the confusion in her mind. 'This is all happening far sooner than I ever supposed. What was the reaction of your father and the family to your wish to marry me?'

'Not good,' he answered honestly, 'but that need not concern us. Ahead lies a time of change and untold difficulties, but when everything begins to improve we can think of making long visits to France whenever you wish.' Gently he held her by the arms. 'In the meantime, as I've said, it's not going to be easy. I can't offer you the life I once thought we would have and yet I want you with me always.'

She turned her face away, feeling as if she were being torn apart. 'What chance would you have of doing any good if you were ostracized by our being married?'

For a moment he hesitated as his conscience took control, but he was too determined to keep her to let anything stand in his way. He dismissed the question immediately. 'I've many good friends and there's too great a need in Russia today for men like me for that to happen. I can be a bridge, serving both the government and the people as I have done in minor ways whenever I've been home on previous visits. The workers trust me.' He leaned towards her, making her meet his searching gaze again. 'So what do you say, my darling? I love you. You're everything to me. I'll not leave Paris until you agree to meet me in Brussels next week and then we'll travel to St Petersburg together.'

Her eyes were tortured and her mouth tremulous. Her heart seemed to be crying out that she could not refuse him. He meant too much to her. She could see how witnessing that terrible scene of slaughter had jerked him out of the easy attitude that he had been holding in the west. In a way she was glad that this metamorphosis had taken place, bringing to the fore the deep qualities in his character that she had long known were there. He had spoken of his country's need of him, but there was also his need of her. How could she turn away from this loving man for the sake of her own selfish ambition? Not even the bond of her birthplace could be considered in the light of being with him. She pictured the coldness of others in his homeland that she would have to face, the turning aside, perhaps even the open scorn of some such as his sister, but that was nothing compared with the alternative of parting from him, perhaps for ever. With time when she had learned the language she could even help him in his crusade.

Slowly she cupped his desperate face between her hands. Nothing that lay ahead should daunt her. Love was sharing the hard times as well as the good. 'I'll meet you in Brussels.'

Exultantly he embraced her, although his kisses were tender, for he understood the sacrifice she was making. 'You'll never regret it, my darling! I swear it!'

There were some practicalities to discuss. She would need all the available days to see Denise through the transition of her departure. He spoke of where they would live in St Petersburg. There was no question of their living in the apartment he had always had in his father's mansion, but he also owned a town house where they would reside. It had plenty of rooms from which she could chose the one she wanted for a studio where she could carry on with her textile designing. He had already arranged that his sculpture of her and others, together with all his tools and equipment, should be shipped to that address.

When they were both dressed and ready to leave they stood together quietly, their arms wrapped around each other, her head on his shoulder, as they savoured these last sweet moments after the life-changing decisions made. She knew she would always love this

152

place that had been a retreat from his diplomatic duties and her world of fashion.

'In time to come,' she said softly, 'a plaque will be placed on an outside wall of this building, stating that this was the studio where the Russian sculptor, Nikolai Karasvin, created some of his early famous works.'

He laughed quietly at her fantasy. 'I think that's unlikely.'

She raised her head to look at him. 'But it could happen! Because whatever else you do with your life you must always keep on with sculpting.'

'Well, if such a plaque should ever appear none will ever know how much this studio meant to me for other reasons.'

'That will always be our secret.'

'Yes, it will.' He kissed her lips lovingly. Then they went from the studio and he locked the door behind them.

CHAPTER THIRTEEN

Juliette stemmed Denise's tirade over her night's disappearance by breaking the news that she was going to St Petersburg with Nikolai to marry there. It was as well that there was an outer office to block off the sound for Denise screamed, cried and shouted her outrage. Finally she collapsed in tears and temper into her chair. Juliette, deeply distressed, tried to comfort her with an arm about her bowed shoulders, but it was shaken off.

'I had such plans,' Denise wept self-pityingly. 'I foresaw Maison Landelle established through you and your children and grand-children throughout the century and beyond.'

'But that could never be taken for granted. Children grow up to decide their own path in life.'

'Not yours! I'd have seen to that,' Denise shouted wildly.

'Listen to me! Please!' Juliette urged in deep concern at the tempestuous outflow. 'My leaving Paris must inevitably cut me off from Maison Landelle, no matter that I might wish it otherwise. I'll no longer be at the pulse of fashion and whatever textile work I get will have to be aimed at the Russian market. All I can promise is that I will always send you any ideas I have for a new line or detail that I believe would be right for Landelle clothes.'

Denise looked up with wet and swollen eyes, glaring furiously. 'Where would you ever find inspiration in that God-forsaken land?'

'From the icons with their gold and rich colours. From the great paintings there. Why not a Russian line for a future winter collection with Cossack coats and fur hats and swirling cloaks? You mustn't think I'm cutting myself off from France for ever. I could never do that. Nikolai has even promised that at some time in the future we might reside for long periods in Paris. Meanwhile there are just ten days before I leave for Brussels. Let's not waste time being at odds. There's work I want to finish and we've the London deal to discuss.'

Denise knew that if Juliette had wished she could simply have walked out after all the verbal abuse to which she had been subjected in this interview. Yet Denise felt no gratitude. She was wallowing too much in her own disappointment to make any allowances for Juliette's wish to marry the man of her choice. Only one spark had managed to penetrate. A Cossack collection. In the depth of her misery it had caught her imagination. It was not an idea to turn aside.

On a ray of hope Denise began to realize what it would mean to have Juliette and Nikolai in Paris for weeks and even months on end. Their children would be with them. She herself would introduce her nephews and nieces to the world of fashion and pick out the one most susceptible to its fascination and spectacle. She could see herself playing the role of a devoted aunt, even persuading Juliette to let the young person stay on with her when the rest returned home.

Sitting up in her chair, Denise forced herself to become more agreeable to Juliette, even though red-hot resentment still burned within her. 'As you say, we must make the most of the time you have left. We'll keep in constant touch after your departure. I'd like you to work on that Cossack theme in St Petersburg and send everything to me. Now tell me about London.'

In relief Juliette pulled up a chair.

The following days were busy for Juliette from morning to night. Extra trunks were purchased, for Denise was insistent that she take all her clothes, wanting her to be a walking advert for Maison Landelle. Nikolai sent her a first-class train ticket to Brussels, his accompanying letter full of love.

155

It was the morning before Juliette was to leave for Belgium that Denise sent for her to come to the office. Juliette had finished all her work there and was tidying her drawing table when the message came. She supposed Denise had thought of another last minute task and fortunately she had time in hand. Happily she went downstairs to her sister. Now that only a few hours separated her from seeing Nikolai again and the new life ahead she was filled with excited anticipation.

To her surprise Denise stood in front of the desk, waiting for her. There was a strange expression on her sister's face. Juliette experienced a sudden rush of foreboding.

'What is it?' she asked falteringly.

Denise hesitated, but was still unable to conceal entirely the note of jubilation in her voice. 'Prepare yourself, Juliette. You'll not be leaving for Belgium or Russia or anywhere else. Nikolai Karasvin's fiancée is here from St Petersburg with her stepmother to choose her wedding gown and her trousseau.'

Juliette made no sound. She stood as if frozen, all colour draining from her face. Denise, thinking she was about to faint, guided her to a chair where she sat upright, staring unseeingly. Only her hands, clenched together in her lap, gave any outward sign of her reaction to the knife-like blow that had been delivered. Going to the door, Denise told her secretary to bring some hot coffee. It came in a pot on a tray and Denise took it in. Juliette still had not moved.

'Drink this,' Denise urged, extremely concerned, holding out a cup of coffee to her.

For a moment Juliette stared at it as if unable to comprehend what it might be. Then she took it and sipped twice before speaking in a clear, low voice. 'What's her name?'

'Natasha Berberova.'

'Have they been here long?'

'About twenty minutes. The *directrice* informed me as she always does when new and distinguished clients come here for the first time.'

'Have you seen Natasha Berberova?'

'Yes. I was told that Countess Dolohova had recommended that they come here.' She did not add that it was the last recommendation she had ever expected in view of what had happened previously.

'The young woman spoke of her forthcoming marriage to Count Karasvin, who is presently in Belgium before going home.'

'When is the marriage to be?'

'She did not say, only asking if delivery would be possible in six weeks. She and her stepmother are staying that length of time with Prince Vadim and his wife.'

Juliette put down her coffee cup and stood. 'Where are they now?'

'In the Blue Salon, looking at designs for wedding gowns. The girl has her own ideas of how she wants her ensemble to be.' Quickly Denise darted across to stand with her back to the door as Juliette moved towards it. 'You're not thinking of going to see her?' she asked in alarm.

Juliette, her face still expressionless with shock, regarded her with disturbing calmness. 'What else would you expect me to do?'

'Promise me you'll not make a scene! Think of other clients within earshot.'

'A scene? Why ever should I do that? It's never been my way in any case and it may be that Natasha Berberova is as ignorant of my existence as I was of hers until a few minutes ago.'

'If she is?'

'I'll not disillusion her, simply say that delivery can't be made within six weeks and send her elsewhere. What I have learned is a matter between Nikolai and me.'

'You're not behaving rationally. You don't know what you're saying or doing!'

Juliette closed her eyes briefly on a heart-breaking wave of anguish before she could speak again. 'I know only too well. Stand aside, please.'

Reluctantly Denise did as she was asked. Then she followed Juliette to the door of the outer office and stayed there to watch her sister disappear in the direction of the salon.

Natasha Berberova, looking through a number of designs, sat beside her stepmother, an austere and haughty-looking woman, who was studying them through a *lorgnette*. The *vendeuse* in attendance drew back as Juliette approached. Intent on the designs, Natasha did not notice her at first, enabling Juliette to study her for a few moments. She was about Juliette's own age with a provocative bosom and a tiny waist, her hair pale gold and worn in a coil at the back of her

157

head. The wide brim of her hat shadowed a pretty face with fly-away brows over long-lashed eyes that were presently looking downwards, an uppish little nose and an unmistakably stubborn chin.

'*Bonjour*. I'm Juliette Cladel.'

Had her name not been known to the two women there would have been no untoward reaction, but Natasha became tense immediately, although she did not glance up from the designs she was holding. The older woman had looked up automatically and then, as the significance of what she had heard dawned on her, crimson flooded her high cheekbones. She was about to rise in her outrage, but even as she shifted in her chair, opening her mouth to speak, Natasha shot out a hand to clamp down warningly on hers in a signal that this development should be left entirely to her.

'But—'

'Please, Stepmother!' The clasp on the older woman's fingers tightened still more. Then Natasha lowered the designs she held in her other hand onto her lap and raised her head slowly to turn azure eyes, glacial with hostility, on Juliette. 'Is there anywhere you and I can talk privately?'

'Yes. Follow me.'

Almost contemptuously Natasha brushed the designs from her lap to the floor as she stood up, her pleasure in them gone. The older woman shook her head anxiously, but made no move to counteract her stepdaughter's wish, remaining in her chair as the two young women left together.

In one of the small private viewing rooms Natasha took a few paces up and down as if stress made it impossible for her to sit down yet as Juliette had done. Then she spoke.

'Had I known that this was the fashion house where you worked I would never have come here. I've always admired Countess Dolohova's clothes and when I said I wanted my wedding gown made by the same designer she gave me no warning.'

'No doubt the harm she intended was directed towards me, never supposing I would speak to you. How long have you and Nikolai been engaged?'

'It is a long time since it was agreed between his father and mine that he and I should marry.' Natasha sat down. 'I have loved Nikolai for as long as I can remember. We were officially betrothed with the Tsar's blessing five years ago.'

158

Juliette's heart contracted agonizingly. 'But since you know of me he must have asked you to release him.'

'He did. I refused.'

'Yet it is I whom he loves.'

'At the present time he does, but that will pass. I'm not a fool, mademoiselle. I've never expected him to live like a monk in Paris of all places, but I was not alone in supposing that he would conduct his *amitiés amoureuses* in a sensible manner. Naturally I was upset to hear that something more serious had arisen, but as my father and stepmother emphasized it is not the first time, and neither will it be the last, that a man loses all common sense momentarily over a lovely face in a foreign land.' Her voice took on a note of sympathy. 'He will soon forget you, mademoiselle.'

'I happen to believe otherwise.'

Natasha leaned forward slightly in her chair as if to emphasize her words. 'But you'll be far away here in Paris and I as his wife will be with him. He has always found me intensely attractive and his memories of you will fade quickly in the pleasures of marriage and the birth of his children and mine.' She saw by the way Juliette's tragic eyes dilated that she had struck the final fatal blow and found it was possible to feel pity in her moment of triumph. 'Your love for Nikolai was doomed from the start. Even if I had been willing to release him my father would never have permitted it. It would have been the greatest scandal if his daughter had stepped aside to make way for a seamstress!'

Natasha went from the room. Juliette sat on, her hands loosely clasped in her lap and her head bowed down under the crushing weight of her despair. She was remembering all that Nikolai had said during the last hour they had spent together. It came to her now that he had no longer spoken of marriage. There was his regret that he could no longer offer her the life that he had hoped for originally and that nothing would be easy. She saw now that he had been afraid of losing her if he had told her that he had not returned free to marry her as he had planned. Instead he had meant to get her to St Petersburg, perhaps telling her the truth on the way and counting on all they felt for each other to keep her there in spite of everything. He, who had always had everything he had ever wanted, had been unable to let her go.

It was a *vendeuse*, supposing the room to be empty and about to

159

show in a client, who interrupted her privacy. Juliette left at once, smiling automatically at the client, and returned to Denise's office. 'Would it be possible for me to go away for a little while before I start work again?' she asked.

'Yes, of course. Where do you want to go? Back to stay with Gabrielle?'

Juliette shook her head. 'No, I need to be quiet. I must have time to adjust to all that has happened. I'll go back to the convent and stay with the nuns. It will be peaceful there.'

'That's a good idea.' Denise nodded approval. Her sister should soon recuperate in those environs and return with plenty of fresh ideas and renewed vigour. Love was a temporal emotion. 'When shall you leave?'

'Tomorrow morning.'

'No need to bother with trains. After I get to work I'll send the Mercedes back for you. Courtois, the chauffeur, shall drive you all the way.'

It was a generous gesture. Denise regretted it as soon as it was made, remembering it would mean the inconvenience of taxis for herself, but it was too late to withdraw.

On the way home Juliette went into a post office and sent two telegrams. One went to the convent. The other was to Nikolai to let him know she would not be joining him in Brussels and that she had met Natasha. It amounted to very few words when the counter assistant added them up, but by the very brevity all had been told. As Juliette paid the money required she thought to herself that it was a wonder that all her movements were not as jerky as those of an automaton, for she was in such a daze of anguish that she could scarcely see or hear. That night she barely slept.

In the morning Juliette, ready to leave, secured her hat with a pearl-headed pin. The Mercedes had returned from Maison Landelle and her luggage was being strapped to the rack at the rear of it. A maid tapped on the door.

'Count Karasvin is here to see you, mademoiselle.'

For a second or two Juliette felt quite panic-stricken, but she forced herself to be calm. He must have set out for Paris as soon as he had received her telegram and travelled all night.

'Tell the Count I'm unable to talk to him as I'm going away.'

While the maid returned to deliver the message Juliette fastened

160

the buttons of her coat with shaking hands, drew on her gloves and took up her purse.

'Juliette!' Nikolai's voice boomed loudly up the stairs. 'I'll not leave until I've seen you!'

Taking a deep breath, she went out onto the carpeted landing and came to a standstill at the head of the curving flight, looking down at him. He was wild-eyed and unshaven, standing with one foot on the lowest tread and a hand on the newel post as if he would have rushed up in search of her if she had not appeared. Behind him the door stood open to the street in readiness for her departure and she could guess how he had charged in. Before she could speak he shouted angrily again.

'Where the hell do you think you're going?'

Until this moment she had been beyond tears, the lack of release adding to her torment, but now, seeing him so wretched and with her love for him unquelled, she had to fight to keep from weeping. 'It's over, Nikolai.'

'It can never be over between us. We are life-bound.'

'That's not so!'

'I'll never let you leave me!'

The butler, alarmed by the passionate fury of this visitor, had sent the maid to fetch the other menservants, but Juliette raised a hand slightly, shaking her head to cancel his command and indicating he should leave the hall. She could not endure others to witness any more of this terrible and final parting.

Alone with Nikolai, she took a few of the stairs down towards him. 'How could you have expected me to share you with someone else?' she asked brokenly.

'You wouldn't have to! The marriage to be imposed on me will be in name only. I'll make sure of that. You'll always be first with me. As long as I live.'

'You must have loved Natasha once to have become engaged to her.'

'Good God! It was all arranged when I was a schoolboy and she was in plaits! Yes, I liked her. Yes, I became engaged to her when the time was considered appropriate. I was nineteen and she was sixteen. Love doesn't usually count in such matches. Couples think themselves fortunate if they can get along well enough. Natasha and I were always friends. I thought we still were, which is why I was

161

so sure she would release me when I went to see her.'

'But she is in love with you. Naturally she wouldn't agree.'

'I didn't know how seriously any more than I knew she'd take it into her head to come to Paris! I loved you too much to accept that any obstacle stood in our way. Her refusal was the last thing I expected. I even went to the Tsar himself to get his permission to put my case to Natasha!'

'Did he give it?'

'No! But I went anyway. The ultimate decision was hers.'

'You should have told me the truth long ago!' It was a heart cry.

'I never lied! And I'd truly believed that I would return to Paris able to make you my wife straight away. Then I would have told you everything. Instead there was only one path open to us being together.'

'If you were free I'd have gone anywhere with you, whether we ever married or not, but that can never be.' She was carrying on down the flight as she spoke. Then she halted abruptly as he blocked her way, his face torn by desperation.

'I'll come back to Paris whenever I can. The time here will continue to be ours alone. It will be as if nothing had ever happened!'

'Stop dreaming, Nikolai!' She was frantic, fearful her knees would buckle and then he would sweep her into his arms as he had done many times before. 'Go back to the woman who's waited five years for you. I never want us to meet again!'

'You can't mean that!' He reached for her, his voice so imbued with love and yearning that the panic she had subdued earlier flared again as her strength of will was snapped by all she felt for him. Tears she could no longer hold back burst from her eyes. Blindly she hit out at him with her hands and her purse, striking the side of his face and his arms. As he stepped back in disbelief, she threw herself past him to run out of the house and down the steps. The motorcar was purring.

'Quick!' she cried to the chauffeur. 'I have to get away. Drive as fast as you can!'

He slammed the door shut after her and threw himself behind the wheel. She was sobbing helplessly but somehow she managed to look back through the rear window as the vehicle gained speed. Nikolai was running behind, his arms wide, his coat flying out, but as the motorcar accelerated he was gradually left behind. She saw him finally come to a halt, his arms falling to his sides in total dejection. It was the moment when she understood fully the meaning of heartbreak. Her tears hid him from her sight before traffic came between them.

CHAPTER FOURTEEN

Juliette stayed six weeks at the convent, having one of the rooms available to parents who needed to stay overnight at any time. She wanted to be sure that when she returned to Paris neither Nikolai nor Natasha was still there, for he might well have decided to stay until they could journey home together.

It was less peaceful at the convent than she had anticipated, for all the nuns were excited to see her and wanted to chat at every opportunity. Even those who had not particularly liked her in her school days, thinking her too independent for her own good, welcomed her as a breath of the outside world. Kindly old Sister Berthe was overjoyed at her visit and showed her photographs of the altar cloth, which they had embroidered together, in its place in Chartres Cathedral. At the Mother Superior's request Juliette gave several lessons in textile design to the pupils. In all, the days went by quickly. It was the nights that were long and sad when sleep refused to come and memories of Nikolai were so vivid that she wondered why she did not die of anguish.

Towards the end of her visit she had a twinge of uncertainty about herself, but dismissed it, blaming the emotional upheaval she had been through. When she set off for home again it was with the determination to work harder than ever, for it would be the only antidote to the emptiness of Paris without the man she loved.

Denise had been impatient for her return and loaded her with work. The first silks, satins and velvets had arrived from London with her designs and there was much to be decided about the gowns that were to be made up in them.

Juliette had been back in Paris for a week, steeped once more in routine, when a wave of nausea attacked her as she left her bed one morning. In her bathroom she vomited copiously before returning to her bedroom where she sank down on the dressing-table stool. There was no longer any doubt about her condition. She was pregnant! What was more, she knew exactly when it had happened. In her ecstatic reunion with Nikolai after her return from London they had been so caught up in passion that for the first time he had failed to protect her from pregnancy, neither in that immediate and glorious coming together nor later when they had made love again and yet again. She had been too lost in love and maybe her belief that they were soon to be wed had added to her own abandon.

Suddenly a tremor of renewed shock rippled through her as she realized that sooner or later the possibility of her being pregnant would occur to Nikolai too. One thought after another crashed into her brain as the significance of what that could mean came to her. He would see it as a way to retain a hold on her through his parental right to see his own child. He would come back again and again into her life, making any kind of future impossible for her and ruining all chances for himself. She thumped her fists on the dressing-table. That must not happen!

Wearily she finished dressing. There was so much to think about, not only concerning the baby's birth, but afterwards. Denise would not tolerate a child in her immaculate house and neither would she herself want to be there. She remembered with fresh gratitude the small legacy she had received from the will of Denise's late husband and which she had kept untapped. She had never thought when first told of it how helpful it would prove to be at what was surely the most difficult time of her life. It would enable her to live independently and bridge the immediate needs that would follow the birth of her child.

She pressed her fingers to her temples. How was it possible for the mind to race on sanely making plans so soon after a traumatic event had been comprehended? Maybe just the certainty of being pregnant instantly sparked a desire to protect the yet unborn in every way. At least it should be a few weeks before anyone became suspicious about her condition. It would give her plenty of time to choose the right moment to tell her sister, who would be certain to react with disgust and tempestuous outrage.

Throughout the day, whether Juliette was at her drawing board or talking to clients, her thoughts would leap unbidden to what had happened. Still in an agonized state of mind, she could not conceive yet what it meant to be having Nikolai's child. There were still too many layers of pain and sorrow and despair to know if the baby was to be balm to her or a constant torturing reminder, particularly if this son or daughter should grow up with features marked with a likeness to him.

The morning sickness continued for its alloted spell, but Juliette's secret still remained her own.

It was when Juliette was being fitted for a new gown that she realized the time had come to break the news to Denise. In the mirror she saw the fitter frown at the tape measure after putting it around her waist and then check again. Fortunately the boned corset Juliette had started wearing to disguise her condition made the difference too slight for suspicion.

Juliette chose her moment when she and her sister were on their own at home one evening, drinking coffee after dinner. For the first time ever Denise did not react as Juliette expected. Instead she nodded her head resignedly and went on stirring her coffee.

'I thought so.'

Juliette looked at her in surprise. 'How did you guess?'

'You had a spell of looking very pale at breakfast and lately you've been avoiding the chef's richest sauces at dinner. But apart from that, I'm probably quicker than anybody else in Paris at seeing the slight changes in the face and figure. The fashion business has given me a sharp eye.'

'I thought you'd be furious.'

'I'm far from pleased!' Denise snapped back dangerously with a rapier flash of her eyes. Then she took a deep breath to bring herself under control again and continued in normal tones. 'How could I be surprised at what has happened? Count Karasvin is a handsome, attractive and virile man of considerable reputation. I never supposed he would be content to hold your hand and you were so obviously head over heels in love with him. I foresaw trouble from the start. It's why I disapproved so strongly of your association with him, but you wouldn't listen.'

'I've no regrets.'

'Hmm. Not yet perhaps, but you must realize what it means to be a single woman with a child.'

'I do.'

'He will have to pay you a lavish allowance and provide generously for his offspring.'

'No!' Juliette's protest was fierce. 'Nikolai is not a man to give up easily and I fear he will come back to Paris before long just to discover if I'm pregnant.' Her voice broke. 'I can't re-build my life if I'm never to be free of him.'

'Are you considering adoption?'

'No! I'll never part with my baby.'

'Fostering?'

'No!' Juliette exclaimed again. 'I'm going to raise my own child away from Paris where Nikolai won't find us. Claude's legacy will enable me to have my own apartment and I'll hire a competent nursemaid to take charge when I'm at work.'

'What work would that be?'

'I shall teach design. I enjoyed the teaching I did again at the convent recently. I can also offer English and Italian lessons.'

'Very commendable,' Denise remarked drily, 'but quite impractical.'

'What do you mean?'

'Claude's legacy won't be enough to keep you indefinitely and you'll never get work that will pay an adequate wage.'

'Why not?'

'No respectable school would ever employ you. With no wedding ring and a baby you'd be seen as a bad example to the pupils. You'll both be outcasts. Is that what you want for your child? The world's cruelty descends on those who bear the stigma of illegitimacy.'

'I'll buy a ring to wear if needs must!' Juliette gave back with spirit. 'My baby shall not suffer for anything I have done.'

Denise sighed. 'Brave words. So what role shall you play? The deserted wife? The young widow? The sailor's spouse awaiting the return of her husband, which never comes about? Employers in

167

any sphere know all those tales. I've heard them often enough myself.'

Juliette twisted her hands in her lap. 'All I know is that I can't stay in Paris,' she cried determinedly.

Denise paused for a few moments before speaking again. 'Why are you so certain that Count Karasvin will give up pursuing you if he doesn't find out about the baby?'

'Because then he'll have no hold on me through demands to see his child and he knows he has no other way.'

'You seem very sure.'

Juliette nodded, looking down sadly at her hands that were bare of the beautiful ring Nikolai had given her. She had carefully wrapped and addressed it before taking it to the Russian Embassy where she had asked that it should be delivered personally to Count Karasvin in St Petersburg. She had been assured most courteously that this would be done speedily. She guessed that Nikolai had gone there after their parting and left instructions for any mail to be forwarded without delay in the hope that she would at least write to him.

Denise broke into her troubled thoughts. 'Fortunately the plans you've made run almost parallel to all that I've had time to think out. There's no need for you to leave Maison Landelle.'

Juliette raised her head in astonishment. 'But you have such a fear of scandal. I thought my employment would be terminated from the second you knew of my pregnancy.'

Denise carried on as if her sister had not spoken. 'I suppose you've been thinking of having your baby in some place where none will know you, but I don't want you to have a clumsy delivery from some ham-fisted midwife. This baby is too important to me for the future of Maison Landelle. I have the perfect solution to all these problems. You shall go to my Tuscany villa.'

'I thought you had a tenant at the Casa San Giorgio.'

'He left some time ago. My caretaker and his wife, Antonio and Candida Bonini, would look after you. When Claude was taken ill there once a young local doctor named Morosini saved his life. I know from Candida's letters he is still in practice in the nearby town of Lucca and he shall attend at the birth.'

Juliette was taken aback that so much had been worked out unbeknown to her. The clarity of thought in which she herself had

168

made her plans seemed to have deserted her. She felt quite overwhelmed. 'I suppose it would be sensible to go there.'

'Of course it would!' Denise could see she had gained an advantage and continued to press on. 'You can soon leave for Italy. In the meantime I'll explain your absence by telling everyone that you did so well in London that I'm sending you on an exploratory tour to various countries with a view to my opening expensive clothes shops abroad. Many people know that I have mentioned this from time to time.'

'So much horrible subterfuge!' Juliette declared unhappily.

'It's for your baby's sake. Not yours!' Denise said sharply and saw with satisfaction that she had silenced any more opposition for the time being. 'For the same reason your child must be given a surname other than your own, which would only be cause for speculation later on in life and a terrible handicap. What's more this must start from the moment of birth if you want to keep the father from ever knowing the truth.'

Juliette felt she was being hammered mentally and physically into becoming a pawn under Denise's direction and yet everything was being arranged in the baby's best interests. She had to remember that, no matter how humiliating it was for herself to submit to these deceits, her unborn child was being considered.

'Although you don't want to be involved in fostering,' Denise continued firmly, 'it would be a wise move for you to leave the baby with Antonio and Candida for a little while. It would give you the chance to take up the threads in Paris again.' It was her intention that the baby should be kept out of the way at the villa for much longer, but she needed to lead Juliette gently. 'Italians love babies and children. Heaven knows why! It's a national trait.'

Juliette sprang to her feet, needing to get some grip on all the arrangements being made. 'I'll never leave my baby with strangers!'

'Of course not! But the Boninis won't be strangers after you've spent the next few months with them and discovered for yourself what good people they are.' Denise stood to put a reassuring arm about her sister's waist, realizing that she must be careful or else Juliette might baulk and ruin everything. 'After all, the journey between Paris and anywhere in Italy isn't so long these days. There are fast trains and good connections. I'd let you take time off whenever you wished to visit your infant.' It was a promise she

169

intended to curtail after a while, for the less Juliette saw of the child the better. 'Remember this is the only way you can ensure a safe and secure future for your offspring. Surely that is worth any sacrifice?'

'But would it be the right one?' Juliette asked with a trapped air.

'Of course it would be! Firstly there could be a convent school – one can surely be found in Lucca – where little ones of either sex can receive first schooling. Afterwards a top boarding establishment in France and then training at Maison Landelle for a brilliant career and eventual ownership. What could be better?'

Denise could scarcely control her greed for the baby's future. Whether boy or girl made no difference, for both sexes could hold equal power in the fashion world. There might never be another child if Juliette should find it impossible to trust any man again after this devastating love affair.

Juliette had pressed fingertips to her temples, full of uncertainties and yet grateful that Denise, instead of turning against her, was doing everything in her power to help. 'Forgive me, but I don't feel able to make any promises or decisions at the present time.'

'I wouldn't want you to,' Denise lied blithely. 'Naturally you're under a great strain and that could distort your judgement on the wisest moves to make. Take your time. Just trust me. All I ask is that you hold on to the knowledge that you and I are the same flesh and blood, able to stand together at this time of crisis. Let your mind dwell constantly on that certainty when you're relaxing quietly in the Italian sun.' Then she added the final inducement that would be guaranteed to penetrate Juliette's state of indecision. 'Count Karasvin would never find your baby at the villa if he should come back to Paris as you fear. You can be certain of that.'

Within a week everyone acquainted with Juliette had heard either from Denise or indirectly about her important assignment on behalf of Maison Landelle. Juliette herself said nothing. At the Casa San Giorgio the caretaker and his wife had been informed of the reason for her forthcoming visit.

Juliette stayed several days in Florence before going on to the villa, needing some time to herself in which to adjust to the changing pattern of her life. Everything had happened so fast at the end of her time in Paris. She found cheap accommodation near the Ponte

170

Veccio and was able to eat inexpensively since she had developed a craving for fruit and pasta. It was early spring and amid the Renaissance splendour flowers blossomed profusely. There were quite a number of other foreign visitors in the city and she was alert to the danger of running into anyone from Paris who knew her. Her hat was veiled, giving her protection against recognition when out of doors while her parasol was an additional shield. She also visited sights of interest early in the morning and at other times less popular with visitors on vacation.

She would have liked to send a picture postcard to Gabrielle and Derek, who had spent part of their honeymoon in Florence, but she had written before leaving Paris to say she was going away for a while, giving no explanation, only an assurance there was no need for concern. She could not risk revealing her whereabouts to anyone and, for the same reason, had promised Denise she would post all correspondence to her at a Paris post office for personal collection.

Having let the Boninis know by letter that her arrival at the villa would be delayed, Juliette set out every day to view yet another museum or gallery. She gazed in silent wonder at many glorious sculptures from Michelangelo's *David* to Donatello's harrowing *Mary Magdelen*, which moved her to tears. There were several paintings in the Uffizi gallery that had a similar effect, for her emotions were painfully near the surface at all times. She concentrated on improving her Italian, realizing how good a grounding she had had in her convent schooldays.

Juliette might have been tempted to stay a little longer in Florence if she had not thought she sighted Nikolai. She was coming down the steps of the Duomo when she saw a man ahead of her with the same fine height, broad shoulders and thick black hair curling under the brim of a panama. Her heart seemed to stop and she pressed a white gloved hand to her throat. Then he turned his head and she saw a stranger's face in profile. Almost blindly she stumbled back into the cathedral and sat on the nearest seat to recover from the upsetting mistake she had made. What alarmed her most of all was that if it had been Nikolai she would have run to him, unable to stop herself. When she emerged again into the sunshine it was to go straight back to where she was staying and start packing to leave for the villa later that same morning.

Juliette took the train to Lucca and hired a horse-drawn carriage to take her the rest of the way. It was a leisurely drive along a winding dusty road amid delightful, undulating countryside with vineyards, the occasional small cluster of russet-roofed houses in sun-faded hues and ancient stone bridges and lush woodland, all set against the grandeur of mountains. Now and again she glimpsed entrances to villas with the occasional sight of windows sparkling in the sun, but mostly all were tucked away behind high walls.

She had never seen a photograph of Denise's villa, but since her sister had always appeared more interested in getting good rents from its tenants than visiting it herself, Juliette had supposed it to be of moderate comfort and size. Once Denise had remarked that the flower gardens were extensive and when the carriage had passed through the gates she saw that her sister had not exaggerated. There were many fine trees, a stretch of formal gardens and an abundance of flowerbeds with a profusion of multi-coloured blooms sloping gently downwards out of sight. Then the villa itself came into view.

Contrary to Juliette's expectations it was not the modest place she had expected to see, but was a small palace, its façade sumptuous with balconies, loggias and statues in niches. Then Juliette realized she should have guessed how it would be, for the late Claude de Landelle had been a rich man and would have wanted the best. Gazing at it, she was enchanted. She felt drawn already to this beautiful and age-mellowed house in which her baby would draw its first breath.

As the villa was set on a rise, giving it magnificent views, Juliette's carriage had been sighted when still a distance away. The Boninis were waiting to greet her on the steps of the arched entrance as the coachman drew his horse to a halt. Both came forward, he to bow and she to bob.

'*Buon giorno, signorina,*' they both said at the same time. He was a genial-looking man, squarely built with merry eyes and his wife was plump and maternal in appearance, her face round and smiling, her black hair smooth and glossy as lacquer, drawn back from a middle parting into a coil. Behind the couple were two girls, not yet twenty, wearing crisp white aprons, who smiled and bobbed when presented as the Boninis' daughters, Lucietta and Katarina, who also helped in the house. Juliette, lingering on the steps to look back across the spread of gardens, asked Antonio if he was the gardener.

'Yes, signorina, but an old man from the village, who's been tending the flowers since he was a gardener's boy here and who trained me in my turn, comes every day to give a hand and make sure I'm keeping up to his standard!'

She smiled at his little joke. Candida was waiting to show her into the villa and she followed to enter the hall with its pale pink marble floor and panelled walls. Everywhere was light and airy, diaphanous white curtains at the windows and shades to draw down against the sun. Her bedroom had a painted ceiling and gilded cherubs held garlands above the ornate bedhead. Later Candida showed her another bedroom that was much plainer with a narrower bed that was to be prepared for her confinement.

During the first weeks at the villa Juliette finished several textile and dress designs, which were sent off to Denise. Until the grip of summer took hold she made a few trips into Lucca. The first time she went to see Dr Morosini, who was to deliver her baby. He wore gold-rimmed spectacles and his attitude was considerate and responsible, which was totally reassuring.

'It's not so unusual,' he said, sitting back in his chair at his desk, 'for a young woman of good upbringing, as you undoubtedly are, to be sent away from her family to give birth discreetly, but you've been left so entirely alone. Usually a trusted nurse or a relative would have come too. Was there nobody the Baronne de Landelle could send?'

'Nobody.'

'The father?'

'He's marrying someone else.' Her voice was curiously toneless. There was no indication of her heartache, the agony of which seemed to be getting worse every day, if that were possible.

'So what is to happen to the baby?'

'I'm keeping my child!' She was unaware that she had cried out defiantly as if already forces were trying to wrest them apart.

'Very well.' He made no further comment. 'Take plenty of exercise by walking daily in the cool of the morning and in the early evening if you're not tired. Rest through the daily siesta hours. Eat sensibly and forget the old wives' tale of eating for two.'

She heeded his advice. Lucca, with its wealth of treasures, open squares and magnificent churches, was a place she could have explored indefinitely, but as summer progressed the heat kept her away. She was perfectly content at the villa and when her morning walk was done she would work on her designs, continuing to despatch them at regular intervals. There were also garments to make for the baby and clothes for herself, which she needed as her figure expanded. The corsets she had worn to hide her pregnancy had been discarded on the eve of leaving Paris. She had bought the fabrics in Lucca; those for herself were of cheap soft cottons and muslins, which she made up in loose styles that were comfortable to wear. At other times she read, played for her own amusement on the grand piano that Claude had installed and learned several new ways to play patience from Candida, who was fond of cards. The two daughters had a gramophone and at their request Juliette taught them all the latest ballroom dances from Paris.

Now that she could no longer go to Lucca, Dr Morosini called on her. Her legacy from Claude not only enabled her to pay for her keep, but also meant that her medical bills presented no problem, although Dr Morosini's fees were moderate compared to what she would have expected to pay in Paris. Generously, he did not charge if he happened to be in the vicinity and looked in to chat with her at the villa.

'How are you today?' he would ask, usually finding her in the garden.

She was always able to tell him she was well. Sometimes they took a stroll together through the groves of cyprus trees and afterwards he would accept refreshment before leaving again. She guessed his purpose was to leaven her isolation, not wanting her to get depressed. He had no knowledge of the onslaughts of heartache that she had to struggle against. She was glad of his company whenever he came, for he was an interesting man, well read and with a wide knowledge of world affairs, enabling them to discuss many matters that arose from the newspapers that they both took daily. Not a printed word about Russian affairs ever escaped her. Having read all the books she had brought from Paris, she was grateful for those he loaned her; most were classics and some were in French, which he spoke moderately well. More than once he expressed the wish that he was as fluent in her language as she had become in his, but as she pointed out she had spoken nothing but Italian since arriving in Italy, which had given her plenty of practice.

In contrast to her schooldays when letters from Denise had been sparse, Juliette received a regular stream of them as she was kept notified of all that was happening at Maison Landelle. It showed Denise's determination to keep her involved. Personal news was always minimal. Instead there were sales figures and details of changes of staff as well as a listing of any new and important clients. The fabrics from London had been made up in the latest floating and layered styles with chemise-like bodices and semi-tunics over underskirts. A few weeks later Denise wrote exultantly with the news that these same gowns were causing a sensation and orders were flowing in. By now Juliette had been over four months at the villa and was just coming into her seventh month. She was still sending Denise new designs and had another two started when her sister wrote again.

When the letter came Juliette left her work and took it out onto the loggia which gave such a splendid view of the mountains. Sitting down in one of the cushioned wicker chairs, she opened the letter, which was shorter than usual. She realized it was one of her sister's rare personal letters and began to read.

Although Juliette had always thought such a letter might come one day, she was entirely unprepared for the way she was to be told what had happened. Without preamble Denise launched into the information that Nikolai had been back in Paris.

I heard that Count Karasvin was combing the city for you, Denise continued, *even though he is now a married man. When he called on me I was well prepared. In your best interests I told him a falsehood that I knew would settle everything. I said you had had an abortion and I had sent you away for several months to recover, which was why nobody else knew your whereabouts. It was easy to see by the effect the words had on Count Karasvin that I have set you free of him for ever. I have heard since that he left Paris that same evening. I know you will wish to thank me . . .*

Juliette had stopped reading, a cry of desolation bursting from her. She dropped her face into her hands, the letter drifting to her lap, and wept silently and despairingly as wave after wave of love and compassion for Nikolai swept over her.

Half an hour later Dr Morosini found her in the same distressed state. The very silence of her tears concerned him. He put down his medical bag and drew up a chair to sit close to her.

'Let me help. Tell me what's upsetting you.'

At first she did not move, but after a few moments she lowered her hands and still without looking at him, half blinded by her tears, she fumbled for the letter on her lap and held it out to him. He took it and saw her turn her face away as if as yet she could not bear to let him view the depth of her private unhappiness. When he had read the letter through he picked up the envelope, which had fallen to the ground, and folded it away.

'Don't read this letter again,' he advised.

Her voice came hesitantly, laden with sadness. 'I feel Nikolai's suffering as my own.'

Dr Morosini sighed at the force of love that possessed her. Few women would still be as charitable towards a man who had deceived them. Most would rant and rave and then be exultant at his downfall.

As if Juliette had read his thoughts she turned at last to look starkly at him. 'Nikolai and I wanted to be together for the rest of our lives. Nothing can change that for either of us.'

'Then the time has come for you to concentrate solely on all that will be best for his child. Any faint hope that you were secretly cherishing that some miracle might yet come about has been finally banished.'

She shook her head uncertainly, brushing away the tears that still ran from her eyes. 'Was that thought really lingering at the back of my mind in spite of everything? I can't be sure. I'll never know.' She stood up slowly and went to the loggia's balustrade where she stood gazing abstractedly at the vista before her.

Dr Morosini stayed where he was for a while, giving her time to come to terms with both what her sister had written and the insight into herself that he had caused her to experience. Then, seeing her silent tears had still not ceased their flow, but continued to trickle down her cheeks, he left his chair and went across to hand her the clean handkerchief he had taken from the breast pocket of his linen jacket. She wiped her eyes. He saw his timing had been right and she had reached some decision. Perching his weight on the edge of the stone balustrade, he waited with folded arms for her to speak.

'I am free now,' she said quietly, turning towards him. 'Not from Nikolai as my sister supposes, because as he said once he and I are bonded for life and I know that to be true. My liberty will be in raising our child in the freedom that Nikolai is striving to gain in his own country for his fellow men.' She gave an apologetic little shrug. 'I must seem to be talking in riddles since you know so little of my life before I came here.'

176

'I can get the gist of it, even though the details are yours.' He had avoided putting her under the slightest obligation to give them, but he hoped that sooner or later she would enlighten him. From the start she had been something of a mystery and he was interested in her.

'I know now that I can't go back to Paris,' she declared purposefully. 'That would involve several partings from my baby. All along I've declared I'd never do that and it's been the right decision from the start.'

'What had put you in a quandary over it?'

'The chance that Nikolai might make claims I couldn't counter.' She saw the doctor's puzzled expression. 'Maybe I should tell you a little of the circumstances that changed his life and mine. I'd like you to understand. You've been so kind.'

'You're my patient. I want the best for you.'

When she had told him the facts quite briefly he agreed with her that returning to Paris would be a mistake. Some of the reasons were his own. He had not liked the Baronne with her arrogant and discontented ways and had pitied her unfortunate husband, whose convalescence had been hindered by her impatience to get back to Paris. The peace of the countryside had not suited her at all. Juliette had been under her control long enough. It was easy to foresee that the woman would mould the baby's life from the beginning towards Maison Landelle. No matter what dreams and ambitions the child might aim for on reaching adulthood, the Baronne would use mercilessly every weapon in her power to destroy them.

'So now that you've set Paris behind you, where do you plan to make a new start?' he asked.

Juliette looked again towards the mountains. 'That depends on several matters that I have to sort out. 'But, Doctor,' she added, giving him a serious little smile, 'I promise you shall be the first to know.'

When he had gone Juliette wrote two letters. The first was to Denise, confirming what she had said originally about never parting from her child and seeking a livelihood away from Paris. She also implored her sister not to sever their sibling ties through anger, for their kinship had come to mean much more to them during their time together. As Juliette closed the letter she thought there was every likelihood of Denise turning up at the Casa San Giorgio in a

177

rage, but whatever the storm created it would be weathered with nothing changed.

The second letter she wrote was to Fortuny, telling him of her circumstances and asking if he had a vacancy in his workshop for a seamstress. She hoped that he, having already approved one example of her skills, might be prepared to employ her. After addressing the envelope she added *Personal* to it, for then it would be for his eyes alone and she was sure he would respect her need for anonymity for the time being.

That afternoon when Antonio drove his wagonette into Lucca to fetch some purchases he posted the two letters for her.

CHAPTER FIFTEEN

Juliette began watching daily for replies to her letters. One came from Denise, which ignored entirely all that she had written and dealt solely with business matters, except for the last line. There Denise stated that she had heard pregnant women get strange fancies and after the baby was born Juliette would soon see sense. A postscript asked for as speedy delivery as possible of the latest designs.

Juliette sighed, weary in the final month of her pregnancy, and felt unable to write any more about the matter for the time being. How could Denise believe so implicitly in her own iron will as to brush aside what was to Juliette the most important letter she had even written? While she continued to work on the designs wanted by Denise she kept hoping that she might still hear from Fortuny, but nothing came.

Realizing time was fast running out, she reverted to the plan she had made tentatively in her mind as long ago as when she was in Florence. There were some elegant gown shops in the city and, as soon as she was able after the birth, she would take a day's outing there to seek employment. She would need to show some examples of her own work and she had some good clothes with her that she had made herself in Paris. This train of thought reminded her of the

Delphos robe, which she had been unable to leave behind in spite of the poignant memories it aroused. It would have been ideally comfortable at the present time, for the wonderful little pleats would have expanded generously over her extended figure, but she could not foresee ever wearing it again.

Although flowers still gave a lovely variety of colour to the terraced gardens, autumn had begun to show itself across the grand landscape. Days were cooler and often wet, the rain not ceasing from morning until night. Nearly a week of wet weather had lifted and some sunshine was showing through in the late afternoon when Juliette came slowly down the steps of the Casa San Giorgio, holding on to the stone balustrade of the parapet. She was eager to get out in the air after being virtually a prisoner indoors since she had finished the last of the designs for Denise and had them posted off to Paris. Now she had only to await the baby's arrival within a few days.

She was only halfway down the flight when she saw a taxi coming from the direction of the gates. Her heart sank. Denise must have had second thoughts and come after all. As the taxi drew up Juliette steeled herself for what was to come. Then, to her dismay, it was Marco who stepped out of the taxi to give her a smiling greeting before he busied himself paying the taxi driver.

She leaned against the parapet in consternation and alarm. Her letter to Fortuny had been personal. The designer had had no right to disclose anything about her, least of all her whereabouts, to anyone else. All she could hope for was that Marco had not chanced to write the news to Nikolai, for she knew they had corresponded previously about books they were trying to obtain for each other.

'So we meet again, Juliette.' Marco had come towards her as the taxi drove away, his face full of pleasure as if her distended figure had escaped his notice. 'It never seems to be in Paris, does it?'

'Now it never will,' she answered emotionally. 'But you shouldn't be here. I haven't had a chance to beg you not to tell Nikolai anything about me. It's his baby I'm expecting and I don't want him ever to know!'

His expression became serious. 'I haven't heard from Nikolai for months and neither have I written.' He did not add that indirectly through Russians in Venice he had heard of the magnificent wedding that had taken place in St Petersburg.

She felt enervated by relief. 'Have you come far today?'

'I left Venice at an early hour this morning. Fortuny and Henriette have been away and he didn't open his personal mail until late yesterday evening. It was Henriette who took matters into her own hands after he had discussed your letter with her in confidence. She insisted that he should agree to her telling me. After all, I had spoken of you to her several times in the past. As she had expected, I said I would come to you without delay.'

'You'll stay here overnight at least, won't you?'

'Would that be convenient? I've already booked into a hotel in Lucca.'

'But I want you to be my guest. I'll send Antonio to collect your luggage.' She half-turned, intending to go back to the villa, but Candida appeared, having sighted the taxi as it left. Immediately she took charge, summoning her husband. Juliette turned back to Marco. 'Do you mind if we stroll a little before you see your room?'

'Of course not. Take my arm.'

She took it, glad of his support, and they left the steps to follow a path through the garden. 'As you can guess,' she said, 'I'm longing to hear if Fortuny is able to offer me any work.'

'Yes, there is a place for you in the studios of the Palazzo Orfei.'

Again relief swept over her and she paused, leaning her forehead against his shoulder, scarcely able to speak. 'How kind of him! And how good of you to come all this way to tell me.'

'I wanted to see you again.'

'Even like this?' she remarked defensively, conscious of her bulk.

'Yes, except that I would have wished to see you married to your baby's father for the sake of your happiness. I never thought it would end between you and Nikolai.'

'Neither did I ever suppose we should be parted as we were.'

He knew she would tell him the circumstances in her own time and he kept the conversation to minor topics, asking her how she had passed the days at the villa and talking of his own travels.

That evening it rained again and when they sat in the flickering glow of a fire she told him what had happened and why she had hidden herself away. His kindliness and understanding were particularly comforting to her, for although Dr Morosini was also a friend now, her relationship with him was on a more impersonal plane and he had never known Nikolai.

It seemed natural that Marco should stay on from one day to the next. There was so much she wanted to know about the work she would be doing for Fortuny. She was to start as a seamstress, but the designer was prepared to take her into the textile workshop when she had fully recovered her strength, for the physical tasks there involved hours of standing.

'The Palazzo Orfei is a gigantic workshop with the Fortuny shop on the ground floor and a showroom, studios and ateliers on the upper levels. Mariano and Henriette have living quarters adjoining.'

'What is she like?'

'A charming, friendly woman. She assists Fortuny in all branches of his work. I'm sorry you didn't meet her that evening at the opera in London, but she and some of the other ladies had already returned to their seats. I know she was disappointed at missing you, because she had been delighted by my account of your salvaging the Delphos robe.'

'I shall have to stay in an inexpensive hotel in Venice until I find accommodation for myself and my baby. Could you recommend one to me?'

'I could, but there is an alternative.' Marco paused. They were in the gardens again, the day being mild and sunny and bright as if the rain had never been, and were seated by an orderly row of tall cypress trees. 'I came to see you for another reason besides telling you that you were being offered employment.'

Instantly Juliette knew what he was about to say and her hand tightened on the arm of the seat. She had known as long ago as their first meeting in Lyon that he was attracted to her as men so often were. Maybe he had never realized how often his lingering gaze had dwelt on her, how quick he had been to assist her in any way, or how special his smile had been when directed at her, his whole expression reflecting his feelings. He was looking ardently at her now and took her hand from her lap into both of his.

'I love you, Juliette. In Lyon you made me realize that the time had come for me to look to the future again, even though tender memories from the past would always remain, but in their rightful place as part of my life that was over. Then Nikolai arrived on his visit, and as soon as I saw the two of you together I could tell how much in love both of you were. I accepted that I didn't have a chance; but afterwards you never left my thoughts.'

'Marco,' she began, but he pressed her hand in appeal.

'Please hear me out,' he urged. 'Then we met in London and I was lucky enough to spend more time with you. I know you think of me only as a friend, but friendship is a good and solid foundation for any marriage. I'm asking you to be my wife, to let me give my name to your child, whom I shall think of as my own from the moment of birth. You will always be my beloved.'

She was deeply moved. He was an exceptional man in being prepared to accept the baby wholeheartedly when so many men would abhor the thought of taking on another's offspring in such a way. She liked him. She even felt affection for him, but never in any light other than friendship. It was impossible to consider marriage. 'I can't accept, dear Marco. Nikolai will always be too much with me.'

'I'm willing to take the chance that with time you'll become fond enough of me to let the past go even as I have done, because it is the only way to go on with life. You and I have both experienced the awful sadness of losing someone who meant everything in the world to us. Surely that should give us unity and understanding as husband and wife that other couples lack.'

'You would be counting on too much,' she insisted, shaking her head at his persuasion, 'and I can see it would be a mistake for me to accept Fortuny's offer of work. You and I would be seeing each other all too often. It would not be fair on you.'

'But I want you to be there! Most Italian men would want you to remain a wife and mother, but I know you're an artist in fabrics and need to be creative. I like that and would be glad to be married to a woman whose interests ran alongside mine. Apart from that, think of the baby, Juliette! Consider what it would mean to the child to have a father, a name to be proud of and a stable home and background that nothing could destroy.'

He saw that at last he had broken through to her. He saw the resolute look in her expressive eyes fade away as she accepted that through marriage to him she could ensure parental love and all the security that it would bring to her child. Her conscience was not allowing her to cast aside all that belonged by right to any new-born human being. Her resistance to his proposal left her. Slowly she nodded in acquiesence.

'You're a good man,' she said very quietly. 'I could tell that when I first met you. You deserve a better wife than I can ever be.'

'I want no other!'

She smiled wanly. 'At least I can promise that I'll always appreciate your love and be ever grateful for what you're doing for my baby and me.'

'I would die for you!' he declared fervently. He bowed his head over her hand, which he pressed to his lips for several moments, swept away by emotion. She leant forward and gently kissed his brow.

They were married before the week was out. The ceremony was held in the fourteenth-century church of Santa Maria della Rosa. Juliette wore a deep blue velvet gown in a loose tunic style under a cape, both of which she had made during her sojourn at the villa, and a wide-brimmed hat that she had brought from Paris. She carried a bouquet of flowers from the villa garden, wanting no others, and these had been picked for her by Lucietta and Katarina. They were at the church with their mother, all three in their prettiest hats and Sunday clothes. Antonio, straight-backed in his best suit, his moustache waxed to fine points, acted as witness with Dr Morosini. At the close of the ceremony Marco kissed Juliette on the lips for the first time.

Afterwards they all went back to the Casa San Giorgio where Candida had left two women in charge of the wedding luncheon, most of which she had prepared herself. Juliette had wanted her to sit down as a guest, but she donned an apron and took over her customary role of waiting on others.

It was a quiet celebration, everyone dispersing as soon as the meal was over. Juliette went to take her usual siesta and Marco walked with Dr Morosini to his parked motorcar where they stood talking. Antonio removed his stiff collar with relief and was soon back at work.

That evening when Juliette and Marco sat again in the firelight he told her of the house he had bought recently in Venice.

'I moved in three months ago, but as yet it's still sparsely furnished, because I've been travelling abroad. You'll be able to add anything you want. I'd like you to take time with the baby until you feel ready to start work at the Palazzo Orfei.'

'I'd originally intended to work without delay, but I would like a few weeks first,' she admitted. 'What made you move from the apartment where you lived before?' She had learned from him in

Lyon that he had sold up his first home after his wife's death, finding it too difficult to stay on there without her.

'It was never convenient, but when I bought it I'd been recently bereaved and was in no mood to spend time going around to a lot of places. The windows looked out on the Rialto bridge and I supposed that appealed to me, although I really don't remember. The new house, which is yours and mine now, hasn't any splendid views of the Grand Canal, but its situated in a peaceful courtyard close to the Palazzo Orfei. When you feel able to leave the baby with a nursemaid, it will take you less than two minutes to go home from the workshop and check that all is well.'

They walked for a while longer until she felt too tired from all that had happened in the day to stay up any longer. Marco came with her to her door. There he took her face tenderly between his hands and gazed into her eyes.

'You'll be happy in the new life you're starting with me,' he promised. 'It may take a while, but the time will come.'

She was unable to visualize ever knowing true happiness again, but she acknowledged his heartfelt words with a serious smile. He kissed her lovingly, but without passion, for which she was thankful. She bade him good night and entered her room.

It was Juliette's decision that a telegram should not be sent to Denise to break the news of her marriage, although Fortuny had been informed. Her sister would know who Marco was from being told about the meetings in Lyon and London, but to telegraph the news would be too abrupt, for it would come as a great shock to Denise. So instead she wrote to tell of her marriage and promised to continue sending designs. She closed the letter by expressing the sincere hope that Denise would visit them in Venice where she would always be welcome.

Juliette also wrote to Lucille, with whom she had kept in touch. Lucille and Rodolphe had invited her to make a new life with the baby in New Orleans with them, but Juliette had not wanted to disrupt the routine of their lives now Rodolphe had retired.

It was still raining on the morning when Juliette awoke to an awareness of new and unfamiliar twinges in her body. When Lucietta arrived with a tray to give her breakfast in bed, which had been the routine for the past month, Juliette asked for Candida to come to her room.

The woman came hurrying with her face abeam. 'Is it beginning?' she asked joyfully, clasping her big hands together.

'I think there's no doubt about it,' Juliette replied with a wry grin.

Her labour was not easy, but she gave birth eventually just before dawn the following day. Marco, who had paced the floor for most of the night, rushed to the foot of the sweeping flight of stairs when he heard the infant's wail. It seemed an interminable time to wait until Candida appeared briefly to smile jubilantly at him from over the landing balustrade.

'It's a boy!'

He put a violently shaking hand across his eyes, overcome by relief. His first wife had died giving birth to a stillborn daughter and he had been racked by fear for Juliette all through the night. When Dr Morosini came downstairs he had recovered himself.

'How is Juliette now?' he asked anxiously.

'All is well! She has asked to see you.'

A spasm of joy went through him. He mounted the flight two stairs at a time.

A cable was sent to Denise telling her that Juliette had given birth to a son. Marco returned briefly to Venice to instruct his housekeeper to get his home ready for his wife and son, for only Fortuny and Henriette knew the truth of the situation.

The day before the christening, when the baby was to be named Michel after Juliette's father, a bulky envelope came for her by post. When she opened it she gave a distressed cry as the torn up pieces of the last designs she had sent to Denise came tumbling from it. Although no letter was enclosed Denise had made it clear that their kinship was at an end as far as she was concerned.

CHAPTER SIXTEEN

Juliette's first sight of Venice was two weeks later and by night. On board a *vaporetto*, smoke puffing from its funnel, she stood with Michel in her arms, he wrapped warmly against the cold wind that was making the glinting water of the Grand Canal slap against the steps of the ancient buildings. Yet even in the hours of darkness the enchantment of the city gripped her, for the lamps, probably radiating no more light than the candle-lanterns of previous centuries, gave glimpses in the will-'o-wisp glow of ancient doorways, streets so narrow that no carriage could pass through and even narrower passageways known as *calli*. There was also the sparkle of chandeliers illuming the exotic windows of the great Renaissance palaces and once there came the sound of a woman singing to an accompanying lute as if time had stood still since the days when Venice had been ruled by powerful Doges.

'You should be seeing this city for the first time in sunshine,' Marco said apologetically, knowing she must be tired after the long journey.

'No,' she answered at once. 'This is unlike anything I've ever seen before and I find it exciting.'

'I'm glad you do. Are you sure you're not getting cold? The next stop will be ours.'

187

They had come from the railway station and sailed some part of the long waterway, passing under the Rialto bridge. On the way he had pointed out buildings of particular historical interest, but had told her there were even more rewarding sights lying farther up where the Doges' Palace looked out to the Lagoon.

'I promised Henriette that I'd take you to the Palazzo Orfei tomorrow morning,' he continued, 'and afterwards we'll go along to my business premises.'

'I'm looking forward to seeing everything.'

As Marco had telephoned ahead there was a porter waiting with a hand-truck when they alighted by the fitful light of one of the lamps. Their luggage was piled onto the truck, her trunk to be collected from the railway station in the morning. Juliette found it strange that the only way to get to Marco's house was on foot, accustomed as she was to the easy transport of Paris, but there was compensation in the lack of hooting horns and in the quietness that prevailed. Marco led the way along the same kind of *calle* as she had seen from the *vaporetto*, the porter trundling his hand-cart behind them. Sometimes they passed a little wall-shrine with a candle flickering at the foot of the Virgin and the Christ Child. Finally they came to a small paved square, the Campo San Beneto.

'That's the Palazzo Orfei,' Marco said, indicating the large and ornate-fronted palace that soared up against the stars and occupied the whole of one side of the square. Its handsome Gothic windows, which Juliette judged to be from floor to ceiling within, sent golden rectangles of light down onto the flags where she stood.

'What a grand building!' she exclaimed.

Marco smiled. 'You'll like all that's inside it. Come now. Our house is only a few steps away.'

She gazed up at the other ancient buildings of the square as she followed him into a small courtyard, wondering if there was any edifice in Venice on which craftsmen of past centuries had not exercised their skills.

'There's your new home, Juliette.' Marco indicated the tall house facing them. Before she could reply the door was flung open, releasing a flood of light and warmth, by the housekeeper, Lena Reato, who must have been watching out for them.

'*Buon sera, Signor y Signora Romanelli!*' Lena drew back smilingly for them to enter, a short, deep-breasted woman in her mid-fifties with greying hair and capable hands. 'Ah! The baby! Let me take him from you, signora.' As he was placed in her arms Michel opened his eyes and blinked, delighting her. 'Oh! what a fine baby he is! I can see the Romanelli likeness! He'll be the image of his father when he grows!'

Juliette glanced at Marco, not knowing how hurt he might be by these well-meant comments, but he seemed unaffected by them. Perhaps he had already banished Nikolai from their lives as if he had never existed. She guessed that it was the only way possible for him to look to the future.

She was relieved to find they were to have separate bedrooms. Lena apparently assumed it was for Marco to escape the baby's crying at night.

'I thought you'd like to have Michel's cot right against your bed,' she said as she showed Juliette into the bedroom that was to be hers. 'Then you can pick him up quickly in the night before his crying gets too loud. I expect you'll want to engage a nursemaid of your own choice, but I have a niece, reliable and conscientious, whom I could recommend.'

'We'll talk of that tomorrow.' Juliette stood looking about her as she took off her hat and coat. Marco had warned her that the house was sparsely furnished. Admittedly there were only outside shutters across the windows and no rugs on the tessellated floor, but she liked what little she had seen. She thought her magnificent bed must surely date from the eighteenth century with its pale green paint decorated with flowers and a border in faded gilt. There was a matching chest of drawers as well as a dainty chair set at a delicately-shaped table with a swing-mirror on a gilded stand. The house itself, its carved doors darkened with age, was surely much older and well suited to the other antique pieces she had seen when coming up the stairs. Lena had noticed her appreciative survey.

'Signor Romanelli inherited all the furniture in the house from his grandmother last year. It was still in store when he returned to Venice recently and told me you were coming.'

'Did you know his grandmother?' Juliette asked, unbuttoning her blouse, for Michel had begun to wail hungrily and it was time she put him to her breast.

'I worked for her many years. After she died I had a post I didn't like and it was my lucky day when Signor Romanelli asked me if

189

I'd like to housekeep for him in his new home. I knew already that he was always coming and going on business travels, but it was quite a surprise to discover he had a wife whom he would be bringing to Venice with his new-born son.'

'I'm sure it was.' Juliette had seated herself and when the woman handed Michel to her she cradled him in the crook of her arm. 'Does it put your employment here in a different light?'

'Not at all, signora. I'm glad to see him with a family and I'll do my best for you.'

'I'm sure you will. I've heard that you are very capable and an excellent cook.'

The woman looked pleased. 'I have a good supper waiting for you when you've finished feeding little Michel. While you're downstairs I'll unpack for you.'

She went out of the door, closing it quietly behind her. Juliette gazed down at the suckling infant and stroked the black down on his head with gentle fingertips. She had not realized until he was born that in him she would find a new kind of love to ease the emptiness that Nikolai had left in his wake.

When Michel was tucked into his cot she went downstairs to where Marco was waiting for her in a large salon with cushioned high-backed sofas of Venetian design. The only other furniture was a carved cupboard and side tables.

'I never knew I should find such beautiful furniture here,' she said wonderingly. 'You spoke of the house being so empty and yet these pieces demand space to set them off. So they're family heirlooms that your grandmother bequeathed to you?'

'Yes, every one of them. I suppose the furnishings seemed sparse to me, because there are boxes of clocks and paintings and other things in a room at the top of the house that haven't been opened yet.' He poured her and himself an aperitif of white wine.

'May I unpack them one day?' she requested eagerly, wondering what other lovely items lay waiting to be rediscovered.

'Yes, indeed. That's what I've been counting on.' He handed her a glass. 'Let's see if you like this *ombra*. It's quite a dry wine.'

Juliette raised her eyebrows. 'Why do you call it a "shadow"?'

'It's always known as that in Venice. In the past when wine used to be sold on stalls in St Mark's Square people always moved out of

190

the summer heat into the shade to drink it.' His eyes dwelt on her as he raised his glass. 'May shadows of another kind never fall across us in this house.'

She sipped from her glass, echoing the toast in her mind. All her shadows belonged to the past. For Marco's sake and her own they must remain there.

They had their supper at one end of a long table, seated in two ornate, high-backed chairs, the rest of the dozen set back against the walls. She felt that to do her chair justice she should have been robed in velvet with jewels in her hair like a Venetian woman of the Renaissance. When she said this to Marco he laughed and replied that when she had been in Venice for a while she would only be surprised by anything that was new. This amused her and eased the strain of being in alien surroundings. As always, he kissed her good night at her door. She wondered how long it would be before this changed.

In the morning Juliette looked out of her bedroom window and had her first sight of Venice by daylight. Although the wintery sun was bright and the sky a clear pale blue there was nothing much to see, for the courtyard below was shut in by the walls of other buildings and the only outlet was the narrow passageway through which she and Marco had come from the square last night. She looked down into the garden where the trees spread branches over a patio and statuary set amid bushes. She remembered Marco telling her that Venice was full of lush gardens hidden away and this was also a private place, its walls concealing it from passers-by. She could see that it would be cool and shady when the summer sun scorched the city.

When Juliette went down to breakfast only one place was laid, but Lena, coming to pour coffee for her, had a message.

'The signor has gone to work and said he would come back for you in the late morning. He thought you would wish to rest after your journey yesterday.'

'I had more than enough rest during the last weeks of my pregnancy,' Juliette replied, unfolding the linen napkin and spreading it on her lap. 'Now I want to make the most of the time that Michel allows me.'

Later, when Juliette had bathed and fed Michel before putting

191

him in his cot to sleep again, she explored the whole house. In a top room she found the boxes, but opening them would have to wait for another day. It was still not ten o'clock when Juliette, dressed for outdoors, went to ask Lena to listen for Michel as she was going to make her own way to the Palazzo Orfei where Marco would join her later.

In the square she stood by the mushroom-shaped well that had long since been covered over while she looked long and steadily at the Palazzo Orfei, letting her gaze wander over the balconies supported by maned lions and the ornamental stonework. Over the grand entrance was the coat-of-arms of the powerful Pesaro family, who had built the Palazzo all those centuries ago. In one of the houses behind her someone was playing a piano and the music danced lightly in the air, adding to the atmosphere. In the morning light she could see, as she'd been unable to discern by night, that the Palazzo's great windows were made up of tiny leaded panes of what was surely medieval glass and these shone blue, silver and gold in reflected sunlight. With a sigh of satisfaction at the Palazzo's ancient beauty she watched two fashionably-dressed women ring at the door for admittance.

It was opened by a fine-looking woman with patrician features, magnificent dark eyes and a maze of soft brown hair worn in the Greek style. She was wearing a green velvet skirt with a hip-length tunic printed with an oriental pattern, its sleeves floating like soft wings and unmistakably Fortuny-designed. She greeted the two arrivals by name, but formally, which made it apparent to Juliette that they were known clients.

It was as the woman was about to close the door again after admitting them that she caught sight of Juliette and hesitated. Then she moved forward onto the step and spoke with a smile.

'I'm sure you must be Marco's wife. I'm Henriette Negrin.'

Juliette came across to her, full of smiles herself. 'Yes, I am. How did you guess? I supposed Marco described me as a redhead.'

'Titian was the word he used. Please come in. Where is Marco?'

'He was going to bring me a little later this morning, but I was eager to see the Palazzo by daylight,' Juliette replied as she was ushered inside.

'That will give me a chance to show you around before he comes. This is such a pleasure for me to have a fellow Parisienne so near

192

as a neighbour. I know we'll have much in common. Marco has talked so much about you. This is the shop where we are standing now, although I doubt if you'll ever see another one like it anywhere.'

She had seen that already. Juliette was enthralled by her surroundings, for exoticaly patterned fabrics in Fortuny designs presented a vista of rich Renaissance colours of sapphire, ruby and emerald, many of them subtly aglitter with gold, silver, copper or bronze. Every inch of the walls under the enormously high ceiling was covered by multi-hued fabrics either under glass or hanging in abundant lengths. As Juliette moved forward she saw that the great curtains, hanging from rods across the width of the area, were there both for display and to create partitions.

'I've never seen so many glorious silks and velvets in all my life!' Juliette exclaimed.

'Ah! Of course you haven't. They are all unique in that after long research into the processes used by Venetian weavers centuries ago Mariano discovered their secrets and uses the same vegetable dyes to recreate similar glories.'

'How well he has succeeded!' Juliette fingered a cloth of scarlet and gold that might have clothed an early Doge.

'Marco has told us of your exceptional designing skills,' Henriette said, 'so I can guess how much all these fabrics interest you. In fact,' she added with a twinkling glance, 'when he came back from Lyon he talked of little else except meeting you.' She had begun leading Juliette towards the aperture at the side of the first dividing curtain, its motif of Persian origin. Beyond it the delights continued with the additional enhancement of Delphos robes and other Fortuny gowns on *mannequins*, which struck Juliette as odd since no *haute couture* house ever displayed its clothes publicly in such a way and these garments were no less exclusive in their own right. Other wares for sale included cushions in Fortuny designs, his silk shawls, Knossos scarves and evening jackets of dazzling splendour.

'This is not like any shop I've ever seen,' Juliette remarked with pleasure as she continued to look around.

Amid sumptuous drapery long antique tables served as counters, the young male assistants in black velvet suits with flowing cravats, the girls with wide collars of Burano lace spread out over their shoulders, their dresses also of black velvet. Juliette thought their attire entirely in harmony.

193

'*Buon giorno*,' she replied to their greetings, the young men bowing. As yet there were only three customers in the shop. Henriette explained that the busy hours were about to start as visitors to the city found their way there.

'There's always a demand for Fortuny textiles and the items on sale here, and women of discernment have fallen in love with the gowns, but mostly wear them as tea gowns. Several actresses have worn them on stage. Apart from you in Paris and myself here, the American women have been the first to appear in a Fortuny creation at social functions in public venues. Yet so far they have remained cautious enough to wear an evening jacket or mantle at the same time!'

'I'm proud that I was the first with you to wear the robe unadorned, although it was only once without my chiffon dévoré coat, because I had caused a scandal! My sister accused me of appearing *en déshabillé* in public!'

Henriette laughed. 'Thankfully those views show signs of changing. Mariano has created a timeless style that's beyond the dictates of fashion. I'm sure you've thought that about yours.'

'Right from the start,' Juliette admitted quietly, 'I knew for more than one reason I'd never discard it.'

'Mariano replaced the missing label for you, I believe. I suppose that as you came by your Fortuny gown in unusual circumstances – I never heard where or how – you haven't had one of the small round boxes normally supplied with a purchase in which to keep the pleats stored properly when not in use.'

'No, I haven't.'

'Customers always get one. You shall have one too.' Henriette went to speak to one of the male assistants and then returned to Juliette's side. 'It will be waiting for you when you leave.'

'Thank you.' Juliette had paused by one of the Delphos robes to touch the silk, seeing it must have been dyed more than once to create a silvery, blue-grey effect. 'This is extraordinarily beautiful. I've seen that several other silks used for robes have been given the same treatment in different colours.'

'That is another process Mariano has perfected himself. Often a fabric is dyed and treated many times before he gets the exact delicate combination of shades and the effect he wants.'

Juliette became aware that in spite of all the time she had been

194

looking at everything they still had not reached the end of the shop. She had lost count of how many partitions they had passed through. 'This is an enormous place.'

'It's one of the largest areas under a roof in Venice.' Henriette talked then about the Palazzo Orfei's centuries-old history, telling her that the powerful Pesaro family had lived in it for over two hundred years before moving to another palace, after which it had continued to be the setting throughout the passing years for splendid occasions, such as great banquets, balls, concerts and plays. Eventually Fortuny was able to buy it and maintain its grandeur with his own displays.

While talking, Henriette had brought Juliette within sight of a pair of draped doors flanked by huge flowering plants in Oriental pots. Even as she explained it was the rear entrance from a side canal a bell rang and a male assistant hurried forward to open one of the doors. He held it wide for a woman and her escort, who were alighting from a gondola.

'What a romantic way to go shopping,' Juliette remarked as she and Henriette turned to retrace their steps.

'I remember thinking the same when I first came to Venice, but it won't be long before you'll be taking every kind of water transport with no more thought than if you were riding in a taxi or catching an omnibus in Paris. I'll show you over the rest of the Palazzo now and we'll start with the salon-studio. We call it that because Mariano likes to paint at one end and we entertain and hold parties in the salon area. Our quarters adjoining the Palazzo are quite small.' Henriette began leading Juliette towards the stairs. 'You'll see some of Mariano's own paintings, etchings and sculptures in the salon-studio. Photography is another of his interests and he has his own darkroom.'

'What does he like to photograph?'

'Everything from family portraits to city views. He has files of them in his library. I need hardly say there are scores of Venice in all its wonderful changes of light and many of me in Fortuny gowns.'

They went up the stairs, looking in at a showroom where more gowns were displayed and then came to a room as vast as the shop area with side rooms leading off and glass doors that opened to a loggia. It was similarly partitioned, but here the great curtains were of antique velvet in exotic designs and colours. Yet today not all

195

these had been drawn together and it was possible to see the whole length of this palatial room to the studio area at the far end. There an easel was to be seen, a canvas on it, bathed in the light of the tall Gothic windows that perfectly balanced those behind Juliette where she stood gazing in fascination at it all.

All the way along, suspended from the ceiling, were lamps of Fortuny's design, reminding her of the planet Saturn in its encompassing ring, each with an ornate lustre hanging from it. The furniture was all dark with age, set off by the silk-covered walls, and velvet-upholstered couches, piled high with an abundance of cushions, positively invited good conversation and laughter amid gatherings of friends.

'I feel as if I've entered the palace of some great Eastern potentate,' Juliette remarked with pleasure. The illusion was heightened by the magnificence of heavily embroidered and begemmed, centuries-old cloaks and vestments displayed on *mannequins*, softly swathed silk concealing the mahogany tops.

Henriette explained that many of the treasures on display, including the draperies, the armour, the equally old Venetian glass and the Persian rugs, had been inherited by Fortuny from his late father and he had continued to add to the rare collection.

Here Fortuny's own paintings were further enriched by their surroundings as were his sculptures. Juliette, studying everything with interest, suddenly found herself face to face with a large framed painting on an individual stand. She felt almost choked by her startled reaction to it. 'What is the title of this one?'

Henriette, seated on a nearby couch, saw how spellbound Juliette seemed by it. 'It's one of Mariano's Wagnerian scenes and called *The Embrace of Siegmund and Sieglinde*. I'm sure you'll recall that it happens in the first act of *The Valkyrie*.'

Juliette continued to stare at the violently passionate embrace of the couple locked together in kissing as wild as the wind that was streaming the woman's hair and whipping Siegmund's tunic. He had crushed Sieglinde to him so powerfully that he had ripped her garment, making her half naked. Juliette felt a tremor pass through her. It was exactly as Nikolai had clasped her to him the evening she had come home from London and run frantically to him at the studio. She seemed to feel again his strength, his muscled body pressed close and his hungry mouth devouring hers.

196

'Is anything the matter?' Henriette's query jerked her out of her trance.

'No!' Juliette's denial came quickly in her anxiousness to dispel any curiosity. 'It's just that I've never seen a passionate reunion so perfectly portrayed before.'

'Yes, it's a fine painting. You can tell Mariano later how it impressed you. I think he still has someone with him at the moment in a discussion about a Titian he's been asked to restore. He often does restoration work on paintings for both the Church and the City. You can see him when his mother and sister call in later. It will be a good opportunity for you to meet them at the same time.' Henriette made a comical little grimace. 'Their visits are rare, because Doña Cecilia Fortuny doesn't approve of me either as a divorcée or because I choose to live openly with Mariano.'

Although she made light of the disapproval, Juliette made a shrewd guess that it covered many unpleasant confrontations with Fortuny's mother. 'I wish I could have avoided all subterfuge over Michel,' she said frankly.

Henriette frowned deeply and rose from the couch to take hold of Juliette by the arms. 'Your case is entirely different. You're abiding by it for your baby's sake, not for your own. The world is full of cruel tongues and an illegitimate child is marked for ever by society from the moment of birth. It was because I have suffered myself from spite that I wanted you to have a chance to make a new life here. That was before I knew that Marco would have a far better plan himself.'

Juliette inclined her head meditatively. 'I'll be thankful for ever to him for the action he took.'

Henriette gave her an impatient little shake. 'He's worth more than your gratitude. A man like Marco deserves to be loved.'

Juliette jerked herself free and turned away. 'I know you mean well,' she said tremulously, pressing her hands together, 'but I must ask you to say no more.'

Henriette spoke apologetically. 'I went too far. I had no right. Believe me, I spoke as a friend. A new friend indeed, but no less sincere for that.'

'I'm not offended. Truly.' Still Juliette kept her face away.

'But you're upset.' Henriette put an arm around Juliette's waist. 'When you get to know me better you'll find I'm inclined to be outspoken at times. Let's go up to the next floor. You'll see the seamstresses at work and people packing and so forth, which will all be familiar to you from Paris. On the top floor there's the screen and hand-block printing of fabrics just as it is done in Lyon. Are you ready?'

'Yes, of course.' Juliette straightened her shoulders determinedly. On the upper floor they went through a maze of workrooms. Only one door bore the sign *No Admittance*. 'That's where the process of pleating takes place, Henriette explained. 'The secret is known only to Mariano's most trusted workers, who are sworn to secrecy.'

'Did you know that no couturier in Paris has been able to discover how such minute pleats can be made to stay in place as they do?'

Henriette gave a triumphant little laugh. 'Neither shall anyone ever discover it! There are plenty of would-be imitators, but only one exclusive Fortuny method.' She glanced at the diamond watch pinned to her tunic. 'I expect Marco has come by now. We'll look for him.'

But Marco had already heard that Juliette was in the building and was coming to find her when they met him on the stairs. 'What do you think of the Palazzo Orfei, Juliette?' he asked. 'Is it all you expected?'

'Much more!' she replied enthusiastically.

Henriette nodded. 'Your wife has seen everything possible. Has Doña Cecilia arrived?'

'Yes, that's why I came looking for you. She and Maria Luisa are with Don Mariano and they're all waiting for us to join them.'

Henriette pursed her lips in a silent whistle of resignation. 'Here we go!'

Juliette thought Marco seemed a little disappointed that he had not been the one to show her around and she regretted her own impatience that had brought her early to the Palazzo Orfei. On impulse to console him, she put her hand into his and saw by his responding glance how pleased he was by her spontaneous gesture and he fondled her hand in his clasp. She experienced a twinge of guilt that it had meant nothing to her.

The three of them went through a door leading off the salon-studio into a large room that was a surprise in itself to Juliette, for it presented yet another artistic delight. It was painted from the floor to its high ceiling with a colourful *trompe l'œil* of an Italian garden, even to the marble statues standing amid the blossoms and foliage. As she was to learn later, it had been painted by Fortuny himself. He greeted her immediately, immaculate from head to foot in what she knew from Marco to be his daily attire, for whatever the weather or the season he always dressed as if it were summer in a well-cut dark blue suit of finest serge with a white silk cravat. Today his shoes were black patent leather, but he was equally likely to wear red sandals of his own design. In everything he seemed to be a law unto himself, which Juliette supposed was the hallmark of every genius.

'How are you, Signora Romanelli?' he asked in his pleasant, jovial manner. 'Or may I call you Juliette?'

'Please do, Don Mariano.'

'Did you have a full tour of the establishment? Good. Now I'd like you to meet my mother and my only sister.'

Doña Cecilia was an austere, good-looking woman, elegant in a black silk, waisted gown that was not of her son's design, her eyes as dark as his in an oval face with classic cheekbones narrowing to a small chin, her nose long, thin and aristocratic.

'I hope you will soon settle down in Venice,' she said to Juliette, 'and not miss Paris too much. Signor Romanelli has kept you a secret far too long.'

'There were private reasons,' Juliette countered firmly. 'As for Paris, I suppose all who are born there never forget their city, but from all I've seen of Venice so far I'm sure that it holds all I could possibly need.'

'Well said!' Fortuny exclaimed approvingly, taking Juliette by the elbow to guide her to where his sister sat a few feet away. 'I think Christian names are in order here. Maria Luisa, I hope you and Juliette will be friends.'

Maria Luisa was as plain as her brother was handsome. It was as if all the beauty to be shared between the two siblings had concentrated itself in him and all that he created. Her attitude was politely amiable as she invited Juliette to take a seat beside her.

'Are you musical?' she inquired.

'I appreciate music and I enjoy playing the piano,' Juliette answered, 'but not in any exceptional way.'

'How unfortunate! My ear is not accustomed to anything less than the superb. I used to sing and play to acclaim, but I stopped as soon

199

as it dawned on me that there would come a day when I could no longer maintain perfection. Now I channel my energies into a campaign against the killing of even a mosquito or a wasp.' She launched into what was obviously an obsession, her eyes lighting up with the fervour of the reformer.

Only the arrival of refreshments interrupted her flow and the conversation became more general. Eventually Marco and Juliette left, she being handed the small round box for her Delphos robe. He carried it for her when they set off on foot for his business premises. She spoke of how strangely Maria Luisa had talked on certain subjects.

'She told me the only way to get a rewarding night's rest was to sleep in a chair as she does.'

Marco shrugged. 'She's become quite eccentric ever since a love affair came to nothing some years ago, but at least there's no malice in her.'

'I noticed Doña Cecilia's edged remark about our marriage.'

'I hope it didn't trouble you.'

'Not at all. Henriette had already given me an indication that she was not easy to get along with.'

'I think she liked you more than you realized. Your patience with Maria Luisa impressed her. She asked me to take you to one of the *salons* she holds occasionally in the French manner. Fortuny has told me that in the past their home was always a centre of intellectual gatherings. Some of the most well known painters, poets and writers in Paris attended her *salons*. After her husband's death Paris gradually lost its charm for her. Nothing was the same in her eyes without him. Eventually she moved to Venice, taking Maria Luisa with her. Although Fortuny had begun to make a name for himself in Paris in theatrical lighting and other spheres he accompanied her. Then he rented and finally bought the Palazzo Orfei.'

'I can see she has problems with Maria Luisa.'

'It also distresses her – and I'm using her words – that Fortuny and Henriette are living in sin.'

'She blames Henriette?'

Marco raised an amused eyebrow. 'Naturally. Mothers rarely fault their own sons.'

Juliette shared his amusement. 'I must remember that. I don't want to spoil Michel.'

Had the situation been different between them Marco would have said there would be no chance to spoil the boy when there were other children, for his Italian blood, his upbringing and the happiness of family life he had known in his own childhood steered him to that aim. But it could not be said. Not yet. Not even soon when he would have every right to go to her bed. He had to wait for the moment when she would come of her own accord to his arms. His great fear was that otherwise whatever mild affection she had for him might be lost beyond recall. He could not endure to have a wife who took him on sufferance.

Juliette, chatting as they walked along about all she had seen and Henriette's friendliness, had no inkling of his thoughts. It was not far to his premises, which were close to the Grand Canal and were like many other businesses in Venice in being located in a building dating back three centuries. The painted ceilings and wall murals in the outer office and in Marco's own were evidence of the premises' more illustrious past, but everything there and in the vast storerooms that filled the upper floors, were run with up-to-date efficiency, all the employees hard at work.

Marco showed Juliette some of the exotic fabrics he imported from the Far East and elsewhere while his exports included Burano lace, delicate as cobwebs.

When she arrived home again her trunk had been delivered. She unpacked it herself and transferred her Delphos robe to its new box where the pleats curled round and settled into place. She put the be-ribboned lid on and stood holding the box to her for several minutes before she finally put it away on a shelf and closed the door of the closet. It was like parting from Nikolai all over again, the remorseless pain unabated.

CHAPTER SEVENTEEN

Before the week was out Juliette had hired Lena's niece, Arianna, as nursemaid. She was a chaste, fresh-faced girl of twenty. On her third morning she came hurrying to Juliette, who was discussing a menu with Lena in the kitchen.

'There's a delivery man at the door with two large trunks for you, signora.'

'But mine arrived the day after I came here,' Juliette said in surprise. 'There must be some mistake.'

She went at once to tell the delivery man, but when he showed her that he had the right address she saw they had been sent from Paris by Denise. When she opened them it was to find the trunks contained all her Landelle clothes carefully packed between layers of tissue paper. She was grateful to have them and wished she could not discern why they had been sent, but she knew that to her sister the chance of still making her a walking advertisement for Maison Landelle was not to be lost, no matter what the circumstances. Although she sat down at once to write a letter of thanks to Denise, holding out an olive branch once more in a promise to wear the clothes, she knew sadly as she sealed the envelope that it was unlikely she would ever receive a reply.

Juliette passed the remaining weeks to Christmas opening the boxes on the top floor and visiting the Basilica, the Ducal Palace and other grand sights of Venice. Warmly wrapped against the cold, she wandered the quiet passage-ways and squares, lost count of the little arched bridges that she crossed and found small churches rarely seen by visitors where she would study the unexpected treasures within, experiencing the same pleasure as when viewing the master-pieces in the Accademia.

In the Church of the Scalzi, which people hurried past on their way to and from the railway station, she found ceiling frescoes by Tiepolo that were of immense spiritual beauty and covered hugely the entire vaulting in the most sumptuous colours. She sat for a long time gazing up at them, doing no more exploring that day. Afterwards, whenever she was near the church, she would go in to sit quietly, particularly when she had something on her mind.

Marco was in his office all day and when he came home he always wanted to know what more she had seen of Venice. In the evenings they went quite frequently to a concert or a play. On special occasions they would be among those arriving by gondola at the grand water entrance of *La Fenice* to take their seats in one of the tiered boxes and enjoy a superb opera. Two theatres had been converted into moving-picture houses and these they also patronized. After-wards they had supper, often at Danieli's with a view of the Lagoon twinkling with the lights of ships and other water traffic, or else they would stop at Florian's to drink delicious hot chocolate topped by mounds of cream. It was the pattern of a courtship and they both knew it.

The wives of Marco's friends were curious to meet Juliette and invited them to parties and to dine. As a result Juliette made some new women friends, some of whom had babies and young children themselves.

On New Year's Eve Doña Cecilia held her *salon*. It was Juliette's wish that the invitation be accepted, although she and Marco had received others to parties he would have preferred. As usual he gave in to her. She did not enlighten him as to why she had made that choice, but in her own mind she did not want the kind of evening she had spent with Nikolai on previous New Year's Eves. She wore one of her Parisian gowns and, smoothing the pearl-sewn cream satin down over her hips, she was relieved to see that she had almost regained her figure, the under-stiffening of the waist tight enough to maintain the illusion of her original measurements.

Marco in his evening clothes, already in his cloak, was waiting in the hall for her. She glanced into the lighted salon as she came down the stairs. The boxes had revealed chandeliers of Venetian glass, portraits of Marco's ancestors, some delicate porcelain and other fine pieces that she had arranged in the various rooms, all complemented by new curtains throughout in some of the best Fortuny fabrics.

'You look very beautiful.' Marco was regarding her admiringly. 'You haven't worn that gown before. I expected to see you in the Delphos robe.'

He had taken her velvet mantle from her arm and she was glad to turn away from him as he put it around her shoulders, never being sure how much he guessed of her feelings at different times. 'I have several other Landelle gowns that you haven't seen,' she answered lightly. 'As for the Delphos robe, I've had it a long time and put it away.' Her shrug was casual as she faced him again, her confidence and composure regained, and took his arm. 'Let's go. We don't want to be late.'

At the Palazzo Martinengo where Doña Cecilia lived on the Grand Canal, they found an international gathering of people in the three great rooms that had been opened out into each other. The walls were hung with priceless antique draperies in time-faded hues that still glinted with gold and silver threads. Although Fortuny was at his mother's home, Henriette was not present, never having been invited there, but he was only staying a short while before returning to her for a party with their own friends. Before leaving, Fortuny took Juliette on a tour of the rooms, telling her about the origins of the most interesting fabrics, and he also talked about his father's paintings that were there in plenty.

Marco knew a number of people present, and he and Fortuny between them introduced Juliette to all the guests. Some were connected with the arts, others with politics and many were foreign nationals rich enough to live anywhere in the world who had chosen to reside in Venice. Juliette made sure that Fortuny's sister, Maria Luisa, was drawn into lively conversation by gently suppressing the woman's favourite, well-worn topics of discussion to which people reacted with boredom. This thoughtfulness did not escape Doña Cecilia's notice and she saw ignited in her daughter through enjoyment some of the sparkle and charm that had once made her sought after by suitors until her eccentricity drove them away.

'I like Marco's wife,' Doña Cecilia remarked to her son when they could not be overheard, 'but I've drawn my own conclusions about their marriage.'

'Oh? What's that?'

'They were indiscreet and when Marco learned that a baby was coming he made an honest woman of her. I shall invite her here again.'

'But you're such an upholder of morality, *Mama*,' Mariano jibed wryly.

'She is a respectable wife and mother now, my son,' she said with emphasis, never missing a chance to show her disapproval of his liaison. 'I shall take an interest in her and the baby. Remember, I'm one of those unfortunate women who have neither a daughter-in-law nor grandchildren.'

With a sharp flick of her Spanish lace fan she swept back to her guests. He made his departure with a resigned sigh.

When it drew near midnight champagne glasses were refilled and Marco looked for Juliette. She came to him, bringing Maria Luisa with her. The clock struck and the bells of Venice began to chime throughout the city. Glasses were raised amid cheers and laughter. The year of 1913 had dawned.

Juliette wanted to walk home instead of taking water transport. There was so much celebrating going on along the Grand Canal. Boats were lit up, passengers on board the *vaporetti*, many dressed in colourful costumes, blew whistles and waved to every passing gondola. Fireworks were filling the sky, competing with snow flakes that came wafting down in a hint of more to come. In the square people were dancing to bands and Juliette and Marco joined in several dances before they eventually arrived home.

They entered the house quietly, not wanting to wake Michel, who slept now in a nursery adjoining Arianna's room. Marco switched on a lamp in the hall and Juliette removed her mantle, the melting snowflakes sparkling on it as she began to go upstairs with it over her arm.

'Wait, Juliette! Let's drink a glass of champagne on our own before we say good night.'

She looked back at him. He had tossed his cloak and hat onto a chair and was holding out a hand to her. She hesitated. 'I've really had more than enough champagne. I felt quite dizzy during that last dance.'

He let his hand drop to his side. 'Then do something else for me instead,' he said in the same even tone. 'Throw that Delphos robe away. Now. Tonight. I want us to start this New Year unencumbered by trappings from the past. I'll buy you other Fortuny gowns. Have them in every colour and style if you wish. At least I'll know that none of them will hold the same significance for you.'

She had stiffened, her head jerked back. He had not spoken out of jealousy since Nikolai was lost to her for ever and neither was he angry. Nothing in this house had connections with his late wife and he had expected the same dispensing with the past from her. She had given herself away, admitting she still had the robe, at the beginning of the evening when he had questioned her choice of gown.

Wordlessly Juliette let the mantle fall into a soft heap on the stairs. She turned and descended to go into the salon. There she came to a standstill, her back to him, and the light from the hall showed her a champagne bottle in ice and two glasses, which he must have asked Lena to leave ready for them. He followed and switched on a couple of lamps. Only then did she speak.

'My sister once told me to get rid of the robe. I wouldn't do it then and I can't do it now.'

'Then give it into my charge.'

'No!' Wild-eyed, she spun round to him. 'You'd destroy it!'

'You have my word that I'd never do that.'

'Then why?'

'I want it removed from our lives until such time as you take it back again as a gown associated with memories faded to extinction by all the good happenings since.'

'What you suggest is pointless. The robe is already stored away in its box, but Michel is a living, breathing reminder in his cot upstairs!'

Marco's face tightened, a nerve throbbing in his temple. 'He is my son! He has been since the moment of his birth. I love him, this child that is yours and mine. Never say anything like that to me again!' He drew in a deep breath. 'Now drink that glass of champagne with me.'

Grimly he lifted the bottle out of the ice, uncorked it and poured the champagne into the two glasses. She took the one he handed to her. If he had intended originally to make a toast he must have thought better of it. He took only a sip from his glass and watched her with narrowed, furious eyes as she gulped down her champagne as if it were water. She believed she spilled some, but did not stop to look. Then she banged down the emptied glass, flashed him a glance as enraged as his, and rushed out of the room.

She almost ran up the stairs, snatching up her mantle as she went. As soon as she reached her room she shut the door and turned the key, which was something she had never done before. Distractedly she prepared for bed. When she lay on the pillows in the darkness she was tense as she listened for him to come upstairs, fearful that he would try the door.

When at last she heard him on the flight she sat up breathing rapidly, but his footsteps went past and straight into his own room.

Outwardly there was no unpleasant aftermath to the quarrel. Neither Juliette nor Marco referred to the incident, but each knew it was uppermost in the other's mind, for it had created a gulf between them that was seemingly unbridgeable. It was also the only time he had not kissed her good night, even as she had never on any other occasion locked her door. Although he had resumed his fond attitude as if it had never been interrupted his embraces were even more restrained than they had been previously.

His intense desire for her had never been in doubt. She had known from the time of their arrival in Venice that he had been waiting for her to give him some indication that she was ready to be his wife in every way. But she had been unable to do that prior to the quarrel since her whole being had shied away from the prospect. It would have been easy to blame her maternal absorption in the baby, for she had heard that after giving birth many women lost all interest in love-making, often for months on end. But it was more than that. The fault was not in Marco but in herself, for as long ago as in Lyon she had been aware of him as a very attractive man.

On the surface Juliette and Marco continued to maintain the illusion that all was well. They talked as before, exchanged news and laughed freely when one of them had something amusing to relate. Important to them both were the times shared with Michel. Marco took an Italian father's immense pride in the baby boy, failing to see a resemblance to Nikolai in the black curls and the fading of the blue eyes to a clear grey that would never match the Romanelli brown.

There was no shortage of social engagements for Marco and Juliette. Even when Marco was away, sometimes visiting Monsieur and Madame Degrange whenever business took him to Lyon, Juliette was never lonely.

Juliette and Marco dined with Fortuny and Henriette, attended soirées at the Palazzo Martinengo and entertained frequently. Doña Cecilia became very fond of Michel and liked Juliette to take him to see her whenever it was not too cold. When he developed a fever she sent a servant every day to inquire after him. It was an anxious time for both Juliette and Marco. The doctor was attentive, but the medicine he prescribed had no effect. Suddenly Michel was desperately ill and rushed to hospital by water ambulance. Juliette and Marco kept constant vigil by his cot and although they told each other there was hope their harrowed faces revealed their deepest fears. It was a timeless spell of crisis before there came the first sign of improvement. One morning the doctor in charge nodded approval.

'Michel is a fighter. He wasn't going to give in. He's still very weak, but his temperature has dropped and the signs are promising.'

Although Michel made steady progress from then onwards, Juliette continued to be more at the hospital than at home. Marco went to work, but made straight for the baby's cotside afterwards. Finally they were able to take Michel home again.

Arianna, who with Lena had also been in a constant state of anxiety about Michel until his recovery, implored Juliette to leave him in her charge that first night.

'You've had so little rest these past days and nights, signora. You need to sleep. I'll watch over Michel.'

Although Juliette agreed, going early to bed and thinking she would sleep like the proverbial log, she only dozed fitfully. At midnight she slipped on a robe and went to the nursery. She found that Arianna, sitting in an upholstered chair at the side of the cot, had her head dipped in sleep. Yet the faint creak of the door made her wake at once and she looked quickly in the cot before she realized that Juliette had entered the room. They whispered together and when Juliette saw that Michel was sleeping peacefully, she tiptoed out again.

It was on her way back to her own room when she heard a faint sound like muffled sobs. Juliette stopped and listened, thinking she must be mistaken, but as she moved on again she heard it once more. Since Lena's room was on the top floor it could come from only one direction. She went to Marco's door, listened for a few moments and then knew she was not mistaken. She pressed down the handle and went in.

As with Arianna he did not see her enter, but sleep was not the reason. He was fully dressed, except for his jacket, and sat in his shirt-sleeves with his elbows on his knees, his head in his hands. Another terrible sob racked through him. She went forward, her robe whispering about her. He heard her then and dropped his hands to raise his dejected, tormented face as she came to stand before him.

'It's all right,' she cried to comfort him, putting her hands on his shoulders. 'Michel is well again and there is nothing more to worry about.'

Marco answered her brokenly. 'I know, but reaction to those past nightmare days suddenly caught up with me. I'd thought I was going to lose him as I've lost you.'

Compassion and something close to love for him in his distress moved her deeply. 'You haven't lost me! You never will! I've needed time. Maybe more time than either of us first realized. I'm here and I always will be.'

His groan broke from his heart and he clasped her about the waist, arching her back, and pressed his face against her. She looked down at him and folded his head in her arms, continuing to murmur soothing, reassuring words. Finally she whispered his name and when he looked up at her she took his face between her hands.

'Marco,' she urged gently, 'take me to bed.'

Her one thought was to give him greater reassurance by becoming a wife to him at last, but for herself she expected nothing. All her sexual feelings as a woman had been drained away over a lengthy period of heartache and maternal devotion. There was no longer any need or wish in her for a return to such yearnings.

When Marco came to the bed, strong, naked and powerful, passion vibrating through him, she took him into her waiting embrace out of pity, blocking her mind to the past. She was prepared to submit to whatever he wanted of her, but nothing happened as she

209

had supposed. There was no pent-up hungry searching, no fierce possession by a man tormented by long waiting, but an exquisite tenderness from patient hands and lips that made tension ease away. Tears trickled from under her closed lids at his consideration for her when she had failed to show any to him since their marriage. She glimpsed the depth of her own affection for him that she had kept to herself, depriving him in another way.

She began to tremble under his stroking touch. With sensitivity and understanding he was slowly and surely using all his mastery as a lover to reawaken her long dormant sensuality and draw her into a sphere she had never expected to enter again. She experienced surprise when after a little time all her natural desires stirred unexpectedly and then suddenly flared. Her young and healthy body, long deprived, seemed to escape all mental control and was borne along as if of its own volition by his increasing passion. He crushed her close as she almost fought against him, even as she succumbed to a sharing of his physical ecstasy.

Afterwards she lay with her face turned away from him and he held her quietly in his arms. Finally she rolled her head round to look into his loving eyes.

'You've been so tolerant, Marco.' Her voice faltered. 'All these months—' She left her sentence unfinished, looking away from him again.

He turned her face back to him with his fingertips. 'There are more ways than one of showing one's love, my darling wife.'

Yet again she thought what a good man he was and this time she accepted that he deserved some part of her heart in their future together.

They did not sleep apart again. She knew it was no fault of his that she never reached the heights to which Nikolai had taken her.

On reflection, as the days went by, Juliette could pin-point exactly when she had stopped looking back at the past and turned her mind to the future. It was when she had opened Marco's door and seen him in that state of utter despair.

Gradually she adjusted fully to living in Venice, letters from Lucille and Gabrielle making up a little for never hearing from Denise. There was also the anticipation of a visit from Lucille during the trip she would shortly be taking to Europe. There was

210

no chance of seeing Gabrielle, who was finally pregnant after four years of marriage.

Juliette looked forward to showing Lucille around Venice, which had become as familiar to her as her native Paris. She had heard it spoken of as a city too locked in its timeless beauty ever to be concerned with the troubles afflicting the rest of the world. Although that was the illusion she knew it was not true. Venetians were as anxious as anyone else about the growing tension in Europe, the talk of war and the mad arming by various nations. At social gatherings conversation always turned to it at some time, making people look grave and shake their heads.

Among lighter topics discussed among the fashion-conscious Venetian women was the hobble skirt that had been introduced by Paris and which gave an elegant line, but made it so difficult to walk when wearing these narrow sheaths. Such talk and any other mention of *haute couture* made Juliette increasingly restless to get back to work. She raised the issue with Marco.

'Originally, before we married,' she said, 'I'd never expected to be at home as long as I have. Michel is over six months old now.'

They were in the room she had made into a library, for he had a great number of books and her own had come in the trunks from Paris.

'The choice is still yours,' Marco replied. He would have preferred her to stay at home, regretting the promise he had made when offering marriage, but he would not go back on his word.

She leaned back against the shelves, her arms folded and her fingers dancing. 'I admit it's been wonderful being with Michel all this time and I like the freedom of attending daytime events with no ties to be elsewhere, but somehow I feel compelled to be in touch again with fashion in one form or another.'

'I guessed that would happen when you began working in that little studio fitted up for you in the top room,' he said resignedly. 'I didn't think you'd keep to painting views of Venice for long and you'd soon turn your thoughts to design again.'

Her eyes queried his. 'Do you mind?'

'To be honest I've come to feel differently about it since we married, but I'll not stand in your way.'

'You've no need to worry. I'll only work for a few hours daily if Fortuny agrees. Working full-time is out of the question. I'll

211

never neglect you and Michel. Both of you will always be first with me.'

'I'm sure of that.'

At the Palazzo Orfei Fortuny listened to her request. Both he and Juliette knew there was no question of her starting as a seamstress, which had been intended originally as a trial period for a new employee whose skills had yet to be tested. He had seen some of her textile designs, which she had created in her studio. These would have confirmed her instinctive eye for pattern and texture, even if he had not known it already from her knowledgeable appreciation of his own designs, which she had expressed at various times. He liked her enthusiasm and was sure she would work well.

'Henriette needs an assistant in the work of colouring the engraved blocks, but having seen your designs I feel it would be unfair of me to engage you only to carry out mine. You'd no longer have any outlet for your own creative activity. What I can offer would not be suited to your talents.'

'This wouldn't be the first time I've redirected my interests. I've moved from sewing by way of being a mannequin to designing clothes and then textiles. Just to be linked with fashion again is enough for me at the present time.'

'Very well. As you've most surely heard, this is the time of year when Venice fills up with the visitors of wealth and distinction and their custom alone makes a seasonal demand on my gowns and fabrics. Would you be prepared to sell gowns for me?'

Juliette was surprised but agreeable. 'I was never a *vendeuse* at Maison Landelle, but I learned a great deal when I was there. I'd be glad to do it.'

'Good. Think of yourself as being more the equivalent of a *directrice* in some ways, because you'll be in charge of the showroom with assistants to fetch and carry for you.'

'You're putting an enormous amount of trust in my ability.'

'You've had plenty of working experience in one of the best *haute couture* places in Paris, and Henriette took more note than you realize of what you told her about your time there.'

'Such as—?' Juliette questioned smilingly.

He grinned. 'For example, how you showed your initiative when you dealt with those women who came clamouring for a Fortuny gown at Maison Landelle.'

Juliette shared his amusement. 'At least here I'll be able to sell them as many as they want!'

'Yes, indeed. There's one more thing I'd like to ask you. Tomorrow morning I'll be taking a series of photographs of Henriette in some of the new gowns. It was her suggestion that you should pose in the rest. Would you agree?'

She hesitated. It would be the first time she had worn a Fortuny gown since her own on the last occasion she had dined with Nikolai. It would not be easy, but it was a hurdle she should overcome in the re-settling of her life. She gave a quick nod before her spirit failed her. 'Yes, I'll do that.'

'Thank you. Could you come along about ten tomorrow morning and would you mind bringing your own Delphos robe with you? I'd like very much to have a photographic record of it for my files.' He smiled broadly. 'It's the only one of my garments that has ever been re-made.' He took her answer for granted. 'I'm sure you'd like some photographs of yourself in it and you shall have them.'

Juliette felt dazed that he, all unwittingly, should have made such a devastating request regarding her gown. She couldn't do it! It was too much! But as she drew breath to turn down his request there was an interruption by Henriette.

'Mariano! Could you come quickly?' Then she saw Juliette and apologized for bursting in. 'I'm sorry. I didn't know you were here. There's a minor crisis that's not in my department.'

'Henriette will settle your hours of work when you see her tomorrow,' Fortuny said over his shoulder as he followed Henriette out of the room.

After leaving the Palazzo Orfei Juliette went on foot to Marco's office and told him she was to start work the next day.

'That's what you wanted,' he acknowledged, 'and I agreed.'

'Thank you, Marco.' She was sitting in front of his desk and hesitated before she spoke again, looking steadily at him. 'There is something more I have to tell you. First of all tomorrow Henriette and I are to model some of the new gowns for a photographic session. Don Mariano also wants me to wear my Delphos robe.'

He raised his eyebrows slightly and sat back in his swivel chair. 'What did you say?'

'I didn't answer him, but I'll not do it.'

Marco rose to his feet and came round to the front of the desk to

213

put his hands on her shoulders. 'I'd like you to do as he asked. Why not? Nothing stands between us now. Least of all anything that happened in Paris.'

She was still uncertain. Yet if it were true that Nikolai no longer stood between Marco and her in the relationship they had built up together maybe she should make a decisive move towards diminishing the importance of her Delphos robe.

'I'd like to choose one of the new Fortuny ensembles for myself – gown, cape and matching purse.'

He regarded her calmly. 'Why not choose two? It would make a change for you not to wear something you've designed yourself. I'll be pleased to foot the bill.'

'That's very generous, Marco! Thank you.'

He raised her up and she looped her arms about his neck as he kissed her. She had come to care for him more than once she had believed possible. When she had first disclosed this to him she had been startled by the triumphant force of his love-making. It had been as if he were exulting in what he had seen as her total submission to him rather than her giving freely of love to complete their marriage. Until then she had wondered sometimes whether if she had never met Nikolai, never experienced such a complete unity of heart and mind and soul, she might have found a comparably rewarding love with Marco on another plane. But the pattern of his passion that night had shown her that she was mistaken. Perhaps he had not realized previously that his wish was not to share but to dominate.

Yet, as today, in spite of his having admitted his change of attitude when they were in the library, he continued to show unselfishness whenever her happiness was concerned and she was grateful, if a little unsure how long it might last. Overall she was far too conscious of her own shortcomings ever to care less for him because of his.

CHAPTER EIGHTEEN

When Juliette arrived for the photographic session Henriette had just finished posing and was in her own clothes again. She showed Juliette the selection of gowns in her size hanging on a rail behind a changing screen.

'As you'll see, all are slight variations of the same design, which in turn follows the basic shape of the Delphos robe, because Mariano will never stray from that. These new ones also adjust with silken chords and are similiarly ornamented with beads of Venetian glass.'

Left on her own to change, Juliette took the first gown from its hanger. It appeared quite shapeless until she put it on and tied the dainty cords. It was in black silk velvet, soft as the bloom on a peach, the gold silk of the bodice imprinted with a delicate design, tiny beads aglitter.

'Are you ready?' Henriette called, having returned.

'Yes.' Juliette emerged from behind the screen. 'Am I all right for the camera?'

Henriette smiled to herself. The young woman, fussing with the cords and looking critically in the full-length cheval-glass once again, never failed to imbue anything she wore with extra style. 'I think you'll pass inspection,' she commented drily.

'Oh good. Marco wants me to choose two of the gowns I like best. He knows how I love Fortuny designs.'

She was thankful that Marco felt able to give her a free hand in choosing garments with a label that previously had been associated in his mind solely with the Delphos robe.

'The one you have on is my favourite. It's inspired by a gown worn on a famous occasion here at the Palazzo Orfei in the sixteenth century when one of the wives of the dignitaries present wore a gown of gold tissue and black lace. It was said to be the most magnificent ever seen in Venice.'

'Perhaps until now!' Juliette declared, stroking her fingertips down the soft velvet.

'Mariano would appreciate that compliment. But we'd better not linger. He is waiting for you. Go ahead to the photography studio. I'll come later. Good luck!'

With the hem rippling like little wavelets about her feet, Juliette went along to the studio. Fortuny was under the camera's black cloth when she entered, but reappeared at the first tap of her heels.

'There you are, Juliette. Oh, yes.' He nodded in approval at her appearance. 'Very good indeed. Just as I'd expected. Stand in front of that curtain and raise your elbows as you clasp your hands gracefully in front of you. That will show the batwing sleeves.'

After taking a number of photographs he asked her to put on the evening jacket designed to go with it. Henriette had come to hand it to her. It was in the same black velvet as the gown with a lining of gold silk. Juliette soon lost count of the times he disappeared under the camera-cloth to photograph her yet again in every one of the other gowns and jackets chosen for her to display. There followed more posing in full-length evening coats and mantles so richly stencilled in silver on sapphire-blue velvet, bronze on purple and gold on crimson that each might have been a robe of state from a Bellini painting. Again and again it was possible to see how Fortuny drew his inspiration from great Venetian masterpieces as well as from Islamic and Oriental art.

Finally Juliette was photographed in her own Delphos robe. Wearing it was like being caressed by the past, the nestling of the silk against her skin a poignant reminder of hands that had stroked, revered and loved. Curiously all her dread of putting it on again was lost from the moment the mirror reflected her in it. Somehow it only

216

seemed to evoke memories of the good times she had shared with Nikolai. She hoped this meant that she had finally conquered all regrets and could concentrate on her marriage and the future.

When the Delphos robe was back in its little round box and Juliette was dressed again, she made her selection of the new gowns for herself. Inevitably she chose the black and gold one and the second had a green silk tunic with a pleated silk underskirt. Both had sumptuous cape-like jackets to match. Marco, arriving to see Fortuny on business, found her with Henriette, both leaning on their arms as they gazed down into the larger of the two courtyards of the Palazzo.

'What's the attraction?' he asked, unable to see anything unusual as he looked down too.

Henriette answered. 'I'm showing Juliette where the origin of one of her new gowns created a sensation.'

'Oh, yes. At the grand performance of *Miles Gloriosus*.' He was equally familiar with the history of the Palazzo. 'My guess is that the courtyard looked much like the salon-studio when all the walls were covered with rich hangings for such events.'

Juliette straightened up with a sigh. 'I was thinking the same. One is only ever a breath away from past centuries with anything under Fortuny's influence.'

'You like that, don't you?' Marco commented.

She nodded. 'Although I'm far too contemporary in my outlook to draw inspiration from a bygone time, I can see why it suits him so well to live here in Venice. I don't think he'd be content anywhere else in the world.'

Marco looked questioningly at Henriette. 'Would you agree with that?'

'Completely. There's nothing on earth could uproot him.'

None of them saw anything prophetic in her statement, but Juliette was to remember it much later.

Fortuny had been right when he foretold a busy time ahead for Venice. Foreign visitors to the city were of every nationality. They patronized the best hotels, filled the theatres, the concert halls and the moving-picture houses. It was often difficult for local people to get seats, but Marco always made sure he secured tickets early for anything Juliette would enjoy, even the moving-picture costume

217

dramas in which Italy had begun to excel, although he preferred a contemporary plot and setting himself.

Juliette often thought that the Palazzo Orfei had a look of the setting for a costume drama with so many rich draperies, some of which even adorned the ceilings in vast loops of gleaming splendour. Any moving-picture vamp could have lain on a tiger skin spread on a couch's silken cushions and not looked out of place. Except, of course, that fur never appeared at the Palazzo Orfei since Fortuny seemed to have no liking for it as ornamentation.

Many rich women came to the Palazzo Orfei. Some were difficult and demanding, no different from those who had come to Maison Landelle. Juliette let nothing they did or said disrupt her composure and found selling to these women a challenge. Whenever there was a pernickety dislike of a certain colour she would produce cards of the same silk or velvet in subtle variations of shades selected by Fortuny for each particular gown. No other change could be made, no matter what the customer's whim might be.

'After all,' Juliette would explain with satisfaction, 'each gown is a masterpiece in itself. No-one has any right to add or take away from it any more than if it were a Titian or a Rembrandt.'

Nobody argued after that statement and sales were made.

Customers often confided to Juliette that they would gladly leave off their boned under-garments if their breasts were the shape they deemed to be perfect, failing to see in self-criticism that the Fortuny gowns could flatter as well as reveal. A young American wife mentioned hearing of a support for the breasts alone that a New York debutante named Mary Phelps Jacobs had made for herself out of two handkerchieves, but there was nothing like that on the market and so the boned support had to suffice.

Chaperoned parties of American girls, touring Europe in a final flourish of their education before becoming engaged, frequently wanted to buy Fortuny gowns that Juliette showed them in all the softly shaded colours. Invariably they were forbidden to purchase, the chaperones considering the gowns to be far too sophisticated.

The first time it happened and the party of young women had departed, the assistant, who was helping Juliette put the gowns away again, made a casual remark.

'There'll be sales yet from those young ladies, signora. You'll see.'

'What do you mean?' Juliette asked.

'Didn't you notice that two or three of the girls neither expressed frustration nor argued? They'll be back on their own to purchase as soon as they can give their chaperones the slip.'

Juliette uttered a surprised laugh. 'I'd do the same myself if I were in their shoes,' she admitted.

Although Juliette did not work later in the day she heard next morning that three girls had been back and also one of the matrons to purchase for herself. Fortunately they did not all come at the same time. After that Juliette was able to spot the girls who would return and put aside their choices in readiness.

She was draping a cape on a *mannequin* one morning when Henriette handed her a large envelope. 'Here are the photographs of you in your Delphos robe. Mariano also put in some of those that have gone to the press, which he thought you might like to have.'

'Yes, I would. Thank you!'

That evening Juliette showed the photographs to Marco. He selected one of her in the new green Fortuny gown, which she had already worn twice with great success. When the photograph was set in a silver frame, Marco stood it on his desk next to the one he already had of her with Michel.

Juliette had been working at Fortuny's for two months when she and Marco went to a picture house to see Mary Pickford in *The New York Hat*. Included beforehand in the programme was a newsreel that showed the King of Italy reviewing troops, a begoggled racing driver winning a race in a Bugatti, the Pope in Rome and finally the Tsar and Tsarina of Russia with their son and daughters processing to take seats for an open-air celebration of three hundred years of Romanov rule. In the Imperial family's wake came a number of top-hatted dignitaries and their wives. One of the men turned his head somewhat sharply as if on the alert for trouble, perhaps even an assassination attempt against the Tsar, for it was not long since the Russian Premier had been killed by a thrown bomb. Juliette recognized the man even before the camera caught him full-face and seemed to dwell on him for minutes that in reality were only seconds. It was Nikolai!

She had stiffened and jerked forward involuntarily to the edge of her seat, gripping the arms. Marco had seen Nikolai too and he drew her nearest hand into his and held it tightly, able to feel its trembling.

'Are you all right?' he asked, low-voiced. The newsreel had ended to the last lingering notes of Russian music played appropriately by the woman pianist and the male violinist in the orchestra pit below the screen.

'Yes,' she whispered hastily, sitting back in her seat. 'I was surprised, that's all. One never expects to recognize anyone on a picture-house screen.'

'Do you want to leave?'

She shook her head and drew her hand away from his clasp. The pianist and the violinist struck up a piece suitable for the main picture. Juliette watched, but saw nothing of it. She was trying to cope with the rush of love that had caught her unexpectedly. It forced her to face the stark reality that the passing of time had done nothing to lessen her love for Nikolai, no matter that she had deceived herself into thinking that somehow she had mastered her yearning. On the screen Mary Pickford received the new hat from the young minister, causing gossip to rampage, but Juliette saw only Nikolai's face, handsome as ever, a slight frown across his eyes. She had a vague impression of a woman on his arm. It must have been Natasha sharing the Imperial occasion with him as she shared his life. This more sobering thought enabled her to get a grip on herself by the time the performance ended.

When she and Marco walked home she was able to say quite casually that she thought Nikolai had looked well and it was surely a sign of his Imperial godfather's favour that he had been given such a prominent position among so many older high-ranking officials. Marco agreed with her, but remembered with jealousy her deep reaction. Neither of them mentioned the incident again, but he did not forget.

When Lucille arrived on her visit Juliette was waiting to meet her. They embraced with happiness. At the first opportunity Lucille looked anxiously into Juliette's face.

'Have you forgiven me for withholding Count Karasvin's letter?'

'Of course I have! Has it been preying on your mind?' Juliette had been taken aback to hear Nikolai's name spoken so unexpectedly, but she could not resist hoping for news of him. 'Did you see Prince Vadim when you were in Paris?'

'No. He has closed his residence there and he and his wife have

220

returned to St Petersburg to give their support to the Tsar in the present unsettled times. Several other distinguished Russians have gone home for the same reason. Oh, my dear, how good it is to see you again!'

That evening Lucille enjoyed being present at Michel's bathtime, which Juliette always took over from Arianna. He had just been tucked into his cot when Marco came home from his office and met Lucille for the first time. They were to go out to dine. When Lucille came downstairs after changing she carried a package in tissue paper. Around her shoulders she had a filmy wrap in a pattern that Juliette, ready in her black and gold gown, recognized instantly.

'May I ask where you purchased that wrap?'

'Denise gave it to me. These wraps are a new sideline for Maison Landelle.' Lucille handed her the package. 'She has sent this one for you.'

Juliette sat down to open it on her lap. The wrap was in another colour with a different pattern, but as with Lucille's the design was her own.

'But these designs are among the last I sent to Denise,' she said flatly. 'After hearing I was to marry Marco she sent the drawings back to me torn into pieces.'

Lucille sat down beside her with a sigh. 'You should have known that Denise wouldn't throw away some perfectly good designs without taking copies first, even though she wanted you to think she had destroyed them at the time.'

'I've not received a word from her since then.'

'So she told me. I've come as a peace-maker apart from my wish to see you again and also to meet your husband and baby.'

Juliette's expression hardened. 'You'll think I'm cynical, but I can only say that Denise must want something of me.'

'Only for matters to be mended between you. She regrets her anger and what she did. I know you have every right to toss her request back at her, but she has had her troubles recently. She told me that Monsieur Pierre had a heart attack and may never work again. The man who took his place is not proving satisfactory and through his errors she has lost several valued clients.'

Juliette made a weary gesture. 'You don't need to say any more. Denise wants me to design for her again, but instead of being

221

straightforward about it she is trying to soften me up first by making out how much she misses me.'

Lucille sighed again. 'I'm not trying to make excuses for Denise, but I truly believe she would have written to you before all these catastrophes happened if her pride hadn't stood in the way. My visit gave her the chance she has been waiting for. She had begun to rely on you more than she realized at the time. You were her hope for the future.'

'Surely she understands that I'd never go back to Maison Landelle? My life is here now.'

'I pointed all that out to her. She accepts that the situation can never be as it was. All she asks is that you design for her again – clothes and textiles.'

'All she asks!' Juliette repeated hotly, springing to her feet and taking a few paces across the room. 'I work for Fortuny now. Didn't you tell her that?'

'Yes. I said your letters were full of your enthusiasm and pleasure at being back in the world of fashion again. Don't think Fortuny hasn't won her respect for his gowns. She has seen several important women of high rank wearing his creations, some of her own clients among them.'

'But how can I design for Maison Landelle? When I thought once I was going to Russia I told Denise then that I'd be too far from the pulse of fashion to keep up with it. Italian women are very fashion-conscious, but the same yardstick applies to me here.'

'She thinks your ideas will be all the fresher for it.'

'But I spend every morning at the Palazzo Orfei. It wouldn't be ethical to design for one fashion house while working in another.'

'Your sister knows all that, but she's in trouble. I've never seen her so cast down. I think all her zest for work left her after her accident.'

Juliette spun round anxiously to face Lucille. 'What happened?'

'Her motorcar skidded on a wet road and crashed into a wall. She broke both legs and is still on crutches.'

'Why didn't you let me know at once?' Juliette demanded.

'It happened just after I'd set sail for France. I went to see Denise in hospital and since she came home I've been staying with her instead of at the Hôtel Bristol. That's why it's taken me such a long time to get to Venice and also why I've postponed my departure for home. I'll go back to her in Paris when I leave here.'

Juliette sat silently, looking down abstractedly at the rings she was twisting on her fingers. Finally she spoke. 'What exactly does Denise want me to do?'

'She wants a whole new collection for next spring. You're to provide the sketches and ideas for it.'

'I can't decide anything before I've spoken to Fortuny.'

'What of Marco? Would he agree to your returning with me to see Denise when I leave?'

Juliette raised an eyebrow. 'I do everything I can for Marco, but I'm not his chattel. I would visit Paris if I took on this new work.' Then she smiled. 'In the meantime, I'm going to show you Venice, but you'd have to be here for many years to see even a quarter of its treasures.'

When Juliette told Fortuny what she had been asked by her sister he heard her out before he said anything. He was at his easel and had put aside his palette and brushes to listen to her.

'Since I don't consider myself to be part of the Parisian fashion world,' he said amiably, 'I see no hint of rivalry in your taking up this obligation that has been placed on you. If it's what you wish, then it's right that you should do it. I would never stand between two sisters.'

'You're being very understanding.' She thought of Marco who had approved this new venture with some reluctance.

'Have you any special ideas in mind yet for this Maison Landelle collection?'

'Yes, I have.' Juliette's face lit up. 'Naturally my designs won't be in any way related to your creations, but inevitably you will have influenced me.'

'I consider that a generous compliment.'

She knew she could confide in him and he would keep it to himself. 'I've been across to the lace-making island of Burano several times and I'll take Lucille with me for the day when I go again. I want to study some of the lovely lace patterns, because I picture an all-lace collection for the day and evening clothes. After that, for the next season, Venetian glass will give me the most marvellous colours for winter woollen cloths and velvets. Think of that strong blue and rich red!'

Fortuny smiled. 'Whether you realize it or not, you are returning to your rightful path in life. An artistic mind like yours should never be allowed to stagnate.'

'That wouldn't have happened all the time I was working here!'

'But it must have frustrated you at times that the gowns you handled here were not of your design.'

'No, because I was so glad to be dealing again with lovely clothes that make women feel better and more beautiful for wearing them.'

'You'll always be welcome at the Palazzo Orfei, Juliette. I hope Henriette and I will continue to see you and Marco as often as before. Remember if ever you want any advice when you're designing again I'll be ready to help.'

'You're a good friend indeed, Don Mariano.'

Lucille enjoyed her visit to Burano, which started with a short voyage across a stretch of water as blue as the cloudless sky. Women were lace-making in their homes while the daughters and granddaughters of some sat in rows learning the exquisite skills in the lace-making school.

While Juliette did her investigating, talking prices and delivery with vendors, Lucille made her own purchases of cobweby lace shawls, veils, cuffs and lace-edged handkerchieves as gifts to take home. Finally she bought a bridal veil for a granddaughter that was a full three yards long and in a delicate rose pattern.

'I'm glad all has turned out so well in life for you,' Lucille said to Juliette when they sat side by side on a slatted seat as they sailed back to Venice, the *vaporetto*'s smoke making a wispy trail in its wake. 'Marco's a fine man and you have a bonny son. You're soon to be reconciled with Denise and that pleases me so much.' She put a maternal hand on Juliette. 'Count Karasvin would never have made you happy, you know.' Then she drew her hand away sharply as Juliette turned and looked at her with tragic eyes.

'Do you suppose I've found happiness without him?'

'But you have so much!' Lucille pointed out falteringly.

'I count my blessings every day, but the kind of happiness I knew with Nikolai is something that comes only once and never again.' Juliette's voice softened and she managed a half-smile. 'Forgive me. I didn't want to make you look so sad after the splendid day we've had together. I shouldn't have spoken.'

There was a pause before Lucille answered. 'I'm pleased you did. I almost told you when we were in Paris that I'd once loved someone who devastated my life. I realized afterwards that even if we had married I could never have kept him faithful to me.'

'Have you ever seen him on your return visits to Paris?'

'No, he died when you were a little girl.'

There was a moment of stunned silence. 'Were you in love with my father?' Juliette exclaimed incredulously.

Lucille gave a weary nod. 'He was quite a philanderer in his young days. I was demented with love for him. We had a very passionate liaison and then one fateful day I introduced him to my best friend.' She shook her head quickly in reassurance. 'Your mother never suspected what had been or how I felt. He and she took one look at each other and from that moment onwards all other women ceased to exist for him. I saw all I'd hoped for crumble away.'

'You were a bridesmaid at their wedding.'

'Yes, that was the hardest day of my life. Rodolphe proposed again that same evening and I accepted him.'

'Did you ever stop loving my father?'

'No, but that doesn't mean I haven't done my best for Rodolphe. If it's any comfort to you, I can promise that such love mellows and time heals the anguish and the pain.'

Juliette was deeply moved. 'I always felt we were kindred spirits, no matter the age difference between us, but I had no idea until now why you were so concerned that I might fall in love with Nikolai.'

'I think this has been a good day for both of us. It's also the right time to tell you to stop calling me *tante*. It makes me feel centuries old! In future my Christian name will suffice.'

Together they laughed and their mood lifted. The *vaporetto*'s blast on its siren announced its return to the Venetian quayside.

Juliette had made up her mind to take Michel with her when she and Lucille set off for Paris. Marco was having to go away on business at the same time and she did not want to leave the child without one or the other of them at home. Marco strongly opposed her plan.

'Travel and strange surroundings would disrupt Michel's routine,' he argued. 'It wouldn't be fair on him and you'll be busy.'

'I've explained why I don't want to leave him behind. Arianna can come with us. It's a sensible arrangement.'

Marco finally acquiesced, but only after he had tried to change the dates of his business trip, which would have enabled him to be at home with Michel, but this did not prove possible.

The journey to Paris went smoothly. Michel at ten months was a good-tempered child and undisturbed by the travelling. Juliette told Lucille that as soon as they arrived she would telegraph Marco to let him know all was well. When they reached the house in the faubourg St Germain Denise came to meet them in the hall with the aid of a cane. She had dispensed with her crutches, but explained she still had to rest. Otherwise she was on the mend. Reassured by the letter Juliette had written agreeing amends could be made and buoyed up as usual when getting her own way, Denise embraced her sister exuberantly.

'This is a new beginning! No more misunderstandings!' After she had greeted Lucille she viewed Michel in Arianna's arms. Her immediate thought was that the Karasvin likeness was unmistakable. 'He's going to be handsome when he grows up,' she conceded speculatively.

'There'll be no trouble with him, signora,' Arianna said in Italian. She had not understood what had been said, but she had seen no warmth for her charge in the Baronne's eyes, only a curious calculating study of the child.

Denise turned to Juliette. 'I don't know what your nursemaid said, but I've allotted two rooms on the top floor for her and the child.' She became full of smiles again. 'As soon as you and Lucille have tidied up after your journey we'll have some refreshments and talk. Be sure to bring down whatever sketches and the list of ideas you've brought with you. There's no time to lose.'

As Juliette and Lucille went up the stairs they exchanged a tolerant glance. Denise had not changed and never would.

It was a busy time that followed. Juliette visited Monsieur Pierre and found him almost fully recovered and eager to return to work. He had heard from Denise that Juliette was to contribute to the Landelle designs again and became as enthusiastic as Denise had been about the all-lace idea. At Maison Landelle Juliette soon discovered the root of his replacement's lack of interest and co-operation. Denise had failed to tell the new designer at the start that he was only there on a temporary basis until Monsieur Pierre was able to return. She understood the man's feelings. Denise had also deceived Lucille and herself to gain her own ends. Nothing was as drastic as had been made out, neither had Denise used a cane since the day of their arrival. She had also lost within the first hour the limp she had adopted.

'I should have known that Denise would be up to her old tricks, aiming to manipulate everybody and everything to her own satisfaction,' Juliette remarked resignedly to Lucille. 'I just wish she could come straight out with what she wants and not always turn to subterfuge.'

'You would be within your rights to withdraw if you wished.'

Juliette smiled, shaking her head. 'It's too late. Denise knew that even if I hadn't given a promise to work for her again I'd be hooked by the exhilaration of Parisian fashion as soon as I was back here once more.'

It was while talking over the new designs with Denise that Juliette told her about the American woman's idea of making a separate support for the bust. 'You produce such lovely lingerie and instead of the metal-strips rising up from the corseted hips and stomach to a stiffened brassière, let the two sections be separate. It would allow women's breasts to retain a natural shape in keeping with the softer fashions being worn. I've drawn several of these separate brassières and made some for myself with the support coming only from the cut and stitching.'

Denise was intrigued. 'Tell me more.'

Juliette unbuttoned her blouse and drew it down over her shoulders with the straps of her lacy chemise to display what she had made. She had not used the handkerchief basis, but her own design in silk. Denise, who prided herself on the seductive lingerie she sold, was sure it would be well received by the young and the well-formed.

'I'll consider it,' she said, able to see that her sister had given her another highly marketable idea and she intended to follow it up.

Within twenty-four hours of Juliette's being back in Paris friends and acquaintances contacted her, wanting to see her again. She had little free time but did manage to see some of them, the rest she

227

talked to on the telephone. All wanted to know how she liked living in Venice and what she missed most of Paris. On a more serious note, wherever she went she heard talk of the threat to France from Germany's increasing military might. Every young man who discussed the situation with Juliette declared his intention to enlist at once should hostilities break out.

'We'll fight to the death!' was the fervent vow.

She hoped desperately that such a terrible catastrophe would never arise.

On her last day in Paris Juliette walked alone to Nikolai's studio. The city had been full of memories for her. When riding in Denise's latest new motorcar, a replacement for the one that had crashed, she had looked out at restaurants where she and Nikolai had dined and danced, cafés where they had sat under awnings drinking coffee or wine and talking of everything under the sun as well as how much they loved each other. She passed the theatre where he had spoken to her in the foyer and also the splendid venues where they had seen Nijinsky dance and Sarah Bernhardt act, as well as countless other performances and concerts. When she reached the studio it was padlocked, its shutters closed over the windows and a deserted air about it.

She set the palms of both hands against the door, not to push but to rest there as she stood quietly, her head dipped and her eyes closed as if willing the clock to turn back. Her outward calm revealed nothing of the turmoil of emotion within her. She could almost hear Nikolai approaching the door to fling it wide and then scoop her into his arms.

Several people stared at her as they went past. She did not notice. When finally she turned away from the door she knew that she would never go there again.

When Juliette arrived back in Venice Marco was on the platform to meet her. She saw him before he saw her, for her compartment went past where he stood and he failed to get a glimpse of either her or Arianna. She alighted from the train with Michel in her arms, ready to see him turn with a smile to greet her, but he went hurrying along the platform away from her as he looked almost desperately for them. She had thought his frown was worried and she guessed that even though she had arranged to return on this day before leaving Venice, he was afraid she might have changed her mind at the last minute. Quickly she handed Michel to Arianna.

'Wait here.' Juliette began to walk swiftly in Marco's direction, making her way through the crowd of disembarked passengers streaming past her towards the waiting *vaporetto* and the gondolas. When she was near enough to see his anxious face again a wave of pity swept through her. She understood now that his reluctance to let her take Michel to Paris had been due to his secret dread that she might never return. Was he still so uncertain of her? Maybe her distressed reaction to seeing Nikolai again on the newsreel had unnerved him more than he had shown.

'Marco!' she called, breaking into a run and waving to attract his attention. Still he did not see her as he peered into carriages and became more frantic in his search. She increased her pace, bumping into people in her eagerness to put an end to his torment. How thankful she was that she had not allowed either Lucille or Denise to persuade her to stay longer as they had wanted!

It was not until Marco reached the end of the train and turned in despair that he saw her. Relief and joy flooded his face. He rushed forward to crush her to him.

'Thank God you're home!'

She could feel his hands were shaking as he cupped her face and kissed her mouth.

That night she dispensed with the simple method of birth control in which Dr Morosini had instructed her before she left the Tuscan villa. She had not intended to have another baby yet awhile, but the time had come to give Marco the ultimate assurance that nothing could take her from him.

CHAPTER NINETEEN

In the spring of 1914 Denise launched her all-lace collection in a natural figure line that was complemented by flower-hued silk coats and plain hats with wonderfully curved brims. It was an instant success and women flocked to buy. Marco had supplied Denise with all the Burano lace that had been used as well as the silks selected by Juliette for the coats. Denise still had Juliette's textile designs woven in England, including a recent set of new ones, but otherwise she took her fabrics from Marco, who dealt fairly with her and whose prices she found favourable.

Juliette had been unable to attend the launch of the collection, for she was in an advanced state of pregnancy. Denise sent her copies of *Le Figaro* and other Parisian newspapers with reports on the success of the collection, but there was much else too. As with the Venetian newspapers there was ominous reading in every edition. The European arms race was gathering momentum. In Russia ten thousand workers had gone on strike and there was fear of war between the United States and Mexico after fighting at Vera Cruz.

Marco came into the room when Juliette was folding one of the French newspapers that she had been reading. She gave him an abstracted smile from where she sat, still mulling over all the news she had studied.

230

'There is nothing like reading one's own national newspapers,' she remarked. 'The main news items are the same in every country, but one discovers snippets only reported at home. I suppose King George V's State visit to France shouldn't be classed as a snippet and I did find a few lines about it in a Venetian newspaper, but *Le Figaro* described in full the way all Paris turned out to greet the royal couple.' Her face was very serious. 'It demonstrated how closely France and Great Britain are allied against the threat of Germany's might.'

'I'd like to read through those newspapers too before they are thrown out. Were you pleased with the reports of the Maison Landelle spring collection?'

She rose to her feet. 'Yes, although it seemed a very frivolous topic in the midst of so much depressing news, but maybe that's one of the reasons for the collection's success. Women want to reassure themselves that by looking beautiful and elegant they can retain a note of sanity in the present mad state of the world that men have created.'

'Then let's hope that sanity spreads out like oil on troubled waters.'

'You're not very hopeful, are you?' she questioned gravely.

'My dear, I don't know what's going to happen any more than the next man.' He cupped her elbows, drawing her as close as was possible without causing pressure on her swollen figure, and looked down into her upturned face. 'But all the time no fool fires a hasty shot there's a chance of everything settling down again.'

'You mean that the slightest skirmish on any border could act like a spark to tinder?' She did not need a reply. 'It's what I've thought myself for some time. I've always kept abreast with the news, but at times like this it's not conducive to sleeping well at night.' Her eyes were troubled. 'I worry about you. If there's a war would Italy be drawn into it?'

'That's highly unlikely. The general mood throughout the country is that Italy should not get involved. You've nothing to worry about as far as this nation is concerned.'

'France might not be so fortunate,' she said soberly.

'We must hope for the best.' He chose to change the subject. 'The reason I came looking for you is that I've brought home those samples you wanted from the new consignment of oriental silks that arrived yesterday.'

231

'Oh, good!' With an effort she returned her thoughts to the new winter designs for Maison Landelle that she had been working on in her studio.

'I think you'll like those with the embroidery.'

'Where are they?' she asked.

'I took them up to the studio, expecting to find you there.'

'I was taking a break.' She smiled as she linked her fingers behind her head and stretched her back. 'I'm getting lazy.'

'No. I think you work too hard in your studio.' He never lost a chance these days to persuade her to give up her designing.

'I'm sitting down and no physical effort is involved.' She regretted her light-hearted remark. 'I'll go and look at those patterns.'

Leaving him, Juliette went up the stairs to her studio. Although on the surface Marco did all he could to help her she knew that he would have preferred her to concentrate entirely on domestic matters. He had changed during their marriage. The most likely cause was a reversion to his roots. She had seen that it had been difficult for him not to forbid her to work for Fortuny, but he was not a man to go back on any promise made and she had truly believed he would come around to accepting it, but his resentment had grown. He had probably never realized how he had shown it in various ways that would have been indiscernible to anyone else. It was that knowledge which had been as instrumental as anything else in her agreeing to design for Denise again. At least she did not have to go outside her own home any more to retain a close contact with fashion. Yet she could tell that Marco was beginning to be uneasy about that too. He had wished her well when she had gone to Paris with Lucille, but even though her being pregnant had made him happier she did not think he would ever want her to go there again without him.

The samples of the fabrics were lying on the studio table. Some were in the jewel-colours she required, the rest too pale, although there was a deep pearly-pink that could be used. She ran the fabrics through her fingers. She believed the winter collection she was completing was her best work to date. At least if war came her designs would keep the flag of fashion flying and that in itself would show Parisian defiance of any would-be aggressor.

In May of 1914 Juliette gave birth quickly and easily to a daughter. The baby became the apple of Marco's eye from the moment he first saw her, but that did not lessen in any way his love for Michel. He wanted the baby named after his late mother and so she was to be christened Sylvana as soon as she was a month old.

Marco knew himself to be a contented man at last. After a long period of unease he had Juliette firmly ensconced in their home with family commitments making impossible any future whim to work beyond its walls. When more babies came along there would be even less time for her designing and eventually that would come to an end. Loving Juliette as he did, he wondered how he could ever have made those rash promises at the villa about letting her keep an outlet in fashion, but then in his desperation to make her his wife he had not realized how possessive he was to become as time went by. It had been an unspoken bone of contention between them, she aware of his increasing disapproval and he of her exasperation that he should wish to rein her in.

But all that was over. From now on all would go well. He felt amiable towards Denise, who had at least secured a wedge between Juliette and her work at the Palazzo Orfei. It made him feel even more benevolent towards his sister-in-law to consider how disappointed she would be when eventually no more designs were forthcoming from Juliette.

'Let's ask Denise if she would like to be godmother to Sylvana,' he suggested to Juliette on her first morning down to breakfast after she had convalesced from her confinement. 'It should dissolve any last threads of estrangement between you two.'

Juliette was pleased. 'I'm so very glad you suggested it. I'll write to her today.'

When Denise received the invitation she saw it as an opportunity to play the bountiful aunt after all. Her hopes revived that in time to come one or other of the Romanelli children might be encouraged to take up a career with Maison Landelle. The first step had been coaxing Juliette back into the business; with that accomplished, even from a distance, it was only another small step to involving the children later on. Once again Denise could picture herself indoctrinating them with ideas as to the paths their futures should follow.

She had no idea what to take as a christening gift for her niece. She had given engraved napkin rings to infants in the past when the occasion had warranted it, but she wanted something special for

Juliette's child. Suddenly she knew what to do. Maison Landelle should become a private company. She would allot shares to both Sylvana and Michel as well as to Juliette. Marco could buy his way in, just as she had always planned a brother-in-law should do. She would make it a condition that shares could only be sold back into the family. Her lawyers would arrange everything. She was jubilant. Her net was cast!

When Denise arrived in Venice it did not take her long to see that Juliette's marriage appeared to be satisfactory. Had it not, she would have tried to persuade her to return to Paris, but clearly that would not be considered. She had a further setback when her offer of the shares was opposed by Marco.

'It is most kind and generous of you,' he said, 'but I should prefer you to withhold them until the children are twenty-one. If Juliette wishes to accept her shares I'll not stand in her way, but for myself I wouldn't consider any foreign investments at this time.'

'But that's absurd!' Denise exploded. 'My *haute couture* house is one of the most successful in Paris and has been ever since I started.'

Juliette intervened. 'Don't be upset, Denise, I beg you. Let's not fall out again. Marco doesn't want to hurt your feelings any more than I do. I'll take the shares if that will please you and thank you for them, but I agree with Marco that the children shouldn't receive such a gift as yet and also that he must do as he wishes.'

Denise struggled with her feelings. Had her plan been too transparent? At least Juliette was securely ensnared. For the time being she must be satisfied with that and when these rumours of war were over, perhaps Marco might reconsider her proposition. At all costs she must not antagonize him. 'I meant well,' she said.

The next day she bought a diamond pendant for Sylvana and a gold pocket watch for Michel, both to be kept until they were of an age to receive them.

Although Denise could have had every comfort at the Romanelli residence she chose to stay at the Grand Hôtel des Bains on the Lido, wanting to be away from the noise of family life. It was also the best place to show off her lace gowns from the latest Landelle collection since people of consequence were guests there too. Many of her clients had told her that they felt as graceful as swans when wearing these new gowns and she had the same sensation herself as the delicate lace drifted like a billowing mist and clung lightly to her arms and figure. She wore cinnamon lace to the christening, gratified to be a godmother and relieved that the other godmother, a Venetian friend of Juliette's, held the baby. Fortuny and Henriette were also present. Denise had been slightly disconcerted at the thought of meeting them, but Juliette had reassured her.

'Fortuny doesn't know how the Delphos robe came into my possession. All I ever said was that I found it.'

Denise was relieved. She wanted to visit the Palazzo Orfei and take a close look at all the gowns and fabrics on display there, but that would have been impossible if Juliette had given her away. Henriette, hearing of her wish from Juliette, invited her specially.

'I'll show you around,' she offered.

To Denise's disappointment she did not see where the magical pleating was done, although she saw almost everything else. Her jealousy of Fortuny's success flared anew. She thought it unfair that Maison Landelle had to keep finely tuned to every new trend on fashion's horizon, ever fearful of competitors stealing a march, while Fortuny kept to his own original prototype and all went well for him. She had learned that he had even registered a patent for it, considering it to be a revolutionary invention in dress. Yet she had reason to believe that in spite of the interest shown in his gowns and the articles about them in a few selective magazines, his output was extremely small in comparison with her own and that of her fellow Parisian couturiers. One thing was certain. He would never become a serious rival to any of them.

Shortly before Denise was due to leave Venice she returned the hospitality she had received at the Palazzo Orfei by inviting Fortuny and Henriette to dinner with Juliette and Marco at the Grand Hôtel des Bains. Everything was of the best and the evening convivial. After dinner they sat on the terrace in the warm starry night and drank coffee. Musicians played and the wavelets of the Adriatic lapped the shore only a short distance away. As they sat talking a Frenchman in his early fifties, who had been smoking a cigar while strolling the lawns after dinner, came back up the steps of the terrace. Sighting the group he paused with a smile of recognition. Henriette saw him first as he approached the table.

'I declare! Look, Mariano! Here's Jacques Vernet!' She turned in explanation to the others. 'He's an old friend from Paris. We haven't seen him for a long time.'

'Then let us invite him to join us,' Denise suggested graciously. She had seen the stranger, a tall grey-haired man, not handsome, but with a lean figure that set off his faultless evening attire that had the unmistakable cut of a Savile Row tailor. Such men invariably had wives who chose to dress equally well. She never lost the slightest chance to further business.

While the introductions were taking place, a waiter brought forward another wicker chair and Jacques sat down at the place made between Henriette and Denise. The new arrival was too well-mannered, as were those he knew already, to let the conversation dwell on personal news. Denise learned that he was the head of a large engineering company located in Normandy, but he had an office and apartment in Paris. There was no mention of a wife being with him at the hotel or elsewhere, but he most surely had a mistress and the Maison Landelle dressed the mistresses of some of the most distinguished men in Paris.

'You are visiting Venice, Madame la Baronne?' he asked.

'Yes, I came for my niece's christening,' Denise replied. 'It wasn't easy to leave my business, but I couldn't miss such an important family occasion.'

'Indeed not. So you are in business too.' He looked interested. 'May I inquire as to what that may be?'

It was easy after that. They got on well and although the conversation soon became general Jacques seemed very aware of Denise and several times he sought her opinion on some topic being discussed. When Marco suggested that they should have a flutter at the gaming tables as the night was still young, Denise managed to walk beside Henriette into the hotel.

'I haven't heard any mention of Monsieur Vernet's wife,' Denise remarked casually.

'Ah, that's because he's divorced. He married an American debutante in New York when he was on a university vacation and brought her back to France. The marriage lasted tempestuously for about ten years and then she went back home and divorced him there. Since then he has lived alone, but not through any lack of amorous liaisons with women who would gladly have married him.'

Denise smiled. A string of successive mistresses was even better than one, because once a rich man had opened an account at a particular fashion house he would always tell each of the women in

236

his life to get her clothes there. In many ways men were creatures of habit, especially when they grew older.

The gaming room where Denise and her party settled down to play was dramatically beautiful, for it was one that Fortuny had been commissioned to decorate and the walls were lined with his own rich red silk stencilled with Grecian designs in gold. Denise thought to herself that it was no wonder Fortuny pleased himself by keeping to a prototype for his gowns when so much of his income flowed in from such important orders, Marco having told her that art galleries and museums had awoken to the fact of how a Fortuny fabric could enhance and set off exhibits. Even churches had begun ordering large panels to set against stone walls and behind high altars. Three of the foremost theatres in Paris had stage curtains designed by him.

It turned out to be a lucky evening at the tables for Denise and Jacques, although the others lost. It created a kind of companionship between them.

'We must have brought each other luck,' Jacques joked. 'Shall we play the tables again tomorrow evening?'

'Yes!' Denise answered recklessly.

Jacques invited the others to join them, but Fortuny had another engagement and so did Marco. Neither Juliette nor Henriette cared to gamble on their own. Denise realized too late that she should have left her last two evenings free to spend with her sister, but it was too late to back out of her acceptance to Jacques now. Yet there was something she could do to be with Juliette.

'Bring Michel over on the *vaporetto* tomorrow and we'll spend the day on the sands. I have a tent on the hotel's private beach and we can bathe. I've been in the water every day.' Denise turned to Jacques. 'Perhaps you'll come and meet my nephew?'

'That would be a pleasure.'

Jacques did not come down to the beach until the afternoon. By then both sisters had been swimming and then taken a light salad lunch amid tall green plants in the cool of the hotel dining-room. Michel was sleeping in the shade of the tent, having tired himself out playing in the soft sand and toddling in and out of the water as he held his mother's hand. A beach assistant placed a deck-chair for Jacques next to Juliette and Denise. He sat down with a contented sigh.

'What a perfect day this is! Not too hot and a cooling breeze. I've spent the morning in the Frari Church and in the glorious Salute. A converting experience in every sense of the word.'

'Is this your first visit to Venice?' Denise asked.

'No, I've been several times over the years, but one always has to come back to gaze once again.'

'Do you always travel alone?'

He had a pleasing smile. 'No, but this time I felt like getting away on my own.' Then he saw a waiter from the hotel approaching with drinks on a tray. 'I ordered chilled lemonade for us before I came down on the beach.'

There was a fourth glass for Michel and Juliette explained he was sleeping in the tent. 'He'll be awake soon. I'll put the glass in the tent for later.'

'I know you don't remember,' Jacques said when she was seated in her deck-chair again, 'but we have met before.'

'Have we?' Juliette was puzzled. 'Where was that?'

'On New Year's Eve three years ago at the Russian Embassy Ball. You were with Count Karasvin.'

Juliette was taken aback. 'Yes,' she admitted cautiously. 'But how is it that I can't recall our meeting?'

'I was in a group when brief introductions took place. There's no reason why you should remember me since we didn't dance together or talk. But I intend a compliment when I tell you that you're not easily forgotten, Signora Romanelli.'

Although Denise had a jealous nature the interest of men in other women had never caused her the slightest concern since she had never harboured a romantic notion in her life, but she disliked sharing her guest's attention. 'Do you know Count Karasvin well?' she asked, knowing it was the one subject her sister would not want pursued.

'No, but I was acquainted with him through his aunt, the second wife of Prince Vadim. She was a Parisienne.'

'I met her at the same ball,' Denise replied coolly.

'You were there too, my dear lady.' He was apologetic. 'But our paths didn't cross or else I would have remembered, I assure you.'

'I forgive you,' she said, mollified. 'There were at least six hundred people present. Have you seen Count Karasvin since he left Paris?'

'I have indeed. Only a short while ago I happened to meet him in Vienna.'

'Was the Countess with him?'

'No. From what I heard there they go their own separate ways.'

'Dear me.' Denise cast a glance at Juliette out of the corner of her eye and saw that her sister had turned away, her elbows resting on the arms of the deck-chair and her clasped hands pressed against her mouth. With a rush of remorse Denise realized that maintaining the subject of Nikolai might well make Jacques notice the likeness of Michel to the Russian. That must not happen. She flapped a hand at her face. 'Do you know I think I'm feeling the heat after all. Would you escort me back to the hotel, Monsieur Vernet?'

'Of course.' He rose to his feet immediately and helped her up by the hand. Juliette had also risen in concern, but Denise spoke to her reassuringly.

'Stay here, Juliette. Don't disturb Michel. I'll see you both tomorrow.'

When Jacques had taken Denise to her suite he returned to the beach, but Juliette and her son had departed.

When Denise left Venice Jacques travelled with her all the way to Paris. He liked her astringent mind, her initiative in having created for herself a niche in the cut-throat business world and holding her own against fierce competition. Most of all she had not shown any of the amorousness towards him that he usually encountered in widows of her age and that in itself made him feel at ease in her company. In all he recognized someone as selfish as himself. He looked forward to seeing her again. In the meantime he had to visit his workshops, for he had turned entirely to producing armaments for the government. France was preparing fast for whatever was to come.

CHAPTER TWENTY

Everything was back to normal in the Romanelli household after Denise's departure. Once again Juliette's time was her own. She had many ideas in her mind for next year's spring collection, which she had talked over with Denise, but there was no need to set them down on paper as yet and she had plenty of time to spend with her baby and Michel. June was proving to be particularly hot and uncomfortable. Friends, who had gone on a visit abroad, had offered the loan of their villa on the river Brenta for the whole of the summer and Juliette would have gladly availed herself of the opportunity for the children's sake if Marco had not intervened.

'Wait until the beginning of August,' he said, 'and then I'll be able to be with you all the time.'

'But you could come on Fridays for the weekend,' she replied, thinking of how wonderfully cool it would be in the countryside compared with the city at this time of year and how beneficial it would be for Michel to play more freely and the baby to breathe sweet air. But Marco was adamant. He did not want to come home to a lonely house and an empty bed. So the sojourn was postponed until August.

There was still a while to wait when Marco, seated at the breakfast table, picked up his newspaper, which Lena always put ready by his plate, and stared in disbelief at the headlines.

'What a catastrophe!'

Juliette set down the coffee pot. 'Whatever's happened?' she asked anxiously.

'The Archduke Franz Ferdinand, heir to the Austrian-Hungarian throne, has been killed by a Serbian assassin in the Bosnian capital of Sarajevo! His wife is dead too! Now the fat's in the fire! The Balkans have long been a dangerous source of trouble.'

'What will happen?'

'It says here,' he said as he continued to scan the columns, 'that Austria intends to take severe measures against Serbia, no matter what the risk might be of provoking European complications.' Lowering the newspaper, he looked gravely across at her. 'If that means using troops I fear the worst, because Germany is Austria's ally and Russia will never stand by and see the Balkans over-run.' He saw that her face was stricken and he tried to give her some comfort. 'Whatever happens Italy will not be involved. At least we can be sure of that.'

But she was not thinking of Italy, beyond thankfulness for the safety it meant for her husband. If there was war she did not doubt that Nikolai would fight.

Daily the newspapers reported the deteriorating situation. To-wards the end of July Serbia had refused Austria's ultimatum and was mobilizing. On the day after Austria declared war on Serbia, Marco was working in his office when his secretary came in. He was extremely busy and glanced up impatiently. 'What is it, Signorina Massari?'

'A gentleman wishes to see you, signore.'

He continued writing, 'I told you I could not see anyone today who had not made an appointment. Inquire his name and ask him to return tomorrow.'

'I did, signore, because he was insistent. His name is Count Karasvin.'

Abruptly Marco's pen became still in his hand, but he did not immediately raise his head. 'What does he want?' he questioned coldly. 'Did he say?'

'Only that he wasn't here on business, but he was sure you would see him.'

241

Slowly Marco rested his pen in its tray and sat back in his chair. 'Show Count Karasvin in.'

As soon as the woman's back was turned Marco swiftly pulled open a drawer and put both his silver-framed photographs of Juliette into it. He had no idea what this interview would bring forth, but his one thought was to protect his wife from the past. He closed the drawer and stood up as his unwelcome visitor entered. Nikolai, casually dressed, smiled as he approached the desk.

'How are you, Marco?' he asked, extending a hand. 'It's good to see you again.'

Inwardly reluctant, Marco responded to the firm handshake. He thought Nikolai unchanged, the good looks heightened by a summer tan, the athletic build still broad at the shoulders and tapering down with no excess weight. Marco was conscious of the extra pounds he had put on around his waist in the last couple of years.

'This is a pleasant surprise. Sit down. I'm afraid I can only spare you a few minutes just now.' Deliberately Marco snapped open his gold pocket watch and glanced at it as he sat down in his swivel-chair again.

'I know. Your secretary told me.' Nikolai took the chair that had been indicated. 'I won't hold you up for long. You're looking well.'

'So are you. Is your wife with you?'

'No, Natasha is at home, spending the summer at her parents' country house.' Nikolai did not add that she spent almost more time with her stepmother than she had done before their marriage, wanting a constantly sympathetic ear for her woes, real and imaginary. 'I've been on my own for the past three months, first in Budapest and then in Vienna.'

'Why were you there? Were you on a diplomatic mission?'

'No. I was one of the many foreign observers keeping eyes and ears open as we mingled socially at various embassies and at the palace.'

'What is the state of Vienna at the moment?'

'Full of the flush of war-fever. Soldiers are being cheered everywhere. Patriotic ribbons decorate the chocolate tortes and the playing of waltzes has changed to military music. I saw the old Emperor Franz Josef shortly after the Archduke's funeral and he'd aged twenty years.'

'The assassination was a terrible outrage. Have you been to Paris

242

at all this year?' Marco was afraid that Nikolai might have heard there of his marriage to Juliette. Whatever happened he intended to prevent them seeing each other. He was also determined that Nikolai should have no knowledge of Michel's existence or else he could draw conclusions that would disrupt all their lives. Although basically an honest man Marco could lie convincingly in business matters when the need arose and he had no compunction in using that skill now. 'You used to spend most of your time there, didn't you?'

'Yes, but that ended when duties called me home and I married Natasha. I haven't been back to Paris since I returned once to look for Juliette, only to find she had virtually vanished. The Baronne de Landelle refused to reveal her whereabouts. What of you?'

Marco shook his head. 'A planned visit to Paris fell through. Since then a few business trips to Lyon have been the limit of my excursions into France.' He was relieved that Nikolai knew nothing of Juliette being his wife. There would be no demand made to see her, but the danger was not over yet. Already he had decided to send Juliette and the children off to the villa this very evening. Nikolai would never find them there. 'Are you taking a long vacation in Venice?'

Nikolai shrugged. 'Nothing like that. I'm probably making the shortest visit to Venice on record. Just twenty-four hours. I have to leave again tomorrow morning.'

Marco relaxed and breathed more easily while raising his eyebrows in disappointment. 'So soon? Are you here on a lightning eyes and ears mission?'

'Far from it. I made the journey for a personal reason. It's why I came straight to you as soon as I'd checked in at my hotel.' Nikolai put his hand to the inside pocket of his jacket and brought out the folded page of a magazine, which he spread out on the desk for Marco to see. 'Look at this fashion photograph.'

Marco had seen it before. It was one that Fortuny had taken of Juliette in her Delphos robe and it had appeared in several international magazines of quality some time ago. 'I believe it's Juliette.'

'It is she!'

'The caption is in French. Was the picture taken in Paris?' Marco read it through, although he knew the contents already. It did not give Juliette's name or that of the photographer, only the information that it was a Delphos robe by Fortuny of Venice and including a short write-up about his work as a designer. 'No, the caption doesn't say,' Marco added, answering his own question, and sat back in his chair. 'Why are you so interested? I remember hearing it was all over between you and Juliette.'

Nikolai shook his head. 'Not all the time she and I are both living.'

Marco felt savage at what he saw as an arrogant assumption and thought to himself it would be easy to amend that state by despatching this Russian with any weapon that came to hand. He realized he was playing with a pencil on his desk and was on the point of breaking it fiercely in two. Unobtrusively he let it roll away under his fingers. 'As I recall, that was not Juliette's opinion. We exchanged a few letters, but its a long time since I last heard. Then it was to tell me she was leaving France and going to live with elderly friends in New Orleans.'

Nikolai's eyes narrowed incredulously. 'Do you mean Lucille Garnier and her husband?'

'That's right. Do you have their address?' Marco began to fear that perhaps he should not have given a specific location.

'No. In any case a correspondence wasn't what I had in mind. I came here to find Juliette. I knew she would be wary of seeing me, but I was sure you'd know where she would be. I didn't expect to hear she was so far away.' Nikolai flung himself out of the chair and stood frowning, his fists thrust deep in the pockets of his jacket.

'I can see it's a bitter disappointment for you.' Marco rose to his feet too as if in sympathy. 'I haven't seen Juliette since I was in London when she was staying with her friend, Gabrielle. Whatever made you think you'd find her in Venice?'

'It seemed logical that Fortuny, who is a photographer as well as a painter and designer and everything else, should photograph his own gowns and where else but at his own fashion house.'

'I'm afraid you've had a wasted journey. Juliette isn't here.'

Nikolai nodded absently. 'Wherever she is I wish her well. All I'd hoped for was to see her once more.'

There came a tap at the door and the secretary came in. 'Signor Torrisi is waiting to see you, signore.'

Marco made a quick gesture of acknowledgement. 'Count Karasvin is just leaving.' He clapped a hand on Nikolai's shoulder while walking with him to the door. 'I don't like to hurry you off

244

like this, my friend.' Now that all had gone well Marco felt pity for him, for their friendship would have lasted if circumstances had been different. 'Let's have dinner together. We'll meet early at Danieli's and have a drink or two before we dine.'

'That would suit me well.' Nikolai seemed to have collected his thoughts. 'I happen to be staying there.'

'Good. I forgot to ask you if you'd ever been to Venice before?' Marco questioned. They had come to a standstill by the open door into the outer office.

'Once as a schoolboy.'

'Then you would have been dragged around all the sights. Take my advice and spend the next two or three hours in the Accademia. It's quiet there and some of the works of art are among the greatest in the world. Afterwards go back to your hotel and by that time I'll be with you.'

'That's a good suggestion. I'm in no mood to follow a guidebook around the city. Until later then.'

Marco closed his office door as Nikolai departed. The route that the Russian would take to the Accademia and then to the hotel was a safe one with no chance of his blundering into Juliette, who should be safely home after shopping since she was expecting Doña Cecilia and Maria Luisa to call on her later.

As Marco returned to his desk he saw that Nikolai had left the magazine page lying there. He crumpled it up fiercely and hurled it into his wastepaper basket. It had been a mistake to let Juliette pose for those fashion photographs in the first place! There was no doubt about it, he had been far too tolerant in the past. More like a lovesick schoolboy than a husband with his rights.

He opened the drawer and took out the photographs again. The larger was a recent replacement of Juliette and Michel by one of her with both children. His eyes softened. He would still do anything in his power for her except ever to let her slip again from her rightful domestic niche or allow her a meeting with a former lover. She was his alone now, possessed by him in every way, and he was increasingly aware of murder in his heart when other men paid her too much attention.

Carefully he set both photographs back on his desk again at the angles he liked best. Then he sat down and made a telephone call before he pressed his desk bell for his next appointment to begin.

*　　*　　*

Juliette had been playing with Michel under a tree's shade in the walled garden when Arianna brought her the telephone message from Marco. It was unusual for him not to know well ahead when he would be entertaining a business associate, but she supposed that something important had to be discussed unexpectedly. He had said more than once that fine wine and good food could often mellow a hard bargain being driven against him.

Now Arianna had taken Michel upstairs for his nap in the nursery where Sylvana lay sleeping in her cot. Before changing out of her morning skirt and blouse Juliette decided to return a book that Henriette had lent her and which she had enjoyed reading. Although it was such a short distance to the Palazzo Orfei Juliette put on a straw hat, for the July sun during the siesta hour was fierce. Fortuny's would be closed at this time, but she would go in by the courtyard entrance.

Juliette crossed the sun-baked flats of the Campo San Beneto and went past the grand entrance to the Palazzo Orfei to go down the narrow *calle* at the side of the vast building. She reached the ancient door set in a Gothic arch and entered the enclosed courtyard where blossoming plants ranged the old walls and flanked the lower flight of the great stone staircase. Juliette went quickly up to the loggia on the first floor where she opened the door set with glass that led to the salon-studio.

'Henriette!' she called cheerily, taking off her straw hat and dropping it on to a leather-seated chair.

Henriette came into sight from behind some of the lush drapery. 'Oh! You're here,' she said with some confusion.

'This book was a good read—' Juliette's voice trailed away. Coming indoors from the brilliant sunshine she had not noticed immediately that her friend looked strained and uneasy. Then with her whole being she knew the reason. 'Nikolai is here!' she breathed, her heart beginning to pound.

'He arrived about ten minutes ago.' Henriette spoke in a lowered voice. 'He had been to see Marco, who pretended ignorance of your whereabouts, but Nikolai Karasvin isn't a man to give up easily when he's come so far to find you.'

'Did you—?' Juliette could barely voice the question.

'Don't worry. I told him nothing, except that I knew where you

246

lived. When I wouldn't give him your address he insisted that I telephone you. I was on my way to do that and ask if you were prepared to see him. You've still time to leave. These draperies muffle sound and it was only because I was near that I heard you. Even if he heard you speak he wouldn't have recognized your voice.'

Juliette shook her head, curiously in control of herself. 'He knows I'm here,' she stated simply. 'He didn't need to hear me. He's waiting.'

Automatically she put the book she held into Henriette's hand and went past to pause in the middle of the shining floor looking ahead to the studio end of the long room. Nikolai stood facing her across the distance between them, his back to the diffused brilliance pouring through the many tiny panes of the great window behind him.

'I've found you, Juliette.' He spoke without triumph, but relief throbbed in his voice.

She remained very still, remembering how once they had always rushed into each other's arms. Time and all that had happened since their parting had put restraint on them as if they had not known and shared the passion and the madness of an all-consuming love.

'You shouldn't have come here,' she stated levelly. The closing of a door told her that Henriette had left them on their own.

'I had to see you once more.' He did not move other than to raise his hands and drop them again in a gesture of reconciliation.

'What made you look for me in Venice?' She began to take slow steps towards him, her face expressionless as she kept herself rigidly in check.

'Through the photograph of you in the Delphos robe that I happened to see in a magazine.'

'Was that in St Petersburg?'

'No. In Vienna. It happened by chance. A woman I'd never seen before dropped an armful of magazines she was carrying onto the floor of the French Embassy as I was going through the entrance hall. I picked them up for her. One had fallen open at the page of your photograph. When I stood staring at it, saying I knew you, the woman told me to take it. It was my first clue to your whereabouts. I'd say that such a happening showed that we were meant to meet again.'

She did not answer him. She had slowed down to a standstill,

247

leaving a few feet between them. The sun's glow fell full upon her and the fly-away strands of her hair, which she had dishevelled slightly when pulling off her hat, glinted bronze and gold. 'Henriette told me you've spoken to Marco.'

'He was determined that you and I shouldn't meet. I guessed that you had warned him, as you had done Henriette Negrin, that I was not to be told where you were if ever I came looking for you.'

'I didn't have to do that. They've both known all along that everything between us ended in Paris.'

'Don't say that to *me*!' he erupted with sudden vehemence. 'We'll always belong to each other!'

'You seem to have forgotten that you're married to Natasha,' she countered coldly.

'The marriage is as empty as I told you it would be!' he exclaimed. 'God knows I did what I could to make it work, but even if I hadn't loved you it would have been no better.'

'But you made your choice.' Juliette heard her own words expressed as harshly as if by a stranger. It was not out of revenge, but to help them both survive this meeting and carry on with their separate lives. His face was agonized. It was the same expression he'd had on the day he had run after the speeding motorcar that carried her away. As before she wondered that her heart didn't stop beating with the pain it was enduring.

'Why did you get rid of our child?' he burst out, his voice torn, 'I'd have looked after you both. You would have wanted for nothing!'

'You'll have other children.'

'That chance has gone. There'll be no heir for me. The doctors say that Natasha is barren. The child, boy or girl, who would have been yours and mine, would have had everything that I could give. I wouldn't have made demands on you if you had wished to go on without me as you have done. I would have respected that.'

'You say that now!' she cried out. 'But you wouldn't have said it then.'

'You're right,' he admitted. 'I've become wiser than I was. Less sure of always getting what I want. Now I would have loved you and the child from a distance if only that could be.'

She almost broke down. She was thinking of his son only a matter of minutes away, perhaps even now opening those grey Karasvin eyes, an endearing child who always awoke with a smile. Surely she would never do anything more cruel in her life than deny this man the knowledge of the son who would have meant so much to him. But she dared not tell him. She had to think of what it would mean, for he would want to see Michel at least once, and Marco would never forgive her. It would ruin the stable contented home life that she had wanted for the boy and now for her daughter too.

'You and I have both had to adjust to new paths. We have to follow them without thinking any more about what might have been.' Her throat was choked, her voice tremulous. 'All the decisions I made at the time were for the best.'

He thought her distress came from remembering what it had meant to have an abortion. He moved nearer and could have taken hold of her, but still he kept his hands at his side. Her lids were lowered as she struggled to overcome the wave of love and compassion for him that threatened to engulf her.

'Look at me,' he urged gently.

She was afraid he might read all the secrets in her eyes. The time had come to use the only defence she had against him. Her lashes glittered with tears as he repeated his request. Finally she did as he asked. 'I'm Marco's wife, Nikolai.'

He compressed his lips ruefully, showing no surprise. 'That's what I began to suspect when I was in his office. Then his clumsy attempt to control my movements in Venice virtually confirmed my suspicions. I'm not attempting to snatch you away from him. As I said, I needed to see you again to say farewell. After all, you gave me no chance in Paris. I had to know that all was well with you.'

'Does it mean so much to you?' It disturbed her that he was so calm, so resigned.

'I'd have journeyed anywhere for the chance.'

Then she knew why. 'You're certain that Russia is going to war!'

He gave a deep nod. 'That's why I'm leaving for home at once. I've been recalled. The Tsar has ordered mobilization. I foresee a long struggle ahead.'

'But any fighting will be settled quickly,' she protested. 'So many outbreaks of hostility between various nations over past years have been of short duration.'

'Those were little more than skirmishes. Everything will be different this time.'

'You speak as if it were inevitable.' She tried a lighter note.

249

'Remember I used to tease you about Russian gloom sometimes.'

He caught both her hands in his, his eyes searching hers. 'I remember everything about you. Your laughter, the hours we spent together, your loving body—'

'Don't!' She snatched her hands away, moving swiftly to stand with her back to him, clutching a handful of the drapery, her head bowed. He followed and waited to give her time to recover.

'Try not to be angry as you were that last time in Paris,' he asked quietly. 'Not now. Not today.'

She swallowed hard. 'We were talking about the possible imminence of war,' she managed to say, wanting their conversation to resume on a level with which she could cope. 'Russia has nothing to fear. No nation would attack her.'

'Napoleon did,' he remarked drily.

'But that was over a hundred years ago!' She swung round to face him.

'Lessons are never learned. Now it's Germany that Russia has to fear. My concern is that as a nation we have manpower in abundance, but we have not kept pace in the arms race.'

'You'll be in the army?'

'I shall enlist as soon as I'm home.'

Now everything was clear to her. He had wanted to see her once more in this life because he did not expect to survive the war when it blasted forth. Any doubts in her mind about the conflict occurring had been banished by his serious words. She realized that both of them had always believed at the back of their minds that at some time in the future their paths would most surely cross again. Maybe he had never thrust down the possibility as she had done and when he had seen it slipping away for ever he had come in search of her.

'I'll pray for your safe-keeping, Nikolai.' She could not take her eyes from his.

'I'm thankful I need not be anxious about your well-being. You'll be safe here. Even Napoleon never turned his cannons on Venice.' A smile touched the corners of his mouth.

Somehow she managed a smile too. For a few moments longer they gazed at each other. Then all her love for him, which she had suppressed determinedly since leaving Tuscany, defeated her. When he reached out his arms she fell into them. Her mouth received his in a home-coming and their kissing was wild and passionate, both

250

unable to assuage the long hunger for each other that had tormented him and haunted her.

When Henriette returned to the salon-studio she saw that the glass door stood open and she went through to the balustrade of the loggia. Looking down into the courtyard, she saw that Nikolai and Juliette were saying goodbye. He was holding her in his embrace, lovingly and protectively as if nothing could ever come between them. Even as Henriette would have turned away, allowing them their last moments of privacy, they kissed tenderly and drew apart. He opened the door into the *calle*, turned once more to look at Juliette and then went out. Juliette stayed where she was, listening no doubt to the fading echoes of his departing footsteps. Then she flung herself against the door, her cheek pressed to it and stood as though held by torturing chains.

Henriette's first inclination was to hasten down to her, but she checked herself in time. There was nothing she could say or do that would ease anything for Juliette. For the moment the past had been brought hurtling back with all its turmoil of love and pain and Juliette must take her own time to re-gather her courage and will to carry on with the next minute, the next hour, the next day and then the rest of her life.

Re-entering the salon-studio, Henriette paced slowly up and down as she waited. Eventually Juliette came in again. She was ashen, but dry-eyed. Henriette went at once to put a comforting arm about her shoulders.

'Would you like a cup of coffee? Or tea perhaps?' she asked solicitiously.

'Nothing, thank you. It's time I went home.' Juliette picked up her hat, but did not put it on. Instead she stood turning it by its brim. 'Nikolai has gone back to his hotel to check out. He was to have had dinner with Marco, but he'll leave a message that he couldn't stay after all. It's best for Marco if he never knows that Nikolai found me in spite of all his efforts. It would only worry and distress him.'

'I agree.'

'Nikolai and I will never meet again. By now he should be on the *vaporetto* taking him to the railway station.' Juliette looked gratefully at Henriette. 'I was so glad that Nikolai and I were able to meet here in this beautiful room away from all other aspects of our lives,

251

especially since it was our shared interest in Fortuny's achievements and my Delphos robe that first brought us together.'

'I'm glad for you too.' Henriette threaded her arm through Juliette's to lead her downstairs to the main entrance, not wanting her to retrace her steps so soon by way of the courtyard.

Juliette had almost crossed the Campo San Beneto when she stopped, looking towards the *calle* that ran on the opposite side of the Palazzo Orfei. It led to a bridge and then through buildings to a gondola jetty on the Grand Canal. She would be able to see Nikolai from there when he went past on the *vaporetto*. Just one more brief glimpse, one last loving sighting before he was lost to her for ever.

But she wouldn't go alone! Nikolai knew nothing about Michel, but that was no reason why her son should not see his father once in his life. Michel could not understand and would never remember the occasion in later years, but she would know and be thankful she had given him that single moment.

Breaking into a run, she covered the last stretch of ground and rushed into her house. 'Michel!' she called out from the hallway, 'Where are you?'

She ran upstairs to the nursery. Sylvana was sound asleep in her cot, but Michel was not lying on his bed and the covers had been straightened. Thinking she would find him playing in the walled garden, she descended the stairs with equal speed. Before she was down the final flight Arianna came out into the hall and looked up at her.

'Signora—'

'Where's Michel!'

'In the salon, signora. Doña Cecilia has brought him a new toy. They've been waiting for you for almost an hour.'

Juliette paused in dismay. 'I had forgotten completely that they were coming!' Too late she recalled that she had intended to be no more than ten minutes away from the house when she went to return the book. 'Has Lena served them refreshment?'

'Yes, signora.'

Realizing that she was still carrying her hat, Juliette threw it aside as she crossed the hall and smoothed both hands over her hair. Michel came running to her as she entered the room.

'Look, Mama!' He held up a wooden monkey on a stick, laughing as he made it turn somersaults again.

She swept him up in her arms. 'What a lucky boy you are!' Then she faced her guests. 'Please forgive me for not being here to receive you. It was unavoidable.'

Doña Cecilia and Maria Luisa sat side by side on one of the brocaded sofas. A silver tray with dainty refreshments, served in the best crystal and on the finest porcelain, were untouched.

'I'm sure it must have been,' Doña Cecilia granted graciously, even though she was considerably put out at being kept waiting. Nobody ever kept *her* waiting! She was also surprised by her hostess's appearance. Juliette's hair was hanging in untidy tendrils and instead of an afternoon gown suitable for the occasion she wore a striped cotton skirt and a plain blouse.

'Michel has been entertaining us,' Maria Luisa said reassuringly. 'We waited for you to come before taking any refreshment.'

'I'm afraid I have to go out again,' Juliette burst out. 'Do pardon me once more! I'll try not to be long.' She darted out of the room. There was not much time left. Michel had dropped his new toy and he uttered a wail. Arianna rushed to pick it up, but she was too late to hand it to him, for his mother was fleeing hatless with him from the house. Bewildered, Arianna turned to glance back into the salon. Doña Cecilia and her daughter were looking aghast at each other over this further breach of good manners by their hostess.

Juliette sped with the sobbing child out of the square and into the long *calle* by the Palazzo. 'It's all right, Michel,' she exclaimed as she ran. 'The little monkey will be waiting for you when we get home again. We're going to watch the boats for a short while.'

He liked boats. His sobs eased away and he clung to his mother with his arms around her neck as they crossed the bridge and rushed onwards. When they reached the narrow wooden jetty she sat him on the top side rail and held him protectively while she regained her breath.

She was not too late. The *vaporetto* was still a little distance away. Michel, who had his back to it, was watching the gondolas go by. Shading her eyes with one hand, Juliette tried to scan the passengers on board, but the little steam-boat was not near enough as yet for her to discern Nikolai. If he should be standing midships on the starboard side the saloon would be between them, but at least she and Michel would be near him for this last time. She did not expect or want him to spot her and Michel, but that was easily avoided, for

253

they were both in deep shadow. All the brilliance was in the sun diamonds dazzling on the water and there was so much to distract Nikolai's gaze with the glorious palazzos on either side and all the activity of the gondolas and barges plying the Grand Canal.

Now she could see him. He was on the fore deck, his light-coloured suit and black curly hair marking him out. Fortunately, he was leaning on the starboard rails and looking away from her and Michel, which made it safe for her to move farther up the jetty for a closer view. She lifted Michel up and sat him on her hip.

'Big boat!' he cried out, pointing to the *vaporetto*. He liked these vessels with a funnel and smoke better than all the others and he bounced excitedly.

Then, when the *vaporetto* was almost level, Nikolai stirred from where he stood and strolled across to look up at the grand façades of the palazzos soaring up from where she stood with Michel. She held her breath, certain that if she made any quick move to get away he would see her. Yet even as she eased a step backwards he gripped the top rail as he stared across at her and the young child she held in her arms. She no longer attempted to hold out against what was clearly meant to be and lifted Michel higher.

'Wave to the man with the black hair like yours, Michel.'

Eagerly the boy obeyed her and chuckled happily when there was an immediate response. Nikolai's wave was slow and questioning at first, but became exuberant when Juliette's nod and her wave confirmed that this was their son whom she held in her arms. He cupped both hands about his mouth. 'What's his name?'

'Michel!' she called back, knowing he would remember that it was her father's name. 'He's two years old in September.'

Nikolai threw back his head in exhilaration, his whole reaction one of rejoicing that Juliette had borne his child after all. By now the *vaporetto* was going swiftly past and she saw him break away from the rails to thrust his way through the other passengers to reach the stern. There he stood waving again to her until they could see each other no longer.

'Goodbye, my love,' she whispered, the tears flowing down her cheeks.

Michel peered anxiously into her face, his lower lips pouting and becoming tremulous at her grief. 'Don't cry, Mama,' he begged, almost echoing the very words his father had spoken earlier, and tried clumsily to wipe her cheeks dry with his palms. He had never seen her cry before and he was alarmed.

She hugged him tightly for a few moments and then wiped her eyes with the back of one hand as she conjured a reassuring smile for him. 'There! Everything is better now. Did you enjoy waving?'

'Yes.' His smile had returned with the cessation of her tears. As she carried him off the jetty he twisted in her arms to wave generally at the water traffic. 'Michel come again soon. Mama too.'

'We'll do that,' she promised. In spite of knowing she still had guests waiting for her it was impossible to hurry homewards. Somehow she was forced to take her time. Her thoughts were too full of all that had taken place in a short while. Apart from the unexpected reunion with Nikolai she had given him and his son sight of each other. It was as if the whole event had been inevitable and she was glad. Surely it was some comfort for any man about to face death in battle when he knew he had a son, especially by the woman he loved.

She put Michel down on his feet and he trotted along at her side, talking of the boats. His vocabulary was advanced for his age, but frequently French words were mixed with Italian, because she wanted him to grow up bi-lingual and always spoke French to him when they were on their own. She picked him up again when they were nearer the house, smiling at something he said, and kissed his cheek. As they entered Arianna appeared at the top of the stairs, thankful to see her home again after her extraordinary flight.

'Are you all right, signora?' she asked with concern.

'Yes, of course.' Juliette saw that the monkey on a stick was lying on a side-table and picked it up to hand to Michel. 'Wait for me and then we'll go in to our visitors.'

She took a quick look in the mirror. There was no time to comb her hair. She tucked up a few tendrils and then smoothed her hands over her hair once again. Taking Michel by the hand, she opened the door of the salon and went in. But her guests had gone and the tray had been removed. Behind her the door closed and she turned to see that Marco was standing by it. Michel ran to him.

'See the monkey, Papa!'

Marco smiled down at him. 'That's fun, but go and play with it. I want to talk to Mama.' As the child sat down on the floor Marco crossed to Juliette and looked at her with hard eyes. 'Where on earth were you all the afternoon? I arrived home early after my dinner engagement was cancelled and found Doña Cecilia and Maria Luisa just leaving. They were most displeased and offended. I know myself that you invited them today and then you weren't here to receive them!'

'I know. It is inexcusable for a hostess to forget she was expecting guests, but that's what happened. I'll call on them tomorrow and apologize.' Juliette raised a restless hand and tucked back nervously another wisp of her hair.

'But there must be a reason why the visit went out of your head,' he persisted.

'I returned a book to Henriette and forgot the time and everything else.'

'Doña Cecilia told me that when you did appear you dashed out again, taking Michel with you.'

'Yes. I took Michel to see the boats.'

'The boats?' Marco exclaimed incredulously. 'When guests sat here in this room!'

On the floor Michel looked up happily. 'Michel wave to boats. Mama wave. Mama cry. Big tears.'

Marco gave Juliette a long, dark look. Then he went to the child and picked him up. 'I want you to go upstairs to Arianna.' Opening the door, he put Michel down and watched him go across to the stairs and start climbing. Then he closed the door again and faced Juliette across the room. 'Tell me whom you saw at Fortuny's apart from Henriette.'

'Nikolai Karasvin.' She sat down sideways on a chair, all strength seemingly gone from her legs, and held on to the back of it. 'I'll not lie to you as you did to him.'

Marco's whole face congested with rage and he clenched his fists as he strode across to stand over her. 'How dare you see him again! What I said to Karasvin was to protect you. I didn't want you upset. Or persuaded to leave me!'

'Have you so little faith in my promise to be with you always?'

'But I knew he'd come to try to take you from me! How could I be sure of anything when he spoke as if you were bound to him for ever?'

She leaned her brow wearily on her hand. 'The past can't be changed, but the future belongs to you and me. I thought when

256

Sylvana was born that you'd finally trust me, because I believed you knew me well enough to know that I'd never do anything to cause my children any unhappiness, least of all would I desert them.'

'But you could have taken Michel from me at any time!'

Her anger flared and she sprang to her feet 'Never! He has your name! I won't listen any more to your jealous tirade.' She would have swung away, but he grabbed her by the wrists.

'You took Michel from the house today! To see the boats! Or was it for both of you to join Karasvin on the *vaporetto* to the railway station? You meant to go away with him!'

'No!' She screwed her body away from him, but could not release herself from his painful grip.

'Why did you weep then? Were you too late? Had he already left Venice? Did you miss your chance?'

'No! No! No!' She struggled in vain to get free. 'I thought Michel had a right to see his natural father just once in his life, even though it was from a distance.'

'Did Karasvin see him?'

'Yes!'

He hit her then with such force that she reeled back, her eyes wide with pain, and fell, hitting her head on the corner of an ebony-inlaid table as she went down to lie sprawled untidily on the floor. Stepping back, his anger unabated, he waited for her eyes to open. He was ready to threaten that he would throw her out, toss her to her Russian, never allow her to see the children again and many other wild and empty utterances that sprang from his own unendurable jealousy that seemed to be driving him to madness.

'Get up!' he roared

But she did not move. Bending over her, he saw to his horror that there was blood on her hair. Instantly he was on one knee beside her, full of remorse, and raised her gently to a sitting position, supporting her neck with his arm.

'My darling! Dear God, what have I done!'

Gathering her up in his arms, he hastened with her to the door. Levering the handle with difficulty, he managed to get it open and rushed with her into the hall. He shouted out, his voice echoing. 'Lena! Arianna! Telephone the doctor. Your mistress has had an accident!'

He heard the women scurry as he swept up the stairs and carried

257

Juliette into their room where he laid her on the bed. Pulling open a drawer he found a stack of his starched handkerchieves and made a pad for her gashed head. Then he sat on the edge of the bed, holding her limp hand. He had never felt more helpless or more ashamed in his whole life.

Although the doctor lived nearby in the next square it seemed hours to Marco before he arrived.

CHAPTER TWENTY-ONE

'Will my wife recover soon, doctor?' Marco asked agitatedly as he and the doctor went downstairs. Juliette had taken four hours to recover consciousness and a nurse had come to take care of her.

'Let us go into the salon where we can talk, signore,' the doctor replied.

Marco led the way. He was still in shock from what he had done. 'Would you like a brandy?'

He felt desperately in need of one himself and to his relief the doctor, although declining, told him to go ahead. As he poured he shot a glance towards the place where Juliette had fallen and was relieved to see that the blood had been wiped away.

'I never interfere in domestic matters between husband and wife,' the doctor began, 'but the swelling on the right side of Signora Romanelli's face could only have been caused by a hard blow and her cheek was cut by a ring. She's going to have dark discoloration and probably a swollen eye.'

Marco groaned and took a gulp of brandy. 'I've never struck her before. I don't know what possessed me.'

'Temper is the most usual cause,' the doctor commented pithily. 'The speed of her recovery depends on your patience and understanding. Forget whatever caused the dispute. She must be kept quiet for a few days and not upset over anything.'

When the doctor had gone Marco telephoned a florist and ordered all the red roses in the shop to be delivered. When they came he took the blooms up to Juliette, who whispered they were lovely and closed her eyes again.

By the next day her room had become a bower of flowers as friends heard she had had an accident. She asked to see the children. The baby was put in her arms for ten minutes and Michel was intrigued by the bandage around her head. He bawled with rage when Arianna took him away again and escaped from her in the nursery to come running back to bang his hands for entry on his mother's closed door. The sounds pierced Juliette's aching head and his distress upset her. She feared he would not be let in at all and asked that he be brought to take his siesta nap on the bed beside her on the morrow. She was allowed no visitors and apart from the doctor Marco was the next one to see her when he came home from the office. She had been sleeping when he left in the morning and he had telephoned four times during the day to inquire about her.

He sat down in the bedside chair that the nurse had vacated for him, leaving him alone with his wife. It was no more than twenty-four hours since Juliette had been injured and he was still wretched with remorse and another worry that had been troubling him since that time.

'Are you feeling better?' he asked, taking her hand that was lying on the coverlet and enclosing it in his own.

'Yes,' she whispered with difficulty, for the swollen state of the right side of her face tugged at her mouth. The curtains were closed to spare her eyes from the light. In the gloom she could see he looked dejected and anxious, but as yet she did not feel very forgiving. 'I'll soon be up and about again.'

'Yes, indeed,' he said with the forced cheerfulness frequently used at sickbeds. Then he shook his head despairingly, engulfed by a rush of emotion, his eyes brimming. 'I might have killed you!'

'I'm not so easily dispatched. I can't regret what I did, but you had no cause to hit me. It must never happen again.' Her eyes warned him.

'I lost my reason.'

'I know that and I understand, but nothing will be as you suppose.

260

Nikolai will never make any claim to Michel. I'd been going to tell you that in the salon. If Nikolai survives this threatened war, as I pray he will, he'll never come back into our lives.'

He narrowed his eyes in disbelief. 'But he *saw* Michel! You said that! Didn't he realize?'

'Yes, he did, but he also accepts that his path and mine have taken different routes for ever. He and I said our final goodbyes. It's enough for him to know that I am safe and that he has a son.'

Marco knew that he should ask no more questions and let her rest, but there was something else churning and tormenting his mind and he could no longer hold back from seeking an answer. 'Were you and Karasvin alone at all during the time you were at the Palazzo?'

She closed her eyes wearily. Was she going to have to contend with that doubt preying on his mind? 'Henriette was there when I arrived, but she went out to give us the chance to talk on our own.'

'Where were you?'

'In the salon-studio.' She knew he would be thinking of the sheltering drapery and the cushioned couches. 'I'd gone in by the loggia door.'

'How long were you on your own with Karasvin?' He knew he was firing questions like a prosecuting counsel, but as on the previous day he was being driven by jealousy he was unable to control.

She opened her eyes again and looked directly at him from where she lay on the lace-trimmed pillows. 'I lost count of time. That's why I didn't remember that visitors were coming here. Why don't you ask me outright if I was unfaithful?'

He had the grace to look discomfited. She was so weak that her whispered query had been almost inaudible. 'We'll talk another time when you're stronger.'

'No. Let's settle this matter now.' She forced herself up into a sitting position, almost fainting from the effort. 'What you fear didn't happen. I'm *your* wife. Nothing has changed between you and me. Neither is Michel any less your son.'

She collapsed back on her pillows, putting a forearm across her eyes as if to shut herself away from all further turmoil. Marco sprang up in concern and leaned over her solicitously.

'I believe you. I just wanted your reassurance. Any husband would have demanded the same.' He drew her arm down and kissed her closed eyelids. 'I must let you rest now.'

When he had gone from the room Juliette opened her eyes sadly. She had told him the truth, but would he ever be able to clear his mind of suspicion? It was like seeing a thread-like crack appear in the framework of her marriage. She would do everything in her power to mend it, for no matter what would be for ever between Nikolai and herself, the caring feelings she had for Marco were not changed.

Juliette came downstairs for the first time at mid-morning on the August day when the newspaper headlines proclaimed Italy's intention to remain neutral. It also announced that Germany had declared war on Imperial Russia and the first exchange of fire had taken place. She thought with compassionate understanding of all the women on both sides, comprehending their feelings through her own farewell to Nikolai.

The telephone rang and she went to answer it. As she had expected, it was Marco wanting to know if she was not too tired through being dressed and downstairs. She reassured him and it was his insistence that she should lie down again on the sofa and rest that prevented further conversation beyond his comment that the news was bad, but at least Italy was keeping out of the conflict.

She returned to the sofa. There was a smaller dressing on her injury since the stitches had been removed the previous day and she had covered it by swathing a soft chiffon scarf about her head, knotting it at the side and letting the ends waft. Her face was no longer swollen, but some discoloration remained. A covering of tinted face powder helped to disguise it a little. Henriette was coming to see her later, but earlier in the afternoon she was expecting the formidable lady who had been neglected on her last visit. Juliette was not looking forward to the meeting, but there had been a written request.

When Doña Cecilia arrived she cut short Juliette's apology, showing the warmer side of her nature that was not always obvious. 'Say no more about it, Juliette. When I thought about it afterwards I remembered that young mothers who have recently given birth often behave unlike themselves and, after all, Sylvana was only a few weeks old at the time. It's no wonder you ended the day with an accident. You slipped, I was told, and hit your head. That's why I advised Maria Luisa to wait until another day to see you. One visitor at a time is enough at first.'

'Perhaps your daughter could come tomorrow?' Juliette did not want Maria Luisa to feel abandoned by her for a second time.

'Very well. That will please her.' Doña Cecilia smiled.

The breach was healed. Juliette hoped it was a sign that at least in her daily life everything was getting back to normal. Marco could not have been more at ease in her company since their talk in the sickroom and she began to wonder if her original misgivings were unfounded after all.

He showed consideration for her the following day when he came to tell her some bad news before he went to the office. She had finished her breakfast in bed, a luxurious indulgence she hoped to dispense with as soon as the doctor permitted, and was in a négligé about to have the bath that was being run for her.

'There are headlines in the morning paper that will be particularly distressing to you,' he said gravely. 'I want you to be prepared.'

She took a few steps towards him, her cheeks hollowing. 'Is it what I have feared?'

He nodded regretfully. 'Germany has declared war on France.'

'My dear country!' she whispered in distress.

She appreciated his having told her and also for taking her into his arms and giving her the comfort of an embrace.

Inevitably the Kaiser, ignoring Great Britain's warning that it would protect Belgium's neutrality and the French coast, sent his troops thundering onto Belgian soil in the first move to invading France. Great Britain's declaration of war followed. Austria did the same towards Russia and Serbia towards Germany. It was as if a terrible madness had been released.

Foreigners had been flocking out of Venice like migrant birds ever since July. Now any ship that put into Venice was beseiged by those of the same nationality wanting to get away to their homeland. Hotels became empty of guests, waiters stood idle in restaurants, souvenirs were unsold and gondoliers saw the greater part of their livelihood fade away. Even those Venetians who had resented the annual flood of overseas visitors from spring to autumn, making a museum and honeymoon venue of their city, would never have wished an exodus to come about through such a cause. The majority of foreigners remaining were those who had transplanted themselves to Venice years ago and had no wish to move under any circumstances. Fortuny was among them. Although he took an immense pride in being a Spaniard and in his Spanish heritage, his loyalty rooted in the land of his birth, he was forty-three and above the age for active service even if Spain had not resolved to stay neutral, and there was no call for him to return.

'His devotion to Venice,' Henriette remarked to Juliette, 'will only end when he draws his last breath here.'

When Juliette was able to go out again she went at the first opportunity to the Church of the Scalzi. By now fighting was taking place on several war fronts, and there had been heavy casualties on all sides. Under Tiepolo's glorious frescoes she prayed again for the safety of Nikolai and the young Frenchmen known to her who would undoubtedly be engaged in the fighting. With the thought in her mind of recent German and Austrian threats against Italy for having failed to give them armed support, she prayed also for a swift return to peace and a better understanding between nations.

After sitting for a while in the tranquillity of the church, Juliette emerged into the sunshine again. She had arranged to meet three women friends, Angelina, Isabella and Elena, at Quadri's in St Mark's Square. In normal times it was difficult to get a table in the height of the season, visitors occupying every seat as they enjoyed the vista of the Basilica gleaming with its gold and jewel colours and all the comings and goings amid the encompassing colonades. Yet today her friends had had a choice of tables and there were plenty to spare as they waved upon seeing her approach, pigeons fluttering up out of her way.

'What is it to be?' Isabella asked after greetings had been exchanged. 'An ice perhaps, or coffee?' She was one of the first friends Juliette had made in Venice, a lively, animated woman, dark-haired and amply-curved, who was the wife of a prosperous businessman and the mother of five young children. 'Or both?'

'Both!' Juliette declared. 'I've time today.'

'No designing at the moment?' Angelina queried. She was an artist herself, and always dressed in the flowing styles that suited her. In her early forties and sharply intelligent, she was older than the others with a grown-up son at medical school and a husband serving as a

264

captain in the Italian navy. Juliette had first met her at the Palazzo Orfei, for she was a friend of Henriette.

'No, Maison Landelle had my winter designs long ago and I've done most of the re-designing on what I originally intended for the spring collection.'

'What changes were those?' Isabella had ordered the ices from the waiter, the coffee to be served later.

'It seemed to me that by the spring the war will have affected the pattern of life for all the women concerned. The hobble skirt is doomed. I've kept the skirts narrow, but with pleats at the back that will give complete freedom of movement. The whole collection follows simpler lines, except for the evening wear. I know nothing of the effects of battle, but I'm sure that men on leave will want to see their women looking more beautiful and feminine than ever before.'

'Naturally they will.' Elena, who was the same age as Juliette, was a pretty, bird-like young woman who always dressed in the height of fashion and the hobble skirt she was wearing was so narrow that she could take only small steps when walking. Childless as yet, with two stepchildren older than herself, she was happily married to a leading Venetian engineer more than twice her age. She had news to tell. 'My husband is seeing yours today, Juliette. There's a big conference with representatives of all the museums and art galleries and the churches.'

'Marco told me he had a busy day ahead, but he rarely says much when he has his morning newspaper.'

Elena knew more. 'As Marco is an expert in all sorts of cloth he's to be asked to supply literally miles of a certain kind of protective covering for all the works of art in the city.'

Isabella, about to put a spoonful of strawberry ice into her mouth, lowered it again in dismay. 'Does that mean what I think?'

Juliette, seeing how upset she looked, tried to reassure her. 'It's a sensible precautionary measure. Those threats by Germany and Austria may only be sabre-rattling, but we can't be sure.'

'But I read that all Europe expects the war to be over by Christmas.'

'I'm sure the Kaiser doesn't,' Juliette remarked succinctly, remembering Nikolai's words.

'I agree,' Angelina commented crisply. 'Although our country is

265

divided between those who think we should side with Germany and save ourselves that way, while the other half is defiant, determined not to be bullied, we shouldn't forget that Austria would like to get its claws on Venezia again. This city is vulnerably close to that old enemy.'

Isabella flushed an angry red and pushed her ice away, all taste for it gone. 'They needn't think they're going to fly their Imperial eagle over Venice again! It's not fifty years yet since their hateful occupation ended. My mother remembers curfews and not being allowed here in St Mark's Square when a military band was playing. Such arrogance! My grandmother had worse tales of the earlier days. Rapes and imprisonments and much else. According to the newspapers, the Germans are behaving no better against the poor Belgians and they took Brussels yesterday.'

Elena regretted having brought their conversation to the subject of war. It was spoiling their get-together. 'It should be different now the British have landed. How are your children, Isabella? Has Lorenzo recovered from his cold?'

Isabella loved to talk of her children. Her expression changed and she resumed eating her ice. When eventually the little party broke up it was on a happier note.

Contrary to all hopes the war did not end by Christmas. Nineteen-fifteen dawned with bitter fighting. Already Venice was changing her appearance as the possibility of involvement in the hostilities loomed dangerously near. The four bronze horses of Venice were removed from the façade of the Basilica for the first time since Napoleon had annexed them, but which France had duly returned.

Juliette and Marco were among the silent crowd who stood watching sadly as the horses were lowered one by one by crane from above the Basilica's great entrance doors. That same morning he had taken her into the Doges' Palace to see how a veil of one of the fabrics he had supplied was stretched over priceless ceiling paintings before the laborious and careful work of removing them could take place.

'What of the Tiepolo frescoes in the Church of the Scalzi?' she asked, thinking to see them once more before they were taken down.

'They're to stay where they are,' Marco replied. 'Experts have looked at them, but they're on thin plaster and would crack to pieces

266

if any attempt were made to remove them. There are others elsewhere that will also have to be left.'

With the horses gone, work commenced to protect the façade of the Basilica itself. Gradually it vanished behind protective cladding and sandbags. To Juliette and many others it was as if with all its glory lost from sight a lamp had been extinguished in the very heart of Venice. Other buildings received similar protection, but not on such an extensive scale. Everywhere the stone lion of St Mark and all outdoor statuary disappeared under sandbags. Irreplaceable medieval glass was removed from churches as well as from the Basilica itself.

In a city built on water with no cellars or vaults, the removal of priceless works of art and church treasures to a place of safety away from Venice was a seemingly endless task. Dry seaweed was used for much of the packing and bushels of it were required. Vast canvases were rolled around rollers and slotted into cylinders, smaller paintings packed into flat crates. Some valuable items, too awkward in shape to be transported anywhere without the risk of damage *en route*, were stored at the Palazzo Orfei in Fortuny's care.

It became a common sight to anyone out after midnight to see the specially built pontoons being towed along the Grand Canal. When other water traffic was at a minimum, these vessels transported freight wagons to the nearest landing stages for the collecting of precious cargoes for transportation by railway.

Juliette, returning home with Marco in the early hours from a party at Angelina's, paused on the Accademia bridge to watch one of the packed wagons pass below. As with every one of these cargoes there were armed soldiers on board to escort it all the way to its secret destination. It was a warm May night and she leaned her arms on the wooden parapet, being in no hurry to move from there.

Marco, who had continued walking down the steps, stopped when she did not catch him up and ascended again to where he could see her. She was wearing the Fortuny black and gold gown, the cape thrown back, the gilt beads glittering, and her arms were milky-white in the glow of the bridge's lamps.

'Why have you stopped?' he asked impatiently.

He had not enjoyed the party. Angelina's husband had been there, his ship presently anchored in the Lagoon, and three of his fellow officers had been invited for the evening. All three had flirted with

Juliette and one had paid her what Marco had considered to be excessive attention, dancing with her at every opportunity. Although Marco could not fault Juliette's behaviour his swift jealousy had refuelled the doubt he could not entirely banish from his mind. Often he forgot it for weeks at a time, for Juliette could be a very loving wife, but something about the naval officer's height and profile had reminded him of Nikolai and he feared she had been responding to that likeness with her smiles and laughter.

Juliette had rejoined him. 'I was watching one of the wagons, that's all.'

To pacify him she put her hand on his arm as they continued on their way. She thought he had been unreasonable to glare at her as he had done whenever she and the officer were dancing. What should have been a delightful party for her had been spoiled unnecessarily. It was far from the first time. She had done everything she could to make their marriage whole again and then, just when she thought she had succeeded, he would get upset about nothing.

They walked all the way home without speaking, the silence rising up between them like a wall. Her heart sank despairingly as they went upstairs, she just ahead of him. Something seemed to snap in her. As soon as the door of their bedroom was closed behind them, shutting out all chance of being overheard, she rounded on him angrily.

'When are you going to stop punishing me?'

He did not have to ask her what she meant. Glowering, he slipped off his evening coat and tossed it across a chair. 'So you were remembering him!'

She was bewildered. 'What are you talking about?'

'That Russian is never out of your thoughts, is he?'

'It seems he's never out of yours,' she retaliated fiercely. 'Is the rest of your life and mine to be ruined because you will not put the past away?'

'I did that when I brought you here from Tuscany,' he gave back. 'It was you who revived the past for both of us. You had a lovers' reunion with the Russian! You took Michel from this house to see him leave!' he turned away, his voice bitter. 'Don't speak to me of wiping out the past. It's you who are keeping it alive!'

She moved swiftly and stood between him and the chest of

drawers on which he was about to place the pearl studs from his stiff white shirt-front. 'I can see you will always hold what happened that afternoon against me.'

'None would blame me.' He moved to the side of her and put down the studs in their velvet-lined box.

'I blame you for not accepting the truth from me! But it makes no difference. I'm staying on here and you'll not get rid of me, heedless of whatever you say or do! Our children are not going to grow up with a parent in one house and the other in another. I will have Michel and Sylvana together with us both and we'll behave in a civilized manner, no matter how much you may come to hate me!'

'What are you saying? I could never hate you!' He was severely taken aback. Her words had conjured up momentarily what the house would be like without her. It was like feeling his heart cut out. 'I'd never want you to leave,' he roared, taking hold of her by the arms and shaking her until her head fell back. 'I love you! If only I could be sure of you!'

The ringing of the telephone, coming at such a night-time hour, took them both by surprise, seeming to pierce the crisis that had erupted between them. He released her, taking a step back.

'Don't let it wake the children,' she urged with an odd return to normality.

He nodded and hurried away down the stairs to answer the commanding ring. She crossed to her dressing-table and sat down to remove the emerald necklace and earrings that Marco had given her as a wedding gift and placed them in the top layer of her jewellery casket. She had meant what she said.

By the time she heard his footsteps come slowly back up the stairs she was in her nightgown and supposed he had stayed downstairs to smoke a cigarette. When he entered the room she could see by his face that he had heard some dreadful news. She guessed the cause even before he told her.

'That was Angelina,' he said heavily. 'Her husband and his fellow officers have been recalled to their ship. Italy has abandoned neutrality. We are at war with Austria.'

She ran forward and threw her arms around him. 'It's a courageous step, but I'm so sorry it has had to happen.'

He held her close. 'Perhaps it's as well. At least we'll all know at last where we stand. It's always easier to face the worst than to keep wondering as we've all been doing for quite a time now.'

'You spoke before of bringing me from Tuscany,' she said urgently. 'The seeds sown when you asked me to marry you, have grown to all I feel for you now and have done for a long time. Surely the fact that we have come along a hard and difficult way makes what we have all the more worthwhile? Let us mend the differences between us once and for all. Now more than ever we have to be united by love.'

It was an impassioned plea. He looked deeply into her eyes, doubt easing away. None could have hoped more than he that eventually it would disappear altogether.

'Yes, Juliette,' he answered huskily. Drawing her to him, he held her in a long and loving kiss. Afterwards he made love to her as tenderly as on their first night together.

CHAPTER TWENTY-TWO

At his office during the next few days Marco made preparatory moves towards his enlistment. All the orders for protective coverings had been fulfilled and had been a boost to his business, which had dwindled away almost to nothing since the German invasion of Belgium. Most of his male staff had volunteered for military service already and his only option was to close down until the war was over. He had talked about it to Fortuny, whose profits had also plunged over recent months, but at least the designer had plenty to occupy him in another sphere. The Palazzo Orfei had become the Spanish Consulate for the duration of the war and Fortuny himself appointed Honorary Consul for Spain.

Marco spoke of his enlisting to Juliette. 'I'll be given a commission,' he said, 'because in my youth I trained in a voluntary capacity in my spare time. How did you get on today with your offer to nurse at the hospital?'

She shook her head in disappointment. 'I was turned down because I have no experience and there, as at the other hospitals, all the nurses are nuns.'

'There'll be other voluntary work that you can do.' He took hold of her hands where they sat. 'I want you to know that my finances

271

are all in order and you and the children will always be well provided for if I should not—'

'Don't say it!' she interrupted quickly. 'You're coming back to us when this war is over.'

'Of course I am,' he declared cheerfully.

The door opened and Arianna came in carrying Sylvana, who was clutching her rag-doll from which she would not be parted. He grinned and held out his arms to his daughter. Having been put down on her feet, Sylvana managed a few unsteady steps until her father picked her up and set her on his knee. He kissed her on the cheek. She was a pretty child with a bronze tint to her dark hair and was as brown-eyed as he.

'When do you expect to leave?' Juliette asked, dreading his departure.

He looked across at her. 'As soon as possible, but we'll have a little time together yet.'

'We'll make the most of every minute!' she declared, hoping the days would not fly past too quickly.

Recently, when the involvement of Italy in the war had become imminent, another much smaller exodus of foreigners, shortly to be in the category of enemies, had taken place. A local wag pinned a notice on the doors of the evacuated German and Austrian Consulates, which read, *Properties for Rent*.

The city was to be well defended. Anti-aircraft batteries had been installed for some time and with the great fear of enemy submarines penetrating the Lagoon a network of subaqueous telephonic detonators had been set in place. Watchmen were to take shifts on the roof of the Doges' Palace as well as at other vantage points and the whole city was soon as full of soldiers and sailors as it had ever been with travellers from other lands. Martial law was announced and a total black-out was imposed.

Venice, never ablaze with lights except in its cafés, restaurants and night-spots, became so dark on moonless nights that some of the first war casualties in the city were those who missed their bearings and fell into the canals, drowning before anyone heard their flounderings and their cries. The furnaces of the *vaporetti* were dampened down after sunset and the gondolas and other boats forbidden to show a light, resulting in more accidents when warning shouts were not heeded in time. Juliette was among those who found it stiffling to have the shutters closed to hide lights in the evenings when normally they were left open to the cooler air.

Only days after Italy's declaration of war many residents awoke, Juliette among them, to hear an unfamiliar sound as if a flight of some unknown breed of insects were approaching out of the golden dawn. Realization as to what it was soon followed as Austrian aeroplanes dropped bombs on the Arsenal. Almost no damage was done, but shock prevailed in the city, for whereas everyone was prepared for gun bombardment, attack from the air was an entirely new experience for civilians.

'We should have been forewarned by what happened to Ypres and other Belgian cities,' Marco remarked grimly. 'I was wondering, Juliette, if you would reconsider taking the children to Lucille while there is still a chance of getting a passage in an American ship?'

His sister-in-laws in the United States had already written to invite his wife and children to stay with them and Lucille had urged her to do the same in New Orleans.

Juliette shook her head firmly. 'I've told you already that I don't intend to leave. Italy and France are my countries. I'm not running out on them and, most of all, I want to be here whenever you get leave to come home.'

He did not try to persuade her again, able to tell when her mind was made up. Instead he did what he could to provide as safe a place as possible for use in air-raids. The smaller salon, which he used as a study, had only one window by the desk and this was to be permanently shuttered. Some protective veiling used for ceiling paintings was pinned over the window on the inside to prevent anyone being hurt by flying glass.

The day came when Marco had to leave. He made his farewells to the children first and afterwards to Arianna and Lena, both of whom wept. Finally he went to Juliette, who was waiting in the salon. To his relief she showed no sign of tears, although the strain of parting showed in her eyes. She held both her hands out to him and he took them into his own. They smiled, each wanting to cheer the other.

'Finish the war quickly, Marco. I want you home again.'

'You may rely on me.'

Neither was quite sure what else they said before they finally kissed and embraced, making the most of the last moments together.

273

She went into the hall with him and when he had opened the door he kissed her once again. In the square he turned to wave to her.

When he had gone she closed the door and went into the walled garden where the children were playing. For their sake she had to conceal her present feelings. Marco was soon to be in the field of war and she was separated from the two men who meant so much to her, each in his own way.

After Marco's departure two more air-raids followed, one of the enemy aircraft flying so low that those with binoculars could see the aviator dropping the bomb over the side of his cockpit. Many churches suffered damage. In the Tyrol relentless fighting was taking place between the Italian and Austrian troops and the wounded began to be brought in. Again Juliette volunteered to do whatever she could, but once more it was to no avail. Several of her friends were leaving the city with their children, moving to safer places in case there should be more bombing. Isabella was among them and also Elena, who had discovered she was pregnant.

Juliette organized a group of those who were staying on and together they rolled bandages and knitted socks, scarves and pullovers for the troops. They all gathered goods for Red Cross auctions and shook collecting boxes about the city in aid of war-linked charities. Juliette also helped the Women's Work Force, which was located in the grandeur of *La Fenice*. There she distributed the thick grey-green army cloth to women, who took it away to make clothing in their own homes for soldiers. As it was paid work for the government she did not sew herself, there being far too many women, previously employed in hotels, restaurants and elsewhere, even at Fortuny's, who were desperately in need of the money.

The war news continued to be bad everywhere. Juliette read with dismay of the success of Austro-German troops, who had over-run Serbia and broken the Russian front in Poland where they had taken many prisoners. She hoped that Nikolai had not been there. London was suffering Zeppelin air-raids; there were ceaseless bombardments between the trenches of the British and Germans in Belgium and Italy was now also at war with Turkey.

In October there was another air-raid on Venice. A bomb fell on the Church of the Scalzi and the glorious Tiepolo frescoes were lost for ever. It was some time before Juliette could bring herself to view

274

the damage. Tarpaulins covered the gaping hole in the roof and the nave was still full of rubble. At least nobody had been killed, although four women were injured. Juliette was well aware that there might have been a fifth if she had been there that day as she had intended, but both children were recovering from measles at the time and Sylvana had been particularly fretful.

When an official appeal went out for those with empty properties to allow them to be used as hospitals for the wounded, Juliette took it upon herself to offer Marco's business premises. After an inspection it was deemed suitable. She consulted the caretaker and he arranged for all the remaining stock, office files and everything else to be moved to the spacious top floor, which would leave the rest of the building free. There had been no time to ask Marco's permission, for mail was often delayed or else freshly written letters arrived long before those with earlier dates. She wrote to tell him what she had done, but by the time she received his approval the building was in full use. Since all operations were done in the main hospital the patients were mostly men on the road to recovery, who had been transferred from beds urgently needed for the newly wounded.

Juliette visited, taking books and magazines to interest the convalescents, and often sat by bedsides writing letters from them to their families. This was not always through their injuries, for sometimes they were illiterate, simple men of peasant stock who, until being called up into the army, had lived in villages, often remote, where virtually nothing had changed over the centuries. They did not understand the causes that had brought about the war and missed their little vineyards and farms and animals as much as they missed their wives and families.

Juliette spoke of them to Angelina. 'There must be hundreds of thousands of such men on both sides of this awful war, who normally would not wish to harm another human being, all fighting because their country has need of them. What a hell has been created by power-mad leaders!' She thumped her fists on the arms of the chair in which she sat. 'When is it all going to end?'

The year of 1916 had arrived with no sign of an end to hostilities. The flood of wounded had increased to such proportions that notices were posted up offering a short nursing course. Juliette immediately enrolled, several of her friends, including Angelina, doing the same.

275

All went well. A nun instructed them in bandaging, how to take temperatures, give a bed-bath and all the elementary duties that would have to be done. When all this had been practised and mastered to the nun's satisfaction Juliette and the other women, wearing their auxiliary uniforms for the first time, were taken into the wards of a new hospital, formerly the Hotel Victoria, and each put in the charge of a nursing nun, who would supervise them until they could be trusted to know exactly what to do. Juliette's nun was named Sister Ursula.

'You can start, Nurse Romanelli, by changing the dressings on that patient's legs.'

Juliette looked in the direction that the nun had indicated and her heart contracted with pity. He was young, no more than seventeen, white-faced and hollowed-eyes, wearing a striped night-shirt too big for him with a plaid rug over his knees. She fetched the dressings the nun had told her she would need and put them on a sterile cloth beside him on his bed.

'You're a beginner, aren't you?' he greeted her. 'This your first day?'

'That's right,' she answered smilingly. 'But I was taught how to change dressings and so you needn't be alarmed.'

He looked wryly amused. 'I'm not scared, but I bet you will be.'

She was taking away the plaid rug as he spoke and she only just managed to hide her shock. He had no legs below the knees. 'Where did this happen?' she asked, kneeling to commence her work, her tone even.

'In the Tyrol.'

The old dressings were stuck by dried blood and as she tried gently to free them she saw his hands clench, his knuckles showing white, but he did not cry out. Instead he taunted her.

'You'll faint in a minute!'

'I bet you I won't!'

'The last beginner did. She went flat on the floor.'

When his wounds were fully revealed it would have been easy to follow her predecessor's example, but Juliette carried out her task doggedly, retaining control of herself by continuing to exchange banter with him. It helped them both through the ordeal.

It was a heart-breaking day. There were so many shattered men, their courage humbling her, and what might otherwise have been onerous or distasteful became a willingly undertaken task to help them a little in their suffering. Many had the additional agony of frostbite contracted in the bitter cold of the mountains. Some were too deep in pain to comprehend what was happening, but the rest were touchingly grateful, some making jokes when their injuries caused them to be clumsy. Soon she became accustomed to three full days a week at the hospital, for as the mother of young children no more was expected of her. She offered to give more time, but the supervisor of the hospital reminded her sternly that little ones always had need of their mother's own care in their early years.

Juliette had Michel with her on a March morning when she went to the Fortuny shop. She had decided that one of the designer's wall-hangings should replace a painting she had never much liked on the dining-room wall. The hangings came in a variety of sizes and she would choose one a little larger than the present painting. Michel did not like shopping as a rule, but he was always eager to accompany her to the Palazzo Orfei where he could play hide-and-seek amid the long curtains and draperies. At three and a half he was tall for his years and sturdy, his angelic looks deceptive to those who did not know how easily he could get into mischief.

'Be good,' Juliette admonished as they entered the Palazzo shop. 'Yes, Mama.'

There were no other customers and only two women assistants, who were bored with nothing to do and happy to play with him. All the young men had joined the army and there was only a skeleton staff left in the workroom through lack of business.

She had almost decided on a cream hanging shaped like an *H* in one of Fortuny's Persian inspired designs, the colouring red, dark blue and gold, when she heard the sirens wailing. Another air-raid!

'Come Michel!' she urged quickly, reaching out her hand for his. 'We're going home.'

Overhead came a clatter of footsteps as the few workers still employed in the ateliers left their tasks to go downstairs where it would be safer. Juliette was soon hurrying with her son across the square. The thud-thud of the anti-aircraft guns resounded as they fired into the pale March sky. Ahead she saw an army officer, supporting himself on a single crutch, coming from the direction of her home. It was Marco! He had seen her too!

'Juliette!' he yelled jubilantly. 'Michel!'

She covered the distance betwen them far quicker than he could have done. 'What happened to your leg?' she asked anxiously when he had kissed them both.

'Nothing very much,' he replied as he hurried with them to the house, 'but it's given me sick leave. We can be glad of that.'

Indoors Michel, who was wildly excited to have his father home again, broke away as soon as Juliette had removed his outdoor clothes and ran ahead to the shuttered room where Lena and Arianna would be with his sister.

'Papa is home!' he announced, jumping up and down. 'Sylvie! Papa's here!'

Arianna and Lena regarded him with amusement, having directed Marco as soon as he arrived to where he would find his wife and son, but they did not spoil the child's excitement by telling him. 'Isn't that good,' Arianna said, taking Sylvana onto her lap, for the child had shown signs of being shy of her father after his long absence.

Still bounding, Michel returned to the hall where his parents were embracing and at the same time the vibration of a bomb made the windows rattle. Marco turned smilingly to take the boy's hand into his.

'Come along, Michel. We'll join the others.' To Juliette he added, 'Do these raids ever happen at night?'

'Very occasionally. It's said that the waters of Venice highlight the target areas, but luckily the enemy is never very accurate.'

It proved to be the same with the current raid. Later in the day they heard that a warehouse had lost its windows, a slip-way had been damaged and the rest of the bombs had vanished into the Lagoon. By then Juliette had learned how Marco had been injured. A bullet had pierced his leg, breaking the bone, but it had been well set.

'The worst of it as far as I was concerned is that it happened the day before I'd been due for leave. So it set back my coming home.' He chose not to tell her of the amount of blood he had lost and how close he had come to death, which was why his recovery had taken far longer than she could suspect.

'But where were you nursed?' she asked, dismayed that he had not been brought to Venice.

'I was in a field hospital under canvas at first and then transferred

278

to a hospital converted out of an ancient building in a village quite a distance from here. How are you getting on with your nursing these days? You don't write about it in any detail.'

'Only because much of the work is harrowing and you experience plenty of those times yourself.'

He gave a heavy nod. Like all soldiers briefly home from the horrors of war, he did not wish to speak of anything remotely connected with it other than giving whatever news was possible of fellow officers who were known to Juliette. 'How about the designing? Any new developments there?'

'Only that mail to and from Paris has become so erratic that sometimes letters are weeks on the way and sometimes never arrive. I find designing very relaxing and snatch whatever spare minutes I have to be in my studio. I'm still making my day clothes practical, the skirts two inches above the ankle.'

'It must be difficult for Denise to get certain fabrics.'

'I'm sure it is. To judge from my sister's letters,' Juliette added with a smile, 'one would imagine that the Kaiser had declared war specially to annoy and inconvenience her personally! Like Fortuny, her sales have fallen disastrously. Some of the top couturiers in Paris have enlisted and are serving on the battlefields.'

'Dear God! What a contrast for them!' he exclaimed wearily.

She was sitting next to him on the sofa and put her arms around his neck and kissed his mouth to drive away whatever thoughts of the fighting had come into his mind. During the night he woke twice in the grip of nightmares, thrashing his arms and yelling orders, and she had held and kissed him again, soothing the horrors away. Once after making love to her he wept, his face buried against her breasts, the warm bouquet of her in his nostrils, and did not know how he would ever be able to leave her again.

Yet the time came. By then he had dispensed with his crutch and one of the medical officers in Venice had declared him fit to return to the front. Juliette had made his time at home as happy as she could. She had had her duties at the hospital, but he had been content to be with the children, taking them out with him sometimes for a ride on a *vaporetto*, which both children enjoyed, or to see a battleship anchored in the Lagoon, which meant more to Michel than Sylvana. He set them free in toyshops to choose within reason whatever toy they wanted, and before taking them home again he

279

never failed to treat them to an ice or a sticky cake or anything else that took their fancy in a café. In all he spoilt them completely, ruined their appetite for meals and annoyed Arianna far more than he realized, for she could see what a task she would have to get them back to routine once he was gone again.

Sometimes he had the children with him when he met Juliette as she came off duty, but at an evening hour he was always on his own. It was during one of these walks home that the only discordant moment of his leave occurred. Quite unexpectedly he voiced a question that caught her unawares.

'Have you heard anything from Karasvin?'

She looked at him incredulously. 'No. That's over. He wouldn't write to me even in the unlikely possibility of a letter getting through from Russia in the midst of this war.'

'I understand it's possible sometimes through the Red Cross. Karasvin would also have access to diplomatic channels.'

'Not is he's in the thick of battle somewhere along the fluctuating Eastern Front. I've had no letter and neither do I ever expect to receive one.'

Outwardly Marco seemed satisfied with her answer, but she realized sadly that it would always be as she feared. Doubt was never going to leave him, always re-surfacing throughout the rest of their lives together.

On his last day Juliette changed her duties at the hospital to be with him. They spent the time with the children as he wished, taking them to a puppet show. In the evening they dined alone and at night he made love to her.

When Juliette woke next morning he was gone. An envelope addressed to her was propped on the bedside table. She sat up, pushing her hair back from her eyes, and read it through. He had written that she was not to be upset, but to say farewell this time would have been almost beyond his powers. He closed by saying he had kissed her and both children before leaving.

She flung back the bedclothes and hastened to the window just in case he was still in sight, but there was no sign of him.

CHAPTER TWENTY-THREE

When the news came of a new Austrian offensive in the Tyrol Juliette was consumed with anxiety for Marco. Sometimes, unable to wait for the morning newspaper, she went to St Mark's Square where a crowd gathered every evening to hear the latest communiqué read out. She joined in with the cheers and the tears of relief when the announcement told that the Italians had broken through the Austrian lines at Trentino. More Italian successes followed, but the toll was in the columns of casualties listed in the daily newspapers. Among the wounded who arrived by the train-load in Venice were Austrian prisoners-of-war, who were treated with the same care, but were segregated into wards on their own with sentries mounted at the doors.

As the summer advanced there came further news of Italian minor triumphs. Juliette was reading about the latest, taking a rest in the salon with her feet up, which did not happen often, and was alone in the house. Lena had taken the children out with her, for Arianna had recently married a sailor, whom she had known for some time. They had all been to the wedding. Although he had gone back to sea Arianna had moved into a small apartment and was working with other women in a small factory attached to the Arsenal.

When the doorbell rang Juliette put aside the newspaper,

wondering who had come to interrupt her solitude. She crossed the green marble floor of the hall to the door and opened it wide to see a woman dressed entirely in mourning black on the doorstep. For a fleeting second Juliette felt an inexplicable qualm assail her as if this stranger might be the bearer of bad news, but in the same instant the woman smiled, dispelling the sensation. There was a gentleness in her face, which was marked by time to reveal she was in her mid-sixties. Her hair was grey, her features aristocratic and her demeanour very dignified.

'*Bonjour*,' she said at once and continued in French. 'I believe I have the pleasure of addressing Signora Romanelli. Yes? I am Signora Ottoni, widow of the late Carlo Ottoni of Venice. Doña Cecilia gave me your name. Forgive me for calling unannounced, but I was most anxious to make your acquaintance.'

'Please come in.' Juliette stood aside for her to enter.

'It is many years since I was last in Venice,' the widow explained when she and Juliette were seated opposite each other. 'That was not through choice, because once we used to spend three months of every year at our Palazzo on the Grand Canal. Sadly my husband's health began to deteriorate and on his doctors' advice we settled in Switzerland where the mountain air is beneficial to invalids. Although I'd long been prepared, it came as a shattering blow to me when I was recently bereaved.'

'Pray accept my sincere condolences.'

The widow inclined her head in grateful acknowledgement. In spite of her Italian name her French bore no trace of accent and yet Juliette was convinced she was not a fellow countrywoman.

'Carlo was an adventurous traveller,' the widow continued. 'Whenever possible I would go with him. I used to tell him that he must surely be a descendant of Marco Polo.' Her little smile showed that it had been a favourite joke between them. 'But wherever we were in the world his heart was always in Venice. It upset him very much when Italy became involved in the war, but he was also proud of the brave step that had been taken and made generous donations towards the war effort. I've come to Venice to fulfil his last wish, which is that I should see the Palazzo Ottoni turned into a hospital for the wounded, all equipment from the beds to an operating theatre to be funded from a special bequest under my jurisdiction.'

'That will be a marvellous benefit!' Juliette exclaimed. 'I speak

282

from my own experience as I nurse three days a week at the Hotel Victoria hospital.'

'So Doña Cecilia told me. I went to see her as soon as I arrived in Venice yesterday. Years ago in Rome my husband and I became acquainted with Doña Cecilia and her late husband, Fortuny y Marsal, who without doubt was one of Spain's greatest artists. Carlo bought a number of his paintings, which he bequeathed to the Prado Museum in Madrid to add to their collection of Fortuny y Marsal's work.'

'Another munificent gift! So you must surely know Don Mariano and Maria Luisa too.'

'Oh yes. Maria Luisa was at the railway station to meet me when I arrived, but I have yet to renew my acquaintance with her brother.' She linked her gloved fingers on her lap. 'I still haven't explained the purpose of my visit to you this afternoon. Doña Cecilia told me that you had supervised the converting of your absent husband's business premises into a hospital for the duration of the war as the Palazzo would be.'

'All I did was to offer the place to the medical board and then arrange for the removal of stock and equipment to the top floor of the building. After that it was just a question of getting women to wash and scrub the building throughout to bring it to the standard required in readiness for the taking over.'

'That alone tells me that you're practical and would know whom to employ for such work.' Signora Ottoni made a little gesture of appeal. 'I'll be frank with you. I'm not a young woman, which is only too plain, and I haven't the first idea how I should go about donating this hospital. Naturally there has to be a legal arrangement, but in the first instance I'd like you to help me. I had counted on Maria Luisa to fulfil that role, but sadly she has changed a great deal in the years since I last saw her and it would be out of the question.'

'Before I can give a reply I have to point out that a local lawyer could organize everything on your behalf and keep in contact with the medical board at the same time.'

'I'm sure of that and I'm also certain it's what my husband expected me to do, but then the whole venture would be taken out of my hands.' The widow spoke emotionally. 'It's the last thing I'll ever be able to do for Carlo and I want to be personally involved throughout.'

283

'I understand.'

'So what is your answer to all I've put to you?'

Juliette's face bloomed into a wide smile. 'It will be a pleasure to help you in any way I can.'

Signora Ottoni threw up her hands in relief. 'How splendid! That is what I'd hoped to hear. You have my grateful thanks.'

'Is the Palazzo furnished?'

'Yes, an old caretaker and his wife live there.'

'Are you staying there now?'

'No. I'm Doña Cecilia's guest. She invited me as soon as I wrote to say I would be coming. I haven't been to the Palazzo yet. Perhaps you would accompany me in the morning? I'd like us to start as we mean to go on.'

'Yes, of course. I shall not be on duty until the following day. I can't begin to tell you how much it will mean for the city to have the benefit of another hospital.' Juliette spoke with feeling. 'The stream of wounded is never ending. So many poor men are shell-shocked in addition to all else that has happened to them.'

'Would you consider nursing at my hospital?'

'I'd like that very much. There would be no problem about my transferring there.'

Signora Ottoni gave a nod of satisfaction. 'It will be good to know you're there. You see, Carlo and I never had children. It was a great sorrow to us both. When I knew of the task with which he had entrusted me I thought again how wonderful it would have been to have had a daughter to help me with everything. Now you have stepped in.'

'I'll do my very best.'

Suddenly there came the sound of the two children's voices in the hallway as they arrived home. A few minutes later the door of the salon burst open and Michel came running in, Sylvana following. They behaved well and the widow was clearly fond of children, but Lena soon took them away. Juliette and her visitor were left discussing Paris, Maison Worth having been the clothes-buying venue for Signora Ottoni whenever she was there. When Juliette had answered her question as to where she and Marco had met, Signora Ottoni went on to tell her how she had become engaged to Carlo within days of their first seeing each other.

'It was in Nice. I went there annually with my parents and brothers and sisters to our villa. We were like so many others in court circles who chose to escape the freezing winter blizzards of Russia for the balmy warmth of the Mediterranean.'

'So you are Russian, signora!' Juliette exclaimed. 'That explains why you speak French so naturally.'

'Ah. So you know that French is the language of the educated in Russia and that one only addresses the servants in Russian. I remember questioning the custom when I was a girl, because Russian is a powerful and descriptive language, but I was told to hush at once. The matter wasn't even to be discussed.'

'Do you still have family there?'

The widow nodded. 'Those of my generation are depleted in number, but I have plenty of nephews and nieces. Just before the war broke out Carlo and I were visited by the son of my youngest sister. Alexander is one of my favourite nephews and I have quite a few, all of whom are now fighting on the Eastern Front. I haven't seen anyone else from my family since he came, although I have a brother-in-law who is one of the Tsar's ministers and he sends his wife's letters and any from my other sisters through diplomatic channels. At least he did when I was in Switzerland and I hope that will continue while I'm here, because then the mail is not delayed.'

'Did your nephew stay long?'

'Unfortunately not. He had been in Vienna with a friend, who had come to Venice on a short visit, and they were meeting again at a midway railway junction to travel the long journey home together.'

Juliette was aware of feeling no surprise at this information and what it was likely to mean. One could not escape destiny. 'Were you acquainted with your nephew's friend?' she inquired evenly.

'Yes, indeed. Russia has millions of people, but court circles are relatively small and sooner or later one knows everybody else, at least by sight. I've been acquainted with Nikolai Karasvin's family for many years. Alexander and Nikolai and several of their friends joined the same regiment when they arrived back. In the last letters I had from one of my sisters before I left Switzerland I learned that Nikolai's father had died recently. It's a sad state of affairs when the heir inherits while at war with no son to inherit in his turn should the worst happen.' She broke off in concern, having seen Juliette press her fingers over her cheek as if to smooth away her paleness. 'Are you not well?'

Juliette dropped her hands into her lap. 'A little tired perhaps.'

Signora Ottoni was reassured. 'That's not surprising when you lead such a busy life. Now I've come here this afternoon to give you still more work.'

'I like to be kept busy,' Juliette answered quickly. 'I welcome the extra tasks more than you can possibly realize.'

'The least I can do now is to leave and let you have some rest.'

'No, please stay and have some refreshment.'

The widow had risen to her feet. 'There will be plenty of other opportunities.'

Arrangements were made for the following day and then Juliette saw the widow to the door. Returning to the salon she saw her own colour-drained face reflected in a gilt-framed mirror. If she had known that Signora Ottoni was linked in any way with Nikolai, no matter that the connection was very slight, would she have shouldered the task so willingly? It would have been easy enough for her to find an official to take over, even though that was not what the widow, nervous and unsure of herself in this new sphere, had wanted. But there was no going back after the commitment had been made.

She drove her fingers into her hair, cupping her head in desperation where she stood in the middle of the salon. Was Nikolai's will so strong that she was forever to hear of him when she least expected it? Even Marco had talked angrily of him when last at home. Could it be that this was what she had to face for the rest of her life, any contentment of the heart forever denied her?

Next morning Juliette went shopping early as she always did these days. With rationing imposed and many foodstuffs in short supply much time was spent in queues, often in vain when supplies ran out before she reached the shop door. When she arrived home with her few purchases a young girl, Catarina Bellini, was waiting to see her. The previous evening Juliette, knowing she would be extra busy with the new hospital venture, had asked Lena if she knew of anyone who would give a helping hand in the house and with the children. Lena had called in Catarina, who had been working for a family that had left Venice for a safer area without taking her with them.

'Would you like to start work straight away?' Juliette asked after reading her references and asking some questions.

286

Catarina, shy, brown-haired and smiling, had already made friends with Michel and Sylvana. Now she dimpled as she replied. 'Yes, please, signora.'

Juliette, relieved that Lena would have reliable help, left the house again and went to the office of the medical board where, as she had anticipated, she was invited to return with Signora Ottoni that same day at four o'clock. That left plenty of time to look around the Palazzo Ottoni. She called for the city's new benefactress as arranged and together they went by gondola to their destination.

'How eager the gondolier was to take us,' Signora Ottoni whispered to Juliette as they sailed along. 'So often in the past it was difficult to get one at all at this time of the day.'

'I'm afraid there's little business for them any more,' Juliette replied. She knew that those still left on the canals were virtually destitute and they and their families relied on a daily meal at the soup kitchen, which had been opened by volunteers.

'I'll tip him well.'

'He'll appreciate that.'

'We should find the Palazzo in good order. The caretaker is in his late seventies, but his wife is over twenty years younger and has always kept everything spotless. I sent them a note after I arrived in Venice to let them know I should be viewing the property, but that I would not be staying this time.'

'Shall you be returning to Switzerland when everything is settled?'

'Only until the war ends. I've a yearning to go home to Russia. One of my nieces and her husband live in the house where I was born, but it is large enough for all of us to reside under the same roof without ever crossing each other's paths if we wish not to do so.'

'Russia was a troubled land before the war. What if that unrest should flare up again in peace time?'

'It won't,' Signora Ottoni stated confidently. 'Nothing unites people more than a common enemy and the peasantry have proved themselves the bravest of soldiers.' She glanced upwards. 'Here we are!'

The Palazzo Ottoni loomed above them with its glorious fifteenth-century façade inset with Gothic windows and enhanced by stone balconies delicate as lace. The caretaker had opened the door and, in spite of his age, stepped forward nimbly to hand the two women in.

'An honour to see you again, signora,' he said with an old-fashioned bow.

'Are you well, Giovanni?'

'Yes, signora, but I miss my wife.'

'Oh, dear. Have you been bereaved?'

'No, not that. She had been unsteady on her legs for some time and not able to do much. Then she fell on the stairs over a year ago and broke her hip. She lives at my daughter's home now and there she'll stay, because she'll never walk again.' He did not seem unduly perturbed. 'I've been managing well enough on my own.'

Proof that his attempts at housekeeping were not as good as he supposed was spotted first in the deep green border on the dust-sheets covering the furniture in the vast hall.

'What happened here?' Signora Ottoni asked in concern.

'The Grand Canal flooded last winter.'

Signora Ottoni shook her head in dismay as she led the way up the ornate staircase, hung with cobwebs, to the great ballroom. Her long black skirt made a swathe in the dust across the rose-hued tessellated floor as she entered and stood looking nostalgically around her. Juliette reached her side. The vast room was magnificent with gilded panels, a turquoise ceiling and two chandeliers of Venetian glass, each five foot in diameter, that glittered in spite of a coating of dust. A painted *trompe-l'œil* of several smiling people, grandly dressed in clothes of an earlier century, looked down over a balustrade amid urns of flowers.

'I'm remembering so many happy times here,' Signora Ottoni said wistfully before abruptly straightening her shoulders. 'There will be many more of a less frivolous kind when soldiers and sailors recover their health and strength here. How many rows of beds could be accommodated in this ballroom, do you think?'

'Three,' Juliette replied. 'Two at the sides and one in the middle. There'll be plenty of space between the rows.'

It was the start of all that took place to change the Palazzo into an efficient hospital. The caretaker gave notice. He approved of what was being done, but declared himself too old for such changes. Juliette had no difficulty in getting labour for furniture moving or for cleaning, for hospital work took priority. There were many fine paintings throughout the Palazzo and Signora Ottoni had these left

288

in place for the pleasure of all those well enough or, in the case of the hospital staff, with time to appreciate them. Juliette in her uniform was among those on duty when the first of the patients arrived. After a few initial mishaps the new hospital settled into routine.

Signora Ottoni had changed her mind about returning to Switzerland. She knew few people there through having devoted all her time to her sick husband, first at their home there and afterwards at his bedside in the clinic. The Palazzo Ottoni hospital became the sole focus of her interest. She took an apartment nearby and went daily as a visitor, talking to the men, reading to them and writing their letters as well as giving them sips of water or feeding those unable to hold a spoon themselves. It was as if everything she did for a patient was something for her husband's last wish and it was a solace for her.

Among the second batch of wounded to be taken in were a number of Russian soldiers. They had been taken prisoner by the Austrians, but in passing from one temporary camp to another they had become involved in cross-fire during an Italian break through of the Austrian lines. Juliette went from one bed to another, looking into the face of each man or, if they were swathed in bandages, reading the names that had been taken from their identification tags. Nikolai was not among them. It had been an unlikely chance, but stranger things happened.

Then, as she was leaving again, one of the other nurses told her that a Russian officer was in one of the smaller wards on an upper floor. She ran up the stairs, but even from the ward's doorway she could see it was not Nikolai who was lying there. She went to the officer's bedside, read his name on the temperature chart, and spoke to him in French.

'How are you feeling, Captain Rostov?'

He had lost an arm and was weak, but pleased to talk to her. 'Much better now that I'm in this bed. Hearing you speak makes me feel I'm back in Paris again.'

'You know my city?'

'I was there on my honeymoon.'

She smiled. 'I can think of no better place.'

'Why are you so far from home?'

'I married an Italian. May I ask if you have ever met Count Nikolai

Karasvin? I knew him in Paris. He is in the Russian army and I wonder if you know whether all is well with him.'

The officer frowned meditatively and then shook his head. 'I'm sorry, but that name isn't personally known to me.'

They talked a little longer, he telling her about his wife and children. When she left it was with a promise that she would visit his bedside again since he was not in her ward. On the way back downstairs she thought that this time it was she herself who had chosen to speak of Nikolai, but she still saw his will behind it.

Signora Ottoni was called in to act as interpreter, for even Captain Rostov could speak no Italian. Several of the Russians died in spite of all that was done for them and she held their hands during their last moments. Those with minor wounds were thankful to talk to a fellow countrywoman, even though she was of the class to whom they had always had to bow their heads. That was forgotten in her kindly words and some, who were wandering in their minds, thought she was their mother. She had hoped that the Captain might be able to give her some news of her relatives presently in the army but, as with Juliette, he was unable to help her. To her surprise, even shock, he spoke openly to her of his disappointment in the Tsar.

'He put himself personally in charge of the Russian army with disastrous results. We've suffered terrible losses through his incompetence that should never have happened. Hundreds of thousands of our men have been killed already. The hardships our army is enduring defies belief. Admittedly not everything can be laid at the Tsar's door – the failure of ammunition supplies, the lack of food that leaves men starving, the boots that leak and the inadequacy of bayonets alone in the face of pounding artillery. Did you know that famine prevails in many places at home? It's not only the army that goes hungry.'

'What a sad and terrible state of affairs!'

'It will get worse. The old grievances of the peasants haven't been forgotten. There are many rebellious elements in the army. I know of officers whose loyalty to the Tsar is no longer certain. Not even such successes as we have attained against the Austro-German forces and the Turks can nullify growing discontent in the army ranks and at home.'

Signora Ottoni kept all he had said about the Tsar to herself, her own loyalty sealing her lips on anything spoken against him. She

290

only told Juliette about the hardships the army was enduring and saw the young woman's eyes deepen with distress.

Juliette continued to write regularly to Marco, knowing how much he liked to receive her letters, and he was always pleased when she enclosed drawings that the children had done specially for him, even though Sylvana's efforts were little more than scrawls with wax crayons. Juliette had no idea when he would be home again.

On the morning two overseas letters were delivered there was also one from him, which she read first. He believed he would be given a new posting very soon, but hoped for leave first. The second letter bore a French stamp and was from Denise. She had written in wild despair. Her last mannequin had left months ago to do war work as had almost all the seamstresses, only half a dozen older women left. Her few remaining clients were wearing their clothes from season to season and new orders had dwindled to almost nothing. She could no longer continue producing the brassières of Juliette's design, which had sold so well at top prices, because nobody was buying enough expensive lingerie to keep that particular workroom open any longer. More *haute couture* houses had closed down and she did not think she would be able to carry on Maison Landelle after the next month. She finished her letter with the furious comment that the Germans had ruined everything for her. Amid the complaints she mentioned Jacques Vernet was still mostly at his armaments factories, but he did get to Paris quite often and always took her to wherever it was still possible to dine and dance in some style.

The third letter was from Gabrielle and written in August over three months ago. It gave her the sad news that Derek had been killed on the Somme and had been posthumously awarded the Military Cross. Gabrielle went on to say that all Derek's family had been wonderfully supportive, she and his mother able to comfort and sustain each other. Her little daughter was her only joy. The last line expressed the heartfelt hope that all was well with Juliette and it would not be long before the war ended and they could see each other again. Juliette folded the letter and wept for her friend's bereavement.

The war ploughed on. It seemed to Juliette and other Venetian housewives that everything was rationed or in such short supply that a delay in getting early to the market and the shops meant no fish

291

or vegetables or fruit that day and meat was rarely available. They knew it was the same everywhere and that even in Germany women were facing the same problems.

Many foreigners in Venice had other difficulties beside the shortage of food, Fortuny and his mother among them. Unable to tap their financial resources overseas they found themselves desperately short of money. Doña Cecilia parted with some of her antiques, Signora Ottoni moved into an even smaller apartment and Fortuny himself had to sell one of his most treasured possessions.

'Not the Goya drawings!' Juliete exclaimed in dismay when Henriette spoke of the matter to her. He had shown them to her once, each as powerful and beautiful as the next.

'Yes,' Henriette gave a deep sigh, folding her arms as she rested her weight against the edge of a carved table in the salon-studio. 'It had to be done. All the workrooms are closed now. The shop is still open, but it's rarely that anyone comes and then I do the serving.' She glanced about at the vast room. 'Isn't it quiet? Do you remember how this place used to sound like an aviary when Mariano and I held parties here before the war?'

'I do indeed. I also recall how Don Mariano was pressured by American contacts to go to the United States when the war first started and carry on producing there. How does he feel about it now?'

'That was partly because of the successful exhibition of his gowns in New York, but he has no regrets. In spite of everything he'd still make the same decision to stay in Venice.'

'He's a remarkable man in so many ways. Does he still design?'

'Yes, he does.' Henriette gave a quiet smile. 'He's biding his time. This war will end one day. Wars always do. In my opinion his Delphos robe will still be admired when the Kaiser has faded from people's memories.'

'I'm sure you're right.'

Juliette rarely entered her own studio these days, having so little spare time. She was busy from morning to night, for when not at the hospital there was much to do. She tried to visit Doña Cecilia whenever possible, for she and her daughter were following Fortuny's example by staying in Venice. In spite of all Juliette still tried to do for Maria Luisa it was in vain, the woman having retreated completely into a world of her own obsessions.

At night Juliette always fell asleep at once through physical tiredness. When the New Year came she slept right through the arrival of 1917 and in the morning she awoke to wonder yearningly if it would bring peace back again. A letter from Marco was a welcome sight when she went downstairs. It was to let her know that he would soon be coming home on leave.

Juliette, knowing the time of his arrival, was able to meet him at the railway station. He looked tired and drawn, but after two weeks at home he was much improved. He was passionate and frequent in his love-making, starved for her, and it was not long after his departure that she began to wonder if she was pregnant again.

The certainty came on the first day of April, shortly after the Tsar had abdicated and the Bolsheviks had announced their intention of ruling Russia. A dangerous touch-paper had been ignited.

CHAPTER TWENTY-FOUR

Owing to her pregnancy Juliette could no longer continue nursing at the hospital. Reluctantly she handed in her uniform and took home the few things that were hers. These included a postcard one of the patients had given her. It showed a pretty red-haired nurse about to give a male patient a glass of medicine, but being kissed by him instead. It was entitled *Not in the Prescription*. She smiled over it again and put it with other keepsakes she valued, for the sender of the card had been only twenty years old when killed during an Italian offensive at Trieste.

Marco's reaction to the news of the forthcoming baby was exactly what she had expected. His letter was full of how much a third child would enrich their lives. Apart from his immense pride in fatherhood it was clear to her that the thought of a new life in the midst of so much death had renewed his hopes for the future. For herself she had not thought of adding to their family until the war was over, but it had happened and she knew she would love the infant when the time came.

She frowned over his letter when she read on to his insistence that she and the children should leave at once for the villa in Tuscany where she would be well looked after as she was before. It had worried him far too long that they had stayed on in a city being bombed from time to time. Juliette would have done as he wished, especially as the official advice had long been for residents to leave for safer zones, for Venice would be a prime prize for the enemy with its great Arsenal and sheltered waters. But she could not leave the city yet. She was still in bed after the worrying threat of a miscarriage.

'You're to stay there until I come again,' the doctor had said on his last visit when she had asked if she might get up. 'Then if all is well I'll allow you to leave your bed only if you rest for long periods with your feet up throughout the day. That will be until I can be sure you'll carry the baby the full term. In my opinion you should have finished nursing at the hospital sooner than you did, but that can't be undone now. We must put matters right as best we can.'

When Juliette replied to Marco's letter she did her utmost to reassure him about the occasional bombing. Italian aeroplanes often took over from the anti-aircraft guns and she reminded him that Venice had its own air ace, who was hero-worshipped for his active defence of the city with his squadron. Finally she promised Marco that later on, after the baby was born, she would leave the city with the children as he wished if it should prove necessary. When Marco wrote back he did not question the doctor's advice or her decision. She was aware how much he hoped for a son of his own this time.

To Juliette the main benefit of her pregnancy was the opportunity it gave her to enjoy leisure time with Michel and Sylvana without the pressure of other matters. She and Marco had always encouraged the children to appreciate books and she was able to give full attention to teaching Michel to read whereas previously these sessions of instruction had been brief. She also introduced him to simple sums. With her help Sylvana was able to identify all the letters of the alphabet and pick out the capitals for her own name and those of the household, *P* for *Papa* not being overlooked.

Every month of her pregnancy seemed to be marked by dramatic events in the war, including the entry of the United States into the conflict. From August to September a state of high tension had existed in Venice as fierce battles raged on the defensive Italian lines at San Gabriele and Bainsizza. When the Austrians finally retreated Venetians breathed again and there was general rejoicing that once more the city had been spared an enemy attack by land.

Juliette thought sometimes that even without the personal

295

reminders of Nikolai, the newspapers continued to give her plenty of information in the daily reports. She read with sympathy that the Tsar and Tsarina with their children had been sent to Siberia for their safety. Moreover there was concern among the Allies that Russia might withdraw from the war to settle its own growing internal troubles, especially since the Russians had suffered a disastrous defeat at the river Riva, which the newspapers blamed on a malaise of discontent in the ranks and mass desertions.

Towards the end of October Juliette rose awkwardly from her bed to bathe and dress. She paused, listening. An ominous sound was rolling towards Venice from the distance. Hurrying to the window, she threw the shutters wide. It was gunfire!

It had happened before that sometimes when the wind was in the right direction guns had been heard faintly like the rumble of far-away thunder, but this was louder than she had ever heard before. She went to look at the children, but they were still sleeping, Catarina having not yet come to get them up. As soon as she was dressed she went downstairs to find Lena and Catarina coming back indoors after talking to two workmen. Hastily Catarina bade Juliette good morning and darted past her upstairs to the children, aware of her duties neglected.

Juliette remained standing by the bottom of the stairs, alarmed by Lena's serious expression. 'What's happening?'

'Nobody quite knows, but according to rumour there's a great battle going on at Caporetto.'

'My husband is in that area!' Juliette's face became ashen. 'He was posted there only recently.'

Lena tut-tutted in sympathy and went to her. 'Go and sit down at the breakfast table, signora. I'll pour you a cup of coffee. All will be well, I'm sure. Try to eat a little. You have your baby to think about too.'

Later in the morning Lena went out to St Mark's Square to see if any communiqués were being issued and it was confirmed that a battle with a large engagement of forces was in progress at Caporetto. All the city knew that the outcome of the battle was vital, for from there the Austrians could turn their guns on Venice.

'We must pack hand-luggage ready for an emergency flight,' Juliette said at once, determined to keep her promise to Marco that she and the children would leave for Tuscany as soon as it proved necessary. She had no wish to travel in the final days of her pregnancy, although all was normal with her now. At least she had enough leeway left to get her to the villa for the birth.

'I'll pack for you, signora,' Lena offered. 'Catarina can see to the children's things.'

'I'll gather some baby clothes together. We shall surely know soon how the tide of battle will turn.'

All through the day the bombardment rumbled on. Juliette's thoughts were constantly with Marco. During the afternoon she took the children to see Henriette.

'Did you come to see if we'd flown?' Henriette joked. She had poured coffee for Juliette and herself and given the children each an apple.

'No, I knew that would never happen. I came to tell you that I'll be taking all my brood off to Tuscany tomorrow.'

'I'm relieved to hear it. If the worst happens Venice won't be taken easily. It will be no place for you and the children.'

'I'd like you to keep a key to the house. If Marco should come home while we're still away at least he could get in.'

Henriette gave her a reassuring nod as Juliette put the key into her outstretched hand. 'I'll keep it gladly. This is the first place Marco would come to ask about you.'

It was unspoken between them that his arrival would most surely mean a full retreat from Caporetto.

In the evening Lena went again to hear the latest communiqué and came hastening back, full of what she had to tell.

'All foreigners in the city have been given notice to quit. Only the British Consul has refused to leave his post!'

'Don Mariano will undoubtedly be another who will have dug in his heels,' Juliette commented, thinking to herself that neither would Henriette ever leave his side.

'There's a special train leaving shortly for the foreigners, only hand-luggage to be taken. You're French, signora. You and the children can be on that train. I'll help you get ready!'

Juliette made no move from her chair, shaking her head. 'That's not possible. Remember I'm an Italian by marriage. I no longer have a French passport. Instead, as I've always planned, we'll all leave together by the first available train for Tuscany in the morning. As I told you a while ago, I've kept in touch with the caretaker and his wife. They know to expect us whenever we should arrive.'

'There're bound to be hundreds of others in Venice wanting to leave by train tomorrow if they didn't get away today. I'll go to the railway station and get the tickets now. If there's any difficulty I'll see the station-master. He's an old friend.'

Juliette fetched her purse and gave Lena the money. 'That will be more than enough to cover the fares for all of us, because on your way to the railway station I want you to call on Signora Ottoni and see if she would like to accompany us. She is Italian by marriage too and there would be no place on the foreigners' train for her either.'

'I'll do that. May I ask a favour? Could Arianna have the same chance too? She is my niece and I've kept a maternal eye on her ever since she lost her parents.'

Juliette took more money from her purse. 'Of course. I should have thought about it myself. Catarina can go now to her apartment and ask her.'

'Mind you, I don't know if she'll come. Umberto, her husband, is home at the moment. His ship put in for minor repairs and she may not want to leave until he sails again.'

'She shall be given the address of the villa and then she can always join us there later. I'm sure her husband would wish her to do that.'

The velvety Venetian night had descended when Lena went out again, taking Catarina with her. On the narrow ways along the edge of the canals they were alert in case anyone approaching might bump into them in the darkness, and gave the gondoliers' cry, rarely heard otherwise these days, of '*Scia ohè*'. It had become the custom since the accidental drownings in the early days of the blackout and the usual reply came back clearly. '*Premi eh!*'

Soon they parted company and Catarina went to Arianna's home. Lena called on Signora Ottoni, who expressed appreciation of Juliette's offer, but said she was staying with her hospital. At the railway station Lena saw that sentries were guarding the entrance and preventing access.

'The station is closed for the night,' a sentry told her when she asked to go through to speak to the station-master. 'Go away now, signora. A hospital train is being unloaded.'

'That's why I'm here.' She lied glibly, determined to get through. 'He sent for me. I'm a nurse.'

She looked convincing. A short, square, full-bosomed woman in her neat clothes and sensible hat. The sentries let her in and she hurried onto the platform only to halt at the sight that met her. There was just enough glow from the shrouded lanterns to show the vast numbers of stretchers being lifted from the train and conveyed in a stream to the waiting water ambulances and *vaporetti* that would convey the wounded to the landing stage nearest each hospital. There were heart-rending groans, some men crying pathetically and so many seeming to be coughing up their lungs. Nuns moved like pale ghosts among the stretchers that were manned by soldiers and civilian volunteers, the station-master among them. All the wounded were in their filthy uniforms straight from the battlefield, caked in mud and blood. Some, who could walk assisted by nuns, had lost their boots, many had their faces and eyes bandaged.

Lena sat down helplessly on a seat, there being nothing she could do amid this organized chaos, and fearful of getting in the way. The scene told her more about the battle at Caporetto than any communiqué could have done. Normally the wounded passed through field hospitals first, but this time the ghastly wave of casualties had swamped all the facilities nearer the front line. Venice itself had become a field hospital.

When the last of the casualties were aboard, Lena saw her friend go into his office. She jumped up from the seat and hurried in after him.

He had sunk down into a chair at his desk, his elbows propped on it and his head in his hands. At the sound of her entry he sat back and looked up, his face haggard.

'Those poor boys,' she said in a quavering voice. 'That coughing!'

He shook his head at the tragedy of it all. 'Didn't you guess the reason, Lena? The enemy is using mustard gas at Caporetto.'

She clamped her fingers over her trembling mouth and sat down abruptly in the nearest chair, taking a few moments to recover from what she had heard. 'I mustn't let Signora Romanelli know. Her husband is there.'

'Has she had her baby yet?'

'Not yet. That's why I have to get her out of Venice quickly to the safety of a villa near Lucca.'

'Don't ask me for advance train tickets,' he insisted wearily. 'It's a case of first to come on the day is first served. I've had people pestering me all day, here and at home, all wanting priority in getting away.'

She pulled her chair nearer and rested the flat of her hands on his desk in a demanding manner. 'You and I are old friends, Roberto. Our late mothers of sweet memory were friends. We played together as children. Am I not godmother to your married daughter in Naples? Are you still going to refuse me?'

He regarded her with mild exasperation. 'I can't do the impossible. When the foreigners' train pulled out earlier that was the last I could guarantee. Priority is being given to all the hospital trains and, judging from what just arrived, there're going to be plenty of them.' He glanced at a clock on the wall 'There'll be another in shortly. What other trains will come and go within the next few days is a matter for speculation.'

'You must have some idea,' she persisted.

He sighed. 'According to the time-table a train you would want should be departing from here tomorrow evening at eight o'clock, but you'd have to chance your luck.'

'I'll have six open tickets all the way to Lucca,' she declared immediately. 'Then if there are any delays they'll still be usable.' In triumph she watched him pull open a drawer, take out the book of special tickets and fill them in.

'Change at Florence,' he said automatically as he handed them over. Then, seeing she was opening her purse to pay, he made a dismissive gesture. 'I don't even know if you're going to get away on any train. Pay the railway company after the war if you do.'

'Thank you, Roberto.'

When she arrived back at the Romanelli house Catarina had already returned. As half-expected, Arianna did not wish to leave Venice until her husband sailed. Lena sent Catarina out again to deliver a train ticket to Arianna for whenever she could travel.

The next day was spent in stripping beds and dealing with the final laundry. After the first air-raid on Venice Juliette had stored away the most valuable porcelain items in the house and when she would have begun packing silver to store away as well, Catarina took over from her, enlisting the children's help to fetch the smaller pieces. Food and drink were put in a basket for the journey and the house began to take on an austere tidiness. Still the distant guns kept up their incessant pounding. At midday Austrian aeroplanes

300

flew in over the Lagoon, but three Italian ones swept in and vanquished them after a short air battle that was watched with excitement from below.

In the late afternoon Lena went to see Roberto again to check that the train would be leaving at eight o'clock. He affirmed that it would be, for whereas hospital trains would hold priority it had become vitally important to get people out of Venice too, in whatever time was left.

'Is the latest news so bad?' she asked fearfully.

He nodded, dashing out of his office as another hospital train came in. With a heavy heart she returned home and found that Fortuny and his French lady had called to say goodbye to the family.

Henriette and Juliette hugged each other. 'We'll miss you,' Henriette declared fervently.

'We hope to be back soon,' Juliette replied huskily.

Fortuny kissed her on both cheeks. 'I echo that hope. In the meantime take care!'

There were no other visitors. Most of Juliette's friends had departed over the past months. Evening came at last and the little travelling party with hand-luggage left the house. Sadly Juliette locked it behind her.

As they stood on the landing stage, waiting for the *vaporetto* to take them to the railway station, Juliette wondered if Nikolai was on the move anywhere too. Bolshevik troops seemed to have found a leader in a man called Lenin. With the Venetian newspaper reduced to a double page, Italian war news was inclined to crowd all foreign news into tiny paragraphs. The report about Russia she had read earlier in the day. Lena interrupted her train of thought.

'The *vaporetto*'s almost here! Are you sure that piece of hand-luggage isn't too heavy for you to lift?'

'No, it's quite light.' Juliette picked it up in readiness. As the steamer stopped she shepherded the children and Catarina on board first before waving on Lena, who was carrying more of the luggage, including the food for the train journey. She was about to follow herself when it came to her startlingly, triggered by those thoughts of Nikolai, that she had omitted to pack her Delphos robe. Abruptly she took a step back.

'Hurry, signora!' Lena called anxiously.

Juliette withdrew still further. 'I've forgotten something! Go

301

ahead! There's plenty of time. I'll catch you up at the railway station!'

She turned on her heel and hastened back as fast as she could by the way she had come. As a precaution earlier she had given Lena all the tickets except her own, just in case in her condition she should be slower getting through to the platform if there were a lot of other passengers. Why hadn't she thought about the gown before? It must have been because Lena packed the hand-luggage for her while she had only dealt with requirements for the baby.

But her gown could not be left behind! If the Austrians bombarded Venice the house might be destroyed. There was always the chance if they took the city that they would loot from deserted properties. Without pause Juliette hurried on down the long *calle* at the side of the Palazzo Orfei. Only the square left to cross. Yet what a distance it seemed!

She arrived breathlessly at the house and let herself in. The electricity had been switched off somewhere in the kitchen regions, but there were candles and matches in the hall. By the light of the flickering flame she started up the flight. Halfway she paused, having to rest and gulp the air. The house was extraordinarily silent, without even the creaks that were normal in the night when the furniture and other woodwork settled. Yet the warm silence was full of memories that were almost audible, totally unlike an empty house when most of the contents had been cleared, the owners gone for ever. She seemed to hear Michel's running footsteps, Sylvana's new-born cry, the conversation of good friends gathered around the dining table, the clink of wine glasses, Marco's deep laughter and the sound made when he had struck her in his rage, that at the time had seemed to go on echoing for ever in her head. Even Nikolai was there, haunting her as he had done vividly for months after her last sight of him, causing her to lie awake when Marco slept after making love to her.

Her breath recovered, she continued up the flight. In her bedroom she stood on a low stool to take the Fortuny box from its remote corner at the back of a closet shelf. Stepping down again, she took off the lid and removed the Delphos robe, its softness crowding into her hand. She thrust it into her hand-luggage, swiftly tossed the box back on to the shelf and closed the closet door.

She left the bedroom and had reached the head of the stairs when a knife-like pain of such ferocity seared through her that it almost tossed her down the flight. The candlestick flew from her hand as she grabbed the newel-post and clung to it. The flame extinguished itself upon contact with the wall. She was left in total darkness, hearing her dropped hand-baggage go bumping down from stair to stair.

Slowly her pain subsided, but another struck before she could move. Somehow she would have to get to the telephone down in the hall! Her difficult descent began. She gripped the bannister rail with both hands, fearful of falling, and found the next tread carefully with one foot before bringing her other down beside it. The pain only subsided to return again in full force, making the sweat run down her face and trickle under her clothes. Would this have happened if she had not hastened back as she had done? She had counted on having at least another eight or nine days. Was she ever going to reach the hall? In the inky darkness it was like descending into a bottomless abyss.

Compelled to pause between pains to regather her strength before moving on again, she thought of the children arriving at the railway station, excited by the prospect of the journey ahead. At least they were in safe hands with Lena in charge. Juliette was certain that when she failed to arrive at the railway station Lena and Catarina would continue with the journey and take the children on to the safety of the villa. Lena would be angry at not having been told what she would conclude to have been a pre-arranged plan by her employer not to accompany them. Juliette could see only too clearly that everything would point to that conclusion. There was the almost theatrical manner, all unconscious at the time, in which she had suddenly drawn back from boarding, keeping the baby clothes with her. Her apparently pre-conceived action would be seen as a way of avoiding a distressing scene with the children, who would not have wanted to leave their home without her. Lena would expect her to follow with the new baby in her own time and would pacify the children with the promise when the novelty of travelling had waned and they had begun asking for her.

How quickly would she be able to follow them, taking with her the baby to whom she was about to give birth? Would circumstances of the war even permit it when she was strong enough to travel? Juliette felt mild surprise that her brain should function so clearly between the mind-blanking spasms of torture that she was enduring.

Surely she must be near the bottom of the flight now? The midwife who had attended her at Sylvana's birth did not have a telephone, it being a luxury generally beyond the financial reach of many people, but a call to Henriette would set everything in motion. Fortuny himself would go to fetch the midwife. There was no chance of getting a doctor, for every one of them would be at the hospitals, trying to deal with each influx of wounded before the next arrived.

Her hand met the carved surface of the bottom newel-post. She was safely down! With relief she stepped from the last tread, but instead of the marble floor her foot encountered something soft. In the same instant she realized it was her fallen hand-luggage, but already she had stepped down with too much confidence and it slid under her weight, taking her with it. She screamed as she went flying, throwing out her arms instinctively to try to save her stomach from full impact with the hard surface. Landing on her side with a heavy thud, shocked through from head to foot, she was propelled by the force of her fall to crash against the legs of the hall table.

For several minutes she lay helpless, tears running from under her closed eyelids. A clock on the wall began to chime in deep tones the hour of eight o'clock and other clocks began to echo its announcement with melodious tinkling behind the doors of various rooms. At the railway station the train would be departing. She could picture Lena looking from the window in the chance that she might have changed her mind at the last minute.

No chance of that! Juliette waited for the few precious moments of respite between pains and levered herself slowly up into a half-sitting position. The telephone was on the table by which she had fallen. Taking hold of the edge of the table with one hand she reached out searchingly with the other until she found the telephone and could pull it forward. It was an elegant shape with brass ornamentation and the ear and mouth piece connected. She put the receiver to her ear and waited for the operator to ask what number she required. Nothing happened. She had to wait until another bout of agony had passed before she could bang the receiver's rest several times, but the line was dead. The reason was easily guessed, for with the military situation so precarious all lines were being kept open only for calls of national importance.

She sank back onto the chill floor again, hearing herself shriek out as a yawning cavern of pain swallowed her into a deeper darkness from which it would have been easy to escape into oblivion, but somehow she struggled back again. Her baby was being born. It would die if she lost consciousness! She must be having a boy, because only the male sex caused women equal agony of the heart and mind. Her thoughts tumbled and twisted as if keeping pace with her thrusting and her screams. She did not hear a key turn in the lock, but in a final body-tearing effort her infant slithered with a rush into the world and she heard his lusty wail.

It was morning before Juliette received a full account from Lena of what had happened when she had failed to arrive at the railway station. By then she had slept for several hours in her bed that had been hastily made up to receive her. The night before Fortuny himself had carried her upstairs to it as effortlessly as if she were a child in his arms.

'Tell me first if there is any fresh news about Caporetto,' Juliette asked from her pillows, looking across at the cradle where her son lay.

'I haven't heard anything,' Lena lied. This was no time to repeat a neighbour's information that Caporetto had fallen and Italian soldiers were in full retreat, thousands already taken prisoner by the enemy.

'I've noticed that the guns are quieter. Do you suppose that means the Austrians have retreated?'

'Let's hope so,' Lena said quickly. 'May I ask what name you're going to give your son.'

'It's my husband's choice. He wanted a son to be named Riccardo after his father.'

'I like that. It's a good, strong name.'

'I like it too. You know, all I can really remember your saying to me last night is that Arianna had taken charge of Michel and Sylvana.'

'You were in quite a panic thinking I'd left them to travel alone with young Catarina.' Lena removed a breakfast tray from the bed and deposited it on a table outside the room, talking all the time through the open door. 'I would never have done that. The train was packed, many passengers having to stand, but Roberto had secured seats for us. It was just as we were about to leave that Arianna came running along the platform looking for us.' Lena came back

305

to the bedside and smoothed the top sheet. 'I was still watching out for you, which was how she found us.'

'What of her husband?'

'He'd been recalled to his ship sooner than he'd expected and she'd just had time to see him off and get to the train. I told her to take over and that you and I would follow when you were fit to travel after the birth. I never expected when Madame Negrin used her key for us to enter the house that we should find the baby had just arrived.'

'What made you come back?'

'Suddenly I guessed what had happened. You hadn't left anything behind! That was an excuse, because you had felt your first labour pains and didn't dare to travel. Naturally I thought you would have gone straight to the Palazzo Orfei. But when I called there first Madame Negrin became as anxious about you as me.' Lena was quite smug in her astuteness at deducing what she believed to be the true facts. Juliette did not enlighten her.

'I was so relieved to see both of you bending over me in the lantern light.'

'Afterwards I've never moved so fast in all my life!' Lena threw up her hands expressively. 'Switching the electricity back on! Finding scissors and twine! I shouted to Madame Negrin to fetch some linen from the nursery to wrap the baby in and a blanket from the cupboard for you. She ran about as fast as I did. As soon as you could be moved she rushed back to the Palazzo and fetched Don Mariano. They'll be calling in later to see how you are this morning.'

When Fortuny and Henriette arrived Lena forewarned them before they went upstairs that she had told Juliette nothing of the disastrous retreat from Caporetto. 'To be honest, I hadn't the heart. Maybe it would be best coming from you, Madame Negrin. But tomorrow perhaps? She's exhausted today.'

'Yes, you're right,' Henriette agreed. 'A full day and night's rest is what she needs. I'll look in again this evening and then tomorrow morning I'll tell her whatever the latest news may be.'

She went ahead up the stairs and Fortuny held up the bottle of champagne that he had brought with him. 'Please bring four glasses up to Signora Romanelli's room. I want you to join us in a toast to the new baby.'

As Lena took the glasses up on a tray she thought to herself that even with the Austrian guns only fifteen miles away, perhaps even less by now, Fortuny was his usual immaculate self from his white silk cravat to his patent leather shoes, just as he had been last night when summoned without warning from his fireside. She believed he would look the same in the midst of the enemy bombardment that was sure to break upon Venice before long. Not even dust would dare to settle on that handsome slouch hat that he had swept off upon entering the house.

Juliette, in spite of her physical tiredness, enjoyed the time her visitors spent with her and thanked them for all they had done the night before.

'It's Lena you should thank,' Henriette countered, sitting on the edge of the bed. 'If it wasn't for her I daren't think what the end result might have been.'

'I'm forever in her debt.' Juliette smiled gratefully at Lena, who was embarrassed by the praise.

Fortuny proposed toasts to Riccardo, to Marco and to victory. Such was his charismatic presence and air of supreme confidence that even Lena was half persuaded that things might turn out all right after all.

For the ten days after giving birth that every woman was expected to spend in bed, Juliette was cocooned in her room; a delayed telegram from Arianna, which arrived on the fifth day, relieved her worry about the children. They were safe and had settled down at the Casa San Giorgio.

Meanwhile the Italian navy was increasing its defences all around Venice and only soldiers were to be seen on the Grand Canal. The market stood deserted and whole streets presented shuttered shop-fronts where once all had been busy. Churches had become temporary shelters for the thousands of refugees pouring in from the war-wasted mainland. When the first time after her confinement Juliette walked to St Mark's Square she paused in dismay at the pathetic sight that met her. More refugees had landed that morning with their children, their bundles and some with pets, every new batch gathering there much as foreign visitors always did upon first arriving in the city. Priests and nuns and volunteers were handing out emergency rations.

The strain on Venice with all these extra mouths to feed was eased as various vessels came to transport civilians down the coast to safer areas. Juliette with her baby and Lena were alloted passes and were making ready to depart when Signora Ottoni called. She was in great distress, her eyes red-rimmed.

'Whatever has happened?' Juliette exclaimed compassionately, putting an arm about her and leading her into the salon where they sat on a sofa together.

'I've terrible news.' Signora Ottoni could scarcely speak. 'I felt I had to tell you before you left. My nephew, Alexander, has been killed.'

'Oh, my dear friend!' Juliette was overwhelmed by compassion.

'The British Consul himself broke the news to me. I don't know by what means it was conveyed to him except that it had come from a mutual acquaintance in diplomatic circles in Switzerland.'

'Were you told where this tragedy happened?'

'No, only that Alexander and two of his friends, Anatole Suchkin and Nikolai Karasvin were shot down by enemy machine-gun fire when trying to rally their men from a retreat. Three fine young men cut down like sheaves.' She broke down into hopeless sobbing.

Juliette sat numbed through by shock, feeling her heart split apart. Then silently she swayed, tipping slowly forward from the sofa onto the floor in a deep faint.

CHAPTER TWENTY-FIVE

Juliette had been reunited with Michel and Sylvana for several weeks at the Casa San Giorgio before she received military confirmation of what had happened to Marco at Caporetto. Candida Bonini came running to her with the telegram.

'This has just been delivered, signora.'

She watched anxiously as the younger woman's trembling hands ripped open the envelope. Then she saw Juliette's eyes shut with relief as she crumpled the telegram to her.

'My husband is all right, Candida. He's a prisoner of war, but he's safe!'

'I'm so happy for you!'

Candida ran to tell the others the good news. She liked having guests in the villa again, especially the children, for she and Antonio missed their own daughters who had married and moved away.

By the time summer came, bringing a golden heat haze over the Tuscan hills, it seemed that at last the tide might be turning for the Allied armies in the fields of battle. In Russia revolution was raging. The tragic Tsar and his wife and family had been massacred before the White army, led by aristocrats, could save them, and the life or death struggle with the Bolsheviks, re-named the Red Army, continued unabated.

Juliette's mourning for Nikolai was private and intense. She had nobody to whom she could talk about it; even Dr Morosini was away, serving as a medical officer in the army. Sometimes, when she went out onto the loggia and gazed at the sweeping view, all that had happened since she first came to the villa for Michel's birth came back to her. For the second time in her life she had to gather all her strength for the future. The war had changed everybody and everything. Reason told her that she and countless other wives on both sides of the conflict would have to build up a new and secure existence for homecoming men shattered by the horrors of the battlefield. But women had changed too, the whole mode of their pre-war lives altered by coming out of their homes into war-work and replacing men in many fields of employment. It would be better for both sexes to be on an equal footing, but it was most likely that the returning men would want everything to be exactly as it was before they went away. Perhaps even more so.

She had written to Marco through the Red Cross to let him know of Riccardo's birth and a long while afterwards she had received his reply in the few lines allowed, expressing his joy. She was thankful that he would not be coming home to find his house damaged by bombs or shell-fire, for when everything had seemed at its blackest for Venice the situation had suddenly improved. Sections of the Italian lines had rallied, and British and French troops had arrived to strengthen offensives. The Italian Flying Corps, which had done so much to protect Venice from the worst of the bombing, was supported by Allied aviators and together they had wreaked havoc on the enemy.

In November, shortly after Riccardo's first birthday, the Armistice was signed and the war was over at last. Juliette was unable to join in the celebrations for she had succumbed to Spanish flu, which had begun sweeping through Europe.

Delirious, she did not hear the church bells ringing in the distance or know that Michel and Sylvana were lying equally ill in a neighbouring room. Lena and Candida did most of the nursing with Arianna's help, for Catarina was looking after Riccardo in another part of the house in the hope they would both escape infection. An elderly doctor had come out of retirement to help with the epidemic and one night he shook his head gravely.

'I fear Signora Romanelli and young Michel will not survive until the morning.'

'That's only his opinion,' Lena said grimly as soon as he was gone. 'I'll make sure he's wrong.'

All through the night she and Candida sponged down the patients, for before midnight Arianna had begun to sway on her feet from the early symptoms of the flu and had taken to her bed. When dawn came hope revived for the sick child and his mother. By the next day it was certain they would pull through and Sylvana was already well on the way to recovery. Before Arianna was on her feet again Candida collapsed and, although everything possible was done to save her, she died within a week. Antonio was the next victim and his wife's funeral was over before he recovered. As soon as he was well enough his daughter, Lucietta, and her husband came to take him away to live with them in Rome.

It fell to Juliette to lock the door of the villa when she and her children with the trio of women left to return to Venice. The key was handed to a solicitor in Lucca, who had always arranged the renting to tenants in the past. He was newly returned from the war and was not quite reorganized.

'Does the Baronne de Landelle want me to find another caretaker for her?' he asked.

'I'm sure she will, but I haven't heard from her for several months. Now that everything is getting back to normal you can write to her.'

The last letter Juliette had received from Denise had told of Maison Landelle's final closing, which had left her sister deeply in debt and wallowing in self-pity.

Venice looked pale and ethereal under a layer of snow, the lights gleaming softly again in the falling flakes. It was early evening and bitterly cold as Juliette and her little party followed the familiar narrow *calle* by the side of the Palazzo Orfei, Michel and Sylvana tired and fretful after the long journey. Riccardo had matched their behaviour earlier, fast developing a will of his own, and even at thirteen months able to show his resentment at the disruption to his routine. But he had eventually worn himself out and was fast asleep as Juliette carried him, warmly wrapped, in her arms.

She glanced up over her shoulder at the façade of the Palazzo Orfei as they entered the old square again. Henriette had written

311

that she and Fortuny had married quietly with only two witnesses. Juliette wondered what had prompted them to take this step after sixteen years together, but that was their private decision and was to be respected.

Juliette and the women with her had expected to find her home closed and shuttered, a cavern of icy cold after being unheated and deserted for such a long time, but the windows were warmly aglow.

'Doña Henriette is showing herself to be a good neighbour and not for the first time!' Juliette exclaimed. 'I'd no idea when I let her know the time we were coming home that she would make the house welcoming for us!'

She handed Riccardo over to Catarina and opened the door with her key. She had thought it would be Henriette coming quickly into the lighted hall at the sound of her entry, but it was Marco who rushed from the salon. With a cry she threw herself into his arms.

'Oh, my dear!' she exclaimed, her eyes tight shut in thankfulness as he hugged her to him after they had kissed. 'You're home! You're safe! I should have been here for your home-coming!'

'I've been back barely a week, my darling,' he answered smilingly, as they drew apart, 'and there was no predicting when I could return.' He turned to look down at Michel, who was tugging at his jacket, and lifted him up. 'How you've grown, my boy!'

'I've been in the country, Papa!' Michel had wrapped his arms about Marco's neck. 'Don't ever go away again!'

'No, I won't.' Marco stooped down and scooped Sylvana up with his other arm, holding both children and kissing their cheeks. Juliette took Riccardo from Catarina and waited. She watched as Lena and Arianna greeted her husband, then Catarina. Marco and the two children he held were directly under the full light of the chandelier, enabling her to see how much weight he had lost and that there was grey in his hair, which had never been there before. He was not in uniform and the dark blue suit he wore no longer fitted him as perfectly as it had done before the war. His face bore an expression of immense happiness in this reunion with his family, but when he set Michel and Sylvana down on their feet again and looked towards the child she held an almost ecstatic joy transfigured his features. He held out his arms and she placed Riccardo into them.

'My son!' he breathed, gazing down into the child's sleeping face.

Michel darted forward angrily. 'I'm your son too, Papa!'

312

'Of course you are!' Marco ruffled the boy's curls, but did not take his eyes from the child he held.

Juliette, seeing the sudden misery in the boy's face, ushered him and Sylvana into action.

'Let's go upstairs and remove our outdoor things.' She took Michel's hand as they went up the flight, leaving Marco carrying Riccardo into the salon, still gazing at him. Sylvana was already near the top of the stairs, eager to see all her dolls again. 'You must try to remember, Michel,' Juliette said gently, 'that although we've had Riccardo for over a year this is the first time Papa has seen him.'

'He called him his son.' Michel hung his head unhappily.

'So he is. Papa calls you his son too.'

'But he only called me his boy.'

'He meant it in exactly the same way. Papa is going to find things difficult after being away so long in a dreadful camp where he didn't get enough to eat. Did you notice how thin he is? We have to do all we can to make it easy for him to settle down again. Promise me you'll do your best.'

'Yes, Mama.' He nodded, but his dejection had not abated.

Upstairs all the beds had been aired and made up. Henriette had played her part from the moment of Marco's return. He had had his meals with her and Fortuny until this evening, and when Lena went into the warm, bright kitchen there was a pan of pasta and another of sauce ready for serving.

They all sat down together for supper at the large kitchen table. Marco had never eaten there before, but this was an exceptional occasion. He opened some good red wine and served it. By Michel's chair he paused to pour a little into the boy's glass of water.

'You've been the man of the family whilst I was away and you deserve a taste of wine.'

Michel beamed at this special attention and the adults all laughed kindly at his obvious pride. Juliette, regarding him with love, knew well enough that he was thinking that Riccardo had not been given this special treat.

Over supper some news was exchanged, Juliette hearing that so far both Fortuny and Henriette had escaped the Spanish flu raging through the city, as had Doña Cecilia, although Maria Luisa had been very ill. Marco wanted to know about the time spent at the villa and was saddened to hear that the Boninis' days there had come

313

to an end through tragedy. It was not until the elder children were in bed and Riccardo in his cot in the nursery that he and Juliette were able to talk alone in the salon where a fire blazed. There was some mail for her on the table and although she would have left it until the morning, ready to give all her attention to Marco, he pointed out that there was a letter from Denise, which he had read since it was addressed to them both.

'Is she well?' she asked anxiously, taking up the letter.

'Yes, indeed,' he replied drily.

The first sentence informed Juliette that Denise had married Jacques Vernet not long after the closure of Maison Landelle and he had settled all her debts.

He and I both enjoy the good things in life, Denise wrote, *and he made a fortune in munitions during that hateful war that is over at last. You cannot begin to imagine all the hardships I have endured. Thankfully that is all over now and Jacques is the most generous man. It is a relief to have finished for ever with temperamental clients, mannequins screaming at one another in the* cabine, *crises in the ateliers and all the other hassles of running a* haute couture *house. In future I shall be the difficult client!*

Juliette read through the rest of the letter. Not even the war had changed her sister in any way. She folded the letter again. 'Denise has finally achieved her ultimate aim in life. She has money to burn at last!'

Marco was standing in the firelight that accentuated the gaunt hollows of his face. 'There'll be no orders from Maison Landelle any more,' he said despondently. 'One more buyer that has gone for ever.'

She went to him and slipped her hand into the crook of his arm. 'Try not to worry. Conditions are bound to be difficult for a while, but that will change.'

'But when? How soon?' His mood was deep and dark. 'I've spent a couple of days at the office checking the contacts that I might be able to pick up again without too much delay. The premises are empty now, the convalescents and the nursing staff left a while ago.'

'You shouldn't have gone there. You're not well enough yet!'

'I couldn't stay long, I admit. I seemed to lose all strength after a while.'

'That will soon pass too.'

'It was disheartening to see how the place had been left. Patients

314

pinned pictures or photographs up on the frescoes. In other rooms nails have been driven into the walls and temporary shelving has been left.'

'I didn't know. I'm so sorry!'

He put his hand over hers. 'Don't blame yourself. You did right to let the premises be used for the sick. I wouldn't have had it otherwise. But there's more to tell. The top floor was broken into and all the stock I had there stolen. The police think the theft might well have taken place when shortages were at their worst. So I'll be starting from scratch again. It's early to speak of it when you've just come home, but we'll have to watch expenses for a while. Arianna spoke at supper of returning to her own home tomorrow and I'm afraid Catarina must go too.'

'Oh, no! She has no other home.'

'Then she must find employment where she can live in.'

'Very well.' She knew how upset the girl would be. 'It must be somewhere she'll be happy. I can't let her go otherwise.'

He frowned impatiently. 'I've said we must dispense with her services and that means as soon as possible.'

'Are things so bad financially?'

'I simply said we must economize in the present circumstances.'

'Yes, of course. You can rely on me. Tomorrow you shall rest and I'll organize the putting to rights of the premises. After that I'll help you at the office. There will be many things I can do. It shouldn't take me long to learn how to type.'

He embraced her with one arm as he shook his head. 'No, that's my domain. Yours is here under this roof.'

With a flash of insight she realized he had come home determined that never again should she step out of the role he had always wanted her to play and that in the future everything should be as he decreed as head of the house. The months of idleness in the miseries of a prison camp had given him plenty of time to mull over his life and the mistakes he believed he had made. She saw now that his determination that Catarina should go was not wholly for financial reasons, but to anchor his wife down more securely. She had expected to find him suffering from all he had been through, but not embittered towards her. She understood that the task she had foreseen of helping him build up his life again was to be even more difficult than she had anticipated.

315

It was unfortunate that when they went up to bed she found that Lena, having unpacked the hand-baggage, had lain the Delphos robe across the bed, not knowing where it was normally kept. Marco snatched it up, the coppery silk shimmering its fiery shades.

'What's this doing here?' he demanded, his eyes blazing.

Juliette became pale, afraid he was going to rip it apart. 'I took it with me. Let me put it away.' She held out her hands, but his grip clenched tighter on it.

'You were only able to take what could be carried on your flight from Venice, and yet you found space for this garment!'

'It weighs so little!'

'But something of more use could have been packed instead!' His face was congested with wrath. 'You couldn't leave your precious keepsake behind, could you? You didn't take the Fortuny gowns I gave you!'

'I had a photograph of you!'

'And plenty of Karasvin no doubt!'

'I destroyed those long ago at the villa when I agreed to marry you. I didn't keep one!'

'You should have rid yourself of this robe as well! I'll burn it myself now!' He made for the door, but her cry made him halt.

'No!' She had flung her arms over her head as she began to sob. 'Nikolai is dead! He was killed in action!'

Her grief, which she had hidden and controlled for so long, burst forth in an ocean of tears she could not stem. Slowly she sank down to her knees as if the weight of it was too much for her to sustain, bowed over as she was racked through by her terrible sobbing. Marco stood looking down at her and did not move. He was in despair that his nerves and his temper had become intertwined, making him rage even on this night of being with her again. The war had torn him apart and he was tortured by the age-old shame of the returned warrior to be still alive when so many friends and comrades had been killed. Memories of death in the stinking mountain trenches tormented him and could not be driven away. Only with this woman whom he loved and in her warm, sweet depths could he hope for any escape from his mental tortures and her sobbing was more than he could bear.

He threw aside the gown and reached down to raise her up and fold her in his arms. Her brow sank against his shoulder as she

316

continued to weep. He stroked her hair, murmured to her and wept himself. When he drew away from her she continued to stand with her head dipped and made no move as he undressed her and put her into the bed. She fell asleep almost instantly from exhaustion. He held her close all through the night.

When Juliette awoke it was late morning and she was alone in the bed. She guessed that Marco had given instructions that she was not to be disturbed. As she sat up she saw he had retrieved the Delphos robe and placed it on a chair. His returning it to her was a way of mending their quarrel, but she feared that it would be a long time before his shattered nerves allowed him peace of mind again.

Catarina moved in with Arianna for the time being and found domestic work in an hotel that was being changed back from a hospital to be ready to receive visitors again. Other hotels were in the same process or simply redecorating and renewing furnishings. Unlike other cities that had been through the war, Venice could count on a swift return to popularity with those able to travel once the Spanish flu scare had subsided. It was still claiming victims throughout the city as it was everywhere in Europe, but there had been plenty of plagues in Venetian history and none had defeated the queen of the Adriatic as yet.

With sandbags and cladding taken away the Lion of St Mark was to be seen again all over the city and bomb damage was being repaired. Fortuny had reopened his workshops, orders for his fabrics were coming in, including some from the grandest of the hotels to cover walls sumptuously as in the Palazzo Orfei. Marco also found his business beginning to tick over again, but not as swiftly as with Fortuny, for although his Far Eastern suppliers were eager to sell just as he was to import, all prices were much higher than before.

At home Juliette found it impossible to make life for Marco as it had been in the past. All her worst fears were realized. She knew he still loved her and kept her patience when he was being totally unreasonable, but it was often very hard on her. There were times when all seemed to be going well with his recovery, and then everything would change again. He could not control the deep clouds of depression that would descend on him without warning, making him angry with everyone around him. Neither could he hide his concentrated pride in Riccardo to the point of neglecting the other

317

two children. It was Riccardo he always went to see first when he came home from the office, the one he tossed in the air, praised and always addressed as 'my son'. At Juliette's prompting he never forgot to address Michel in the same way, but the boy noticed the other differences as if the feeling of rejection he had experienced at the time of the reunion had been branded into him. Sylvana, always placid and amiable, was not aware of her father's singular devotion to her little brother, but Michel did everything he could to gain Marco's attention. When all else failed he misbehaved deliberately at table and elsewhere until Marco's nerves, always close to breaking point, caused him to explode into temper and dreadful scenes resulted.

'Try to be more patient with Michel,' Juliette begged as she had many times before after the child had been sent crying up to his room.

'He needs disciplining, that's all,' Marco countered sharply. 'He became spoilt all that time at the villa surrounded by doting women.'

'That's nonsense! The trouble lies with you! You make it so obvious that you favour Riccardo more than Michel and Sylvana.'

'I'd never be guilty of that!' Marco was outraged. 'If I was, then Sylvana would be as difficult as Michel is proving to be.'

Juliette thought to herself that it was like talking to the proverbial brick wall every time she tried to make Marco see reason. She could only conclude that when he had received her Red Cross letter telling him that he had a son it was like a torch showing him the way to the future. That feeling had never left him.

In April Juliette and Marco took the children to the celebrations on St Mark's Day when the Basilica, repaired from its bomb damage, once more radiated its golden splendour like a great jewel in the sun. Not all the works of art and other treasures had yet returned from exile in safe places and the four bronze horses were still missing from the façade, but before long they would be home again. St Mark's Square was crowded with rejoicing Venetians, many foreigners among them. With the decline everywhere of the Spanish flu visitors had returned and once again honeymoon couples were hiring goldoliers to sing to them as they floated along the Grand Canal.

Bands were playing and there were all sorts of entertainments.

318

Riccardo, who could only toddle, rode on Marco's shoulders to keep him out of harm's way. To Michel's delight, Marco made sure that he and Sylvana secured good views of the jugglers or the acrobats or the clowns, and afterwards bought him a red clockwork motorcar that he had long wanted. He chose a doll for his sister and a woolly ball for his little brother. They all enjoyed ices at Florian's then later Marco let Michel choose where they should eat and, as expected, the boy wanted hot snacks from one of the stalls. Lena took Riccardo home for his nap in the afternoon, leaving the others to more entertainment. As soon as it grew dark there was a spectacular display of fireworks.

'What a wonderful day this has been,' Juliette said gratefully as they walked home. Marco was holding Michel's hand and she was thankful he had taken notice at last of her entreaties to pay the boy more attention.

'We'll do all this again when the bronze horses come back to the Basilica,' Marco said. 'Did you hear that, Michel?'

'Yes, Papa!' Michel jumped with glee.

When all the children were in bed Juliette went in search of Marco and found him lying back against the sofa cushions in the salon, a glass of brandy in his hand. She thought he looked tired. Sitting down on a stool, she folded her hands across her lap as she smiled at him.

'The children have all gone to sleep with their new toys on their pillows. They had such a good time.'

'I enjoyed it too. Join me in a brandy, Juliette, and give me another.'

'Very well.' Normally she did not drink any alcohol except wine, but she had the impression he wanted her to remain in the salon with him, the decanter and another glass being on a side-table, and not to go off to where the wine was kept. She took his glass from him, stooping to kiss his brow at the same time. With a start at the warmth of his skin she drew back quickly and put her hand on his forehead. 'You're not well! You're burning!'

'Yet I feel quite shivery.'

'You have a chill. It's no wonder you look tired! No more brandy. Go to bed and I'll bring you a soothing lemon and honey drink instead.'

He obeyed her without protest. As she went into the kitchen to prepare the drink she was gripped by an icy fear. Although cases of Spanish flu had been down to no more than two or three the previous week, Marco was displaying the exact symptoms that she and the others had experienced.

In the night she had to telephone for the doctor. Her worse fears were confirmed. Marco grew weaker every day in his raging fever, his time in the trenches and in a prison camp having undermined his previously robust health. He became the last person to die of Spanish flu in Venice. Michel was inconsolable, crying out in protest.

'Why did it have to happen? Papa was just beginning to like me again!'

Juliette thought to herself that she had given Michel a father, only for him to lose that relationship all too soon. Her own grief was deep. Unlike her love for Nikolai, which had been infused with passion from the first glance, all her feelings for Marco had developed from gratitude to a loving friendship on her part of enduring quality. It was not in any way to be demeaned by comparison for that reason. Both men had given her memories.

CHAPTER TWENTY-SIX

Towards the end of the year Juliette went back to selling gowns at the Palazzo Orfei. She had no financial need to work as Marco had once promised her, but fashion remained a magnet she could not resist. Michel was at school and Arianna, who had recently had a baby herself, had offered to take care of Sylvana and Riccardo daily in her own house. It was an ideal arrangement.

For months after Marco's death Juliette had felt as though she were existing in a numbing vacuum, but when at work again she began to revive. Friends were relieved to see her becoming herself again. She had dispensed early with mourning attire, knowing that Marco would have wanted her to make everything seem normal again as far as was possible for the children's sake and to keep his memory alive in a cheerful, natural talk of him. Yet she would never forget Michel's desperate cry of protest that had shown he had seen Marco's death as a further rejection of himself. Once, after she'd been widowed a year, he had asked her wistfully if she would soon marry again.

'There are plenty of men about,' he stated. 'Not all of them have children already. Surely you could find someone who would like a family. Papa wouldn't mind.'

She smiled and yet at the same time she was touched almost to tears by her son's desperate longing for a father in the house. 'I'm sorry, Michel, but I don't want to marry again. As I told you once, I lost both my parents when I was a little older than you are now, and so I understand. All I can promise you is that I'll always do my best for you and Sylvana and Riccardo.'

He nodded, choking back a sob of disappointment, and flung his arms about her waist. She held him close. One day when he was grown and could understand in his turn she would tell him the truth of who his real father had been. It was possible he would even remember the day he had waved to a man on a steam-boat, for she herself had a particular memory that she knew dated back to when she was two years old. If his looks did not change unduly she would be able to tell him how like he was to Nikolai Karasvin.

That same year of 1920 Fortuny had opened an establishment for his gowns and textiles in Paris, not far from the building that had once been Maison Landelle and on the rue Pierre Carron where Nikolai had first seen Juliette, a coincidence that did not escape her. She fully expected Fortuny to take Paris by storm for the sudden rise in orders for garments with his label was almost phenomenal.

Before the war Fortuny had never remotely matched the sales of Parisian *haute couture* houses, his gowns, if not his textiles, appealing only to those able to ignore conventional dress. Yet not long after the Armistice it was as if some invisible grapevine had made women turn their eyes in the direction of the Palazzo Orfei from many parts of the world. Perhaps those who had purchased in the pre-war days praised their gowns for being timeless and still wearable through all the swift-moving changes of fashion, emerging anew in the early days of peace. Others may have remembered the graceful lines of the garments they had seen on others or in an exhibition or even in a printed illustration that had made them think that one day they would have one of those Spanish-Venetian gowns themselves.

Whatever the reason, women began to talk about Fortuny clothes, even those who had never seen them, and the demand for these robes increased in a tidal wave as had never happened before, even though Fortuny found as Marco had done that the pre-war prices of imported silk-velvets from Lyon and silk from Japan had soared beyond belief. He could no longer charge modestly as he had done in the past.

322

Many women still chose the Delphos robe, but there were new and lovely variations in subtle, melting shades as Fortuny's dyeing skills reached new heights of pure perfection, for he was always experimenting. Some of the new gowns had long sleeves that clung softly to the shape of the arm, but most were sleeveless and tubular with a tunic effect achieved with points hanging at hip-length at the sides or with an additional one both at the front and the back. Others had cross-straps over the bodice, such as were once worn by the women of Ancient Greece, that enhanced the shape of the breasts. No woman of taste could resist these garments.

It was fast becoming the mode for actresses of the stage and screen as well as titled women and others of means to have their portraits painted while wearing a Fortuny creation. Many young women were choosing to be married in his pleated, silvery-white, often sheath-like, silk gowns, which were enhanced by classically plain veils and simple and yet sophisticated head-bands worn fashionably straight across the forehead. Fashion editors sent representatives from Paris, London, Milan and New York to interview Fortuny and get photographs. The quality magazine which had published the early photographs that had been responsible for the brief reunion between Juliette and Nikolai, reprinted them with the boast that it had foreseen the future international fame of Fortuny far ahead of its rivals. This time it was Juliette's children who gazed in surprise at the printed photograph of her in her Delphos robe, a garment they had never seen her wear.

Towards the end of that same year the blood-stained civil war in Russia came to an end with the Red Army triumphant, and refugees connected with the opposing side of the White armies were flooding out to all parts of the world. Ten million men had lost their lives in what was becoming known as the Great War and there was no telling how many more, including British and French who had aided the White Russian army since the Armistice, had fallen too, adding to the already awful total.

The highight for Juliette the following summer was the visit of Gabrielle and her new husband, Harry Scott-Moncrieff. They were on their honeymoon and Gabrielle's daughter, Elizabeth, had been left at home with Derek's mother, who was devoted to her late son's child. Harry was a much older man than Derek would have been

323

and had an equally distinguished war record. He was very much the English country squire, for generations of his family had lived in the Sussex manor house that was Gabrielle's new home. Juliette was able to see that Harry had the same protective attitude towards Gabrielle that she always seemed to arouse in men and there was no need to fear for her future happinesss. Juliette would have liked Lucille to visit her too, but her old friend's travelling days were over. She could no longer leave Rodolphe, who had become dependant on her in his declining years. As for Denise, the occasional postcard was all that Juliette ever received from her, usually sent from somewhere such as Monte Carlo where the rich could gather to enjoy themselves.

One such postcard sent by Denise from London, telling her that she and Jacques had been to the Ascot races and Henley regatta, arrived on the morning Juliette went to view the factory Fortuny had opened on the nearby island of Giudecca in what had been a derelict convent. His name in large letters across the front of the building was repeated in an appropriate size on the polished brass door-bell.

As Juliette rang for admittance she had a feeling that Fortuny was going to offer her the chance to work there as a change from selling, which she had been doing for almost two years. He was in the hall, talking to one of the men when she entered, and gave her a smiling nod.

'When you've looked around, Juliette, meet me here and we'll go back to the city together.'

She was interested in all she saw. In the large airy rooms with views of the Lagoon, his workforce had already started using the machinery invented by Fortuny himself for new methods of putting his textile designs onto an Egyptian cotton, which lent itself particularly well to what he wanted. His aim was to bring his products into a wider range by using cheaper material, but with no less care given to the methods of production. She wondered in which department she would find herself and guessed it would be re-touching the fabrics with paint brushes before they were passed as perfect.

When she and Fortuny set off again for the city in a *vaporetto*, she congratulated him on another successful new venture. He smiled, well pleased with the way everything was working out.

324

'I saw no reason why simple cotton couldn't be as beautiful in its own sphere as the silks and velvets I'm continuing to supervise personally at the Palazzo. I wanted to talk to you as I've something in mind that I'd like you to consider. There's no immediate rush for a decision, because I know what an upheaval it would mean for you, but would you consider selling for me in Paris instead of Venice?'

She was completely taken aback. Such a possibility had not occurred to her. Yet at the same time she felt a kind of call tingle through her blood as if, without ever realizing it, she had been waiting for the time when she could go home to France again. 'Why do you wish me to do that?' she managed to say.

'You're Parisian, you're an experienced saleswoman, you can be trusted with responsibility and you probably know more about Fortuny garments than anyone except Henriette and myself. So think it over.'

He did not mention the difference it would make to her financially, because he knew that would not be a consideration for her, no matter how much she would benefit. It would be whether Paris still held a greater appeal for her than Venice and if she felt able to uproot her children from their schools, even though they were bi-lingual, and leave the many friends she had made. For himself the future was presently unsettled, but only because there were so many new projects he wanted to put into motion; so many new ideas to get down on paper, some to include still more revolutionary effects with lighting and design for the theatres of the world, the majority of which had long since adopted those he had established whilst still a young man. Now he was fifty-one with grey taking over his thick hair and well-trimmed moustache and beard, but he could still meet any challenge with the same enthusiasm and joy in beauty that had propelled him since birth.

It took Juliette a week to reach her decision, but she had known what the result would be from the moment that Fortuny had given her the chance to go home. She broke the news to Michel and Sylvana, who received it according to their natures. He was always fearlessly ready for adventure and interested to see for himself the city of Paris about which his mother had told him so much from time to time. He was further attracted by the thought of being able to ride a bicycle in Paris, for none were allowed in the narrow ways of Venice. Sylvana, always placid, did not like leaving her friends, but was consoled by the thought that she would soon make new ones. She was unaware as yet that she had the gift of drawing people to her, a charm that would give her friends all her life and be a magnet to any young man of her eventual choosing. Riccardo was too young at the age of four to hold any opinion as to his whereabouts.

The house soon found a buyer. Juliette let none of the heirlooms go for sale, shipping to Paris some of the smaller items including two family portraits that Marco would have wanted his daughter and son to inherit one day. Her sister-in-law at the mission in Africa had wanted nothing except a beautiful cloth, heavy with lovely Burano lace, to be an altar cloth in the little mission church there. Everything else was shipped to Marco's brothers and their wives in the United States, for they had gratefully accepted her offer to send these family treasures.

Many friends gave farewell parties for Juliette and promises to meet again were made. She said farewell to Maria Luisa and then to Doña Cecilia, who had played such an important part in her son's life, awakening him from childhood to the beauty of art which he in turn had given to the world through silk. Although Juliette would see Fortuny whenever he came to Paris, Henriette likely to accompany him at times, it was still a wrench to be moving away from them. She found it hardest of all to part from Lena, who had been through so much with her, but the woman had firmly refused to uproot herself from her native soil. She came to the railway station on the last day to see Juliette and the children off to Paris.

'If ever you should change your mind,' Juliette urged from the carriage window when they were aboard, 'you have only to let me know and I'll come to fetch you at once.'

Lena shook her head. 'That won't happen, signora. It breaks my heart to let you and the children go without me, but I wouldn't want to be far from Catarina, Arianna and little Emilio. In any case it's time I retired. Umberto has found me a small apartment in the same neighbourhood where I'll be near them.'

The train began to move, Lena hurried along, waving to the children through the window until it gathered speed. She was left wiping the tears from her eyes.

*   *   *

326

In Paris Juliette and the children stayed in the Vernet mansion, which Jacques and Denise had offered her as a temporary abode upon hearing that she was returning. Denise had had to surrender her home in the faubourg St Germain upon her re-marriage according to the terms of Claude's will, but she had an even larger home now and it was even more luxurious with its own ballroom and double the number of household staff. She and Jacques were at present cruising in the Caribbean on a private yacht.

Juliette appreciated having leeway to choose a place of her own at leisure and schools for Michel and Sylvana. She also hired a capable nursemaid for the younger ones. An agent lined up properties for her to view and drove her to them in his motorcar. Once they passed the site of Nikolai's studio, but it was no longer there, having been replaced by a newly-built library. When she had seen all the apartments she decided on one of good size with fine rooms dating from the embellishment of Paris by Baron Haussman and within easy walking distance of Number 67, rue Pierre Carron.

When Juliette first walked into the prestigiously-sited Maison Fortuny she might have imagined herself back in the Palazzo Orfei if it had not been that the salons were smaller. Here Fortuny wall-coverings and decorative hangings, ceiling draperies, exotic lamps and certain effects were all as in Venice. In some of the draped areas his gowns, displayed as was his way on *mannequins*, glowed in tempestuous colours, while others were in delicate candy shades. Fortuny had created another Arabian Nights spectacular in the very heart of Paris.

The manager, pleasant, businesslike and alert, was exactly the sort of man Juliette had expected to find in charge. They regarded each other with respect, for each had heard Fortuny speak highly of the other. They discussed her selling only the silk pleated gowns and their capes and accessories.

The day before Juliette started work she had her hair cut in the new short style. Since the end of the war waistlines had been dropping and skirt-hems rising to become virtually knee-length. Her legs were a good shape with slim ankles and she enjoyed wearing the new length, glad that at last women's clothes were attaining the liberation for which she had always aimed and which Fortuny had achieved long ago within his own range. It gave her a new sense of freedom much like that which she had experienced when coming home from the convent all those years ago with her future stretching before her. Now she was thirty with three children and also one of the widows feared by single girls competing for the reduced number of men left available from the war. Yet although she had no shortage of male company her only romantic commitment was to a love that would never come again.

Juliette had always enjoyed selling at the Palazzo Orfei and nothing was different in Paris, except that there was a greater influx of *nouveau riche*, whose husbands had been war profiteers. Many of the other customers were women she knew from her Maison Landelle days and foreigners were plentiful, especially Americans. Only the Russian aristocracy was missing. Paris was among the cities of Europe and those overseas that had become a refuge for countless numbers of White Russians who had had to flee their country when their cause was lost but, almost without exception, they were impoverished; their land, property and possessions sequestered by the new regime. They had to take whatever work they could get and a doorman at any Parisian restaurant might be a grand duke and the head waiter a prince. A singer drawing customers to a Left Bank café was known to be a Romanov and a close relative of the late Tsar.

When Jacques and Denise came home again it was spring and they gave a party on a grand scale. A jazz band played and two hundred guests threw themselves exuberantly into all the new dances, Juliette among them. Many of her own friends were there. During the evening she was invited to join a group of them going at the end of the week to the evening preview of a special exhibition of the works of Rodin, who had died when she was still in Venice.

The preview was a fashionable event and the tickets had been in demand. Many people of importance were there, including the President himself. All were in evening clothes, the younger women favouring the shorter skirts. Juliette had chosen to wear one of Fortuny's highly successful cottons that wafted softly with every movement in a blending of russet, green and gold.

It was as she was laughing and talking with her friends, a glass of champagne in her hand, that she had the sudden sensation of being watched. It was oddly familiar and yet it made her uneasy. She turned her head casually. Then her heart gave such a lurch that she almost cried out, dropping her glass, which smashed at her feet. In

328

a gap in the milling throng around the sculptures she saw Nikolai, older in his looks and yet the same, standing by the statue of Balzac. He held her startled, anguished eyes with his across the distance between them. Then people broke their line of vision and he was lost from her sight.

'Whatever is the matter, Juliette? What's wrong?'

She turned to her friends almost unseeingly. 'Nothing! I'm all right.' The words seemed to be stumbling on her tongue. 'I happened to see somebody I haven't met for a long time. Please excuse me, everybody. I must speak to him.'

'I'll come with you,' her escort insisted, still concerned, and took hold of her by the elbow.

'No!' she exclaimed again, drawing sharply away from him. 'Wait for me here. I'll be back.'

He stared after her in consternation as she stepped over the shards of broken glass and left him to weave her way through the gathering. When she reached the Balzac statue Nikolai was no longer there, but she darted beyond it and, as she had expected, he had withdrawn to a quiet area away from the crowd. Tall potted palms gave the illusion of a more exotic clime and there were several gilded chairs set in pairs.

She went swiftly to him. They faced each other amid the green palms, each still in disbelief that they were meeting again. Briefly she stepped forward and in speechless relief that he was still alive she laid her cheek lightly against his shoulder, her eyes closed for a moment, and then withdrew again almost at once. They did not kiss. Too much time had elapsed, too much had happened to set them apart. He spoke first.

'You've cut your hair, Juliette.' His gaze roamed over its shining neatness before he smiled slowly at her. 'It suits you.'

'Oh, Nikolai!' Her voice was choked, tears swimming in her eyes. 'I was told you were—' She was unable to finish her sentence, but he understood.

'So many people have come back from the dead. When our army fell apart through mutiny and desertion and the upsurge of revolution there was total chaos.'

'I'm so thankful to see you safe and well!' She struggled to speak calmly. 'I can't express—' Again she broke off helplessly, shaking her head.

329

'It's difficult for me to realize that I'm seeing you too. I thought you were far away in Venice. Are you and Marco visiting Denise?'

'No. Marco came through the war only to fall victim to the Spanish flu.'

'I'm truly sorry to hear that. He was a good man and once I was able to count him as a friend.' Nikolai hesitated. 'Natasha and my sister, Anna, both lost their lives in the revolution.' His face had grown strained at the memory of managing to reach his home, hoping to get the two women safely away, only to find the palace ransacked and deserted. His frantic search had ended nearby when he found them lying raped and murdered with the bodies of the servants who had fled with them. When he had buried them all he had left the Karasvin estate for the last time.

Juliette, seeing his thoughts were painful to him, placed a hand compassionately on his arm. 'You have my deepest sympathy,' she said fervently, 'in the loss of all those near to you and also in losing your own country.'

He appreciated her words and took her hand into both of his. 'Are you living in Paris?'

'I have been for some time. I work for Maison Fortuny.'

'Ah, Fortuny.' His tone was a reminder of the memories that the Spaniard's name evoked for both of them. 'I often pass his establishment on the rue Pierre Carron. It never crossed my mind that you would be there.'

'How long have you been back in Paris, Nikolai?'

'Five months. Seeing you again it's as if I'd never been away.'

She slid her hand from his clasp, wanting to warn him that nothing could be as it was before. 'But we were both away from Paris for a long time.'

'Tell me about my son,' he requested.

It was the question she had been expecting. Before answering him, she went across to a pair of the gilded chairs and there they sat down together.

'Michel is strong, healthy, intelligent and sensitive too. Sometimes he needs reassurance and at others he's too adventurous for his own safety. He resembles you and his dark hair is curly and grows to a point at the back of his neck in the same way.' A smile tilted the corner of her mouth. 'He would do much better at school if he was less keen on sport!'

330

Nikolai gave a quiet laugh. 'That was my failing throughout my schooldays.'

'My daughter was still a baby when you and I met in Venice and now I have a younger son too. All three children are with me in Paris.'

'Would you let me see Michel?' There was deep appeal in his eyes.

She had known this request would come. 'You may, but only on condition that you don't let him know you're his father. I want to tell him when he's old enough to understand.'

'I'll do whatever you say. I was anxious for your safety and his when Italy came under threat from Austria. I wished all the time there was some way to get news of you.'

'As it happened,' she commented on a sigh, 'it would have been much better if I'd never heard anything of you.'

'How did you hear of my presumed death?'

She explained and then asked if the report about his friends had been false too, thinking how much it would mean to Signora Ottoni if her nephew should still be alive. But Nikolai shook his head with regret.

'It was correct. They were killed instantly. I only survived my wounds because my sergeant crawled to me through the mud and dragged me to safety with him. By then we were in full and disorganized retreat. That man carried me on his back until he reached a peasants' hovel and there I was left with an old woman who nursed me. For weeks I didn't know who or where I was. She also hid me from the Germans in their advance. I owe my life to her in more ways than one.'

'I feel equally indebted to her.' The trauma of their reunion almost overwhelmed her and her voice caught in her throat.

Nikolai leaned towards her. 'We can't talk any more here. Leave with me now.'

'I can't,' she declared. 'I must soon go back to those I'm with.' Her voice still faltered, but she was desperate to learn as much as possible about him in the time that was left. 'What happened after your recovery?'

'By a roundabout route I eventually reached the White army and I fought under the Imperial flag until the last battle. Then I had to flee for my life. After a very varied journey I reached French soil and made my way to Paris.'

331

'Are you sculpting again?'

'Yes, I've always had funds in a Paris bank, which enabled me to set myself up in another studio. My work hasn't been forgotten and commissions have been coming in. I'll be holding an exhibition of my own work at the end of the year.'

'I'm so glad for you.' For a few moments they smiled at each other as something of the old intimacy seemed to hover between them, making the years fade away, but she could not let it last. 'I must go, Nikolai.'

She rose to her feet, he with her, but blocking her way. 'Would you pose for me again?' he asked. 'I'd like to replace the head I did of you that's been lost somewhere in Russia.'

'That wouldn't be wise.' Her attitude was firm.

'There's nobody else, is there?' He was looking hard at her.

'There never has been as you mean it and there never will be. But nothing could ever be between us as it was before. It's over eleven years since we parted in Paris.'

'But later in Venice nothing had changed between us!'

'You're wrong, it had. Even though we knew our feelings for each other were the same, our love already belonged to the past. We didn't speak of it then, but there was no need, because we both understood that was how things had to be.'

'But neither of us could have foreseen what was to happen! That we should both be free when we met again. I hadn't expected to get through the war alive!'

'Yet you have and we're not the same two people whom we were before. The war changed us as well as everything else. Marco came home a different man. I saw Michel thrust aside for not being his own son. I'd never risk that happening to Sylvana and Riccardo. As I said before, Michel is sensitive and it would distress him to feel his sister and brother were being left out.'

'You expect me to treat the two youngest with such disregard?' He was incredulous.

She let her hands rise and fall in resignation. 'I don't know you now as I did in the past.'

At that moment her escort's voice broke sternly in on them. 'Juliette! We're all about to leave for supper at Ciro's.'

Neither she nor Nikolai had noticed him come to stand a few yards from them, making no move to be introduced.

332

'I'm coming!' she answered quickly. Nikolai gripped her by the shoulders even as she moved.

'Listen to me!' he urged fiercely. 'You and I have been given a second chance, Juliette! It's the rarest of all gifts. Don't throw it away! I would be starting afresh with all three of the children, doing for them all what once I would have done for Michel, not as lavishly as would have been possible before the war, but with the same loving care. Each one of them is yours! How could I not love them equally for being part of you? Because I love you as I've always done. It was your name I repeated constantly when I lay between life and death in that hovel. I've always kept with me the photo of you taken in Montmartre. You will always be everything to me!'

He swept her hard against him and kissed her with passionate violence as if to drive away all her doubts and fears. She responded totally, snatching briefly at the remembered joys and ecstasies of the past. Then, as his embrace eased and he withdrew his mouth from hers she broke away, hurrying to her waiting escort.

Nikolai stood looking after her. 'Tomorrow, Juliette! The same time at Larue's!'

She had heard him. He could tell by the last swift glance she threw over her shoulder at him before her escort clamped a jealous arm about her waist, hastening her away.

Juliette went to Maison Fortuny as usual when morning came. It was not easy to concentrate on her work, Nikolai's words running through her mind as they had done for most of her restless night. In those last few minutes with him she had realized that her life was beginning to cleave to his again just as it had done in Paris once before when she had paused on a staircase and seen him for the first time. She knew there would be difficulties ahead, problems to overcome and readjustments in every way, but nothing had ever run smoothly for them in the past and this time they would be facing everything together.

Later, after work, Juliette spent time with the children as she always did and told them a little about Nikolai, whom they were soon to meet. She was about to get ready for her evening with him when a corsage of orchids, pearly-white with green flecks rising from the calyx, was delivered. With a smile she put the exquisite blooms

333

lightly to her lips. Nikolai had thought of everything in this new beginning.

In her bedroom Juliette took her Delphos robe from its box and slipped it on. Its gold and coppery sheen rippled around her, reclaiming her figure once more. Timeless and beautiful it transcended all the years between as it always would in the future. She pinned on the corsage. Lastly she picked up her Knossos scarf and took it with her.

Looped over her arms, it floated out behind her as she alighted from the taxi-cab at Larue's. Once she had caused a scandal under this roof through appearing there in her Fortuny gown. All that was in the past, together with so much else. Nikolai was waiting for her. Full of hope, she went to him, taking that second chance.